TREADING ON SHADOWS

TREADING ON SHADOWS

Timothy Wilson

GRAFTON BOOKS
A Division of the Collins Publishing Group

LONDON GLASGOW
TORONTO SYDNEY AUCKLAND

Grafton Books
A Division of the Collins Publishing Group
8 Grafton Street, London W1X 3LA

Published by Grafton Books 1989

A CIP catalogue record for this book is available
from the British Library

ISBN 0-246-13249-3

Printed in Great Britain by
William Collins Sons & Co. Ltd, Glasgow

For June, Niv and Jim

We two kept house, the Past and I.

THOMAS HARDY

CHAPTER 1

You only drank gin to get drunk.

Whisky and brandy were ruddy and festive, suggestive of tots by an open fire and deep leather armchairs. Vodka still bore traces of the fierce and outlandish, rum remained colourfully nautical. Port and sherry were antiquely quaint, to be drunk wearing a powdered wig. Pernod and Cinzano and other such concoctions were frivolous. Wine was what people drank in restaurants. Beers and stouts and cider were bucolically social, lager thirst-quenching. And there were oddities like advocaat and Irish cream which effectively hid the fact that they were alcoholic altogether under an innocuous, nursery sweetness.

But gin . . . gin was squalor, seediness, Gin lane, clean straw for nothing, mother's ruin and the scalding bathtub, the cheap banal stink of it like the cheap banal emotions, old as the world, which it fed and fed on. It did away with all the hopeful associations – cheers, good health, here's looking at you – with which people hoped to costume the small sour naked truth: that drink depressed, but made misery your friend instead of the nagging companion who trailed after you with his monotonous remarks right round the sober world. Gin introduced you to that friend without preliminaries and left you alone with him, to enter that instant intimacy of those who know they are bound to each other in spite of quarrels and incompatibility just as surely as two lovers buried six feet under in a coffined embrace. And he had drunk a three-quarter bottle of gin already and was still drinking, as friends will stay together, mute, yawning, their dull familiarity not so much a statement of loyalty as of rejection of the murderous hostility of people who do not know each other.

Mother's ruin. Bathtub gin. His mother had never touched a drop. The lips that touch liquor . . . Towards the end, at Marian's suggestion – she was always meekly obedient to Marian – she would sip a little Scotch as a medicine, wincing and shuddering as if at the primitiveness of the relief rather than its taste. Six feet under. Three sheets to the wind. One over the eight. He started to laugh, starting to cry. He was free.

How she would have liked to be there, today! She always fancied herself as the matriarch, in a quietly humorous way. At family gatherings she would sit back a little from them, reserved, watchful, cherishing her years and her knowledge, like a resource that must be carefully husbanded in case of need. 'Airs' Uncle Alan called it, thinning further his pale Methodist lips. She and Uncle Alan had never got on. 'Funny' she called him, and in rare moments of vindictiveness pronounced her private anathema on him – 'there was something the matter with him.' Something, that is, more than the double incapacitation of asthma and anaemia that made him a thin and white and resentful man for whom funerals were a signal pleasure horribly sweetened with apprehension. Fifty-nine now and never married, kept a house that was too big for him filled with model steam-engines like a schoolboy. It wasn't right. Oh, he had been in his element today. Even though it was a church funeral – or perhaps that had been better, as representing not only a victory over a woman of whom he had always been afraid but a victory for chapel; one less churchgoer in a town where a great cathedral sneered down for ever at the shabby foot-soldiers of Nonconformity. He had been expansive today, patronising, like the rest of the family, the solicitude barely veiling a current of inquisition. 'How are you feeling now David? I know this is a terribly upsetting time for you *but* . . .' What was he going to do with the house, how would he cope alone, would he not rather leave a place which, after all, must be full of memories for him . . . ? And his unspoken, gloating corollary – now you're like me, now you've joined the misfits, the livers-alone, the roamers of silent houses who missed the marriage boat and lie in single beds listening to the ticking of the alarm-clock measuring out the dimensions of a wasted life. Yes, she should have been there today, she would have put them in their place.

But of course she had been there. Guest of honour. Except she had not been sitting in a corner, patient, deceptively relaxed, the pouchy dewlaps of her face powdered like marshmallow, but laid in an improbable posture in a wooden box where she could not watch them all with her shrewdly gentle eyes that said: I know you, I know you. She ought to have hammered on the lid and cried Let me out, only she would not have done that. She would have climbed carefully out herself with the same concentration and silence – no exaggerated grunts and apologies about old bones – with which she levered herself out of her armchair, until the day she could not do so and he had lifted her soft, uncomplaining bulk and put it to bed.

'Pull the curtains to, David. We don't want people peeping in.'

His mother's voice sounded so clearly that he started from his doze and was on his feet peering round the room in one movement. The fire had gone out and only the street light outside sketched a few chalk details on the black outlines of the furniture and, with unsubtlety, as of a Hollywood image of bereavement, picked out the glint of his mother's spectacles folded on the mantelpiece. Obediently he closed the curtains and sat down again and groped for the gin bottle and his glass. The house had a large front garden with a tall privet hedge. No-one would ever peep in. When someone died you were supposed to regret never having said something terribly important to them. Hollywood again, the deathbed, the broken voice welling up: 'I love you Moooommy!' – You did not, most emphatically not, break in on the heavenly chorus with, 'Mother, why the hell did you always have to have the curtains closed the moment it got dark in a room where nobody could possibly see you anyway?'

Because . . . because I am old and you are young – at least, I am dead, but I was sixty-seven, and you are thirty-five, which is young – though I don't expect you to understand that. Because I was born just after the First World War, and you were born well after the Second, and though I am not – was not – an old-fashioned woman, and I quite like the pop music because at least it's lively, and I think the freedom the young have nowadays is healthier, far healthier, and so on – this is not my world. And perhaps because – who knows? – you lived at home with me all your life and I deliberately wanted you to be aware of, and irritated by, my old, suffocating ways. But I don't think it's worked, has it? I don't think it's worked.

Ethel Barber, née Russell, late of this parish, widow of Harold and loving mother of David and Marian, had been buried at St Mary's cemetery on a December afternoon so cold that the ceremony briefly threatened to become a double one when Great-Uncle Bob Russell had keeled over in a faint, colliding with Uncle Alan, giving David a vision of the whole lot of them toppling like dominoes into the open grave. A few spadefuls of earth and the entire Barber and Russell clans would be dispatched. But the old man had soon revived, and later when they had all assembled at the house – David's house now – for the spread, whisky had perked him up so far as to set him off on an endless train of reminiscence about the manners of death of various members of the family. His grandfather had died whilst up a stepladder painting a picture-rail, and had left a perfect diagonal streak of paint across the wall describing the trajectory of his fall; David's father had lain in the sanitorium on the hill at the edge of town looking better daily until one evening his lungs had simply exploded; his cousin Wally had got halfway out of bed for a glass of water one night –

'and he never moved again.'

David's friend Ron told him the rest of this story privately. Ron had been a policeman at the time and had been called to

Wally's house that morning. The old man had indeed been found by his wife when she woke, sprawled halfway out of bed motionless like a waxwork. He had gone so stiff that there was no way of carrying him down the narrow stairs of the terraced house, so in the end they had to push his head between his knees like a jointed doll and bowl him down the staircase. 'Terrific noise it made,' said Ron. 'And the air came out of him as well, if you see what I mean. Cruel old world, really.'

David had wanted to laugh, and had laughed, noisily, till the family had coughed and frowned at him and put it down to a grieving hysteria and then felt sorry for him. It wasn't hysteria, he simply wanted to laugh: what else could you do but laugh, after that freezing church with everybody's ears and noses pinched red, and the intolerably maudlin tune of 'Abide With Me' – it was in his head now, a woeful supine keening, the litany of small and pathetic creatures wretchedly abased before some entirely cold God of stone pillars and paraffin-heaters in the nave and dirty stained-glass windows and monolithic suffering. Cruel old world, as Ron said, Ron being one of that lucky few who could perceive simultaneously both this fact and its humour. Not cruel to David though, now. He was free. Didn't they see that? If only they would stop feeling sorry for him. Mr Carelli the other day, coming round from next door with some stew between two plates. 'You got to eat,' he said gravely. 'Though I know, you don't feel hungry.' In fact David had been ravenous. His sister Marian, helping him clear away in the kitchen, looking steadfastly at him with her swimming eyes until he felt he could scream, and then placing her hand on his, a gesture too theatrical to be anything other than sincere. No-one had really commiserated with Marian; it was all for him: but of course she was married, her centre of gravity had shifted in both senses.

And that was when, for the first time, he really comprehended his isolation. The Family: the scent of them was still in this room, lingering and amorphous like a folk memory – smoke and perfume and talcum and old suits reclaimed from sepulchral wardrobes – where they had gathered, drawn together by threads longer and looser than those of love or affection voluntarily cultivated, but stronger, and unbreakable. And yet now he was as free of them as it was possible to be, could rove as far as the threads would let him. Perhaps this was what had made him – bleared with whisky and slightly sick with cold ham and greasy bread-and-butter – aim his shot at their complacency.

'Why isn't Auntie Aldyth here?' he said. 'Couldn't she come?'

Marian had had the ordering of everything; it was she who had summoned the mourners here; it was at Marian that everyone looked, including David, feeling suddenly belligerent.

'Oh – you know she doesn't have anything to do with us,' was all she said.

'We don't have anything to do with her you mean,' said David. 'You mean she wasn't invited.'

'Your mother wouldn't have wanted her here, David,' said Uncle Alan, and distributed his thin sandy hair a little more evenly over his scalp.

'Dear God – after all this time . . . her own sister,' said David, spluttering, and was firmly talked down by Auntie Jeanette, who burst with supernatural brightness into a peroration on Christmas shopping.

They had squashed him and he did not wriggle. His mother would not have wanted her here. He had to admit the truth of that. Aldyth's name, if anyone should be foolish enough to mention it, would transform the soft rosy lines of her face into something unapproachable, alien and frightening. It was frightening that such intense bitterness should last so long and not kill you. There was only one photograph of Aldyth in the house, in his mother's chest of drawers amongst lavender crumbs and little odds and ends – plastic keys from twenty-first birthdays and horseshoes from weddings – things so useless they could only be hoarded like treasures.

It was a studio portrait, hand-tinted and taken, he guessed, during the war. In front of some painted clouds in an absurd state of storminess Aldyth smiled in a wide-shouldered suit. Her eyelashes were pronounced, as in a child's drawing, and her dark hair was rolled on top. It was a very dated picture and apart from her exceptional beauty he could glean little about Aldyth from it. But he liked it and with a sudden inward movement of identification he put down his unfinished glass of gin and went unsteadily upstairs to find it.

His mother's room was bitterly cold and filled with a merciless light from the street-lamp outside the window. Someone – Marian probably – had stripped the bed and rolled up the mattress and it lay, a fat sausage, on the sagging metal springs.

Mother, a firm bed would be better for your back, you know.

No, I wouldn't be comfortable.

The small portable television he had bought for her was still on the cabinet, and on her dressing-table there was the orderly platoon of bottles of scent and bath-salts and medicine.

He left the room again and closed the door quietly.

CHAPTER 2

Christmas suited the town, and the snow, when it came, softened and blurred the edges and incongruities of a place that was somehow, in spite of careful civic planning, less than the sum of its parts.

It lay in a river valley marking the spot where the fenland of the east gave way to the chalk upland of the midlands to the west. In pre-industrial times it had been a moderately important market town of thatched buildings clustered round the skirts of a beautiful cathedral; but it had not grown, or only grown imperceptibly. The *Gentleman's Magazine* of 1820 noted it as a place of four thousand souls, 'of no great extent, and indifferently built, though with a fine bridge.' Then in the 1850s had come the railways and, after a brief and bitter wrangle with a larger and more prosperous town twelve miles to the west, the little city had won and the main line from London to the North had been ploughed through it. The rival town had died almost instantly, and the city had expanded. Big families of agricultural labourers like the Russells came in off the land to work on the railways, and spent their good wages with the small Methodist shopkeeping families like the Barbers.

The wheels of David's car spun out little fusillades of melting blackened snow as he braked at the traffic lights at the bottom of the hospital bridge, waiting to cross into the centre of town with an impatient convoy of Christmas shoppers. An Inter-City 125 flashed by beneath them, sending a hum through the arching girders of the bridge, and he thought of standing on the bridge when he was a boy, watching the last steam trains that threw up a cloud of delicious smuts as they passed beneath him.

By the end of the nineteenth century, 40,000 people lived in the town. The core of elegant Georgian houses and an old corn exchange and a florid town hall with stone pillars and a few fragments of medieval wall was encircled by a waste of railway yards and sidings and warehouses and factories, and then beyond them row upon row of terraced cottages for railwaymen, blackened with furnace smoke and doomed to become slums as surely as if the word had been picked out in white paint on their slate roofs; and beyond them still sprang up crescents and cul-de-sacs of square-bayed villas and avenues of semi-detached half-timbered houses screened from the railway cuttings by clumps of chestnut trees. And now, after the added impetus of a government expansion plan in the 1970s and the creation of a development corporation, the town had a population of 140,000 and the flat fields that had formerly marooned it were eaten away by estates of spanking new houses, arranged in closes with rural names, and interlaced with a latticework of parkways and carriageways whose high verges were staked out with infant trees in geometric ranks like crosses in a war graveyard.

David, with a lifetime's knowledge of the town, swung the car into a short cut to the centre, passing down sidestreets of terraced houses nearly all inhabited by Asians. Here blobs of incongruous colours glowed against the snow: men with red beards ambled by in shalwar chemises, followed a few paces behind by women swathed in flimsy turquoise and cerise with gold sandals on their feet. A little girl gave him a V-sign, and to her delight he gave it back.

Yet it was still at heart a small town. In spite of industries, two hospitals, three municipal parks, big office-blocks amongst green-field developments, a college, covered marble shopping malls cunningly integrated with the old buildings which the council, having spent the previous ten years energetically knocking down, were now just as energetically sprucing up, the town wore its size uncomfortably. Even the presence of the cathedral, a pleasant anachronism like a stately dowager with a vast bosom of pearls, had never really accustomed the town to calling itself a city; and privately it still did not take to the name. As if wishing to contract into parochial miniaturism wherever possible, it called its estates townships and ranged them around mock village-greens and hid them from the motorways with embankments and impromptu copses that had all the authenticity of the bright green grass used in the windows of butchers' shops. It named its streets after long-dead aldermen and in the shiny arcades placed blown-up Victorian photographs of the old market-square with sepia ladies pushing coach-built perambulators eyed by men in boaters. And Christmas came to its aid, the uniformity of tinsel decorations and glimmering afternoons lending to it a cosy unity that was complete when the snow came, blowing up the valley on dark winds that scoured the wide flat streets, dignifying the chimneys of factories and brickworks and giving ash-heaps and cinder paths and the tarred roofs of sheds a feathery discretion and even delicately pencilling the striated mess of railway-lines and sidings around the station.

The snow was early and heavy this year. It began two days after David's mother was buried, quickly and competently muffling the town with a whiteness that made dingy the whiteness of cotton-wool snowmen in shop windows and the Pickwickian snowscapes on Christmas cards that were ferried endlessly around the town by mail-vans and came in flurries through letter-boxes to pile like snowdrifts on doormats that were themselves miniature tundras of melting snow. On the east side of town, where the agricultural land crept up to the walls of gaunt factories, it came stinging and horizontal across a sky choked with masses of cloud, bringing the gathered momentum of an unimpeded flight across miles of fens to do its work on this most sturdy ugliness. Here were the last remnants of back-to-back housing, the sewage farm, and the big gasometer. It stood on David's right as he queued to drive up to the multi-storey car park and he thought of the story his father had told him of one evening forty-five years ago.

Working late in his office at the old brickworks – where the war told him to remain because of the weakness in his lungs which was tuberculosis and fourteen years later would impatiently fling them across the whitewashed walls of the sanatorium hut – David's father had watched a lone German plane with its muttered throbbing circle this gasometer and spray bullets at it while the anti-aircraft guns made panicked sputterings from the park across town. Now his son gazed from his car at the gasometer which German bullets had failed to penetrate and saw the top of it disappear into whirling eddies of snow, rendering it enigmatic, as if it might be a tower of infinite height.

In the echoing heights of the multi-storey the wind was freezing and tossed handfuls of crystalline snow down the back of his neck and he was glad to cram into the human warmth of the lift. With their bodies pressed intimately together everyone chose a spot of space to stare at; the middle-aged lady next to David drew in breath in little conservative gasps to minimalise their contact.

It was as if this determined privacy were calculated to remind him – as if he needed reminding – that now he was a solitary and rootless being. Which was what he wanted, wasn't it? Freedom. At the office this morning he had been, as he had always been, part of the workforce, individuals yoked together by circumstance into one body. Not unlike a family. But when work was over, each left his desk and disappeared into a world of his own making: except David, who went home to his mother. Now was his chance to be like them.

The lift doors opened into the covered precinct and its cargo spilled out, scattering immediately in different directions. Carols played on what sounded like xylophones were relayed from speakers around the base of a thirty-foot Christmas tree. David hesitated, decided to go one way and then changed his mind. As he turned something small and yielding collided with his legs and he found he had bumped into a little boy. The child fell back on his bottom and set up a wailing that boomed round the marbled walls. 'I'm so sorry,' he said to the mother who bent to scoop him up. 'I just didn't see him . . .' and he smiled ineffectually, looming and adult and frightening, at the child, making him cry louder.

'It's all right, he never looks where he's going,' said the mother, hoisting the boy on to her shoulder, and he wanted to say something more, something which would somehow convey that he really was sorry, that he knew what it was like dragging kids round town, that he was from the same world – but the mother, not interested, had disappeared into the milling shoppers. He went on, disliking children and disliking the fact that they disliked him. He caught sight of himself in the mirror-glass that covered one side of the mall, a tall stooped figure moving amongst the others with dusty-fair hair too long at the back, and felt bleak. So this was the other, self-chosen world he turned to after work – going into town to buy presents for a family he had made up his mind to be free of.

Freedom and fear: those were the reactions expected of him now that his mother was dead and he faced the prospect of starting life at the age of thirty-five, and he wanted to reject them. He had not been tied down by the years of living at home looking after his mother; he did not believe himself to be a mother's boy or a sterile emotional cripple or a latent homosexual. That classic unarticulated scenario that featured him growing older and older and contracting fastidious mannerisms which would multiply until he was a lonely, fussy bachelor like Uncle Alan was too pat, too trite, he told himself.

Fear and freedom: he felt both, and the mixture paralysed him.

He blundered his way through the overheated chain-stores, his list of presents going crumpled and damp in his hand. Old ladies ran their trolley wheels over his feet and sturdily planted themselves in front of the goods he wanted to buy, so that in frustration he snatched at things he did not want and paid for them and stuffed them savagely into his bag. He wondered how it was that his mother could always negotiate this festive scrum with such ease: he remembered as a boy following her through crowds like this, her hand holding his and occasionally giving it little jerking tugs, not because she was hurrying him on but, it seemed, to reiterate their claim on each other, to establish that their hand-holding was not merely for convenience or safety, not merely to be taken for granted. But these shops with their carpets and escalators and an astringent smell of glossy perfume-counters were not here then. The shops he remembered as a boy had noisy floor-boards and drawers with hand-written labels behind the counter; they had tea-rooms above them and his mother knew all the proprietors by name and, it seemed, knew all their secrets: Fairlie who owned the big toyshop and drank all day in a back room; Ellis, the confectioner, who supported a half-mad brother who threw the furniture out of the window when there was a full moon; Mr Hendry who with his sister kept the Christian bookshop where David's mother bought her religious, Santa-Claus-free Christmas cards that he always found so dull, and who never took off his muffler because he had been a missionary and caught leprosy and the lower half of his face was not there. Apart from the Co-op, there was only one department store in town then. Lacey's: a place to be entered with something of the solemnity of a church, or even the cathedral, a sleek and hushed and magisterial place where articles were flourished out of glass cases for your inspection and then flourished back in again as if exposure to the air might corrupt them. This was where the rich, driving in from the heavy mock-Tudor houses in the west of the town, bought their food. To have your groceries delivered from Lacey's was just about the most appallingly luxurious thing you could do then. Lacey's was still there now: he passed it as he emerged from Boots. It looked shabby, dwarfed by the steely fronts of the chain-stores where the goods were not only cheaper but more numerous and of better quality. Yet it retained some of its absurd hauteur. It was the old town, rooted, and the chain stores were flashy carpetbaggers beside it, wide boys with gleaming teeth and a suitcase full of bargains.

In Littlewoods David bought a pair of gloves for Marian

and a scarf for her husband Richard and watched a perspiring man choosing red frilly lingerie. For his wife, presumably. What did wives say when presented with that sort of thing? He found himself staring until the man noticed and gave him an unfriendly look. He moved away, feeling childish, nose pressed against the glass behind which a world of adult citizens went about its private mysterious rituals.

At work Jack Erskine, the wag of the wages office, had converted commiseration, like the rugby-player he was, into a kind of admiring, salacious congratulation of David on what lay ahead of him. 'I wish I was in your shoes mate. Young, free and single now, eh? Well, two out of three anyway – no, only kidding. But just think – footloose and fancy free. No-one to answer to. No responsibilities. There's no end to what you could get up to!' And he let out a zipping yell. 'Wa-heey!'

David did not believe this – any more than Jack Erskine did. David had lost his virginity when he was twenty and briefly engaged, and had found it again in fifteen years of celibacy interrupted by a single drunken though enjoyable coupling after an office party which his partner had charmingly, and genuinely, forgotten about the next day. Love had come to him early in life, too early for him to appreciate it: not knowing what to do with it, he had thrown it away like a ticking bomb, and with an instinct for self-preservation had never allowed himself to dwell on this devastating waste. His mother, right to the end, had regretted it. Not that she had ever nagged; he could not even imagine his mother nagging. That was what people, trying to add an upbeat coda to their sympathetic noises with a cheery But-at-least-now-you'll-be-free, could not grasp (no doubt 'meaning well', but wasn't that an excuse too readily sought?). His life and his mother's life belonged to the stock of cliché: he was Anthony Perkins in *Psycho* or nothing. That his mother's occasional, gentle suggestions that he should find himself a nice girl and get married were not the interfering proddings of an old-fashioned woman but the flutterings of anxiety, born of perception, perception that he would have to learn to be young again when she was gone and he would not find it easy, would not occur to them, and it was only now beginning to occur to David.

In the window of a modish gift shop a poster displayed a pair of high-heeled and black-stockinged legs poking out of a Christmas parcel. David stared at it a moment and then left the precinct and emerged into the old streets where real mullioned windows had been sprayed inside with artificial snow whilst real snow came twirling down shaken into damp startled flurries by sudden jabs of wind.

Outside a newsagents an old red setter waited humbly. It was not tethered, for its lead trailed on the ground, but it stood motionless, its bow legs planted apart, occasionally casting a wrinkled glance up at the snow that was settling and melting on its matted conker-coloured coat. A skinny old man in a mackintosh came out of the shop with a newspaper under his arm and a rolled umbrella in the other hand. Bending arthritically, his face expressionless, he gave the dog three blows on its head with the umbrella, slow, feeble-wristed. Then he picked up the setter's trailing lead and set off with the animal waddling behind.

David stood in the snow watching them, with half a mind to go up and call the old man a cruel bastard. Though the blows from those wasted arms could scarcely have hurt a puppy. But the dog, which could probably have snapped its master's calcified spine with one bite, had peered up abjectly, wincing, in an agony of utter submission.

So that was what mutual dependence meant, was it – little cruelties and degrading resignation? Better to be alone then. He marched up Bridge Street with a self-consciously business-like tread. There was a mock-Victorian chestnut-barrow here, and he bought a bag of roast chestnuts from a youth with a gold earring dressed as a coster.

The steaming chestnuts smelt delicious and satisfied a sense of the cosily appropriate in the snowy street of antique buildings that led to the turreted gateway of the cathedral; but they were scorched and tasteless, and David ended up throwing them into a bin. He felt very lonely now, lonelier than he had since his mother died ten days ago; and he did the only thing he could do, which was to go into a supermarket and buy a huge frozen turkey and a Christmas pudding like a cannonball and a lot of drink he could not afford.

'You're going to cook Christmas dinner for the whole family?' said Marian. 'You? You've never cooked a proper meal in your life. Oh, David, I wouldn't do that.'

Marian worked in Marks and Spencers, in the children's wear department, and talking was difficult. People nudged him aside as he stood there burdened with heavy carrier bags and this added to the irritation she unfailingly produced in him. 'Why not?' he said, when he had her attention again. 'Mum always did. Keep up the tradition and all that. Anybody can bung a turkey in the oven.'

A long strand of hair fell across Marian's smooth round forehead: the rest of her hair was tied back but this long strand was always there, where it must surely annoy her, and it had the effect of annoying him. He stared at it impotently angry while she moved away to serve a customer buying dungarees for a bad-tempered child. Marian was good with children. She was three months pregnant now and she already had a seven-year-old daughter for whom every birthday and Christmas David bought a painting-set or a writing-pad, uncharitably feeling that in Marian and Richard's house the child would grow up a moron: he had an obscure notion that if she had the right tools she might, like some Victorian autodidact, improve herself. He said again, 'Why not?' but she merely shook her head.

'Well, I suppose if you've gone and bought all the stuff you'd better go through with it,' she sighed. Marian could make every prospect sound baleful, like a visit to the dentist. 'I shall have to come and help you, if it's going to be eatable.' She looked at him steadily the way women did, with a flat assessing shrewdness. 'Anyway, what's brought all this on? You've always given the impression you can't stand the family and wanted to be rid of the lot of them.'

'Because it's nearly new year, and so I might as well begin this new independent life – which I *am* going to begin – with the new year. Clean sweep. A last traditional get-together before I cut myself adrift. And don't look at me like that. Of course I don't want to spend Christmas alone in that house. But that's not all there is to it.' This was not what he actually said to her – in fact he had made no reply – but what he was wishing he had said as he drove home. Anyway Christmas was for families wasn't it? Mainly because one formal day a year was about all they could stand of each other, he told himself with a willed cynicism. Every Boxing Day Auntie Maggie would walk two miles across town to their house, erect and indefatigable though she was four years older than his mother, with a basket of presents: Auntie Maggie, for whom the word 'spinster' had been coined, turning up in her gaberdine coat as regularly as Santa Claus, until at last she stiffened in her solitary bedroom with ponderous pieces of walnut furniture as attendant shades. Never married, she had by that one omission placed herself at the mercy of the family and laid herself open to the patronising, shameful remark that was like an accusation – 'We're all she's got.' Once she brought him a clockwork motor-car and for what seemed hours – in fact it was minutes but he was a child then and not a grown man, though he could not envisage a point that separated the two – he had zoomed it back and forth across the carpet, and sometimes it had come to rest against Auntie Maggie's shoes below the wrinkled lisle stockings and a glimpse of slipping brown bloomers and she had bent with a creak – corsets or bones? – to send it scooting back to him.

'Today is the first day of the rest of your life,' announced a poster, shredded by the cutting wind on the front of the Eastgate Baptist Chapel. He felt a sudden desire, like a twinge of pain that was as quickly gone, to go to church this Christmas, even though he had stopped going when he was eleven and had no faith to speak of; to be fed some certitudes as you were fed the communion wafer. But even then what he was hoping for might be to recapture some unthinking cosiness such as you felt as a child drawing pictures of the Three Wise Men or rehearsing a Nativity play. 'Today is the first day of the rest of your life' – well, that had seemed to be true for him ten days ago.

He drove on, the windscreen wipers parting curtains of slippery crystals, towards home where he was going to cook a stodgy sort of meal about which he felt a needle of guilt because his mother would have thought it unwholesome, and thought about the rest of his life, picturing it as a segmented cake like the diagrams they used at school to teach you fractions. He left the chapel behind and drove through the railway terraces and then past the council estates with their jagged modernity of flat roofs and metal chimneys and then into the stolid pre-war suburbs with their jealous garden fences and everywhere the town wore its past confusedly and covered its indecision with snow.

CHAPTER 3

'Today is the first day of the rest of your life,' said the Eastgate Baptist Chapel – it was a square brick building that had formerly been the Temperance Tea-rooms and before that a dance hall so dubious that it had been a byword for Going To The Bad when the town was of a size for scandal to be possible in it – and similar notices stared through the snow all over the town.

'For best results follow the Maker's instructions.'

'If you see someone without a smile – give them one of yours.'

'This is a ch--ch. What is missing . . . ? Make us complete this Sunday!'

The town had caught Nonconformity late and, like the measles, caught it badly. The cathedral, built on one of the few eminences the flat land had to offer, dominated the landscape, but spiritual domination was less than complete. Now half the faithful went to their Christmas worship in a variety of chapels, from the Victorian Methodist Hall that could seat a thousand, to the glorified scout hut that housed the Christadelphians; or else rejected Christmas in two synagogues and several mosques. Only in the mosques however were the congregations on the increase, and gone were the days when a prim, 'Is she church or chapel?' had been the dreaded, inevitable question asked of a young man telling his parents he was courting. A certain artificial placidity about Sundays in the town, a certain reluctance on the part even of newsagents to open, was all that remained of a Sabbatarianism that would have given Dickens apoplexy.

This Sunday in December 1937 gives an idea of that Sabbatarianism. The building that is later to house the Eastgate Baptist Chapel is a dance-hall, but it is closed tonight. However, close to it is the Fairfield Road Methodist Chapel, to which earlier today Harold Barber went, and which he now repasses on his way to visit Ethel Russell, to whom he is engaged. She did not go to the Fairfield Road Methodist Chapel today but to St Mark's Church, with white gloves and a prayer-book and a gestural smear of make-up which she borrowed from her sister Aldyth and which did not suit her.

Harold and Ethel are going to get married next year, or the year after, in spite of the fact that he is chapel and the Russells are church. For Harold Barber is very respectable and has an unassuming charm and a good job, and he is a particularly handsome man. He looks a little gaunt as he strides through the empty dark streets of the town centre – there are no lights in the shop windows, except at Lacey's, which is a sufficiently discreet and funereal place to be lit even on a Sunday – but then that is not unusual in this low-lying valley town where many people are gaunt because they are consumptive. Harold is twenty-two and feels even younger, very much in love as he is with Ethel. The thought of her makes him walk a little quicker, his shoes slipping a little on the frosted pavement, hunching in his overcoat against the wind that springs out at him with a hollow whistle as he passes the Arcade. He enjoys going to visit Ethel, not only because of her but because he likes her family and feels a little more at ease amongst them than he does with his own. The Russell house is a semi-detached villa near the railway with a huge garden at the bottom of which they keep two pigs, and the family fills it to overflowing. There are six children, all grown up and all living there still, and a fearsome grandma he has never seen and to whom he knows one day he will be introduced.

Ethel's mother likes him very much and, from the steamy kitchen – where she is a slave in all but name and the great shiny copper and the mangle and the pot-bellied stove the instruments of her bondage: the slavery will kill her finally in twenty years' time – she brings him endless cups of brown tea and slices of lardy cake, thinking he needs feeding up. Ethel's father also likes him, though he does not say as much. He sits in his chair – *his* chair – a big man, white-haired and white-moustached with quick twinkly eyes that express the equal parts of joviality and foul temper that make up his character, and rolls cigarettes. He is in a good mood, for he spent dinnertime in The Locomotive, drinking hugely, before hurrying to the bakehouse to bring home the smoking tin of beef and Yorkshire pudding which he is still pleasantly digesting. He fought in the First World War, and will nearly be the town's first casualty in the Second, for he is a railwayman and a stray German plane will bomb the railway in daylight, miraculously doing him no further harm than knocking him off his bicycle as he leaves work for his dinner.

They talk to Harold, the mother in staccato bursts as she pops back and forth into the kitchen, the father rumbling, merrily and gravely, like the slow trundling of train wheels on iron track. Harold sits on the settee with Ethel, holding her hand. When Ethel comes to his house they cannot do this. Some dusty paper chains are strung across the ceiling and there are sprigs of holly stuck behind the fly-spotted mirror above the mantelpiece. Harold feels warm and comfortable, and this feeling is only disturbed when Aldyth comes clattering down the stairs and into the room. He never feels quite at ease with Aldyth, who is sixteen and tall and extremely pretty, and who does not plump herself down beside him and flirt with gawky, sexless innocence like the other young sister Jeanette. Aldyth is merely polite to him, sometimes slightly brittle and remote, and he has the feeling, somehow, that his being engaged to Ethel, his being there at all, is something she cannot take entirely seriously: almost as if he were a child and she a grown woman. 'Have you seen my mother-of-pearl earrings, Ethel?' she says, without greeting or acknowledging Harold, and when Ethel shakes her head disappears again with a cry of 'They've got to be *somewhere*.' That shake of the head seems cool and dismissive, yet when Harold looks at Ethel she is staring at the door where Aldyth has just departed with a strange intense expression. Harold is disquieted and gives Ethel's hand an extra squeeze. She turns to him again with the lovely soft slow smile he finds delightful and he feels reassured, feels she has come back to him. He also thinks, with an inward movement of urgency he does not understand, that they must get married soon.

Then her father is suggesting that he go up and meet Grandma, and he realises that at last he has been summoned by the old lady. With Ethel he climbs the steep stairs and enters the room where Grandma Russell lies in state. The two six-foot sons, Joe and Frank, share one small bedroom, but this, the largest room, is given up to the old lady. The bed is huge and she lies centrally in it. Heavy chenille curtains are drawn and there is a rosewood commode that smells badly and on the bureau amongst the framed photographs there is a real ostrich egg mounted on a marble base. There must be six, seven pillows on the bed but Grandma Russell sits up rigidly straight and pays no attention to the couple when they come in. She is reading the *News of the World*, using a big round glass off the face of a clock to magnify the print, and her lips mutter as she reads. To Harold's amazement her nightdress has a high lace collar with a cameo brooch.

At last she puts down the newspaper and the clock-glass and Ethel says obediently: 'Grandma, this is Harold.'

'Harold who?'

'Harold Barber, Mrs Russell,' says Harold in his friendly way, extending a hand. 'How do you do?'

'Come a bit closer. Come and sit here.' The old lady screws her eyes up at him and pats a wicker chair beside the bed. 'You're very thin, are you poorly?' Without waiting for an answer she goes on: 'Barber, I don't know any Barbers. What do your family do?'

'They keep a shop,' he says, aware that Ethel has not sat down, 'in Gladstone Street.'

The old lady seems to consider this, and he begins to observe, despite the erect posture and the acerbic firmness of the voice, how immensely old she is. Above the amazing

Edwardian collar her neck trembles in fleshless folds. She snaps suddenly at Ethel.

'Don't stand there like a spare part, Ethel. Sit down.'

Ethel sits meekly on the edge of the bed, saying nothing. 'So you pair are going to get wed,' says Grandma Russell. 'Well, you're both old enough. I got married when I was seventeen. Can you keep her? What do you do?'

'I'm a clerk,' he says, and where he began by being a little afraid of her he now feels amused, and senses too that Ethel's demeanour, subdued even for her, is a matter of indulgence rather than respect. 'At the Stanwood brickworks. We've both been saving for a year. And I should be due for promotion quite soon.'

The old lady shakes her head, and her fingers make vague irresolute searchings on the counterpane. 'I don't know where half these places are. Stanwood, there used to be a horse fair there. My Sam used to get up at four and walk there from Whittlesey to hold the horses' heads for a few coppers when he was a boy. It's all changed. Brickworks now.' He thinks she is going to ramble, but she catches this thought up sharp by suddenly fixing him with a keen look. 'Well, I hope you're serious,' she says. 'Not mucking about. Are you serious about her, this girl of ours?'

'Yes,' Harold says, simply, and looks at Ethel, who is not looking at him. The old lady nods, seeming satisfied.

'And what about you Ethel? I hope you mean it and you're not just being soft over your first chap. I know you young girls, you think you want to get married when you know nothing about it. You think it'll be a bed of roses.'

'No, grandma,' says Ethel, 'that's not how I see getting married.' Harold looks at her, the way she is sitting on the bed, demure without being affected, and feels proud of her.

'I shan't see you wed,' says Grandma Russell, 'I don't suppose I shall.' This time Harold supposes she will grow tearful, but instead she looks at him and smiles and says, 'She's a deep one you know, our Ethel. A bit stiff-necked sometimes. But she's got a heart of gold. Same as the boys. Though Frank drinks too much, and I've told him it'll ruin him. He don't listen.' Harold remembers Ethel telling him that before Grandma Russell took to her bed she would walk every dinnertime to The Locomotive and sit in the snug bolt upright in her long black dress and effortlessly drink six or seven bottles of stout and march back home with complete equanimity. He feels he likes the old lady and feels too, pleasantly, that she likes him and he has been approved. 'Maggie's too prissy,' she goes on, counting on her trembly fingers, 'she'll never get a husband that way. Jeanette's the daft one. Though there's no harm in her. And Aldyth fancies herself.' She laughs, nodding her head. Harold notices her hair is so thin and wispy that he imagines a draught might blow it away. 'Fancies herself too much. A little madam. Don't you think?'

Harold shrugs. 'Well . . . I don't know. She's certainly – very nice-looking.'

'And she knows it. And she knows it. You're not going to say what you really think of her are you? I don't blame you. What's going to become of her I don't know. I wouldn't be surprised if she came a cropper.' Grandma Russell leans her head back and closes her eyes. When after several minutes she does not move Harold assumes she has gone to sleep and raises his eyebrows at Ethel but Ethel only shakes her head. He begins to find the fusty room a little oppressive: his time with Ethel is precious and he is growing impatient when the old lady open her eyes again. They are bluc and briglit but their brightness is metallic: age has taken all the depth out of them. 'I think you pair will be all right,' she says decisively. 'She'll look after you, you can be sure of that,' and Ethel looks down with her gentle smile. 'Yes, you'll be all right. You're so thin though. Don't they feed you? What are you, chapel?'

He says yes.

'And how old are you? Twenty-two? Well, you'll be better when you get to twenty-eight. Fourth cycle of seven. Give me a kiss.'

It is a peremptory command and without surprise Harold bends and kisses the lean cheek. She receives the salute stiffly and then as he is drawing back she puts a hand on his arm and gives him a quick, blundering old kiss and he feels on his own cheek the papery brushing of her lips and whiskers.

The old lady abruptly dismisses them then and on the darkened landing Harold, feeling in a kissing mood, and greatly daring, puts his arms round Ethel and pecks her several times on the lips. She laughs briefly and puts her hand up to his face. 'You're sweet,' she says.

'Can we go out for a walk, d'you think?' he asks, this being fairly acceptable for a Sunday evening.

'I should think so.'

As they are going out through the hall Aldyth appears again, with her earrings and make-up on, and he wonders where on earth she can be going this evening. She looks very tall and mature and there is something glossy and foreign in her deep black waved hair and almond eyes which startles him. She gives him an unusual look as they are leaving and says, 'Don't do anything I wouldn't do.'

'Oh, I don't suppose that's likely,' he says amiably, and she gives him a quick bare smile that leaves him again feeling strangely younger than her, immobilised and awkward like a clumsy boy.

Outside there is a wonderful crisp starriness in the air and the street is quiet except for the soft chugs and wheezes of the shunting engines in the marshalling yards behind the houses. Ethel's hand is warm in his and he is about to try to tell her how much he loves her when she says curtly, 'Don't flirt with Aldyth.'

She does not look at him and by the light of the street lamps he cannot read her expression.

'I didn't know I had,' he says honestly. 'Anyway, she's only a child really – '

'That's where you're wrong,' she says. 'She's not. She never has been.'

'Don't you like her very much?' Harold is surprised, and a little irritated: he cannot see what Aldyth has to do with the two of them.

'She's my sister, it's not a question of like,' says Ethel, shortly, and he is suddenly afraid that she is closing up, withdrawing from him as she sometimes does to some mysterious distance where he cannot reach her. She continues to walk briskly, heels clopping on the pavement, her hand inert in his. 'I'm sorry,' he says, and waves of troubled tenderness move in him. 'Ethel, when can we get married?'

She surprises him again by stopping in her tracks and seizing him in a hug and covering him with kisses, the warm, kindly kisses that are so typical of her. 'Soon,' she says, 'oh, soon, soon, Harold. Let's get married soon.' And he feels giddy and light-headed with a puzzled happiness, standing in the street in the empty frosty evening with her arms clasping him tight and the cold freshness of her cheek against his mouth.

.

It was not because he was afraid of Marian's reaction that David postponed telling her until he had been at her house half an hour and had had a glass of beer with Richard. Marian's reactions to the slightest things tended towards the operatic, and anyway it was done now. But he wanted to prove that not only was he capable of independent action but that it would be the future pattern of his life. So when at last she gave him an opening by asking if he had been busy today his casualness was monumental as he said: 'Oh, did a bit of shopping. And I took some of mum's stuff to the Sally Army shop this afternoon.'

Marian was sitting at the dining-table with her mail-order catalogue open before her, eating wine-gums. She chewed the sweets with jaw-cracking relish, open-mouthed, and instead of a woman of thirty-two he saw her as a girl again, wearing plastic rings she had won on the lucky-dip machine at Skegness, telling him rude rhymes she had learned at school and getting upset because he already knew them. She stopped her chewing and he went on hurriedly: 'It's amazing the things you see in there. I'll bet there are real antiques buried amongst the rubbish.'

'What stuff of mum's?'

He presented to her a face of flattened neutrality. 'Eh?'

'What stuff of mum's?'

'Oh, well, I didn't take an inventory. All that old furniture in the bedroom anyway, except the bed. A lot of her bits and pieces from downstairs. It was only her who liked them after all. Terrible old things most of them,' he added, realising he was starting to justify himself. Of course the idea that he was somehow betraying mum was ridiculous; and of course he had thought of it himself. When he had loaded up the car he had stood for a moment looking at it and had hovered on the point of taking all the stuff out again and putting it back. Mr Carelli next door had watched him from behind his curtains. Accusingly. Barely cold in her grave, look at him Lisa.

'You never said anything to me about this,' said Marian. 'When did you decide to do it?'

'When? I don't know. What's the fuss? Anyway what do you mean I didn't say anything to you, I just have.' He rubbed the back of his neck irritably where the barber had shaved it. He wasn't sure that this haircut didn't make him look rather older. Marian had gone tight-lipped: not what he had expected.

'How much did you get for this furniture then, David?' said Richard.

'What do you mean?' he said. 'You don't get anything. It's a charity concern, you give the stuff free.' Typical of his brother-in-law. David watched the workings of Richard's big face as he wrestled with the strange idea of giving something away.

'Hi David.'

It was Richard's younger brother, Peter: he was a university student and was spending Christmas with the couple. He came into the room in drooping attitude and sat horizontally on the settee next to David and eyed the television with disgust. 'Hi' stuck in David's throat and he settled for 'Hello'. He hoped this interruption would mean the end of the subject.

'I know it's for charity and everything, David,' said Marian, 'but I do think – '

'Mum was always keen on charities,' he said. 'You know that.' He remembered the little girl in Africa for whose schooling his mother subscribed. Once a year she received a brief childish letter from her and she kept each one in an album. He was struck, with great poignancy, by the thought of the little girl, playing under a tropical sun, unaware of her benefactress's slow death thousands of miles away in the haggard winter of an English town.

'That's not the point.' Marian came round and sat in the easy chair, twitching her skirt over her big shiny knees. 'You just can't go and dispose of all that stuff without telling anyone. You've got to consider the family – '

'The *family*,' he said, hearing his voice loud and edgy. He put his glass down on the floor with the excessive care of insobriety. Richard's home-brewed beer tasted awful but it went straight to your head. 'What's it got to do with them? There's nothing there that you'd have wanted, you've said so yourself.'

'You should have asked them. People take fancies to things.'

'Oh, no. That's like some bloody situation comedy – everybody scrabbling over who's going to have grandad's watch or whatever. Better to give the whole lot to a good cause. They're none of them short.'

'Auntie Jeanette might have liked something. Even for sentimental reasons. She is mum's sister.'

'All right. All right. In that case we should have asked Auntie Aldyth as well. Except of course that's out of the question, we've got to keep that bloody skeleton in the closet.'

'Don't start that again, David. How could we get in touch with her anyway? Nobody knows where she is now.'

'Somebody must do. Somebody must.' David realised he was blustering and tried to calm down. 'However bloody scandalous she was we ought to be able to speak her name in this day and age.'

'Don't keep swearing David, Tracey will hear you. She's only in the room above,' said Marian.

'Well she ought to be asleep at this time of night!'

'She won't be if you keep shouting the odds!'

Peter stirred. 'If you're going to play happy families,' he said languidly, 'd'you want me to leave the room?'

'No, no, Peter,' said Marian, 'it's all right,' and David saw that she was genuinely shocked at the idea that they could be having a row. He felt softened and said, 'Well, perhaps I should have mentioned it before. But it's done now, and it'll do somebody some good.'

'I should think that house is even emptier now, David,' said Richard, holding up his syrupy beer to the light. 'You ought to sell it and move out to the townships.'

'Thing is, it won't be that empty.' Time for the second bombshell: he wished he'd never said anything. 'I'm going to have a lodger. In mum's old room. That's a big room, and he can share the facilities. And the extra money will come in handy.'

'Sounds like a good idea,' said Richard. 'Put an advert in the paper. Or go through an agency, more reliable.'

'Oh, I should be careful, David,' said Marian. 'You can get all sorts of funny people.'

'I've got somebody. He's moving in tomorrow.'

'Oh!' Marian stared at him. 'Anyone we know?' and his heart sank at her tone.

'He's just a young chap I met at the Sally Army shop.' He struggled with the impossibility of explaining what he could hardly have explained to himself: how he had got talking to this scraggy peroxided youth who had nowhere to live, who had seemed to represent in one brief meeting everything that was young, that was different, that was not the Family and the dreary iron-bound proprieties that threatened to immobilise him.

'He works there?' said Richard. 'Can't be much of a job.'

'Oh, it's only voluntary,' said David. 'Not paid. He's on the dole.'

Peter raised his head a painful fraction, like an interested tortoise. 'Dosser like me,' he said. 'Only my pittance is a bit more.'

'Oh, David, what were you thinking of?' Marian's eyes widened and she put a hand up to her cheek. She had a range of gestures like those of a bad actress; yet she was a person incapable of dissembling. In spite of himself David understood the horror on her face: it was the mark of a new kind of generation gap. She had walked out of school into a job – so had he for that matter – and she seemed unable to conceive of the dole except in terms of flat caps and mufflers and soup-kitchens, or even the workhouse and the parish beadle. 'He'll never be able to pay the rent,' she went on. 'Can't you get anybody decent?'

David frowned, and it was on his lips to say that just because he hadn't got a job didn't mean the young man wasn't decent, but he realised that he wasn't decent, really, by Marian's standards, and that was what he liked about him. 'They get their rent paid by the council now,' he said lighting a cigarette and standing up, as if that would give him more authority. 'He hasn't got anywhere to live and I've got a house that's too big for me. I can't see any objection.'

'Why isn't he with his parents? How old is he?'

'Nineteen-ish, I should think. He doesn't get on with his mum and dad. Anyway you want some independence at that age.' Did I? Do I now? He sat down again, afflicted by a bleak voice that periodically spoke husky whispers of despair to him.

'I see,' said Richard. 'Probably chucked him out because he wouldn't get off his backside. So he's going to have a nice easy life on my taxes.' David knew Richard was very proprietorial about his taxes. Richard's taxes must have been phenomenal. They kept half the population in luxury. When he was in a bad mood they made up the entire revenue of the United Kingdom.

'Well I don't know. I think families ought to stay together,' said Marian.

'Like ours? God forbid.'

'They're important. Something you've always got to fall back on.'

Yes, the safety net. No matter what you did, no matter what aerial extravaganzas you aspired to, that fine buoyant mesh was waiting to receive you, making all your daring as innocuous as the teetering of a child along a foot-high wall.

The mesh was so fine that once you were in it you probably would not get out again, but then that was the price you paid, the premium on the insurance policy against being alone. And there was the nucleus of a new Family here in this house – Marian and Richard, and the unborn baby, and seven-year-old Tracey upstairs: the threads of another net were spinning out and interweaving beneath the trapezium of the future.

He would not be part of it. When Richard suggested they go out for a drink David was glad with an almost physical relief, as if the house might take him prisoner. It was a nice house, a small new one in a green-field estate, but whenever David visited he was dismayed by the interior, which had a unique chilliness despite the constant warm breaths that sighed up from the central-heating vents in the floor. Marian was simply tidy but Richard was obsessive. Everything but the chairs and table was spirited away into cupboards. A newspaper left lying on the floor seemed to cause him actual pain. David did not much like him, mainly because he did not understand him. He was a man of bland largeness, like a professional golfer. Though he was a couple of years younger than David – they had been at the same secondary modern – David always thought of him as an older man; a person of whom you asked advice, and a person who would never reply 'Christ, don't ask me.' As they drove out to the club in Richard's car with Peter, who had gloomily volunteered to go with them, singing to himself in the back seat, he stole a look at his brother-in-law's face by the dashboard light. It was a square heavy-jowled face which had rejected handsomeness by rejecting expression.

'I think Marian's a bit fazed by your news, David,' said Richard. 'I thought we'd better come out and leave her to mull over it a bit. She'll come round, but she doesn't get used to new things quickly.'

The measured, impersonal tone Richard always used when talking about Marian. No possessive tender fondness there. Was that what eight years of marriage did for you? Yet there was no doubt they were devoted to each other. David felt impatient with him and turned to Peter. 'How are you getting on at university, Peter?'

'S'good. S'good laugh.'

'Bet you don't get much work done, eh?' he said, to his horror finding himself using the stock inquiries of the older generation to the younger and unable to find any way of speaking that belonged to neither.

'That's right, we spend all our time at drug-crazed parties,' said Peter, sleepily. There was no venom in the sarcasm. Peter was of a type unknown to David. He was quiet without the slightest touch of shyness, good-looking in a forgettable way, he had done horrifying, inexplicable things like wandering round Thailand on his own. He seemed to acknowledge none of the vagaries and semi-fatuities of ordinary conversation, declined the common effort that kept the silence at bay. He seemed by some process to have cauterised his nerve-ends. 'Jesus, a real Wheeltappers' and Shunters',' was his reaction to the Barlow Watkins Sports and Social Club, but this was more hopeful than truthful. It was a big shiny place of chrome and mirrors and several bars. Its only archaism was a dance hall with bare boards where members of the Olde Time Dancing Society hauled one another around the floor raising dust like horses.

Louise came to serve him at the bar.

'Hallo, David love. Nice to see you again. I was that sorry to hear about your mother.'

'Oh – thanks, Louise.' He was surprised, and touched; perhaps chiefly by the fact that she came right up and said it instead of muttering in a shifty embarrassed way as most people did.

'Are you managing all right?'

'Yes, not so bad. Oh – two and a half pints of bitter, please.' He added, 'And whatever you'd like.' Louise was a nice girl, shortish and trim with light buttery hair and a clear round face. He did not often meet her, for he seldom came to the club except for meetings of the Painting Society, an appallingly unadventurous little group led by an ex-art teacher who took them on occasional forays by minibus into the country, there to get cold fingers and numb bottoms in a frustrated and untrained attempt to put the flat fenny landscape on paper. He had always liked her and now as he watched her smart deft movements he felt a little distant firing of excitement. 'Busy tonight,' was all, lamentably, he could think of to say but she smiled at him and said: 'Always the same just before Christmas. You'll see, after Christmas they'll all be sick of booze and I shall get a few nights off at last.'

Her smiling face with its smooth milky skin was still in his mind as they went to a table, and he could not be bothered to fully attend to Richard, who was talking about work. Richard was a draughtsman at Barlow Watkins and the intricacies of office politics were of endless fascination for him. Only when Peter stifled a yawn did he stop and say: 'My brother here's bored by all this. He's a free spirit, thinks I've sold out and joined the rat-race. Pawned my soul for a fridge-freezer. Have I got that right?'

'I never said that,' said Peter. 'No doubt I'll be joining you in a year or two, when I've got my piece of paper.' He shrugged and aimed a footballer's header at a tail of tinsel that was hanging above him.

'No need to if you don't want to,' said David.

'Come off it,' said Peter. 'What else should I do? Don't tell me you believe in some alternative lifestyle crap. I'll either have to put the old suit and tie on and knuckle under or go on the dole. And be bored out of my brain and broke. That's reality.'

'I suppose so,' said David. 'Bit of a bleak way of looking at it.' This cynicism in a young man disturbed him. Romance had never really been weeded out of himself, and he recognised it as such without mistrusting it. 'Surely there's more – possibilities to life.'

'If you can find them, good luck to you,' said Peter. He winked at Richard. 'I reckon David's going to do a Gauguin. Throw up everything and go native and screw the dusky nubiles.' The brothers laughed together, Richard a little restrainedly because of the indecency, but collusively. David realised with disappointment that in spite of their differences these two were definitely turned out of the same mould. He was glad to get up and fetch more drinks, brushing aside Richard's punctilious protests that he must get these.

For a moment as he stood at the bar he was afraid the steward was going to serve him, but then Louise spotted him. 'Same again, is it?' she said, smiling once more. Of course, you had to smile for customers in this job. He glanced covertly at himself in the mirror behind the bar. The muscles on his jaw seemed to stick out like a cadaver's and he realised he was clenching his teeth. 'Louise,' he said as she gave him his change, 'you know what you were saying about your nights off after Christmas . . .'

'Yes, love.' A blank, unsurprised face. There were little glinting golden hairs on her arms.

'I was wondering if you'd like to come out one night – '

'Sorry, David, half a minute.' She moved away to serve someone. Nervously he dipped his lips in dark beer. Richard and Peter must be watching. She came back, bright and friendly. 'Sorry, what were you saying?'

'Oh, I just wondered if you'd like to come out somewhere one night.' It came out lamely enough.

'With you? Yes, that'd be lovely. When? Mind you, like I say, it depends on my nights off. Look, I'll give you my phone number.'

He came back with the beer shakily triumphant. Richard and Peter had not been watching: Richard was deep in the subject of the trouble with young people today. 'More opportunities, of course, that's a good thing. But more opportunities to do the wrong things, too.'

'Promiscuity, I presume,' said Peter archly, and winked at David. 'Chance would be a fine thing.'

Richard was flushed and serious. 'If that's what you want to call it. You see when David and I were your age – '

'Hang on – let's hear what you're going to say before you include me in this.'

Richard puckered his lips judicially, one finger poking the

table top. 'All I'm saying is we didn't take – certain things as our natural right. There was a sense of mystery – '

David too was flushed, with beer and excitement, and he burst out, 'Oh, come on, Richard, don't tell me you and Marian didn't before you were wed . . .'

He had not meant to say that – did not in fact believe it – but he was amused at the stony petulance that froze his brother-in-law's face. Peter giggled slurpily into his glass. 'I don't feel you should talk about your sister in that way, David,' said Richard. 'I know you're only joking but – well, she sees things differently. You seem to forget. I know you don't go to church any more but she still does.'

'What's that got to do with anything?'

'The way you were talking earlier, it upset her. Really, you know, David – ' Richard was emerging out of embarrassment into a bearing gravely avuncular which made David want to laugh even more – 'we're a little worried about you. I know you were as upset as we were about your mother, but I wonder whether it hasn't affected you in some way you don't realise.'

'Don't tell me,' said David: he was suddenly flooded with smarting hurt and anger. 'I'm betraying her memory. By trying to live my own life. By doing what she would thoroughly have approved of. Anyway, who was it who bloody well looked after her all these years?' He didn't mean that. Rancour had pricked him into acting the martyr, which he was not.

'I'm sorry,' said Richard, 'I've given you the wrong impression.'

'As Mike Yarwood said to the actress,' said Peter, who was becoming rapidly drunk, or pretending to be.

'What I mean is, you've been going on about your Auntie Aldyth. And you know full well your mother wanted nothing to do with her. Surely you can respect that.'

'Who's this, who's this?' said Peter. 'The Barber black sheep? Baa, baa, black sheep,' he sniggered to himself.

'It just seems pretty hypocritical,' said David, 'all this

family pulling-together. And her out of it. She can't have been that bad.'

'The point is it's all in the past,' said Richard. 'You should let the past be, it's gone.'

'*She* isn't though,' said David. 'Unless my loving family bashed her on the head and hid her in the cellar. All I'm saying is I'd like to get in touch with her if I can.'

He watched Richard solemnly shaking his great head. Somewhere within him there had always been a certain respect for Richard. His assurance was pig-headed but David had always looked on any assurance with something like awe. Now he was relieved to find that respect gone. He imagined Auntie Aldyth flouting a world of stolid Richards: the idea appealed to him. She had found some way of severing those clinging spidery threads. He raised his glass to his lips in a mental toast to her.

CHAPTER 4

The large, doughy-pale bottom of the model was flushing bright pink under the arc lamps and the electric heater. David wondered if he should account for this in the shading of his drawing. He glanced to his right and noticed that Nicholas had already produced an annoyingly fluent sketch and now, his interest flagging, was going into absurd rococo detail in the folds of the blanket on the mattress. Strange, the disregarded, firework nature of this talent. He had even left the woman's right foot as a brief parallelogram of a few lines, but it looked right. In David's sketch the foot was huge and bulbous and literal. It gave the impression of having too many toes, though he kept counting them. He wondered if he dare risk using his eraser, a prohibition he found highly constricting, but he was in full view of the instructor, Miss Lacey ('Call me Ruth', though few people did), and he was already fearful of the moment when she would get up from her desk and come round to look at their drawings.

'Are you still warm enough?' said Miss Lacey.

The model, lying on her stomach, lifted a sleepy swollen face. 'Yes, plenty, thanks.'

'Do say if you get cold.'

David didn't know how they could do it. However, it was really not at all embarrassing, as he had thought. Perhaps it was the presence of Nicholas: he never felt embarrassed when he was around. Well, perhaps at the end of that Christmas day he had been embarrassed, a little, but he couldn't remember because he had been laughing too much.

Nicholas, when he had got up on Boxing Day morning – or rather afternoon – seemed to have forgotten all about it, or didn't care, which came to the same thing with him. Everyone else had been pretty good about it. Only Uncle Alan, whom David had met in town the other day and had only received a curt nod from, seemed still offended. He had to feel sorry for Uncle Alan. After all he had been the only one at the dinner without at least a drop of drink in him. Waking alone on Christmas morning in a chill of temperance and solitude, then off to chapel to assuage his loneliness with a draught of long cold prayer before driving in his Morris-Minor to David's, there to perform the role of skeleton at the feast which life had forced on him so insistently that he had begun to embrace it.

From all over town to share the turkey – for the cooking of which Marian gave him a detailed page of instructions, written in one long periphrastic sentence like the American Declaration of Independence – came the family. Came Marian and Richard, with little Tracey irritable in tow and inclined to kick at furniture legs and human ones if she could get them, together with Peter, who buttonholed David's drinks cabinet like an old friend and went into a huddle with it for the rest of the day. Came Auntie Jeanette, whom David liked best, a horse-faced woman who galumphed about like a schoolgirl, and her husband Reg, bringing with them Great-Uncle Bob Russell and his pervasive fug of tobacco, onions and brilliantine; came Duncan, David's cousin he didn't know how many times removed, a sleek man given to weighty jewellery whom David had only invited because he did not think he would come.

'I didn't realise your lodger would be joining us for dinner, David,' said Marian aside to him. 'I don't think he really fits in, do you?'

'Well, what am I supposed to do? I can't shut him in his room and just let him smell the turkey through the keyhole,' he said. He was just realising this was his first Christmas without his mother, and he still had a hangover from the night before and was attempting to make sense of memories that included standing on top of a post-box and singing carols at garden gates in the small hours with a mouth that seemed to have a will of its own.

And there she let it drop, which surprised him. It was clear she did not like Nicholas, even though he obliged Tracey, who was monotonously shooting at him with a toy gun, by collapsing in dramatic death throes. It was clear that she did not like the little exhibit that he and David, full of beer, had placed next to the Christmas tree. Nicholas, somehow, had got it from a department store: it was the middle section of a mannequin, for displaying underpants; it was an unnatural flesh pink and the genitals were a discreetly ambiguous bump. From the same source Nicholas had acquired a mannequin hand and this he had attached to the buttocks in a prurient pinch. Looking at it again, David could not quite see why it had thrown him into such hysterics, especially when they had placed it on the turntable of the record-player and it had gracefully rotated. But the release of that laughter had been wonderful in itself.

Nicholas was very tall and thin: he wore a leather motor-cycle jacket with a jewelled brooch on it; his peroxide hair was teased into a gravity-defying coxcomb. 'How do you *get* it like that?' Auntie Jeanette asked him, with her frankness that never offended. David was pleased to see her, at least, taking to him.

At the same time he was aware that it was not approval that he was seeking for having taken in this singular scare-crow. That they were all more or less getting on with him – even Marian laughing as he described the woman in charge of the Oxfam shop: 'Great long streak of a woman, tits like chapel hat-pegs – she's always got these dozens of tissues stuck up the sleeves of her jumper, her arms look like Popeye's' – did not disguise the fact, even from David, that in having him here he had committed himself, thrown down a gauntlet.

Duncan came into the kitchen while David was impotently poking at the Brussels sprouts, which refused to soften. It was just about the only job Marian had left him to do unaided. His cousin held a scotch in his hairy fist: a year or two younger than David, he had obviously grown tired of Christmassy chat with aunties and had come for a manly talk. Fastidiously he looked around for somewhere to put his drink and settled for a few inches of clear space on top of the refrigerator. 'Smells good,' he said. 'You must be getting used to cooking for yourself now, David.'

'Yes, I don't really mind it.' His cousin reeked of after-shave, whisky and money.

'Be nice to have a little woman to do it for you though, eh?'

'Or a large woman, come to that,' said David, who himself had topped up his hangover with a few drinks.

Duncan laughed, shortly. 'Sure.' He had a stock of mid-Atlanticisms which David disliked. 'But seriously – ' and Duncan spoke in his straight-from-the-shoulder way that irritated David further – 'ever think of settling down?'

'You can't get much more settled than me. We don't do much jet-setting in the Wages Office of Barlow Watkins.'

'No, I mean – find a nice girl. Marriage, kids, all that. You know.'

'Well, *you* haven't settled down,' said David, fully aware that Duncan's words rested on the premise that settling down was the lot not of the Duncans of the world, with their bachelor flats, expensive leather gloves and good jobs, but of the Davids.

'I like my independence,' said Duncan. 'But who knows? I might get caught one day. We can't play the field for ever.' He flashed David a tanned, practised grin. David knew that 'we' did not include him, and knew that Duncan knew it, but that he was only required in this sort of talk to make an appropriately raffish response. He refused to do so. 'Chance would be a fine thing,' he said.

'Ah, come on, David,' Duncan said, giving him a cigarette that tasted like a cough sweet. 'Time's ripe. You've got this house, could do with repair, okay, but a roomy semi, pre-war, in a popular part of the city – or it will be until the wogs get here. It's a good start.'

'Perhaps I should marry an estate agent.'

'Okay, okay. But all I'm saying is, it's not really a place to be on your own in.'

'It was my mother's house.' Shades of Norman Bates.

'Right. And all I'm saying is it'd be ideal if you had someone to share it with. I mean me-laddo here – ' he gestured towards the living-room door – 'he's all very well, until you can find someone more suitable . . .'

'What's wrong with him? He livens the place up.'

'Oh, I don't doubt that.'

David looked quickly at his cousin, who was blowing out perfect smoke-rings. He put the lid back on the pan, very carefully. 'Say what's on your mind.'

Duncan squared his shoulders further. 'Well you couldn't hear because you were in here, but a minute ago that actor fellow was on the telly, Jeremy Whatsisname, and your young guest was going into raptures over him. Saying how gorgeous he was and all that.'

Duncan swept up his glass and drank from it: a pretentious gesture, suggesting in a single second that he knew the scotch was Sainsbury's-own-brand, that he was used to drinking better stuff, but that he would carry the thing off with style to humour David. David wished for a gesture that would convey the fact that he thought Duncan was a shit, that one scotch was much like another, and that Duncan had polished off half the bottle. He wanted the conversation to end right now. He could not say when it was that he realised that Nicholas was gay, nor could he say that it had been a startling revelation. It somehow seemed merely of a piece with the breeze of unconventionality that the young man brought with him. In the pub the other night with some of his friends, who as far as David could tell were not gay, Nicholas had said, dropping into slumped, slack-jawed Brummy, 'Oh, straight sex is so *boooring*,' and that seemed to sum it up as far as he was concerned. David was not repelled but curious: dim memories of a man down the road, with a big leonine head and small white hands, whom as children his mother had told them to keep away from, constituted the only real yardstick of response he could measure by.

'You did know, didn't you?' Duncan said.

'Of course I knew,' said David; and only the fact that it was Christmas, and a relic in him of a small but solid belief in the bit about goodwill, prevented him going on: 'And I don't care, I don't care if he shags sheep, he makes me laugh and he makes me feel younger, and if you don't approve then that's a very good reason for liking him.' Instead he said: 'It's his life, it's up to him. He's grown up.'

'Well, not strictly. He's not twenty-one, is he? Okay, forget that. Look, David – ' for a sickening moment David thought he was going to say 'We're men of the world' and was afraid that if he did he would not be able to stop himself tipping the whole pan of sprouts over his head – 'what I mean is, some people might think it's a pretty dodgy set-up.'

'They can think what they like.'

'Fair enough.' Duncan stubbed out his cigarette. 'Don't let him have – overnight guests, do you?'

David dropped the fork with a clatter. 'I've heard enough of this – '

Duncan held up his hands. 'All right. I'll clear off again now. Go and listen to old Bob's tales for the umpteenth time. Reckon he makes most of 'em up.' He paused with his hand on the door. 'But I don't think your sister's too happy about it. And I don't think your old mum would be either.'

That remark might have got to David, but the cheap patina of sentimentality that the word 'old' gave to 'mum' cancelled it: it was the sort of meretricious maudlin phrase used by brute-faced criminals. And he was surprised to find himself buoyant now, refreshed; surprised by the realisation that Duncan, for all his mohair-coat rascality, was a prude, and that he was not.

So he played the genial host well. Nobody got food poisoning. Auntie Jeanette got tipsy on sweet white wine, and began playfully slapping Richard's big stolid thighs because he would not wear a paper hat, and her husband Reg, who had married her because he found her amusing and never regretted it, just sat back and laughed. Duncan was all charm, and the only sign of his conversation with David in the kitchen came when Nicholas got up from the table and, making room for him to pass, Duncan shifted his legs back an unnecessary distance.

David could not remember who it was that suggested playing charades; he was himself quite fuddled by then. It was some time after the Queen's speech, which Uncle Alan had insisted on switching on, shushing old Bob who made remarks about the Queen Mother's fondness for gin. But he remembered Marian, who was hopeless at this sort of thing, abandoning an attempt to portray 'The Fall of the Roman Empire' and returning to her seat in half-embarrassed laughter, and then Nicholas – who never slurred or staggered and hence could become deceptively drunk – sprang to his feet and said '*I've* got one' and promptly disappeared from the room. In the surprised silence that followed Auntie Jeanette leaned over to David and said with woozy earnestness: 'He's terrifically good fun, isn't he?' She smelt pleasantly of wine and peppermints. She sat with one foot awkwardly on top of the other and he would not have been surprised to see a big hole in her stocking with a scabbed knee sticking out. Softened and expansive, he began to say 'I'm glad you like – ' when the door was flung open again. Nicholas stood in the doorway, his arms pressed tightly to his sides. He was wearing a red balaclava helmet pulled right down over his face, and nothing else but a pair of off-white underpants. 'Give in?' he cried, his voice a little muffled. 'Give in? A *matchstick*!' David only realised that Nicholas was completely, obliviously drunk in the split second between his saying this and toppling face forward to the floor in a confusion of white ribs and elbows.

David smiled to himself at the memory, and then wiped the smile off his face and studied his drawing because Miss Lacey was looking. Nicholas, who had persuaded him to come along to the evening drawing classes at the technical college, had assured him it was quite informal, but he still found the atmosphere rather schoolish. And the pencil felt as clumsy as a broom-handle in his fingers: he was not used to drawing in anything but solitude. In a countryside where agriculture was so tyrannical even a tree was a rarity he had often felt the need to enliven the landscapes he painted with figures, but they always looked impossibly stiff, and this drawing was not turning out any better.

'Oh, it's not that funny.'

He jumped. Miss Lacey had noiselessly appeared beside him.

'Oh – I wasn't laughing at my drawing,' he said. 'Well – despairing rather.'

'No need for that.' Her voice was soft, just audible, the sort that makes one drop one's own voice in sympathy. 'Especially as you haven't done this before. Try to forget it's a person lying there. Forget you know what a person looks like. None of us do really. Think of it as a collection of shapes. Look.'

In one corner of his paper she began to sketch a schematic version of the figure. He stood back awkwardly, trying to concentrate on her drawing, observing her piecemeal in little darting glances. Her dark hair, cut quite short, had coppery threads in it and her eyes were so dark as to be almost black. He thought she had a Celtic look about her. And he had been deceived by the faintly schoolmarm manner: she must have been a couple of years his junior. Her fingers as she sketched were enviably relaxed: as he watched his own fingers seemed to swell and go numb until they felt like flabby sausages.

'There, that should give you an idea,' she said, stepping back and giving him a brief smile. 'Just relax a little more, don't worry about detail too much.'

He did not feel relaxed and, by the end of the class, twenty minutes later, his drawing looked even worse and was smudged with sweat.

'There, I'll bet you you'll bump into that model in town soon,' said Nicholas as they walked down the corridor. 'Always happens. I never know what to say. I mean you've got to say something. "Hello, didn't recognise you with your clothes on". She's good though, keeps dead still. Some are always fidgeting and scratching themselves. They had a bloke last term, Pedro his name was, he started to get an erection while he was standing there starkers. God knows what he was thinking about. One look at my incredible handsomeness probably. It has that effect. Miss Lacey was brill though, just told him very firmly to control himself. He went down like a popped balloon. I suppose that's the sort of authority money gives you.'

'I wouldn't have thought her job was all that well paid.'

'Oh, God, no, not that. Didn't you know, she's one of *the* Laceys, as in Lacey's department store. Not that they actually run it any more, I don't think, but the money's still there.'

'No, I didn't know,' said David. He felt in his pocket. 'Damn, I left my rubber in there. Wait a minute.' He hurried back to the studio, and Nicholas's voice called down the corridor after him, 'You've got a crush on teacher!'

'You left this behind.' Miss Lacey was holding the eraser up.

'Ah – thanks.'

'Well, now you know my prejudice against those things, you needn't bother to bring it again,' she said with mock severity, but the element of mockery was self-conscious, as if she was aware that her severity tended to be genuine. He smiled and turned to go. 'By the way,' she added, 'it is Mr Barber isn't it?'

'Yes.'

'I was sorry to hear about your mother.'

'Oh – thank you – did you know . . . ?'

'Well, I saw the obituary notice in the *Advertiser*, the name rang a bell. Knew your parents years ago, through my parents really.' She spoke rather quickly.

'Oh, I'd no idea.' He was surprised: could never imagine his mother having anything to do with the Laceys.

'Well, anyway. See you next week – not too discouraged I hope?'

'Not at all. Goodbye.'

'She'd eat you for breakfast, mate,' said Nicholas when he rejoined him in the corridor, and again, laughing, in the pub later, 'She'd eat you for breakfast,' until for the first time David felt a little impatient with him.

*

The winter of 1938 has been a cold one, and this March night the town sleeps among its still frozen marshes and dreams of warmer times. Old Chay, trundling his empty handcart along the slippery pavement, thinks he can sense them coming. A nocturnal creature, he is used to the slow yellow glimmering of dawn and expert at divining what it means for the day ahead, and those first few spreading stains of light above the chimneys and an extra freshness in the air convince him that spring is on the way. Standing on the south platform waiting for the London train he says as much to a railwayman beside him, and the man nods, believing him. The London train is on time, emerging suddenly from beneath the bridge blowing like some fire-eating whale. The railwayman helps Chay load the blocks of newspapers, parcelled up with cord and with a pleasant starchy whiff of print, on to his handcart, and then Chay trundles off again to the newsagent's.

He will be glad to see the back of this winter. His shoes have nearly worn through so he has fixed strips of old tyres to their soles. When Wilks, the newsagent, saw this he looked troubled and the next day gave Chay an extra shilling. Chay is appreciative of this, but the fact is he does not wish to buy new shoes while the uppers are still in such good condition. He is able to get by on what Wilks pays him and what the railway company pay him for knocking-up, which he sets off to do after delivering the newspapers to the newsagent's. He collects his long wooden pole with the metal tip from where he keeps it in Wilks' shed and then crosses the footbridge over the marshalling yards to the Great Northern Cottages.

These rows of terraces, two-up two-down, built by the company for their employees, will in forty years' time be in sad dereliction and crammed with poor Asian families. For the moment, however, they are comparatively smart and well-built, with decent kitchens and outside lavatories to each one, and a step up from the clusters of Victorian monstrosities on the other side of the bridge, where the first rail line was run – where Chay lives. Years of having to be awake in the small hours have never quite ridded Chay of a feeling of regret at having to wake the railwaymen from their warm sleep to go on their shift. But even though the houses all look alike, he has a wonderful memory and has never made the mistake of waking anyone up who is not on shift. He ambles along the terrace, lifting his pole and rapping gently on each bedroom window, and then waiting patiently for a light to come on or for the curtains to twitch before going on to the next one. At last his job is done and he observes with approval the streaks of cadmium yellow in the sky beginning to suffuse with a pink glow before turning for home. He is stopped by a noise of someone sobbing from a lean-to shed at the back of the last house.

He finds inside, hunched on the floor amongst tools and rusting pots of paint, a very pretty young woman with dark waved hair, in a grey coat and smart ruched dove-grey frock which the shed has soiled pitiably. She is crying as Chay has never seen anyone cry, and from the red ravaged state of her eyes and cheeks has been doing so for a long time. 'What's the matter, duck?' he says. 'What is it?' He never knew anyone could cry that much. She seems to take no further notice of him than to turn her head away slightly and to carry on sobbing. He crouches down beside her, which is not easy for his old joints, and searches in his mind. He knows just about everyone in the Great Northern Cottages and is certain she does not live here. 'What's happened to you, pet?' he says, feeling his mouth dry. 'Has anybody hurt you?'

'Nothing,' she says, shaking her head convulsively. 'Nothing, it's nothing.'

There is a handkerchief squeezed into a ball in her hand but he offers her his and is glad to see her take it. He wonders if it might be drink but he cannot smell anything. 'Where d'you live then?' he said. 'Can't I take you home?'

At first he cannot catch what she says for it is broken and breathless with tears but at last he makes out the words 'Fifty . . . Corporation Road.'

'Come on, then, pet. That's not far, I'll tek you. Go and see your mam and dad, eh?' But this last seems to make her worse, so he does not mention it again.

She comes with him, still sobbing. The streets are still

fairly empty, but a couple of men on bicycles pass him with surprised glances, for her steps are unsteady – there was obviously drink at some point – and so she holds his arm as they walk. He feels very strange, going along with this pretty, mysterious girl, with his pole over his other shoulder, and for a moment he thinks what a story this will be to tell the old beggars in The Navigator this dinner-time; but then he thinks that really he ought not to say anything of it. He keeps up a soft crooning of consolation, but she says nothing except, once, 'I want Ethel.'

They arrive at Corporation Road, and though the girl says she'll be all right now he waits while she taps at the back door. 'Knock a bit louder,' he says, but soon the door is opened by another woman, a little older but also pretty, in a dressing-gown and cardigan, with the air of someone who has been waiting up. 'Oh, Ethel – ' the girl begins to say, and then Chay watches in amazement as the woman in the dressing-gown slaps the girl across the face, over and over again, in between each slap holding the girl's face in a convulsive hug, and saying in a kind of screamed whisper 'You've been with him, haven't you? You've been with him, you've been with him.' She does not even notice Chay standing there and at last she pulls the girl inside and the door is closed.

Chay walks slowly back up the path to the street and there turns to look at the front of the house. The curtains in the front room and the main bedrooms are closed and the house has a sleepy, complacent, uncommunicative look, and for a moment an odd fancy flits across Chay's brain to reach up with his pole and rap the house on its big blank forehead to wake it up.

CHAPTER 5

When Nicholas called him to the phone on Tuesday night saying, 'It's Miss Lacey for you, wants you to come and draw her in the buff,' David was so thrown by thinking for a moment he was partly serious that he did not at first recognise Louise's voice.

'David, is that you? Who was that I just spoke to?'

'Oh – Louise – sorry, that was my lodger.' ('What do you mean, "sorry"?' exclaimed Nicholas in the background.) 'How are you?'

'Okay, thanks. Touch of the after-Christmas blues, you know. It's always a bit of a let-down, isn't it?'

'Oh yes . . . yes.' There was a silence. He knew he was supposed to say something, but his mind felt frozen.

'Well, does that invitation still stand then? Or have you forgotten all about me,' she said, with what sounded like a nervous laugh. He could hear her breathing, on the edge of audibility like his own.

'No, no – I mean, yes, of course it does. Well, when are you free?' and he had to turn away out of sight of Nicholas, who was pantomiming lewd gestures across the room.

So Wednesday night was arranged, and Wednesday seemed to crawl by at a deadlier pace than usual. With the pre-Christmas rush of sorting out holiday pay now over, the Wages Office had settled back into a routine that was doubly dreary. There was a strange kind of cocoon-like suspension about this place. The heating was turned up high, not enough to irritate but enough to make you sleepy, and the windows were of smoked glass, so nobody could see in even though it was four floors up. The view from here, over the tops of the cactus plants, would have been a pleasant one of the churches and bell-towers of the old town centre, but the Co-op dairy and the sugar-beet factory got in the way. In the autumn afternoons you could open a window and a delicious smell of crushed beet would waft across; a smoky, nostalgic smell like that of burning leaves, whetting the clean coolness of the air to unbearable sharpness, and inducing an adolescent melancholy of the kind that expresses itself in regret for things you never did, and tenderness for things you never liked, and a general vague feeling that the world is a sweetly-sad sort of place. A place in which the only sensible thing to do is go home and drink hot sweet tea and listen to the maudlin transcendence of country-and-western songs on the stereo, convincing you that you cried all the way to the altar, that it was a good year for the roses, and that you're the world's worst loser, When it comes to losing you – her – whoever . . .

But not in January. David came out of a dream to see Jack Erskine watching him from the opposite desk. 'Penny for 'em,' he said, and winked. 'A quid if they're not clean.'

'Nothing as interesting as that,' said David, and tried to look busy to avoid a quizzing.

'Go on,' said Erskine. He nodded his head towards the boss's door. 'Musso's not around. Who is it, eh? You've been dead close all day.'

'Musso' was Erskine's uninspired nickname for Mr Musson, their Section Leader, as they were supposed to refer to him. He was a yellow silent man who seldom smiled. He had been in a Japanese prisoner-of-war camp during the war. David supposed he didn't feel much like smiling. He was an unexacting boss, and one source for the distaste David felt for Erskine – who was nominally his friend, in the way that people who work in the same office are friends – was his fanciful insistence that they worked under a fire-eating martinet.

'I've got a date tonight, if that's the word,' said David.

Erskine's face, covered with a sparse gingery beard that

gave him a wolfish look, expanded in a grin of delight. 'You've never! Well, you are a dark horse, aren't you, Barber!'

'You needn't sound quite so surprised.'

'Oh, I'm not, mate, I'm not, just pleased for you,' said Erskine. The grin did not fade. 'What's her name then?'

'Mind your own business.' He meant it to come out jokingly; the edge took him by surprise.

The fun went out of Erskine's grin, just leaving his teeth showing. He had small and lashless and sometimes truculent eyes and they stared with dull, baffled affront at David. 'No need to come the old mild and bitter,' he said. 'Go on – what do you reckon your chances are?'

'For God's sake, Jack, can't you think of anything else?' snapped David, guilty and irritated because that was exactly what he had been wondering. Erskine wore the pouting expression of a child that has been refused something and is uncertain whether to try tears or tantrums. It was so long since David had had to talk about this except in the entirely chimerical nonsense that was common between males: one joined in unthinkingly, it was the currency, the masonic handshake by which the elect excluded the dubious and sanctioned the free telling of whopping lies. But with men of his own age like Jack Erskine he had always felt distanced in two contradictory ways: on the one hand assuming himself to be younger, still embedded as he was in the family, unmarried, an incomplete citizen; on the other hand nurturing with an uneasy pride a sense of himself as older, constantly in the company of the old, and granted access to maturer perspectives. Was his only choice now to join the Jack Erskines, embrace their world? It seemed like tunnelling out of a prison cell to emerge in the one next door.

'Of course,' said Erskine, 'if you're ashamed of her we won't say any more. But you needn't be, God knows, I've had some right old dogs in my time.'

'I wonder what your wife would say to that,' said David. It was an unkind, embittering point. A union of slobbish husband and termagant wife, the Erskines' married life was Punch and Judy with blood. The news that Mrs Erskine was seeking a divorce, leaked by one of her friends who worked in Accounts, had not surprised David.

'How d'you mean?' Erskine had coloured, and the points of his collar, which were joined by a little gold chain, were sticking up as if they were bristling.

'Forget it.' David felt he had gone too far already, fuelled by a combustion of nerves and excitement about tonight that constantly threatened to escape in searing blasts of temper. He realised suddenly that he had no friends with whom he could talk seriously about it, not even decent jovial Ron. Certainly not Jack Erskine. The realisation, coupled with an intuition that Erskine would never feel nervous like this and would laugh at anyone who did, had the effect of sharpening the antagonism he felt towards the waggish, dubious man who sat opposite him.

'Well, good luck to you, son,' said Erskine, staring at a file on his desk. 'I don't imagine you often get the opportunity.'

Let that one pass, said David to himself, with a pleasant sense of self-control, and a sense, also somehow sickly pleasant, of having irrevocably made an enemy. Erskine was silent for a moment, his fingers, plump and white, running delicately up and down the spine of the file. 'Oh, and by the way,' he went on, 'if you need any rubbers, I can lend you a pack. If you need 'em that is. Not much use putting a top on an empty bottle.'

David wondered afterwards at his own casualness as he got up from his desk and walked across the office as if he were merely going to open a window. It certainly startled Erskine to find David lifting him out of his seat by his collar. His eyes dilated and his lips pursed almost as if in prudish offence and David looking at the scribbled network of boozer's veins around his nostrils found he did not know what to say.

'Just shut it.' Lame enough, the fury had disappeared leaving only a throbbing in his temples, but Jack Erskine seemed frightened. He blustered a bit when David dropped him again – he was pretty heavy – and called David a loopy bugger and told him to keep his hair on. But for the rest of the day he kept quiet. Whenever David looked up he was bent over his desk, breathing noisily through his nose, the tips of his ears deeply pink. I should have apologised – No I shouldn't – I should have – No I shouldn't – went the chimes of his feeling, on through five o'clock and the congested drive home until the clangings of panic and anticipation drowned them out.

Nicholas tut-tutted at his shirts and hooted at his ties. David submitted to his advice and eventually left to pick up Louise with his neck throttlingly constricted in a shirt belonging to Nicholas. A thaw had descended suddenly on the town and the tyres of his car spun out hissing slush as he pulled up in front of Louise's house. Before he could unfasten his seat-belt a young girl came clopping briskly down the front garden path. She tapped on the windscreen and smiled at him and then got in.

'Ooh, I think we're going to have a mild spell. About time an' all. It's freezing in our house.' Perfume filled the car. She twisted about, fumbling for the seat-belt, supple and laughing in a short herringbone coat and a tight black skirt. It came to him that he did not know her age – twenty-three he would guess – but she was a young girl beside him. He found himself making rapid calculations as the phrase 'old enough to be her father' went through his head. Well anyway it was physically possible. One read these things in the Sunday papers . . .

'Not late am I?' Some reflexive social instinct had forced him to speak and betray no sign of his shock. He started the car and pulled out carefully.

'No, no. I'm always ready ages before time. I don't get that many outings, specially with Terry away.' She shifted in her seat. 'Hope I don't crease this skirt, I borrowed it off Jan. She's one of the girls I share with. You should meet her, she's such a laugh. She's got more clothes than she knows what to do with, I could smash her. Oh, she's dead kind though. Works at Lewis's, window-dressing – damn good job.'

'How do you like sharing?'

'Oh, it's lovely. Fur flies a bit when we get on each other's nerves, but most of the time . . . So you're taking in lodgers now then, David?'

'Just the one, in mum's old room. He has the use of the kitchen and what have you.'

'Makes it a bit less lonely for you, I should think,' she said sympathetically. Headlights of oncoming cars threw roving patches of light across the windscreen, so that the soft ingenuous oval of her face flickered in and out of the shadow. 'You ought to get married, David love.'

That was pretty direct. He pretended to concentrate on the road and laughed and said 'Don't think anybody would have me.'

'Don't be daft.' She got out a cigarette and said, 'Shall I light one for you?' The tip of the cigarette she passed him had a faint sweet taste of lipstick. He felt absurdly elated. 'Have you never wanted to get married?' she went on.

'I was engaged once. Oh, years ago. But we broke it off.'

'We?'

'Well, she did really.' But it was my fault. He recoiled from memory and went on briskly, 'And then Marian got married and left home and mum wasn't well, so . . .'

'Must have been a bind for you.'

'No, not really.' He felt a little resentful inward stiffening. 'I didn't mind it. I wanted to look after her.'

She must have caught his tone for she said, 'I didn't mean it that way. Only it does limit you, doesn't it? She was lovely your mum. I remember you bringing her into the club, must have been a couple of years ago, when I first started there, and she sat there ever so straight and dignified but with these lovely twinkly eyes.'

'Yes, I remember. She was very poorly then, of course, and she never drank, but she liked to get out. "I'm not going to sit in this house any more," she used to say. "The light won't shrivel me all up like Dracula." You know the film where he turns into dust when they open the curtains on him. She always loved those horror films, they used to make her shake with laughter. "How do people get frightened by these things?" she used to say, jogging up and down in her chair. I don't think anything ever frightened her in her life.' To his alarm he registered a tugging sensation below his eyes. Shit, not now, he thought. He put on a little speed as they left the last green banks of the development estates and slipped between dark copses into the country.

'I don't know why, I imagine she was lovely-looking when she was younger,' said Louise.

'Oh, she was. Hers was a very handsome family. One of these big families who came off the land to work on the railways and just got bigger.'

'God, don't talk to me about big families. Nine of us there was, and we all hated each other.' She laughed, a pleasant husky sound coming warmly from the back of her throat. 'Glad to get out of it. Six of 'em left, all in one of those boxy houses on the estates. Terry always says I should go and see 'em more often. I just say I'm afraid if I get amongst all those rabbit-hutches I shall get lost and never get out again.'

'Terry?' The word was out. But already some part of his mind knew.

'You know, my fiancé.'

'Oh, yes.'

'You remember him, used to come in the club a lot. He's in Germany now. And a corporal. He quite likes it out there.'

'Mm. I'm sure there are worse places.' Remarkable how the mouth could go into automatic while the mind floundered, rocked on its heels. Remarkable how you could know something perfectly well but allow a little febrile adolescent excitement to bury it so deep out of sight. He remembered Terry now, a quiet sort of bloke with fair hair and big ears. He could even remember someone saying Louise was engaged to him, someone at the club, quite a while ago. He hadn't taken much notice. Well he would take more notice of things in future, that was for sure, not to be so damned, bloody stupid.

'Can't be easy for you two, separated like that.' Thank you, mouth. Please, please, keep it up for the rest of the evening. That's all I ask.

'Well, you've got to expect these things when he's in the

army. And we've been very sensible about it, I mean I'm not supposed to go into purdah or anything while he's away. He likes me to go out with friends and enjoy myself.'

He glanced at her, her calm blonde candid face, palely illuminated. No, there was no guile or malice. He saw, quite clearly, that if she could know of the fantastic structure of nebulous hopes he had been building on tonight she would have been surprised, and then genuinely sorry at the thought of having misled him. She was that sort of person. And she had not even misled him. He had misled himself.

'Gorgeous houses round here, aren't they?' she said.

They were. The town compensated for its unspectacular architecture with a hinterland of some of the loveliest villages in England. To the east were chiefly scrubby riverside hamlets of clapboard bungalows and chicken-wire and rusting abandoned cars, and an occasional gleaming feed silo standing in for the parish church: from time to time the town would reach out and surround one of these with council houses and effortlessly absorb it. But to the west, where the land dipped into the fertile plain between the valleys of the Nene and the Welland, were picture villages built of grey limestone and thatch with little brooks and manor houses and mills. These were the aces in the development corporation's pack. Into these moved the executives from the new computer businesses in the town, converting barns and chapels and granaries and building limestone carports, bringing with them their polite, jodhpured children and big dogs. On Sunday lunchtimes they crammed the gabled pubs in spanking new tweeds and heavily accosted a few remaining grumpy countrymen encamped around the dartboard, and during the week pounded the narrow roads to and from town in Audis and BMWs and burnished noiseless Daimlers. And somewhere in an unhandsome Palladian mansion behind impenetrable gated parkland lived the local aristocrat, whose ancestors used to nominate a couple of MPs for the town as a periodic diversion from crested boredom, and who now consoled himself for lost glory by still owning all the land and selling the newcomers little parcels of it at enormous prices.

They were having dinner at The Haycock, a big old coaching inn that had swapped the Great North Road for the A1 and done well out of it. The food was of stoutly English kind: 'The thing I like about this place,' said David as they were seated, 'is that I can understand the menu.' This was true. But he realised he would not have come out and said it if the absent fact of Terry had not put the evening on a different footing for him. And he felt relieved. The miasma with which he had surrounded the evening had evaporated, dispersed by a clean breath of reality. He could genuinely enjoy himself now.

'Let's get one thing straight – I'm paying half of this,' said Louise, with humorous severity.

'What do you mean?' he said, and was glad to see her laugh when he added, 'I thought you were paying all of it.'

She asked him what he had been doing with himself, and loosened with a couple of gins and the genial warmth of the restaurant he told her about Nicholas, about the life class and the old gentleman who wore pince-nez and whose drawings, like Disney mermaids, delicately omitted the nipples. They laughed a lot and at last Louise, looking at him with bright and watchful and amused eyes, said, 'A drink certainly livens you up, doesn't it?'

'Ah, so I'm boring the rest of the time am I? Thanks.'

'Now, touchy. You know what I mean. Does the opposite with me, makes me want to flop into bed.'

He laughed, delightfully freed from the necessity of being vigilant for signs of flirtatious innuendo. 'I am boring though,' he said, spreading his arms out wide. 'You are looking at the world's most boring man. I'm so boring I'm interesting.'

'Silly. Only if you make yourself so. You ought to get out more, take a risk. Be a devil.'

Something slipped ticklishly down his shirt-front: that collar-button had popped off at last. It struck him that they were both wearing borrowed clothes. 'What do I do then?' he said. 'Join the dangerous sports club? Hang-gliding?' The tension of fine-drawn frivolity seemed to snap suddenly. 'Go out to dinner with someone whose fiancé's away?'

She was quite still. 'That's not what you think, is it?' she said quietly.

'Daft, I'm joking.' Too late.

'But did you think, before, when I said I'd come out with you . . . ?'

'It doesn't matter. I forgot. Honestly.' He felt the smile still on his face, tense and screwed like a wince.

'Oh, David, I never dreamt . . . If I'd thought for a moment that you – I thought you'd *realise* . . .'

'I know, I know.'

'I've gone all embarrassed now.' Her face was flushed and pained and she shunted a remnant of beef back and forth across her plate.

'Look, it's my fault . . .' He struggled to extricate words that were not spurious from tangled coils of regret and guilt inside him: guilty at having made her feel guilty, and conscious of his own guilt at the centre. 'Anyway – all this doesn't mean we can't have a nice meal together does it? You said yourself Terry likes you to go out and enjoy yourself. We can't go around wearing badges with all our private details written on them.' He was babbling now with a sense of feverishly juggling, keeping the evening airborne, staving off collapse; but it was working. The babble might be unconvincing, but that didn't matter; she was clearly relieved, they had renewed the contract. 'After all, we're mature adults – well, very mature in my case – over-ripe might be the word,' and he was thankful to see her laugh, joining in the effort by laughing at what was not really funny, and lift her head up.

'I'm glad you're not hurt,' she said.

'Oh, I daresay I shall languish a bit,' he said, and then, fearing the fun was becoming a little too brittle, 'Anyway, to come down to more mundane matters, I've got to go to the loo. I'll have the crème caramel if the waiter comes in the meantime.'

If only the toilets in pubs and restaurants could talk, he thought. The haven they provide for many a bursting mind, the few minutes hurried space for mentally running over the implications of many a tight little drama. Men seemed to use these white-tiled glaring places for the most casually confessional remarks, and he had heard women did too. He saw in the mirror that Nicholas' shirt was very obviously too small for him. He looked pretty silly. 'You've got to be able to laugh at yourself' must have been the most frequently given piece of advice in the world, and what rubbish it was. An ability that everyone saw as infinitely desirable, but one that nobody possessed. Well, there was no harm done anyway. Perhaps he and Louise could go out again some time, if she would like to, now that the air was clear. At least he had learned now not to build great structures of possibility on other people in this adolescent way.

He left the toilet and edged his way back through the bar, which was smoky and crowded. An inflection of voice caught his attention and he glanced round to see a handsome woman with cropped black hair holding hands with a man across a table by the open fire. She did not see him and a moment later he was back in the restaurant, his face composed. Maisie.

'Everything all right?' he said to Louise, and they talked amiably about films they had seen. Their desserts came, and he spooned his crème caramel up without tasting it.

Maisie.

Maisie staying the night at their house, sharing Marian's bedroom, and David taking them a cup of tea in the morning. Maisie bounding across the room in her nightie and jumping right off the ground into his arms. And his mother, crossing the landing, looking on with an expression of amazement and of something else, something almost appreciative.

Freckles across her nose – which she hated. And her name too. 'Like something out of the *Beano* or the *Dandy*,' she said. 'I hate it.' She was somehow good-humoured about hating things. Hate was an amusing emotion, she couldn't conceive anyone feeling it seriously.

His friend Ron, charmed by her, absolutely won over. Her giving Ron a kiss once, as they all said good night after a party, and the look of stupefied, transfixed wonder on his face, a fair heavy decent face with eyes of a transparent blue. He was a police cadet then, and he almost stood to attention. When he learned that they had broken off the engagement he nearly went through the roof. 'You're mad,' he said. 'You're a fool to yourself, Dave. A fool to yourself.' He wanted to do something, kept pacing up and down the room, was all ready to drag them back together by the scruff of the neck and force them to make it up. Perhaps he should have. But David was stubborn. Walking home from a football match once on a freezing day, David had fainted in the street. He had a bad dose of flu and shouldn't have gone out. Ron scooped him up and carried him the rest of the way home. He was immensely strong. But he was helpless against David's stubbornness.

She would grab hold of David's ears, tugging them, never hurting. She liked his ears. Hair always covered the ears in those days, and she would poke and push his hair away until she could get at them. He liked her hands, quite pale and soft and fleshy. She bit her nails, and dipped them in all sorts of concoctions in an effort to stop.

Ron's twenty-first, where David met her. She only came by chance, friend of a friend of a friend. The Co-op function rooms, hired for the occasion, with a local pop group playing the recent hits rather well. Those awful tight ribbed sweaters and cravats. Ron's family all huge, hulking, tremendous drinkers. His grandma with the best of them. There was a song with a refrain about waving your knickers in the air: someone told Ron's grandma that everybody did it, so she dropped her bloomers on the dance floor. Then got upset and tearful because people laughed. 'I've got another pair and a panty-girdle on underneath,' she said. Maisie made her feel better. A mightily cheerful party, everyone dancing. The floorboards shook. Maisie dragged him on to the dance floor. 'Come on, misery-guts.'

Soon they were snogging in the cloakroom. All happened so fast.

His mother going to do the washing-up in the kitchen at home. Maisie flapping her away with a tea-towel. 'No, you come on out the way Mrs Barber.' Her accent very broad, every vowel flat. 'Me and muggins'll do that.'

Something different, foreign about her, about the way she talked, moved, laughed, even though she lived just half a mile away. Lincoln Street was mostly Asian even then, already becoming ghettoised. The house was a tip. You had to heave at the front door to get in, shoving aside boxes of rubbish. Her father had the living-room all wired up with sophisticated hi-fi, his hobby; there were gaping rents in the carpet. The family would have screaming rows in front of David, sitting there with a sweet sherry served in a teacup, aghast. No one ever raised their voice at home.

Maisie: she whisked him a world away from his late teens, hanging around with a morose group in the rec, with cigarettes and those big drum-shaped cans of watery beer, and then pubs and dances in church halls, and fumbling assignations. No one serious, before Maisie. Perhaps that was partly the trouble.

They loved each other, and said so. He often said so, because he meant it, and because he liked the sound of the words.

Sometimes she would put her face right up close to him and peer at him and say, 'I wish I could tell what you're thinking.'

Her parents went on holiday and her teenage brother, a friendly boy of precocious discretion, absented himself. David came to sex expecting, and half-fearing, earthquakes and pyrotechnics and was pleased to find tenderness instead. Virginally they blundered together, like skaters taking to the ice for the first time, before kindness and understanding, the stuff of their everyday relationship, came to their aid.

'Well, if you're not completely sure she's the right one,' his mother said when they split up, 'then it's perhaps for the best.' Sewing a button on Marian's stripey school blazer, by the fire, calm. Supportive, but her observant eyes told the tale, told his tale. Oh, she could read him all right.

The old song, 'What are you doing the rest of your life?' It was a favourite of his. Maisie would croon it to herself, her voice huskily a fraction off key. She was learning to play the guitar. The fingertips of her left hand were rougher and harder from holding down the strings.

He was scared. And stubborn. Stubbornly refusing to believe he had found all this so early, so quickly, so easily. A perverse logic, a private mythology, suggested that it must be an idyll. The rest of his life . . . that must surely wear a dim, mysterious shape. Without ever really wanting to, he thus connived at the break.

A couple of years later he heard she had married. Ron told him so, trying not to say I told you so. That was probably the man he had seen her with in the bar. She looked happy. She would perhaps have been happy with David, but of course that didn't mean she wasn't happy with her husband. There were lots of contented couples who could easily have married someone else, if the multiple contingencies of geography and careers and all the rest of it had been different. That didn't detract from their happiness, didn't make it fatuous. And it made his wilful stupidity all the worse.

Going on the bus to Skegness for the day. Paddling in the icy sea. She slipped and fell into a droll sitting position, up to her waist in the surging grey suds, and just sat there, weak with laughter. Her skirt was sodden. Up on the promenade she wrung it and wrung it and still the water ran out in noisy streams, spattering on the concrete and coursing down her bare legs in cold interlaced tricklings, and she gasped in an exhaustion of laughter and shivering.

When they drove back to town the slush was almost gone from the roads and a fine mesh of rain was falling. Louise had forgotten to find out her next week's hours from the club, so they popped in there for a quick drink before last orders. 'We had such a gorgeous meal,' Louise told the other barmaid. 'I've had a lovely time while you've been stuck in here,' and for a moment David was large with vanity. He was aware of a hand waving at him from the lounge.

'He's from your office, isn't he?' said Louise.

'Jack Erskine. Yes.' He waved back, and smiled back. They looked like the best of friends.

'Thanks ever so much, David,' she said when he dropped her off at her house. 'It's been – well, you know – really nice. We'll have to do it again.' She touched his hand. And he patted her hand in return, and watched his own hand, pat-patting, as if it were someone else's, a remote, mechanical, old hand.

CHAPTER 6

The wedding of Harold Barber and Ethel Russell is finally to take place, at St Mary's church. Finally, because there has been some doubt as to whether it would take place at all, and Aunt Minnie began to regret buying a new hat in the spring sales. But everything seems to have been smoothed over now, and as Aunt Minnie shouts into the deaf and uncomprehending ear of Grandma Russell – querulous and bedridden in a houseful of relatives who keep popping into her room to patronise, all fligged up to go to a wedding without her – 'The path of true love never did run smooth, and all that.'

Thursday the eighth of September 1938 is a warm, Indian-summery day, perfect weather for a wedding and, if the international political climate bodes less well, gloomy thoughts are not allowed to spoil the day; Harold's father, who has been crouched at his wireless every night for weeks, has been instructed to keep his ideas about Chamberlain and Czechoslovakia to himself. Thursday has been agreed upon because the Barber family are nearly all shopkeepers. If it was a Saturday nobody would turn up – probably not even the groom's parents, sourly observes Mr Russell, who likes Harold but thinks his family a stuck-up, money-grabbing lot. The night before, he took Harold out drinking with his friends, and though putting away countless pints himself was secretly pleased to find the young man has little taste for it.

Everyone, virtually, is there: even a brood of country Russells, the last of the family to remain on the land, have come in from their Lincolnshire fen on the bus and arrange themselves modestly in a line in the back pew of the church. There are six freckled carroty-headed daughters in descending order like Russian dolls. The youngest is a thirteen-year-old who is nervously excited – her first wedding – and quite overawed at the sight of Ethel, spectral and lovely in white satin, moving down the aisle on the arm of her big, moustached, hungover father. Harold, too, she thinks impossibly handsome, though he has grown even thinner and there is a smoky, haunted look about his eyes as he turns to see his bride arriving, and in the young girl's head vague delicately romantic dreams uncurl which in her empty world of level horizons and beet-fields are unlikely to be realised.

The bridesmaids are Ethel's sister Jeanette, flattered and coltish, and a girl Ethel works with at the printer's.

Not Aldyth, which is surprising. Even more surprising is the fact that she is not there at all. 'She just couldn't get the time off work,' is Mrs Russell's explanation, and if she expects them to believe that, well . . . So thinks Aunt Minnie, who always self-importantly busies herself at such occasions, presiding like some household goddess of ceremonies, and privately she believes that all may not be well amongst the Russells at Corporation Road. And really the young groom looks almost as if he were going to his execution: he is very pale and stumbles over his responses.

But when at last they return down the aisle, arm in arm, it is difficult to believe that anything could be wrong. They both have a charming air of bashful relief. The little country cousin gives Ethel a glowing look as she rustlingly passes her, and at the same time is sadly conscious of having sandy skin and reddened elbows and pale green naked eyes.

There is a single taxi, for the newlyweds, and after Max Haver, who keeps a photographic studio in town with a dusty windowful of portraits of youths in stiff new Territorial uniforms, has taken three photographs – for the days when every occasion takes place to an accompaniment of endless Polaroid clicking are yet to come, and there is a suitably solemn restraint in the creation of these artefacts which in thick embossed cardboard will stand for years on crowded sideboards and, later, television sets – they get into the taxi and the rest are left to make their own way to the reception at The Locomotive. One Barber uncle is very nearly a rich relation – he keeps a large ironmonger's shop in town which is to find itself hopelessly overshadowed by the springing up of great do-it-yourself warehouses in the nineteen-sixties – and he has an old Humber into which he crams Harold's parents and Ethel's gangling brothers and the bridesmaids. The other guests, all hatted, some tearful, go on foot, leaving a couple of children squatting in the church porch picking up and examining pieces of confetti. Their journey is short, but the route makes a tour through the subtle shifts of class that the coming of the railway created and which even advertise themselves in the names of streets: through Laurel Grove where houses secrete themselves behind foliage to Cobden Street where the noise of the railway shivers the ornaments on the mantelpiece in each tiny front room to Huntly's Terrace where pregnant women in aprons and carpet-slippers stand at open front doors. From the world of the managers to that of the foremen to that of the engine-drivers to that of the labourers, and those with no work at all. To The Locomotive, that looks out across the railway itself.

The Locomotive's function room is up a steep flight of stairs above the saloon bar. It is used as the lodge for the town's order of Buffaloes, and real buffalo horns, looking rather mangy, are mounted on the walls. Trestle tables are set along the bare boarded floor and indefatigable Aunt Minnie pokes and nudges people to their places and with the help of an aggrieved-looking female relation who nobody knows serves out warm port wine and sherry. The crockery and cutlery have all been lent by Mrs Barber and Mrs Russell and Aunt Minnie and so that they will know whose is whose afterwards threads of different coloured cotton are tied around the stems of the glasses and the knives and forks and spoons. The country cousins have vigorous appetites and they bolt down the boiled ham and tinned fruit salad with a will, all except the youngest, who feels for the first time faintly ashamed of them and tries to imitate Harold's mother. A tiny, bird-like – and, occasionally, when she darts a glance round the room, hawk-like – woman, she prods with tense finicky movements at her plate as she listens politely to Mrs Russell's anxious flutterings, and she drinks nothing. Harold's father, very tall, bald, grave, talks to Mr Russell who is at his most twinkly and Father-Christmas-like and is wondering if he can slip down to the bar where his railway mates are and from which an occasional belch of beery smoke comes wafting up the stairs.

'They're all Methodists, of course, Harold's lot,' says Aunt Minnie in an undertone to Frank, Ethel's brother, who is now in the RAF and cutting a dash in his blue uniform. 'Won't let themselves go for a minute.' Aunt Minnie's idea of letting go is to loosen her corset a little and take another glass of port wine, but Frank can see what she means. They are not a lively crowd and if he were not still childishly afraid of his father he would accompany him down to the bar for a pint.

As for Harold and Ethel . . . well, they are smiling now, and handsome, and pretty much as perfect a pair of newly-weds as the little shiny figures on the top of the wedding cake. Only to the youngest flame-haired cousin does there seem a peculiar fervency in the way their hands clasp, a need almost of reassurance in the glances they exchange; as if they were a couple abruptly roused from sleepy contentment by some catastrophe like the dropping of a bomb, who after an interval of smoke and fear and darkness stumble into each other's arms again, astonished to find each other still in one piece. It is really very touching, this mute uneasy tenderness, and the little cousin is for a minute again made unhappy by a precocious clairvoyance of what she will never have. Yet there is still something a little peculiar about it.

There are speeches. Harold's best man, his next-door-neighbour, is horribly nervous and driven to fatal flippancy; the father of the bride, a natural speaker with his bass voice, jingles the change in his pockets and speaks of Ethel as the apple of his eye, and the sweetest you could wish for, and then looks at plain quiet Maggie and gamine Jeanette and says amid laughter that he really needs three eyes. There are presents, including much fancy crockery that already wears a dusty, retiring look as if preparing itself for the years spent in cupboards never being used. There are toasts. It is stuffy in the clubroom but they cannot open the windows too wide for they overlook the railway embankment and clouds of choking smuts are liable to be swept in. Something of a lull falls on the reception. Two families covertly eye each other up, as if for the first time aware of the link that the brief ceremony in St Mary's church has thrust upon them. And then there is the sound of loud laughter on the stairs, and escorted by a young man in spectacles Aldyth appears.

Aunt Minnie is an old hand – robbed of her husband after three months of marriage in 1915, she has pulled the family about her like a shawl and devoted her life to the unprized role of mediator: she will die a lonely death of cancer in a cottage hospital just after the war, consigned to a box-room of the mind by each of her relatives – and like a little bustling tug she drags Aldyth and her young man in amongst the groups of guests, hoping to minimise the surprise and the staring. 'Finally got my boss to let me out early, so I wouldn't miss *all* the fun,' Aldyth says to her mother, who looks more than ever vague and harried, and then turning to Ethel and Harold says, 'All the best to you both. Oh, you do look lovely, Ethel,' and after a fractional hesitation the sisters kiss. For a moment Aldyth looks expectantly at Harold but he does not offer to kiss her, in fact seems to draw back a little. 'Oh! well, if that's how you feel about it,' she says laughing, and then pulls forward the young spectacled man who is wearing an almost agonised look of embarrassment. 'This is Tom. You didn't mind me bringing him, did you?' and without waiting for an answer she goes on 'Look, he's brought his gramophone and some records, we can have a bit of a dance. C'mon Tom. Put it over here.'

Peremptorily she supervises the placing of the gramophone on a side table and the young man sheepishly obeys her instructions. The youngest country cousin watches with awe this new apparition: deep black hair, a generous white-toothed mouth that flashes into a disarming and brilliant and also somehow intimidating smile, a slender rounded figure in an oyster-coloured costume with black velvet revers, a dash, a verve, a cool scintillation that makes her feel that if she could be like that she would die happy. She is surprised to hear her mother hiss venomously to her father, 'Disgusting. She's got a damn nerve.'

Aldyth has a brief impromptu dance with the young man Tom, but the rest of the time the little cousin wonders why he was ever brought, and the young man seems to be wondering too. But Aldyth's brother Frank is delighted and is soon pushing back the trestle tables and then waltzing his sister about the floor. There is some similarity in looks between these two and certainly an empathy in gaiety but Frank's handsomeness is of a weak sort and there is something indecisive and petulant about his pink curved mouth. He has inherited his father's temper but not his hollow legs and he is clearly tipsy. For a while they dance alone in a circle of wallflower faces and then Aunt Minnie rallies herself and grabs Mr Barber and forces him to execute a stiff shuffling walk with her and others follow suit and the tension lifts a little.

Presently Frank, observed by the basilisk eye of Harold's teetotal mother, turns yellow and goes clattering down the stairs to the toilet. His father follows him and while he is being sick into the bowl stands beside him and blasts him with words of fierce and terrifying contempt that despite the music from the gramophone can be heard upstairs.

'You stupid bloody sod! You're pathetic, you are, you daft little bugger! What makes you think you're fit to wear that bloody uniform, eh? A couple of drinks and you're bloody well falling about. You make me sick.'

The youngest cousin hears her mother say something about 'a bad example to the young ones' but she is too fascinated to attend. Aldyth is walking with her long confident stride over to where the bride and groom have been quietly sitting like unobtrusive guests. The shrill screeching of the London to York express as it passes through rattling the windows obscures whatever is said but the next moment Harold has risen to his feet and is dancing with Aldyth. Aldyth is smiling but he does not even look at her: his too-bright eyes stare fixedly over her shoulder. Ethel sits with her hands folded in her lap and watches them with a strangely neutral expression. It is a slow tune that is being played and no-one else is dancing now and for a few moments the scene seems to the wondering eyes of the little cousin to freeze into a vivid tableau. Then there is a horrible grating sound as the young man Aldyth brought, who for some time has been moodily drinking a large whisky he fetched from the bar, snatches the gramophone needle from the record. Aldyth releases Harold and goes over to the young man and they mutter together apart and then she gives a little squeal as he throws the whisky violently in her face. The little cousin gasps at the whisky staining that lovely oyster-grey suit. Aldyth with great address slaps the young man full across the face. His spectacles go comically askew across the bridge of his nose and his mouth drops open in an expression of surprise that is somehow comic too. Then he is gone leaving his gramophone behind.

Mr Russell has finished with Frank and now he is ready to have a turn at Aldyth. But Ethel does not let him. Very dignified and calm in her white she puts an arm about her sister and steers her away wiping her gently with her handkerchief.

The little cousin's mother announces that it is time for them to go and they rise as one and disturbed and excited as she is she feels ready to cry with vexation and protest. But as she has often been told, and has found out, she is not too old to get a belt, so she troops along behind the narrow backs of her sisters. Mrs Russell, her hair escaping in greying harassed strands from beneath her hat, sees them down to the door and at the last minute the bride and groom reappear to thank them for coming. The sun is low, throwing attenuated shadows across the street, picking out the traces of orange in the turning leaves of the chestnut trees that line the cutting, and framing the happy couple in the doorway with gold; and there is an almost cruel beauty in the poised suspension of the waning day and the gentle warmth that the sun is about to take with it. There is a last mechanical round of congratulations and then the red-headed brood file off down the street to walk to the bus depot and the youngest one cranes her head round on her skinny neck, unable to bear the thought of letting them out of her sight and tormented too by the thought of the empty clay fields waiting to reclaim her. And all through the bus ride home to the farm she watches the coppery sun dragged into the earth leaving a last smeared stain on the sky and she wants to cry again in frustration at the things she does not understand and fears she never will.

Sunday had become a horrifying vacuum for David, but at the same time he could not quite fathom why. When his mother was alive they would read the papers, he cursorily, she with great thoroughness, have Sunday lunch, and then perhaps drive out to the country for the afternoon, or to Marian's house for tea.

Often he had been bored. But he had not felt this peculiar dread. Now staring out of the dining-room window with its spidery apple-trees hoarily slouching over the tarred fence, he felt he could understand those cases where one day a perfectly normal man blasts his family with a shotgun before turning it on himself. But on the first Sunday of March the winter seemed to get tired of its own rigour and relented to allow a little pale sunshine, and he took the opportunity to get out.

He took drawing materials and set out on foot for The Peacock Inn. Often he had seen the most atrocious sketches of pubs proudly framed and hung above their fireplaces and he was convinced he could do better. 'Have a go,' Nicholas had said. 'These places buy anything as long you make them look quaint and about a thousand years old.' That was before the Mood set in. 'I'm in a mood,' Nicholas had announced, coming in one night and barging up the stairs. He had gone into a monosyllabic purdah, but as far as David could gather, it was over somebody called Bez, who had once called at the door when Nicholas was out. 'Nick in?' he had muttered, a podgy sort of youth with an earring in the shape of a dartboard and glinting wire spectacles that made his eyes seem evasive. David found himself oddly disappointed that Nicholas's boyfriend, as he assumed he was, should be so . . . well, drab; and found himself little able to be sympathetic with his lodger's silent sulks. He was in something of a Mood himself.

He missed his mother now as you miss any stage of your life that has irrevocably gone. A mental effort of recreation would induce a certain sadness, but for most of the time his existence proceeded to the trite sighing tune of 'Life goes on'. It was when the intrusive discord, 'What for?' made its periodic appearance that the fear came.

Some nights he still put himself to sleep with drink.

A listless light embalmed the empty streets and his footsteps seemed to ring out, startling and irreverently loud. His route took him out of the old suburbs to the town's first council estate, carved out of cornfields after the war in Festival-of-Britain spirit. The avenues – no 'streets' here – were absurdly wide with grass verges like hockey pitches. There was a parade of barrack-like shops and opposite it a huge primary school, all low roofs and dome-shaped climbing-frames. He had attended it as a child and Auntie Jeanette had taught there too, dispensing cheer and plastic pants amongst the midget chairs and caged guinea-pigs. When he was little the population of the estate seemed to have an average age of seven and the paths were minefields of dog-droppings and the doors and gates and window-frames and even the clothes-posts in the gardens were painted a uniform shade of saffron. Now there had been a subtle shift: older people bought the council houses, transformed them, with their green settings and solid brickwork, into pleasant retirement homes; and the flocks of screaming children and the institutional paintwork were to be found in a newer estate, beyond this one, of concrete closes and tin chimneys. And perhaps in the future that too would be privately colonised, and the beet-fields beyond it would be replaced by a mass of yet boxier, rattier houses where rows of nappies perennially flapped and rusty tricycles scraped round the unfinished pavements.

In the midst of all this, incongruously, stood The Peacock Inn. Next to a service-station with a giant day-glo sign saying DERV, you came upon a large stone gabled seventeenth-century building with latticed dormers in the roof and a doorway you had to stoop to enter: a country inn that had stayed put while the country around it disappeared.

David had kept up the life classes, and could now at least look at the drawings he did there with a critical eye, instead of the furtive shame of a child contemplating the mess he has made on the carpet; but still he felt – almost guiltily – more at home with the fiddly exigencies of drawing architecture. Seated on a garden wall across the road from the inn, he abandoned himself to the pleasure, like eating chocolates, of fussy scratchings and mannered intricacies that would horrify Ruth Lacey. And he knew he could do it well. Once two young teenage girls in tight knock-kneed jeans drifted past him and paused to look over his shoulder, exuding pink bubble-gum breath. 'Cor,' they said, and 'That's good,' and 'You gonna sell it, are you?'

'If I can,' he said casually, and screwed his eyes up and pursed his lips intently, an Artist.

By lunchtime he had a very passable sketch, and now the inn had opened he took it inside to sound out the landlord. Entering through a tiny panelled snug like a priest-hole he emerged into the lounge where the first thing he saw was a large, execrable watercolour of the inn hanging on the wall.

'Looks like someone else had the same idea,' he said to the landlord who came to serve him, a bald rotund caricature of an innkeeper down to the brick-red face and the towel over his shoulder. He showed him the drawing.

'Eh, that's smashing, that is . . . I saw you doing it from the window. Yes, you've got all the windows right. Why I bought that thing over there I don't know, it all looks wonky, but it seemed like a good idea at the time . . .'

'I don't suppose you'd be interested . . . ?'

'I would, yes.' the man squinted at the drawing. 'Thing is

. . . it's a bit too real, really. What I mean is, what I'd really like is a picture of it as it was originally. The real thing like.'

'I didn't know the building had been altered at all,' said David.

'Well . . . come outside and I'll show you.'

He followed the landlord, who even had a waddling gait – surely he must be acting – and talked on in fruity soothing tones: 'Place was a morgue once, you know . . . they reckon it's haunted, though I've never seen owt – not that I'd go so far as to say there's nothing in it . . . During the war they requisitioned it for an RAF Officers' Mess . . . and they used to hold auctions here – well, that was before the war . . . Now, see this bit here, that's new. Built this century anyway.'

He indicated a square bay window. Possibly, now David looked closely, the stone looked a little lighter here . . .

'Course, it's the original stone, from when they knocked down the coach-house on the other side . . . now, if you could put that in . . . and change the lattices – they're new, the windows had square panes originally – or they did when I took over . . .'

'Hmm . . . I see.' This was going to be very difficult. 'And the porch, that's new?'

'No, that's original.' The landlord smiled. 'I know, looks sort of modern, doesn't it? You can never tell. I mean, don't get me wrong, it's a lovely drawing, but what people really like, you see, is . . . And if you could sort of put a tree half-covering the front – '

'Was there a tree there, then?'

'Not really.' The landlord smiled apologetically. 'But I think there should have been – know what I mean?'

'And what about the sign? They wouldn't have had written signs in those days.'

'Oh, leave that in. So's people will know what it is.'

The landlord offered him a drink on the house, and while he drank it he stared at his drawing trying to impose on its smug lines a version that would reconcile the past and present until it seemed to blur under his eyes and he was overcome by the impotent frustration he felt in the life class. Last week in irritation at Ruth Lacey's comments he had burst out, 'Is it that I can't draw or is there something wrong with my eyes?' It was that insistence of hers that all you had to do was see the object properly and then the drawing would take care of itself. Well, that was an exaggeration, but that was what she seemed to insinuate in her intolerably cool and confident way. That he found her attractive only made it worse, rendering him clumsier, with the dumb abased hopelessness of the backward schoolboy.

And now the afternoon stretched before him . . . at home, only Nicholas reclusive in his room, inaccessible in Mood and headphones, and the empty Sunday rooms in which to wander to and fro trying to fill them up.

Great-Uncle Bob lived near here, just round the corner in fact, in a sheltered housing flat. No more Family, he had decided that. But this was a special case. Anyway, the poor old chap was on his own. He bought some bottles of stout to take to him.

All on his own . . . a vision came to him of himself at ninety, living in sheltered housing, facing the vacancy of Sunday afternoons. But it was not a vision of very good quality; it merely involved floury-white hair and a Mr Chips moustache, like an actor made up to look old. Uncle Bob was really old. His eyes were magnified and watery and startled as they stared at David on the doorstep through thick wire-rimmed spectacles.

'Hello Uncle Bob. Can I come in? I've brought you some Guinness.'

'Aye, lad, come on in,' said the old man opening the door wider. 'Ooh . . . I wondered who it was there for a minute. Go on, after you,' he went on as David stood aside in the hall for him, 'you sh'll get there before me anyway. Go on in living-room where it's warm.' He came shuffling after David in slippers, sighing, wobbly. 'Eh, it's nice of you, David. I don't get a lot of visitors.' This was stated without self-pity. The living-room was very warm from a gas-fire. The television was on and Bob turned the sound down with a remote-control switch. 'Marvellous thing this,' he said, painfully lowering himself into the bottom-shaped depression in his chair. 'My Eric brought it me last time he was down.'

'Still got the shop in Leicester, has he?'

'Aye, he's reckoning on coming back here though. The nig-nogs are buying all the shops there he says. I says to him it's the same here.' He laughed, showing his own tobacco-brown teeth.

'Have you got a bottle-opener? No, don't get up, I'll fetch it.'

'In the drawer by the sink. And there's glasses in the top cupboard. I think that's where Madam puts 'em anyway.'

The kitchen was spotlessly clean, except for a dish of butter speckled with crumbs and a pot of jam with a knife sticking up out of it in the centre of the table. 'Who's Madam?' said David returning. The whole flat, he saw, was fiercely neat: the only untidy thing in it was Bob himself, in an old wreck of a cardigan, smelly, like a tramp wandered into a show-home.

'My home-help. Madam I call her, bossy little cow. It gets her back up.' Bob took the glass of stout and drank it half down. 'Ah, that's all right.' He grinned at David, froth on his blue veined lips. 'You like your beer. You're not like your dad. Course, your mother never drank, but then she were different. It's my side you take after. Not your dad.'

Of course, thought David. It had never seemed to him that he could take after the man who had died when he was a child: he had left no imprint. Whatever was contained within his individuality had been buried with him; he had left no threads trailing in this world.

Leaves of tall chestnut trees thwarting soft autumn sunlight over the narrow avenues between the sanatorium huts; a country smell, although the town was visible from the hill, and on the ground many fat, bulging conkers in their spiky green cases, some that had already split open with their own heaviness, to reveal a peeping crescent of lustrous red-brown nut. There were so many of them and nobody else wanted them . . . but he never picked them up. Not quite understanding that he was coming here to see his father dying, he yet understood that it would be wrong, or rather it would be transgressing that peculiar law of the appropriate that in the child's world is such a dangerous enigma, for him to pick them up and take them home.

'How do you mean, mum was different?'

'Sensible one. Always was. Ten times more sense than your grandad. I'll never forget one night he got sloshed and come home with his mates and they bet him he couldn't lift the rain-barrel out the back yard. Bloody great thing, full to the brim, but he went and had a go and ruptured himself. He were like that right up to the end. He doted on your mother, funnily enough, even though she used to tell him what she thought of him when he'd had too much. Joe and Frank were as daft as brushes, and Maggie was a bit funny, there was summat up with her I reckon. Jeanette was daft, still is, how she can be in charge of kids I don't know. And you never knew about Aldyth. Funny lot.' He fished tobacco and papers from his pocket and began to roll a cigarette.

'What was Aldyth like then? Daft as well?'

'Oh, no! She weren't daft. God, no.' He licked the edge of the paper and sealed it and lit the cigarette with immemorially practised movements. 'No, it were the men she sent daft. Couldn't see it meself, though I suppose she did have summat about her. No, not daft. She went to the County Grammar, and then went to work in the railway offices. That weren't a bad job then, you know.'

'Did she not get married?'

'Aldyth? No. She went in the land army during the war. After then I don't know, that were when I was living in Northampton, and the last I heard she'd cleared off wi' some bloke. Course, we'd all lost touch with her then, and your mother never had nowt to do with her.'

'Why? Why didn't they like each other?'

The old man sucked in great lungfuls of smoke that came pouring out again in dragonish twin clouds: his stubby body seemed to absorb Guinness and tobacco effortlessly, endlessly. 'Oh, they did. They were as thick as thieves when they were gels. People change, especially women. You think they're one thing and they're always damn t'other.'

'Where is she now?'

'Dunno. Families don't keep in touch nowadays,' said Bob, and as if aware that this sounded wistful added, 'Bloody good job an' all. You all had to live in each other's pockets years ago. Jeanette's the one to ask, if anybody. Eh up, there goes Glissy Needles.'

A tall and thin and severely made-up woman was passing in the street outside at a supernaturally brisk pace. 'Always at this time on a Sunday. Glissy Needles I call her, sharp as shit. Don't know where she goes. I like to imagine she goes to a knocking-shop.' He cackled. 'You start to make up tales about people watching 'em from this window all day. All sorts of daft things. Truth about 'em's probably worse,' he added with dry cynical sagacity.

David thought about a life spent here, in this overheated room, with a window in front of which people passed, presenting themselves to the imagination but offering no other challenge. It seemed in a way attractive. He looked at the neat impersonal room. Aside from a couple of china alsatians on the sideboard it had none of the enveloping clutter he associated with old age, the talisman pieces of a life piled up like snowdrifts around its end.

Bob's voice, thin and sexless with age, broke in on him as if aware of the tenor of his thoughts. 'It gets bloody boring you know. It's comfy all right, but could drive you mad. That's the thing about getting old, you don't feel any different. People expect you to be all calm and peaceful, for some reason, but that's the last thing you feel. You'll find that out, David.'

'I feel like I already have. My life's not exactly exciting at the moment.'

The old man watched him narrowly, cigarette clamped between his lips. 'You don't want to start feeling sorry for yourself at your age,' he said. 'You've got the future, that's the main thing.' He sighed. 'I dunno. I've always said it – youth is wasted on the young.'

'I'm not young,' said David, laughing in irritation.

'Course you are, you daft bugger. What do you think you are compared to me? I've lived damn near three times as long as you and I still think of meself as a young man inside. When you wake up in the morning your first thought int, "I'm old". You're just yourself, and that don't change.'

'Well that's just it. I'm neither one thing nor the other. Most blokes of my age are married and settled or whatever, but it's like I'm just starting out – with a thirty-five-year-old body.'

'Y'ought to be grateful. I was married when I was nineteen and got a couple of kids before I was twenty-one.' He drained his glass and belched, an oddly discreet little noise. 'Chuck us that book over here – the album there. I'll show you summat.'

David passed him a tattered heavy photo album and the old man's fingers riffled through the pages with arthritic testiness.

'Here. See that. How old do you think I was then?'

From a sepia photograph, so worn it was like limp tissue, an unrecognisable Bob looked gravely out above a stiff collar. His face seemed composed of hollows, in cheeks and eyes and chin.

'Late twenties?'

'Nineteen. That was just after I got married – just before I was called up.' Bob was triumphant, but in his stertorous smoking breaths that garlanded him with a blue tobacco cirrus and the impatient pawings of his hands there was still an eagerness as of indignation.

'There – that's your Uncle Frank, he'd be sixteen then. Looks like a little old man, don't he?'

A chalk-white youth leant on a bicycle, engulfed in giant trousers, a brilliantined swoop of hair bisecting his forehead. His hands looked oversized on the end of skinny arms.

'There was no such thing as teenagers then. You went straight from being a kid to being an adult. You were old before your time. Talk about the good old days, it's a load of rubbish.' Bob brooded over his photographs, excitement dying away as he became interested. They seemed to be in no coherent order: they flipped past David's eyes in flashes of monochrome, colour, sepia, ladies in cloche hats and little children in toy racing-cars and men in uniform.

'Oh – there's your Auntie Aldyth,' said Bob, and clumsily stopped in his flicking so that a pile of loose photographs slid off his knee to the floor. David impatiently scooped them up and handed them to the old man, who laboriously turned each one over and held it up to his eyes, muttering 'Gone and lost it now . . . only one I had I think . . . really want me other glasses for this . . . no . . . no . . . damn me, it's vanished . . . Ah! there it is.'

David almost snatched the photograph from him. No, it was not the same one as his mother had. This was an amateur snap, showing Aldyth in what looked like a farmyard, with her arms around the neck of a young calf. She wore rough trousers tucked into wellington boots. Her smile was a little mocking; it entered willingly into the spirit of things, but insisted on a residue of reserve, a tiny but appreciable ironic distance.

'That was took during the war, when she was in the land army. Chasewater Farm that is, up Sawtry way. That's still there, you know, about the only one left. Most of the land went when they built the airfield. Where your Uncle Frank was. There's one of him here somewhere, in his uniform. Flew bombers. About the only thing he could do well . . .

'But that's another story,' he sighed, and leaned his head back and closed his eyes, seeming suddenly tired, leaving David holding on to the photograph.

'Well, I'd better be going now, Bob,' he said. 'I don't suppose . . . I could keep this, could I?' And as the old man opened his bleary blue eyes and looked at him he felt himself flush a little, as if he had said something indecent.

'Aye, you're welcome if you want it,' he said. 'Ta for the beer, David, it's good of you.' He began to roll another cigarette. 'I shouldn't bother trying to find what's become of Aldyth if I were you. She wouldn't want none of you. Never wanted anyone really, for all she put herself about. A loner.'

*

The telephone was ringing when David got home. He heard its urgent trill as he fumbled with cold fingers to bring door-key and lock into some kind of relation. Where the hell was Nicholas? He almost knocked the telephone off the table when he reached it.

'Hello?'

'Hello, Mr Barber? It's Ruth Lacey here. I hope you don't mind me ringing you at home, only as you know there's no class next week and I really wanted to ask if you could do me a favour. Well, me and the Amateur Musical Society that is . . . It does depend if you have the free time . . .'

'Oh – well, ask away.' Absurd; he was smoothing his hair and composing his features as if she could see him through the receiver.

'As you've told me what a keen painter you are – ' (Did I say that? I must have.) ' – I was wondering if you'd like to help us out with the scenery. It's *Carousel* we're doing this year. We have a very nice old man who usually does the backdrops, but yesterday he fell off his stepladder and hurt his back, so we're in a bit of a jam – '

David was laughing, light-headedly, and trying to stifle it till his diaphragm ached. 'I'm sorry, it's not funny at all . . .'

She was laughing too. 'I know, I must admit I couldn't help . . . I thought he was going to go right through the stage, poor man. Anyway as I say it depends on your free time . . . Our main rehearsals are on Saturdays, and we really do badly need the scenery completing. But you must say if you haven't the time, I'd quite understand.'

'No, no,' he said. 'I'd love to help, if you think I'd be any good.'

'Would you? That's great. They're nothing elaborate, but the look of this show is quite important. We have the Regal all day on Saturday, so if you could come then . . .'

'Certainly.' Terrified by a fraction of a second's silence that the conversation was about to end, he said hurriedly, 'I had no idea you were involved in that.'

'Oh, it's just for fun. Bit of a family tradition. I'm only in the chorus. I get one solo line actually, in the verse of "June is bustin' out all over".'

For some reason he could not help laughing at this too. He covered the mouthpiece but she heard him and said 'Now don't mock, I think my line is the highlight of the show. I shall expect rapturous applause from the scene-painter when I sing it.'

'Of course.' He could think of nothing more to say, but the tone of that last remark had an effect as of suddenly closing up wide distances, and he felt a keen pleasure cutting a swathe through the murkiness of his day and of his life. From the corner of his eye he noticed an old glass table-lamp of his mother's on the floor.

'Well, we'll meet on Saturday then? Thanks so much, it's very good of you. Bye.'

He stood looking down at the lamp for a while, not seeing it, mentally rewinding and playing over the phone call, like a favourite tune.

Then he stooped and picked it up. The glass was broken, though he had not seen that at first; a sliver went with a sleek jab of pain into his thumb. He swore and set the shattered lamp on the table and ran into the kitchen and washed his thumb under the tap and found a plaster for it.

He banged three times at Nicholas's door before a muffled voice said, 'What?' He was not really angry, but feeling he ought to be he barged open the door. The curtains were drawn and the air in the room was stale. Nicholas sat hunched on his rumpled bed with a book held open before him in a way that made it obvious he was not reading it. He did not look up at David.

'What's been going on?'

Nicholas frowned, his white face beneath drooping yellow hair set into intractable angles. 'Nothing,' he said.

'Why's my mother's lamp broken then?' David noticed he did not say 'my lamp' and was annoyed as if he had somehow given himself away.

'It was Bez,' said Nicholas.

'What – he broke it? What was he doing with it then? This

Bez?' He noticed too that he was giving the name quotation marks – dissociating himself from such a word. What with that, and his hands-on-hips posture, he realised he was blundering into a position he could not sustain; especially before the potential of Nicholas's irony which could come hissing at you like an arrow from nowhere.

Nicholas tossed the book over his shoulder. 'What I mean is, it broke when I threw it at him.' He tucked his knees under his chin and grimaced at David.

'Oh.' David sighed and relaxed, thankfully, letting the air seep out of his puffed attempt at an authority he did not want. 'Oh, dear. Perhaps that wasn't a very good thing to do.'

'Too right it wasn't,' said Nicholas. 'It should have been a brick.'

David smiled, but if it was a flash of the old Nicholas – or what he thought of as the old Nicholas – it was a feeble one, and not unambiguous. 'Think I'm joking don't you?' the young man went on. 'I'm bloody well not.'

'What was it all about then?' said David, looking about for somewhere to sit down. Standing here like this did not encourage confidences; and Nicholas in this mood was giving no help. But both chairs were covered in soiled clothes and magazines and paperbacks. He propped himself precariously against the chest of drawers, noticing he was echoing the posture of Marlon Brando in *On the Waterfront* from a poster on the wall.

'Just the usual row. What are rows ever about? He's trying to give me the elbow, that's all. And trying to "let me down gently", as he puts it. Well, fuck that. He's a straight really, that's his trouble. He's latched on somehow to this half-arsed trendy idea that he's gay, but he's not. God, they're the worst,' he said viciously. He was barefoot and pulled moodily at his toes. 'So I lobbed that lamp at him. I know you're supposed to throw the crockery around when you have a row, but there was none to hand. Right screaming match, it was.'

'Well, look, I don't really know him, but is he worth it, this Bez? What I mean is, you could do better than him, surely?'

Nicholas looked at him with a sardonic stubbornness. 'Buggers can't be choosers,' he said.

David was unsure whether to laugh, as he usually did at Nicholas's salacious epigrams: there was a prickliness here in the semi-dark room that made him unsure of all the responses he had formulated where his lodger was concerned. 'Just tell him to piss off, then. Give him a taste of his own medicine,' he said, opting for a brisk practicality that almost in the same moment he perceived did not fit.

Nicholas rolled over on to his back and stared at the ceiling. 'Go on,' he said. 'Give me some more advice, Uncle David.'

Nicholas had not called him that before nor adopted quite that sarcastic tone, and David disliked it. 'I'm only trying to help,' he said, hearing his voice come out in a despicable whine.

'I know. I know you are. But you don't understand, you can't – '

'Why not? These – problems are the same in relationships whoever they're between – '

'Of course.' Nicholas sat up abruptly. 'I don't mean that. But it's all right for you, Mr Self-Sufficient. You don't know.'

'God, is that what you think of me?' said David, in almost a panic of reaction. 'That's the last thing I am – '

'Well that's the impression you give,' said Nicholas. 'You're on your own because that's what suits you. I'll bet it was the same all them years with your mum – no, I'm not saying you didn't love her, I'm not saying you weren't good to her. It was just the ideal sort of relationship so that you could stay closed up in yourself and yet not be on your own.'

'You've got no right to say that.' He felt faint, and humiliatingly constricted, as if unable to answer back to a teacher.

'I know. Just like you've got no right to start giving me advice when you don't know what you're talking about. I'm not saying it's bad. It's probably the way most marriages work. I just don't like being patronised.'

'Obviously. Obviously that's what your mum and dad found out whenever they tried to be helpful.' The exchange had fragmented into spiteful shards of bad temper, as both of them cooled, regretting things said and turning childish in frustration at the impossibility of taking them back. Nicholas blew out a breath and threw a teddy-bear from his bed up in the air so that its head bumped softly on the ceiling and caught it as it came down again. 'I told you I was in a mood,' he said.

'Yes, you did.' David opened the door.

'Sorry about the lamp, David. I'll pay you for it.' Nicholas was squinting at him with rueful irony, waving the teddy-bear's arm in valediction.

'It's all right,' David said. 'It was only an heirloom.'

CHAPTER 7

Ruth Lacey, dressed in a pink check gingham frock and flat shoes with a ponytail wig, did not look very convincing as a New England virgin of the 1870s. Somehow this incongruity had the effect of increasing her attraction. And the amused self-mockery in the occasional glances she gave him, perched on his ladder above the stage, suggested that she was aware of it too and added to his excitement the delightful sense of a shared, private joke.

He had not reckoned with heights, of which he was more nervous than he cared to admit. He was all right slapping paint on top of the plywood carousel, but above that, at least fifteen feet up, was a half-finished banner reading, MULLIN'S CAROUSEL, and once he was up there his knees started vibrating and sweat coated his palms. He painted some rather wobbly lines and hoped they would not be discernible from the auditorium.

The Regal was a huge and hideous box of brown brick: inside there was a melancholy chilliness. Sex farces whose titles always included the word 'wife' and thrillers featuring soap-opera stars on sabbaticals always filled it. Surprisingly, the yearly production of the amateur musical society always did too. Below him a music teacher pounded out the opening waltz on an upright piano and citizens in poke bonnets and boaters milled across the stage with a noise like a barrage. Everything seemed chaotic and everyone was enjoying themselves in that way that expresses itself as self-importance. Only the young girl playing the lead was very quiet: he had heard her sing earlier with a voice of remarkable beauty. Most of the others were ostentatiously trying out little dance-steps, engaging the director in earnest discussions, over-enunciating their lines like people talking to foreigners. The young woman who was playing Carrie Pipperidge was the worst. She had an affected walk, hands outspread, toes pointing, as if she were balancing something on her head; she spoke her lines in a breathless hand-me-down Blanche Dubois accent that was excruciating and inappropriate; when she sang she pressed her hands to her midriff as if bilious and took the top notes with her eyebrows.

When there was a tea-break, announced by the director clapping his hands and shouting 'Take five, boys and girls' in true Broadway-Melody-of-1933 fashion, David stood around uncertainly for a minute until Ruth Lacey appeared beside him holding two plastic cups of tea. 'Here you go,' she said. 'The people doing the real work tend to get forgotten.' He thanked her, expecting her to move away again, but she brushed her hand across a pile of planks and boards and said: 'This won't collapse under us, will it?'

He rather thought it would but he felt glad sitting next to her and determined not to be tongue-tied said hurriedly: 'I must confess I've never been to any of your productions, but I've been very impressed today.'

'Oh, good. Amateur theatricals tend to be looked down on – you know, thought rather silly.' She seemed really pleased and as she smiled he noticed again the intensely dark colour of her eyes. As if aware of his scrutiny she suddenly plucked off the stage wig and ran her hand through her short black hair. 'That's better,' she said emphatically, almost as if challenging him to deny it.

'I like it better,' he said, and smiled, really in genuine admiration, for she looked marvellous: dark, compact, pale-skinned, with a quality of self-containment that fell just sufficiently short of self-satisfaction not to make you feel superfluous.

She looked away and inclining her head towards the leading man across the other side of the stage said, 'I'm afraid Philip's a bit on the plump side for Billy Bigelow.' The young man had a youthful face but a body that gestured towards middle age and as if to emphasise her point he leaned over at that moment to show a huge backside engaged in a trial of strength with his check fairground-barker trousers.

'More like Billy Big-below,' said David, and they laughed, though there was just enough of reserve about her laughter to warn him against extending the mockery, as would have been so easy: to the man in the chorus, for example, whose idea of dancing was a few langorous flicks of the toe as if kicking off a pair of slippers; to the oblivious egotism that transformed these decent people from the offices and factories of the town into precious primadonnas. He was not perhaps actually on her ground, but he was on ground to which she had invited him, and however much convenience directed her motive the choice had been made.

'No problem with time off work then?' she asked him.

'Oh, no. Flexitime.'

'Where is it you work, by the way?'

'Barlow Watkins – wages office.'

There was a cleft between her brows and she said with a strange diffidence 'Where exactly is that – ?' He caught in her words the mark of a certain isolation, and was fascinated. 'You know, across the hospital bridge. Not far from where I live, actually.'

Her eyes were narrowed as if in an effort of remembrance, or almost as if she were suspecting him of lying to her: then she seemed to relax and shrugged and said, 'Well, I never know where I am in this town now. Especially in those new townships, as they call them – makes you think of Soweto or something. They just go on for miles.'

'You must have lived here all your life,' he said, and then at her neutrally inquiring look went on a little nervously, 'I mean your family – the department store and everything.'

'Oh! yes. And you have too – you've got the accent.'

He was a bit surprised, and not entirely pleased, to be told he had 'the accent' as if it were some sort of disease: he did not think he had any accent and he felt a distaste at the thought of the flat Midland tones which always seemed directly expressive of a dreary sort of stoic resignation. Something of this must have shown in his face for she added: 'That's rather a thought isn't it – we're both natives. One of the many odd things about this place, how few it's got, what with so many people moving here with the expansion.'

'We're a bit of history,' he said, and she smiled, giving him once more a sense of shared joke as of people who have known each other a long time. 'Mind you, I can remember a time when everybody was indigenous, so to speak. People used to stare when they saw an Asian in the street then.'

'That's right, they did,' she said. 'God, now you're making me feel old.' She said this in the manner of someone who never feels old in the slightest.

'You were saying this was a bit of a family tradition.'

'Oh – well, my mother was in the Court Players, you know, when the town had a rep company. Just for a couple of years. She was only ever a maid or something – you know, "You rang, sir?" and exit. She packed it in, but there must be a little trace left in the blood.'

'You – said you knew my mother – or your family did . . .?'

'Yes – well, it was really my mother who remarked when she saw the notice. I don't know when it was . . . people make so many acquaintances in the course of a life, don't they?'

He nodded, and kept his peace, for he knew his parents did not make many acquaintances, if any. There were friends – and really few of those – and there was, more importantly, family.

'Hello, this the new boffin?'

The voice that broke in was pitched as if just a little higher than came naturally to it. It was the girl playing the second lead, whom Ruth introduced as Roberta. 'Christ, I'm exhausted,' she said, sinking down in a swooning way on to the floor. 'Wish I had your job, David.' He disliked the interruption and to the tingling radar-dish of his resentment she managed to suggest both that she was unconventional enough to sit on the floor with nonchalance and that she did not at all wish she had David's job but with an actressy version of *noblesse oblige* was prepared to say so. 'Done this sort of thing before?' she went on. 'You can't be any worse than old Fred. He was senile if you ask me. The other year when we did *South Pacific* he left a great six-inch nail sticking out of part of the set. Bloody Mary's sarong ended up in shreds and she had to make her entrances sideways to preserve her modesty.'

This anecdote was lightly tossed to him, and he laughed obligingly. She sprang to her feet again and swivelled her body round to touch the hem of her frock. 'Ruth, is this hem okay? I keep thinking it's coming down.' She extended a slender attractive leg as she pivoted, and caught him looking at it, as he supposed was the intention, so he merely returned her look. She was very pretty. And she knew it, as his mother would say.

'By the way, Ruth, there's a party at Vic's next Friday. No doubt he'll make a complete fool of himself again but we've got to go – '

'No, I'm teaching Friday night,' said Ruth.

'Oh, but you've got to come! You can come after class. I can pick you up.'

'No, I shan't feel like it,' she said, with a firmness that David liked very much. 'Not after work.'

'Well, if that's how you feel.' She turned to David again, with the same air of generously including him. 'She's so conscientious, our Ruth, you know,' she said, laughing brightly. The director began clapping his hands loudly. 'Ah, well,' said Roberta, 'back to work. No rest for the wicked,' and gave another little laugh in admiration of her own liveliness.

The director was a dapper little man with a white pointy beard like something from the Naughty Nineties. It was funny to watch him in action. Completely without self-consciousness he danced back and forth, acting out a little of each part: one moment swaggering and giving forth in a deep oak baritone, then in a flash switching to Julie Jordan, simpering on his toes and springing out a note as pure and piping as a boy soprano's. Also he had a fine tetchiness, his features crumpling into a rictus of passionate agony when something displeased him. Roberta, David was pleased to see, got the full force of this when she sang her big number 'When I Marry Mr Snow'. Her Mr Snow watched her from the wings, a rabbity little man who was not up to the part and was clearly terrified of her. The director cut her off in mid-song, flapping his arms and groaning like a man under torture. David could see his point. The girl tweed all over the number: the melody was already fulsome, it needed doing straight. Roberta was having none of it. She protested, stamped her foot like a child, and finally marched off to the wings and there made indecisive movements with her costume, suggesting that she had half a mind to walk out on this bloody production, really right this minute, she didn't have to put up with this sort of thing. He watched Ruth Lacey go over and speak to her, in a low voice that he could not hear. Finally she flounced back, sweeping past him as if he were part of his painted scenery. On impulse he gave a deft flick of his wrist and a blob of yellow paint landed on the back of her skirt. It was a childish thing to do and he enjoyed it.

The rehearsal ended at six. The director came over to David and, resting a hand on his shoulder, appraised his work. He had popping eyes of a brittle blue like a doll's and David decided he was not so much a poseur as genuinely loony. A lot of people were. He threw his head back and gazed at the backdrop of curlicued pillars and the wobbly banner as if it were the Sistine Chapel. 'Bravo,' he said. It was not very difficult really, rather a little tedious like decorating. A couple of chorus members helped him lug the great lumps of chipboard downstairs to a store-room and when he had finished he came back to find most of the cast changed and ready to go. He moved in Ruth Lacey's direction in a casual sidelong way and Roberta got there before him. 'We're all going to The White Lion for a drink,' Roberta was saying. 'You are coming, aren't you?'

'Oh, Roberta, do you mind? I really can't, I've got some shopping to get in before they close. Sorry.'

In the theatre car park he lingered, looking at the river where it threaded a muddy course between willow trees and electricity pylons. It was very shallow here and a supermarket trolley poked up out of the water. There was a suggestion of buds on the tendril branches of the willows and a springlike gusty temperance in the air. He felt wistful, and alone. He got into his car and put the key in the ignition and then jumped at a loud rapping on the nearside window.

'Oh, I'm sorry, can I give you a lift?' He opened the door again with a rather too powerful gesture, nearly knocking Ruth over.

'I don't want a lift.' She looked amused. 'I was hoping you would come for a drink.'

'Yes, of course.' He clambered out of the car in haste, clumsily as one must. There was not much room between his car and the next and he stumbled about a bit. She laughed and put a hand out to steady him. 'Sorry, I thought you said you had to go shopping or something . . .'

'To Roberta, yes. They all go to The Lion in a cohort and bitch all evening. It's awful. We'll go somewhere else. After that little display this afternoon I couldn't face the prospect of Roberta again.'

'Won't they bitch about you if you're not there?' he said.

'Yes, that's the Catch-22. And you too, probably. It's such an incestuous little set.'

'God, what can they say about me?' He was genuinely, if mildly, alarmed.

She laughed. 'Oh, they'll think of something, David.' She had not used his Christian name before.

The town centre was still full of Saturday crowds, late shoppers and remnants of supporters from the afternoon football match, a few chanting youths but mostly older men in caps and scarves, diehards of mute Third Division loyalty. He and Ruth walked together with a little space between them, as if to admit an invisible third person, he noticed. First person and second person, I and you. You and I. Thoughts trailed each other round his head, as if he had already had the drink they were going to have.

Inside The Old Workhouse they drank cold lager in front of some cunning gas jets disguised as an open fire. The building had reputedly been used by Dickens as the model for the workhouse in *Oliver Twist*: now in an ironic reversal of the principle of less eligibility the place was highly fashionable and people crammed to get into it. Lace curtains hung prissily at the leaded windows. 'I don't know if that's true about Dickens,' she said. 'He certainly came here several times.'

'I wonder what he thought of the place.'

'Ruskin thought the town was the perfect example of the hideousness of industrial prosperity.'

'Did he? I don't think it's that bad.'

'Neither do I. Still, I suppose as time goes by the ugliness of one age becomes the quaintness of the next. Like this pub. I hope you weren't too bored today.'

This last was added hurriedly.

'No, not at all, I – '

'I mean I did rather plunge you into it. You're probably dreading coming again next week.'

'Don't be daft.' And as that sounded a little peremptory he went on, 'I was delighted to be asked. I'm looking forward to it. Honestly.'

'I enjoy it,' she said diffidently, not looking at him, 'but then sometimes I think it's a bit bloody pathetic. I mean like that business this afternoon . . .' It seemed to have bothered her. 'She's not *always* like that,' she burst out as if in contradiction of something he had said. 'Sometimes she's good fun. Just when she gets like that she invariably expects me to take her side. And I'm not always ready to do that. Not for anybody.'

He nodded, listening. Something about him seemed to encourage people to regard him as a confessor: it was flattering, partly, but he feared also it implied an assumption that somehow he was removed, out of the arena himself. Passive. The confessor had nothing to confess. What had Nicholas said? Self-sufficiency. Surely not.

'I didn't think she was much good in the part,' he said flatly.

'She isn't. She's hopeless. And she realises it, deep down, that's the trouble. I'm sorry – this is hypocritical of me, talking about her behind her back.' She smiled, as if noticing him there for the first time. 'Easter soon. Do you do anything special?'

'I don't do anything really. When mum was alive . . .' He stopped. 'No, nothing really. I'm a bit old for Easter eggs.'

'No, I mean it's just that we have hordes of relatives descending on us. More so than at Christmas, really.'

'We?' he came out with bluntly, unable to stop himself. She lives with a bloke, you fool. Drink your drink and go, you've been through this before. No, why should I?

'Me and mum. I live with my mother. Last of the Laceys,' she said with a laugh. 'Sounds like a historical romance. Well, no, I've a brother in London.'

A big house down Park Crescent, Nicholas said. 'Down Park Crescent, isn't it?' David said.

'You're well informed.' She looked at him, quizzically, but not offended.

'Well, the name's still sort of well known. Sorry, that sounds a bit patronising, doesn't it?'

She laughed again. 'Don't apologise. I think we've had our day. Mum's still got a controlling interest in the store, but she leaves everything to the managers. A lot's let out to concessions now. I never go in there, dreadful old-fashioned place.'

'Your father – ?'

'Dead, ages ago.'

'Mine too.' Now was the time to say something like how much we've got in common. Hand seized across the table, and suddenly they knew and . . . His mind was working cynically – defensively, to counteract an emotional excitement. You didn't go around seizing people's hands.

'You live alone, then?' she said. Not, 'Do you live alone?' Did it show that much?

'Yes. Well, there's the lodger, Nicholas, you know him of course. It was him who persuaded me to come to your class.'

'Oh, of course. Gifted young man. Doesn't really use his talents.'

A young barman came to their table and emptied the contents of the ashtray into a bin. David noticed with surprise that he had smoked two cigarettes already. The barman threw the ashtray down again with a clatter, irritably, don't dirty it again.

'He doesn't get much opportunity to use them. No, I know what you mean. But it doesn't seem to bother him.'

'No. But perhaps it will later. There's nothing worse than regret.'

That struck home to him. Wasted lives . . . 'Bit like me really,' he said, and wished he hadn't.

'What do you regret?' Her genuinely curious look was quite pleasing. Not taking it for granted that he should feel regretful, a thirty-five-year-old failure. Stop it. 'Well, nothing really. Just sort of regret for things I haven't done. Though if you pressed me I couldn't honestly name what I'd have wanted to do.' Maisie? No. No and no. 'Just the usual What have I got out of life? feeling.' He laughed, and drank, squirming out of it.

'I think we all feel that. I do often. What am I – a teacher, and not a high-up one. A trade increasingly undervalued and poorly paid. And I really haven't got any sense of vocation.' He noticed she restricted her emphasis to her career, no personal life. But then some people just didn't have one.

'It was just when mum died I started to feel like that, inevitable I suppose,' he said in a rush. 'Me looking after her . . . like two trees leaning together, you cut the small one down and the big strong one can't survive. I hadn't got any identity. Only Family gave me one . . . the most basic thing in human society. Son, brother. Something to stand in relation to. In both senses I suppose.'

'And now you feel you haven't got anything like that?'

He nodded, feeling a bit worked up and disliking it. He had not intended this.

'You shouldn't feel like that, David,' she said. A tone of mild reproach, as you would say 'You shouldn't swear.' 'It's silly to feel like that,' she said, shaking her head.

'I know. I suppose I don't, really. Not consciously.' He

couldn't explain. You never 'felt' anything really. You put it into words, and that convinced you that you felt it. 'It's just I seem to have difficulty filling in the time nowadays. Don't you find that?'

'God, I wish I did,' she said, veering as if from a frontal attack, which was what it was. 'I don't have time for half the things I want to do.' She looked at him and seemed to repent of such breeziness: it was as if she kept remembering who he was and relaxing, and he felt obscurely pleased. 'Sorry, that sounds awful, doesn't it? Like I lead *such* a busy life, dahling. It's just I seem to spend all my time doing stupid and unimportant things and none left over for . . .' she substituted a shrug for whatever it was. 'I'll get us another drink.'

The pub was only half-full: it was early yet. There was a group, two young men and two young women, seated in a circle on the kind of impossibly low deep chairs that reduced conversation to an Alpine hallooing over a mountain-range of uplifted knees. These people were not talking anyway: he had seen such groups before. They sat wordless, staring at their glasses on the table as if attempting telekinesis, and then at some invisible signal, like the migration of swallows, they would get up in a body and leave. One of the hairy drunks who hung around the cathedral square all day with a cider bottle came lurching in, looked in a puzzled smashed way at his sober surroundings, and went out again in disgust. David was moved with a sudden keen pleasure and pride at being here with Ruth, as he was training himself to call her, and wished acutely for her return.

'Here we go,' she said. 'Sorry, I've forgotten which was your glass.'

'Doesn't matter,' he said. 'I don't suppose I shall catch the lurgy.'

'Lurgy! I'd forgotten that word. We used to say that when we were kids too.'

'I actually used to think there was a disease called the lurgy. It sounds pretty horrible.'

'And "dods" were sweets, remember?'

' "Gi's a dod." '

'Did you have a nickname?'

'Haircut. From Barber, you see. Bit far-fetched. It's not that funny,' he said, in mock offence, for she was laughing loudly, but he found he was laughing too. 'Logical, really. Go on then, what was yours?'

It was good to make someone laugh so much. Tears were starting from her eyes. The simple act of telling her his childhood nickname, after a course of stops and stumbles, seemed to have lifted them with a swoop to a new level of intimacy. 'Sorry, I'm sorry. It's not that funny . . . Sorry. Ah, I didn't have one. Girls don't do that so much.'

'H'm. I'll bet. I'll get it out of you one day.' His words invoked the future, brought it flooding urgently around them. But he did not wish to retract the words and neither, it seemed, did she.

'I don't think I made a very good child,' she said. 'I didn't understand the rules. Like when somebody called you a name and said "No returns" and that meant you couldn't say it back. I used to think Why? Who says?'

'I know. Children are really tyrannical. I remember when I was little there was a sort of game, except it didn't seem like a game to me, where it was bad luck if you trod on somebody's shadow. I hated that game. Some kids got really vicious, stamping on your shadow, I remember I got really upset and told my mum. The thing was there was no avoiding it, you're bound to tread on people's shadows some time.' Even at this distance a breath of that hurt indignation passed through him.

'Who'd be a kid again?' she said, sighing and leaning back in her chair. She looked softly relaxed and comfortable, folded into herself yet not withdrawn. Somehow she was different. It was not so much that her manner had changed: somewhere she had crossed the line between the cool composure which before had torn him with both attraction and a frustrated wish to disturb it and a genuine, and charming, tranquillity. That this calm was directly connected with his presence was a gratifying thought. 'Who'd be a teenager come to that?' she added.

'My mum used to say the thirties were the best time of your life,' he said.

'Your mum was a wise lady.'

She didn't seem to mind him looking at her: her pronounced repose was a gesture of frankness, making it sensible for them to look at each other, silly to look away.

'What do you do on Sundays?' he said.

'Not a lot,' with baffled amusement. 'What should I do?'

'Oh – I mean, you don't go to church or anything.'

'Good God no.' They laughed at the incongruity of that expression and he said, 'No, it's just that my family are very churchy, not me, but I tend to forget . . .'

'Oh, my mother used to go until recently, now she goes and plays bridge instead. Seems just as penitential.'

'Yes . . .' He rallied his thoughts: he was like a man who had plunged bravely into foaming water to find it three feet deep. 'Anyway . . . Come out with me. Drive into the country or something, now the weather's improving. Good Sunday institution.'

A small breeze blew in from an open window behind them, bellying out the net curtain, a slight token of spring and countryside coming as if on cue. 'I'd love to,' she said, and he waited for a But – but that was only a reflex, and unnecessary.

War has come to the town, throwing into strong relief the profile of the Family. For it is after all the most implicitly communal of activities – wars are not fought by individuals. And many an apparent individual who, not called up, not bombed out, not occupied, might expect to sit out the war in the comparative tranquillity of the town, finds a thread snaking out from that knotty, history-book abstraction and circuitously but surely touching and ensnaring him. Via the Family, from which at such a time there can be no illusion of detachment. Perhaps even the war itself is a family matter at heart; so one might think looking at the photograph still on Grandma Russell's cabinet, of tiny ancient Queen Victoria, surrounded by relations who occupied most of the thrones of

Europe, with Kaiser Wilhelm looking dutiful in the foreground. A flashy upstart sort of grandson perhaps, causing great rifts in the family which have never healed, his cause now taken up by an orphaned solitary determined in his own way to bring them all together again.

The declaration of war comes a few days before Harold and Ethel Barber's first wedding anniversary; but they are unlikely, they feel, to be much affected. That weakness of the chest of Harold's, which has yet to show its real malevolence, makes it unlikely he will be called for service. In the meantime they live with his parents above the grocery shop in Gladstone Road, with the exemplary thrift that characterised their engagement and will allow them soon to have their own house in the next street. With something of the same restraint they have postponed having children, and will continue to do so till after the war, while the dwindling manpower at the brickworks means Harold just keeps on getting promoted. His brother Alan, nervous and asthmatic in his early teens and already wearing the defensive look that will stay with him through a lonely adulthood, will see nothing worse than a spell with the Home Guard towards the end of the war. A sensible household, into which Ethel fits perfectly, and is accepted even by little bird-like Mrs Barber, most sensible of all, hovering behind the grocery counter with genteel ferocity, registering her customers for the rationing soon to be law, and being very firm with the weak spirits trying to do a spot of unpatriotic bulk-buying.

Mr Barber is still very grave over the radio-set in the autumn evenings, with fresh memories of the first instalment of this drama twenty years ago, and has become an Air Raid Warden and hangs his tin hat and rattle beside his brown shop-coat in the hall. Still, urgency is not the prevailing sense in the town – everyone has been expecting it too long for that – rather a muffled resignation, almost relief, settles over the streets: the streets which were usually dark and quiet, and are now simply more so, as a few cars and vans, their headlights reduced to a feeble squint by masking-tape, negotiate the blacked-out evenings, and householders retire behind windows covered with old army blankets in what is only a more pronounced version of their insistent privacy. Gangs of labourers dig trenches for shelters on greens and waste ground, and a stretch of the municipal park is torn up for an anti-aircraft battery. A great pity, for it is a very handsome park, gift in 1880 of Alderman R. P. Serjeant, as is recorded on the plaque above the aviary – whose inhabitants are the war's first casualties, every one dropping dead from fright the night the anti-aircraft guns are tested.

A few small parcels of hastily salvaged humanity called evacuees have begun to arrive in the town, to stay a few months in most cases before drifting back to London. A young mother with a new baby is billeted for a while on the country brood of Russells on their fen farm (unmarried I'll bet, goes the vindictive whisper in the frigid ginger-headed household). She leaves after what is to her the last straw – having to wash her baby in rain-water collected in the barrel in the yard. 'Dirty water,' she labels it, 'not like from a tap,' and is gone.

An air-raid shelter has been built virtually opposite the Russell house in Corporation Road, but the family declines to use it, instead walking up to the one at the end of Huntley Street, where they have friends and can be sociable. Mr Russell grumbles at having to go at all – the sirens are always false alarms – but his wife insists, and always takes with her her sheaf of insurance policies in a green leatherette bag. Soon most people will come to agree with Mr Russell, and the shelters become the refuge only of courting couples who leave contraceptives on the floor and dirty old men who dribble stinking pee against the walls. Ironically only then will the bombs really start to fall, the factories and rail-yards making a handy target for German planes on their way to the conurbations of the west Midlands.

Meanwhile the skies are full of reassuring planes, for the town with its flat open environs is ringed with airfields. The RAF is a comfortingly palpable presence, and young Frank Russell finds himself a little more respected in his father's eyes. One evening, home from his station in Lincolnshire, he is having a smoke with the old man in the front garden at Corporation Road when a plane approaches, scarcely, it seems, above the rooftops, droning with a guttural menace. When Frank looks round, Mr Russell is no longer there. He has dived head first into a gooseberry bush and only his boots are visible. Frank collapses with laughter. 'It's one of ours, dad!' he manages to say. 'One of ours!' and this, though he is not aware of it, is the first time he has been able to laugh at, and with, his father.

He also feels a little superior to his brother Joe, who is only in the Territorials and has been posted to a camp in Norfolk amongst the pleasant woods of Thetford Chase. One day a coach party is organised for families of the Northants battalions to go and visit there, which is treated as something of a pleasure outing – at least on the surface, for Mrs Russell is sick with worry over solid, easy-going Joe who, alone of all her children, it sometimes seems to her, has never given any trouble. Mr Russell is privately worried too, chiefly at the prospect of being left beerily alone in a houseful of women, for though he has married one and fathered four, he has never liked them. Upstairs, invincibly old and definitely not ready to depart, lies Grandma Russell, who as a child in the country was exhorted to be good 'or Boney will get you', and who now has an obscure idea that Boney has reappeared. And then there are three daughters left: Maggie, thirty, industrious, unlovable, pious, lacking the family good looks like a changeling; Jeanette, boisterously healthy and getting serious about a young man called Reg; and Aldyth, somehow holding down that very good job in the railway offices and apparently not serious about anyone or anything.

War does not change the railway offices much; it seems nothing ever has. The top office where Aldyth works is a huge unheated room the size of a church hall. Rows of desks, exactly like a schoolroom, face a raised dais on which sits Mr Hutchinson the boss, who has never spoken a word to Aldyth. Tall arched windows look out over the station, or rather look blindly, for the tiny panes are always completely opaque with grime from the trains. Here from half-past eight to half-past five Aldyth works, 'verifying' a stream of pieces of paper with occasional spells as a punch operator. She is the youngest, comeliest and most intelligent person in the office; and this does not make for contentment. 'You're damn lucky to have that job,' her father tells her when she lets slip a rare word of complaint. And she is. Only people who attended the grammar schools, as she was haughtily informed at her interview, are even considered for work here. Her father, however, is unaware of the thousand petty restrictions and snobberies that must be endured in this smoke-stained bureaucracy for the sake of a small social cachet and two pounds a week. The many fine, hardly perceptible gradations of rank which make the officious old bag who collects the twopence a week for buying the tea Aldyth's superior; the single duster with LNER printed on it, always to be replaced after cleaning your desk – one morning she picked it up and to her disgust found a mouse inside it; the degrading business of having to ask permission to go to the toilet; the eagle-eyed checking of your scrap at the end of the day, for if you make a mistake on a punch-card you have to tear it exactly half-way across so that the number of your mistakes can be counted, and there is no possibility of trying to tear it up and hide it.

With her colleagues, Aldyth has nothing in common: the old ladies with their tweeded bums like bags of laundry and thick stockings and narrow sour disapproving faces, and the stooped dried-out males behind their tortoiseshell glasses. She does not disguise her antipathy, and they make theirs pretty obvious. She is a little madam, a little piece, no better than she should be, and all the rest of it. They are stand-offish or icily polite while their fleshless features turn quite vulpine with envy and longing. A sort of exception is Eli Shawcross, a little grey ratty man who works in the office below. His nails are cursory black crescents and his teeth are brown and he moves in a cloud of halitosis. He is a member of the Plymouth Brethren and quotes from the Bible. In spite of, or maybe because of this, he regularly positions himself at the bottom of the staircase and unashamedly looks up the women's skirts as they descend. Aldyth puts a stop to this, or at least puts a stop to her own suffering of it, on a day at the end of November 1939, with a swift knee to the groin, the day she throws up her job and walks out.

This particular day she has endured all sorts of niggling from her section leader, and anyone may tell from her face what sort of mood she is in. But Eli Shawcross has managed to be in his usual position for the lunch break and is leering up at her making no secret of where his eyes are directed as she comes down the stairs. Half-way down she stops and fixes him with a level look.

'Seen enough?' she says.

Eli Shawcross, taking this as mildly flirtatious, if not a downright come-on, leers harder until every one of his ochreous teeth is visible.

'Wouldn't mind seeing a bit more,' he says. 'If you're offering.'

'You are a filthy old man,' she says calmly.

This seems not to actually displease him. 'No harm in looking,' he says. 'Specially not in your case, duck. There's plenty done more than look up there, from what I've heard.'

She comes to the foot of the stairs, smiling, and quite deftly and gracefully knees him in the crotch. His little body folds up like a puppet whose strings are released and as he goes down on one knee with a puff of mephitic breath she fetches him a slap on each side of the face, one, two.

Several of her colleagues are still in the top office tidying their desks and they are surprised to see Aldyth come back in and walk down the long room towards Mr Hutchinson on his dais. Most surprising of all is the echoing noise her shoes make on the floorboards – everyone here tends to tiptoe somewhat – and those shoes of hers – which are strappy and high and really, you know, not quite the thing – make a terrific noise when she is walking so boldly and carelessly. Mr Hutchinson stares red-faced at her and for a moment they form a strange Oliver Twist tableau. Then she tosses him the key of her desk and walks out again.

In the town centre Aldyth goes into a tea-shop and gorges

herself on cream cakes. She tries on the hats in Milady's milliners. She wanders around, looking in the shop windows latticed with tape in case of bomb blasts, at her reflection in the glass, at the police station surrounded with sandbags and covered with posters calling for volunteers for war service. She glances at these idly and passes by and then turns back to read them more closely.

CHAPTER 8

The house in Park Crescent presented a pompous mock-Tudor timber-framed face at the end of a short drive lined with lime trees. It spoke with discreet insistence of a cloistered world, faded now from a brief illumination in the history of the town: a world David had known only by glimpses on the edge of memory and vision; a world of golfing and Rotary club circles, of charity balls and aldermen; of feed merchants and insurance brokers, of company directors and bank managers and school governors; a world that established itself in heavy square-bayed houses with conservatories and cupolas and coach-lamps in porches and bumpy tennis-courts, around the old municipal park and the cemetery. It rose with the town to prominence, savoured the historical moment when the town was of a size in which there was a Set and it was worth belonging to, and then as the town continued to grow fell into abeyance. There was no longer any possibility of a Set; and the Money had shifted to the new green-field suburbs where young couples who were not as young as they looked met over snifters in open-plan pubs. Still, there was not decrepitude. For every conversion into flats or doctors' surgeries a gabled, burglar-alarmed monstrosity remained, and in summer from the park David would catch sight of the liver-spotted denizens of this social Atlantis sitting panama-hatted in canvas chairs on lawns that were like green baize.

A dog yapped somewhere inside when David rang the bell. The door was inlaid with ugly thick stained glass, which made the house seem unfriendly. Ruth opened it to him. She was wearing an old sweater and jeans which made her look bigger and, peculiarly, rather older. 'Come in a minute, David,' she said, 'I'm nearly ready.'

He followed her through a big draughty hall, noticing a hat-rack and two great pot-bellied Chinese vases with dried ferns sticking out of the top. The place was really remarkably ugly, almost boastfully, triumphantly so. The kitchen was as impractically small as the hall was big; there was the familiar, and always strange, other-people's-houses smell of washing and stale cooking.

'There's the culprit that's made me late,' she said, picking up her coat from a chair and pointing to a Pekinese that watched him with animosity from beneath the table. 'Something's wrong with him. He won't eat and he keeps sort of coughing. God, mum'll throw a fit.' She spoke tetchily.

'He's her dog, then?' David crouched down to look into the little squashed face. He made an encouraging sound and was rewarded with a growl.

'Oh yes. Well, I like him too in his way, little sod. Come on Jasper.' She squatted beside David and the dog came waddling forward to her outstretched hand, nosed her fingertips for a moment and then turned and shuffled around in a distraught way, gagging and making tiny snorting noises.

'Perhaps he's got something stuck in his throat,' said David.

'That's what I wondered. He did have some chicken bones yesterday. I've *told* mum not to give them to him.'

'Couldn't we have a look?'

'One of us'll have to hold him.' She looked at David uncertainly. 'Would you –?'

'Well it's horrible seeing him like this. Let's have a go.'

David was not keen on big dogs, but this sort of model was all right. He held out his hand and tried to get the dog to come to him, but when it showed no interest he made a determined grab and hoisted it up before it could bite him. It squirmed and kicked but he wrapped his arms tightly around it, holding down its little stubby legs. He was determined: he felt himself oddly challenged, by this ugly house in which he felt alien, by something unexpectedly brusque and inaccessible in Ruth's manner: he would squeeze the life out of the little brute before he let it go. Ruth hesitated a moment and then using both hands squeezed open the dog's jaws. She peered into the small ribbed mouth. 'I don't believe it – can you keep him all right? – there is a bit of bone there, I can see it, right at the back.' Keeping the mouth open with one hand, she pushed her first and second fingers into it. Her hand, close to David's face, was thin and pale and trembling a little with care. He could feel her breath lightly on his face. 'Little bugger's teeth are sharp,' she said under her breath, for the dog was biting for all it was worth. Then she slowly withdrew her hand and he saw a bone like a matchstick between the ends of her fingers, trailing a filament of saliva. They both sighed, as if at the sight of something extremely moving, and Jasper gave an extra hard struggle. David put the dog down and it was copiously sick on the lino.

Ruth laughed. 'I never thought I'd be glad to see that happen,' she said going to the sink. 'There wasn't any blood, it must have been just stuck and not cut his throat. What a relief. Mum's so attached to him, it's the end of the world if he's poorly.'

'Has she gone to her bridge?'

'Yes.' She knelt down to clean up the mess with a shovel and a plastic bag, and looked up at him, smiling for the first time. 'Thanks so much, David. You didn't bargain for this, did you?'

'I didn't bargain for anything, except seeing you.'

That remark might be taken as irritable, or flattering. He felt himself similarly poised at the apex of two slopes of feeling.

Two people getting to know each other: traditionally a tentative matter of intimations, hesitations and retreats, of small dainty progressions, a fiendish semaphore code out of which understanding was gradually and painstakingly teased.

It was rubbish! People really floundered together like battling dinosaurs raising clouds of dust, their clumsy thrashing bodies imperfectly following the instructions of their tiny petrified brains as they collided and rebounded and collided again.

'Do you play golf?' she asked him as they drove past the golf course northward out of the town.

'Good Lord, no.'

'Why the good Lord?'

'Well, it's just the whole thing of the golf club and the check slacks and it's-my-shout-old-boy and all the rest of it.'

'Oh, come on, you're exaggerating. It's not like that really. Not nowadays.'

'More than ever nowadays, especially here. And you have to shell out a fortune to buy clubs and everything.'

'You can hire them.'

'I suppose so.' He did not know why they were having this pointless exchange about golf. It had never even entered his head to 'take up' golf. The very vocabulary was repulsive. 'But anyway I'm not interested. I think playing games like that is all pretty childish.'

'What on earth do you mean?'

'Well – grown men hitting little balls around. Getting all worked up about it. Bloody stupid. It's not – ' He struggled for a word. 'It's not serious.'

She looked quizzically at him. Because he was driving he could not return her look and it was annoying to have to simply submit to being so scrutinised. 'You're a bit of a puritan really, aren't you?' she said with something of triumphant discovery. You are a puritan and I claim my five pounds.

'Maybe.' A rigid stubbornness was overcoming him: he recognised its onset too well. 'I don't quite see why it's used as such a derogatory word. I sometimes think if I believed in God I'd like to be some sort of puritan if anything.'

'You're joking.'

'Well, I mean all that sort of dignity and responsibility and sobriety, there's something attractive about it, it brings out the stern Protestant in me.'

'As long as you could drink and smoke as well.'

Needled by a note of scorn in her voice, he said: 'All right.

I'm not saying I ever would be. It was you who called me puritanical.' One day he was going to finish with talking for ever. You might as well just shut your mouth, for all the hope of what you say giving anyone the slightest hint ever, ever, of what you meant or what you were really like. 'Anyway I was being hypocritical, I do like football. Watching it, that is.'

'Ah, well, that's different, of course – it's all salt-of-the-earth and flat caps and mufflers and Hovis. And those sixties realist films with Albert Finney or Alan Bates. Going t'see me a'ntie and tekking a drop o' summat.'

She did the Northern voice very well. He was stung, not so much at being accused of being a working-class hero, but at the accuracy with which she hit the target: he really liked those films. 'Yes, I like those films,' he said. 'Must be my upbringing,' deliberately flattening his accent. He found that his ears were burning.

What the hell was he doing, driving out into the country with this stranger? Did he know a single thing about her? How did he get here? What had come over him? Well, he could answer that one. Sex had come over him, that was what. Not raising its ugly head but barging in like a drunk at a party and spiking the drinks. Of course it wasn't 'just' sex – but then sex was never 'just'. For a moment David decided he was going to let the whole thing go. Stop going to the drawing class, the musical society, just drop it. It would be easy, it was easy, ridiculously easy – even though he felt more attracted to her than ever, more than anyone he had ever met. You are thirsty and you want the cup of tea that you are raising to your lips; but it would be so easy to relax the fingers and let it fall to the floor. Just let things settle into their natural inertia.

But they had left the outskirts of the town now, and were driving between empty fields and the windscreen flickered with a little apologetic sunshine, so he was stuck with it. He could see she was smiling, the sort of smile that goes as vanguard to laughter.

'You're easily goaded, aren't you?' she said. He realised that she found that funny, that she found the goading funny, and that any reaction of his that included further huffiness would be funny. It was a mode of exchange – 'only winding you up', as Jack Erskine would say – which was alien to him. His family did not talk in that way. It was the sort of thing to which his mother would say firmly: 'Don't be silly.'

'I suppose I am,' he said. 'Where shall we go, anyway?'

She looked at him and said nothing, and for a while the car was filled with two different kinds of silence. At last, horribly uncomfortable, he began to say, 'I thought we might go up Eltham way. By the river there – '

'David, don't be so prickly,' she interrupted him. 'There's no need. Really. You don't think I came out with you to make fun of you, do you?'

He seemed to feel a stretching of obstinate tension across his chest: like a child, reprimanded and relenting, wishing to make the so easy capitulation.

'You're not a very relaxed person, are you?'

'Well, not compared with you,' he said, trying to counter-attack. At the same time he knew, with a mixed relief, that he was putting himself in her hands.

'What gives you that idea?'

'First impressions I suppose. When I first met you I was a wee bit scared of you.'

She did not seem surprised at that, but laughed. 'Don't say that. Perhaps that's my trouble, I scare men off.'

As she said this he felt sickly jealous at the word 'men' and knew that he did not want another soul in the world to go near her. He was disconcerted at the intensity of his own reaction. 'When I say scared I mean in a nice way,' he said.

'That's how I took it.' He glanced at her. All at once they were both smiling. That was nice to hear – never mind anything else.

A skein of dewy mist still lay in the hollow of the valley as the car dipped towards Eltham and sheep lifted their black faces to watch them from damp fields over ditches choked with nettles and rusted barbed wire. The river was swollen and green and as straight and still as a canal: it ran deep into the flood plain where the limestone houses of the village stood on watery foundations amidst black farmland where in summer wheat and mustard came like an occupying army and imprinted the dazzled retina with Van Gogh yellowness. Through David's open window came a whiff of powerful earth smells that clashed unpleasantly with the rubbery clinical interior of the car.

The sign, Chasewater Farm, registered on David's brain just after they had passed it and he swung the car into the grass verge with a jolt that threw Ruth forward in her seat.

'What's wrong?'

'Nothing. I just remembered – that did say Chasewater Farm didn't it?' He found himself in some difficulty to explain. He fished in his wallet for the photograph of Aldyth that Bob had given him. 'There's an aunt of mine I'm trying to trace – Aldyth, that's her – apparently she worked on this farm during the war. I don't know where she is now.'

Ruth passed the photo back to him with an expression of polite interest. 'So?'

'I wonder if there's anyone at the farm who knew her. Might be worth a try.'

'I wouldn't have thought so. That's a long time ago, it's probably changed hands since then. Were you very fond of her, then?'

'Oh! no. I never set eyes on her.' He smiled a little painfully: this must sound very odd. 'It's just a bee I've got in my bonnet. She's a bit of a black sheep – some scandal apparently. I'm just curious.'

'Oh, I see.' He could tell she was not interested – why should she be?

'Anyway – do you mind? Could we just walk up there and see if anyone's around?'

'OK.'

He got out, suspecting from her tone that she was a bit peeved; but when he glanced across at her she smiled. It was a beautiful smile, but coming from a face that was habitually grave its effect was curiously that of a kind of tightening of tension, a flashing into view of a disquiet that was itself offered as friendliness. As they walked between tall privet hedges up the path towards the farm David was suddenly and acutely filled with an anxiety that could only be expressed as wanting everything to be all right.

The farmhouse was an incoherent building, part brick, part wood, with a shaky verandah from which hideous salmon-pink paint was peeling. It was dwarfed by a huge barn of corrugated iron across a concrete yard: from this came a grunting and stamping and the sweetly pungent, beef-and-shit smell of heifers. David went up the three steps to the farmhouse door and knocked and then recoiled as he noticed the slanting curranty eyes of a dead rabbit hanging by its legs from the lintel staring into his. Ruth made a noise of disgust. He went down the steps again and looked up at the windows. There was no sign of anyone inside. He hesitated and then turned to go round to the back of the house and saw a big collie dog bounding towards him. A barking muzzle seemed to loom within inches of his face and then at a sharp 'Brandy, git down!' from behind him the dog was silent and began sniffing round his legs in a placatory fashion.

'Oh, hello,' David said. 'I knocked but there didn't seem to be anyone in.'

'There isn't. What can I do for you?' The man facing them was sixty-odd, in a flat tweed cap and elbow-patched jacket, big and healthy-looking except for a remarkably white colourless face. He carried a heavy stick and he twirled the end between spatulate fingers as he looked at David.

'Well, I wonder if you could help me – ' he fumbled for the photograph. 'I've been told that an aunt of mine used to work here. During the war, a land girl. That's a picture of her taken at the time. I'm trying to trace her . . .'

'What, she missing, is she?'

'No, no – what I mean is, I'm trying to get in touch with her. Her name's Aldyth Russell.'

The man raised his eyebrows and passed the photo back. 'Land girl you say?' He made a sucking sound. 'That's a long time ago. That was me dad's time really.'

'Oh. It's just that I can't find anything out about her. I

wondered if perhaps someone here might remember her, even what became of her after the war.'

'There's only me here,' said the man. He did not seem unfriendly, but rather a little bored by David's insistence. 'There was a lot of them girls, they came and went. I was called up in 1942 anyway.' The collie, having inspected Ruth, was now frisking round the farmer excitedly. He looked down with a slight frown and fetched it a swinging crack with his stick. David heard the impact of wood on bone. The collie retreated to a little distance whimpering very quietly.

'The war did tend to scatter people,' the farmer said, conversationally. 'Change 'em too. She could be anywhere.'

'So you don't recognise her at all?'

The farmer shook his head, solemnly. 'Sorry. Can't help you.'

'Oh. Thanks anyway. Sorry to have troubled you.' He found himself wishing, absurdly, that he had a hat to lift.

'What *is* that bird?' Ruth said as they walked back to the car. 'There on the fence, look.'

He looked. 'Bullfinch,' he said.

She glanced at him in surprise. 'You know,' she said.

They got into the car. 'It's one of the few things I do know. The names of birds. Can't think why, I'm not the least bit interested.'

'Good. I'm glad you're not into one of those awful anal-retentive things like bird-watching or train-spotting.'

He laughed. 'Hang on. I'm just trying to think if I've got any anal-retentive interests. Drawing doesn't count of course?'

'Oh no. Creative.'

'Drinking?'

'Condition of creativity.'

'What about country-and-western music?'

'Really? Do you?'

'Yes. Oh, don't worry, I'm not one of those berks who dress up in all the cowboy gear and everything. I just like the music, some of it. It's not that strange.'

'No – I'm just surprised. You don't strike me that way.'

'What way?'

'Well, it's pretty reactionary, isn't it? Down-home and good old boys and piety and stand by your man even though he's screwing around.'

'All true. It's just the – sublime miserableness of it I like. The ridiculous melancholy. I love it.'

'But why? I like music to cheer me up, not plunge me into worse gloom.'

'Ah, that's the same,' he said. 'That's still indulgence of emotion. It's still, whatsit, laying that flattering unction to your soul. You ought to go to the country festival in the summer, it's great. No, really. There's all these Brummies in stetsons. "Yow gowing to watch the 'orse-roidin-guh?" Honest. Anyway, why the fear of anal-retentive types? Do I detect some past vindictiveness?'

She laughed softly. 'I'll tell you about it, perhaps. Here, park here, we can go down the bridlepath to the river.'

He swung the car into an opening to the fields between two cottages. 'Pity there was no luck at that farm. Still, I shall keep on, shan't give up.'

'Oh, no?' she said, and he saw again she was not interested.

The river ran past the feet of the cottage gardens and out into pastureland between banks of nettles. At the bend where it turned east stood a deserted mill and beyond that a disused lock. 'We should have brought a picnic,' said David, but it did not feel very picnicky. The east wind that in this part of the world came across the flat land keen and unabated right up to the edge of summer was blowing steadily: he shivered a little in his jacket.

'Are they going to demolish this, or what?' said Ruth, as they stood looking up at the old mill.

'It's been like this as long as I can remember,' he said. It was tall and massive and the bricks were blackened as if with smoke – not at all rural – it put him in mind of Victorian workhouses. Nor was it at all ruinous: solid and intact, filthy and empty, it had the resilience of supremely ugly things. The windows were glassless, but instead of being boarded up they were fixed with heavy metal grilles. 'It's a wonder they haven't turned it into a restaurant,' Ruth said. 'Or a "carvery", whatever that is. Oh, look, there's a cat in there!'

'There's a whole colony of them,' he said. 'Has been for years. Turned feral. They must get a good living here.' At the grilled window a big tom pressed himself up against the bars to catch a ray of sun. His gingery matted fur stuck out in hedgehog spikes and as they bent to peer at him he turned his head, slowly, owlishly, to look back at them.

'What a face,' said David. Yellow slit eyes regarded them neutrally from a fat round head that through countless fights was almost earless.

'Like he's seen all the evil in the world.'

The tom curled back his black lips and hissed at them, languidly. The yellow-flecked pupils of his eyes expanded and dilated perceptibly in the changing sunlight.

'I wonder how they get in and out?' said David. He walked along the side of the building to a barred door and craned up to a small gap at the top. In an instant a streak of black fur shot past his face, hit the ground running and disappeared into the long grass. 'I think that's how,' said Ruth, laughing. He had let out a shout of alarm and gone reeling backwards. 'Come on.' She took his arm, still laughing. 'Country walks are supposed to be relaxing, not scare the life out of you.'

They stood on the lock bridge and looked upstream to the weir where the glassy green water was suddenly seized and twisted into white sparkling ropes and then as abruptly became a flat plane again filled with a bottomless reflection of sky. Below them the lock was a dirty sunken basin where water slopped against walls stained with slime and rust. A depth-post like a giant ruler read eighteen feet. 'Just think if you fell in there,' he said. 'You'd never get out. There's nobody to hear you screaming. Like a rat in a bucket.'

She looked at him doubtfully. 'What's this?' she said. 'The Nashville gloom coming out?'

'The Barber gloom I think. You could probably keep afloat until somebody came along anyway.'

'Not me. I can't swim a stroke.'

'Can you not?' He was surprised.

'"Ee, can you not?"' she mocked him. 'Sorry, sorry – it's just you're so funny sometimes.'

'Not when I mean to be?'

'That's what I like. Men never can understand that. They take being laughed at as contempt or something.'

'I'll remember that.' He kicked a pebble and it fell with a sleek plop into the oily water.

'How's Nicholas?'

'Not too good at the moment. In fact he's being a right pain. Over a lovers' tiff.'

'What, serious?'

'It seems like it, the way he's going on. I keep wondering if there's anything I can do.'

'In what way?'

'Well, go and see this bloke perhaps and – oh, I don't know, say something . . .'

'It's a *bloke*?'

'Yes. Sorry, I thought you'd realise – well, no reason why you should.'

'It never even occurred to me . . .' She looked interested. 'What do your family think about that?'

'They're – not too happy about it.' It depressed him to think about them: they had no place here. 'Anyway what do you think? Should I do something? It's obviously making him very unhappy. I like him, and I feel a bit responsible for him.'

They left the bridge and walked down the river path between the tall clammy nettles. There was not much room to walk abreast and they brushed against each other in regular rhythm.

'I wouldn't interfere,' she said. 'He might take it badly. If he didn't get on with his parents he probably wouldn't appreciate you acting *in loco parentis*. What was his quarrel with them, anyway?'

'Oh, they didn't approve of him. They were disgusted when they found out about him and as good as threw him out.'

'That's terrible . . . It's awful that that can happen in this day and age. Parents can be more bloody irresponsible than kids sometimes.'

Something of suppressed savagery in the way she said this moved him to put a question that he had been wondering about. 'Do you get on well with your mother? You must do, I suppose.'

'Why must?'

'Well . . . you still live there with her.'

'She couldn't manage on her own. Oh, she's not old or anything – she's fifty-six and fit as a fiddle. She's just one of these people – I can't imagine her on her own. She'd go spare. She's often said so.'

He felt sceptical. 'Isn't that just her exaggerating?'

'You haven't met my mother,' she said, a little too firmly.

'Do you not resent that a bit?'

'Oh, but I'm not tied down, not in any real sense. I thought you'd understand this, David. Things like resentment don't quite apply in any normal way when it comes to family. It . . . has its own rules. Anyway – ' she began to speak with the slightly artificial breeziness he thought she had begun to shed with him – 'we get on perfectly well, and I like living there, there's more than enough room for both of us. Damn, is that rain?'

Fine ticklish rain was suddenly falling, and most infuriatingly out of a sky that seemed to have no significant clouds. 'I don't think it'll last,' he said. 'We'll be all right under there.'

They ran up the bank and took shelter beneath a solitary ash tree. At the tips of the twigs that dangled round their faces he could see sticky dark buds. As they stood there a little out of breath she looked out past him at the river in a sort of abstraction which suggested she was more intensely aware of him than if she had stared straight at him. He found himself too thinking about her, her solid impenetrable presence, as if he were away from her. Drops of rain hung separately on her hair.

'Go on,' he said. 'You were talking about anal-retentive types and you said "I'll tell you about it".'

She smiled briefly. 'Well, perhaps I wasn't being fair. I was thinking of Bill. He wasn't a hoarder or anything . . . just obsessively neat. No, that's not true either. Obsessive would make it funny perhaps, more interesting. I went out with him for a couple of years. Finally lived with him for six months or so. I was just thinking of his handwriting, of all things. It was like something out of a teleprinter, you know when the football results come up on the TV. Every trace of character removed . . . Oh, I'm sorry, this is awful, the bitching of old lovers. So tacky.'

'So how did your mother manage to cope alone for six months?' He could not prevent a little nastiness seeping into the question.

She shrugged. 'It was almost as if she was part of the arrangement. She knew him before I did – old family friends, you see. Where do family friends begin, I wonder? Friends are individuals who like each other . . . Anyway – he was Bill Swain – you remember Swain & Sons Insurance? – they got taken over by Pearl. Mum thought he was wonderful. I think she even liked him more than me: she used to get all perfumed and made-up when he called. And though she obviously wanted us to get married, when I said I wanted to try living together that was fine too, whereas normally she's very old-fashioned like that.'

'She really put the pressure on then?'

'Well, not exactly. It was more as if she was enjoying it through me. It was such an eminently suitable arrangement. Anyway living together was a good idea, since I found I couldn't stand it. It was the usual descending spiral of quarrels. Or not even that, he wouldn't quarrel. Just put his damned headphones on.' She sighed. 'Not long after we finished he was in a car crash. He was all right eventually, but he was badly injured. And all I thought was, thank God it's not me having to sit by his bed, thank God I'm out of it. Does that sound bad?'

'What did your mother think?'

'Oh, she kept pressing me to go and see him. Sort of, don't you see, this is the moment to make it up. I think she felt I'd left him out of some sort of loyalty to her.'

'But that was the end of it?'

She nodded, and passed him a cigarette. The smoke snaked out and meshed with the rainy air till it looked like clouds of steam rising.

'But did you ever – well, like him for himself?'

'You mean it sounds like an arranged marriage or something absurd like that? Oh, of course I did. But it's a funny world my family comes from. It's anachronistic and incestuous and I don't suppose you've ever noticed it's there. But it still has its effect. It's like when you see an old photo of your grandma or somebody and there's a certain echo in the face that makes you think God, that's me. All the time you've been thinking you're a complete individual – but there are bits of you going back years and years. And it makes it harder when your name's stuck up on a great monstrosity in the middle of town. Of course mum still thinks of the town as it was forty years ago. You know where the Midgate Arcade is? That's Bassett's Corner to her. Where Bassett's Emporium was. But there isn't even a corner there now.'

'My mum called it that too. She had a different map in her head.'

'Anyway that was Bill. Come on. Your turn. Now I've become a Woman with a Past for you, what about you?' She turned to face him, chin lifted, with a touch of wry catechism.

'Me? Oh, I'm a Man without a Past, I'm afraid.'

She frowned at him, and he perceived that already that sort of thing would not wash, that if he wished to become for her anything but the limiting image he had defensively created for himself then he must shrug off the habit of such evasions.

'You shouldn't get me talking about the past,' he said. 'It's as much as I can do to stop it taking me over completely. I sometimes think I've got a kind of nostalgia sickness, if there is such a thing.'

'What about? You're not old enough for nostalgia.'

'Oh, that's just it. It doesn't make any difference how old you are. I can be nostalgic about last week. Seriously. It's as if something's only got to be in the past for it to take on this golden glow. Not even any particular event, just any period of time that happens to get – summoned up by something. I have to stop myself thinking about it. Because the inevitable result is the feeling "Ah, there'll never be days like that again".'

'That's surely your mother's death that's made you feel like that.'

'No, no – well, it's maybe accentuated it. But I've always been like that. Sometimes I really wish somebody would invent a time machine. Then they could take me back to these times I brood over and say Look – this is what it was really like. You were miserable at the time! Because I probably was. What's alarming is the prospect of always being like this. The fear that good times – well, not good times, I hate that phrase, but happy times, are only ever going to exist in retrospect. Sorry. This really is a bit of Barber gloom coming out.' Wasn't now the time to say, but I'm happy here with you? But he couldn't even trust that to be true, couldn't be sure that it wasn't already a stored kind of happiness, to be retrieved another time.

'Well, you make that sound worse than it is. I mean, surely that means you've had a pleasant life really. If it can make you feel like that. Doesn't it?'

'You're right. I have. I suppose that's very English. Like they say the English national character comes from the fact that we've had it easier than just about any other country. And I've lived all my life here, right in the middle of it. Perhaps nostalgia's the national disease, and I just share in it.' And in a sudden painful panic that he was talking a lot of rubbish he burst out, 'But don't you find that?'

'I know the mood you mean. I don't think there's anything special in that.' He thought he detected a note of reproach in her voice, and inwardly shuddered at the thought that it might appear he had been taking care to represent himself as an Interesting Person. I'm really weird you know. 'You've just got to recognise it for what it is,' she went on. 'And, well, it's an awful cliché, but live for the moment a bit more. Otherwise everything that comes will automatically be a disappointment.'

'That's certainly true. D'you know I still get disappointed at Christmas? Oh, not because Father Christmas doesn't come or anything. There was just this one Christmas I remember when I was, I don't know, eleven or twelve I think. Last day of term the school used to go for this special service at the cathedral, and then you'd walk home in the afternoon. And the sense of freedom, it was marvellous. And I went to the Central Library for a book. I had to have a book that I could read over Christmas: I didn't like schoolwork at all, but this was different, like a ritual. It was *Three Men In A Boat*, of all things. And I loved it. I got really enthralled. Wading through this dim Victorian humour. Mum used to look at me and smile and say, "You still enjoying that?" I finished it on Christmas Eve. There wasn't anything special about that Christmas. I don't even think it snowed. But it's just got fixed in my memory as *the* Christmas.'

'And what about if you look at *Three Men In A Boat* now?'

He grimaced. 'Terrible stuff.'

She gave him a look, not unkind, that for a moment made him think of Maisie when she was about to shake her head and say 'Funny lad' – or more accurately, and disturbingly, of the times towards the end when the fondness of the look gave way to a bafflement that filled him with an entangled prickly stubbornness. Ruth said, both compounding and curiously relaxing this unease, 'Too much introspection, my lad. That's your trouble,' with the defensive humorous sternness that her voice, usually low and quite deep, both belied and suggested.

'What's the cure?'

'Violent physical exercise. Come on. Rain's stopping. Race you to the bridge.'

'I haven't run in years,' he began, but she had already set off.

In the end he caught and passed her: pleased at the discovery that he could still run quite fast, he carried on along the bank with her calling after him, until all at once he realised his lungs felt as if they were filled with sandpaper and he had to stop to cough and stoop and cough again. He heard, or rather felt, her laughing through her arms resting on his back. 'That's the cigs for you,' she said. 'Serves you right for showing off.' She gave him a slap between the shoulder-blades and then a gentler cuff as one would rub a child's head.

When he had recovered she was standing on the crest of the bank at a spot where it plunged steeply down for twenty feet or so and then briefly levelled out before dropping sheer into the water. She turned her head to look quickly at him, and he saw the excitement in her reddened cheeks. 'Race you to the bottom here.'

He shook his head. 'Never be able to stop,' he said, still a little out of breath, and was prepared to pull her back. He did not trust this river: half-swimmers and careless children too regularly lost their lives in its deceptive deep currents. She made a scornful sound and started down the slope.

For a moment he felt absurdly, sickeningly as if this action constituted an irrevocable rejection of him, that he had shown himself to be completely impossible and that she was disappearing out of his life for ever, and panicked by this he had plunged down the bank after her before the fury overcame him.

The grass was slippery, treacherous: with that and the gradient it would be impossible to stop. But somehow she had managed to slither to a halt, without falling, right at the water's edge, and waited with her hands out to stop him, still laughing and exhilarated.

'That was a bloody stupid thing to do,' he said, staggering about in squelchy, rank nettles.

'Yes, sir.'

'What's the matter with you? You can see how deep it is here, I said you wouldn't be able to stop – '

'Well, I did stop, didn't I? Don't be so stuffy. You sound like a heavy father or something. You sound like Bill.'

Stung, blustering with draining anger, he started clumsily back up the slope, not lingering to help her follow. 'Well you're the one who bloody well can't swim,' he stormed, ridiculous now, and seeing the day threatening to collapse beneath the weight of his righteousness.

He was absurdly pleased to find her hanging on to the tail of his jacket, and when they reached the top she did not let go. 'Hold on there King Lear,' she said. 'Look, I'm reproved, I'm grovelling.'

'I'm sorry,' he said lamely, meaning it. It always came out lamest when you were sincere. She looked at him closely, the irises of her eyes impenetrably dark: he had begun to realise that her intent gaze was the result of short-sightedness, and hence it was becoming for him rather vulnerable than intimidating. 'You've gone all tense again,' she said, 'just when I thought I'd got rid of that.'

'If I'm tense with you there's a good reason, Ruth,' he said, anxious now to keep saying what he meant, as if that ensured nothing more would go wrong.

She smiled, and seemed to check a laugh. 'Now that's more like it,' she said, and looked quickly down. 'Mud all over my jeans. Perhaps you were right to tell me off. Oh God, what's that . . .?'

Between the hem of her trouser leg and her short sock was a patch of bare skin to which adhered some globular, semi-transparent water-creature. 'Could you – get it off me please,' she said with the flat dry calm of the utterly squeamish.

He bent and plucked off the little repulsive yielding body and as he tossed it into the river he thought for an instant of the way as a schoolboy one would inevitably first thrust the offending thing towards the girl's face. She caught him smiling at this thought. 'What are you laughing about?'

'Oh, nothing. Not you.'

'You'd better not,' she said.

The rain started again as they drove home. It flung itself against the windscreen with a violent sizzling sound, coursing down and collecting in pools on the bonnet, so that he had to crouch forward in his seat to see the road ahead, and they did not speak much. When he dropped her at the drive to the house in Park Crescent it had increased to a drenching vertical pounding and she took an old magazine from the car to cover her head before sprinting to the house, turning at the last moment to wave to him.

'I'll see you on Tuesday. In my official capacity, that is,' were her last words to him. He thought about them as he drove home, crossing the invisible borders to his own world and to what was – it struck him for the first time – his own house. At the same time, he wished briefly that his mother were there, so that he could tell her about her. Nicholas was too cynical, or at least too sceptical, and too close to adolescence himself not to demolish in gales of scorn what David wanted to say.

Nicholas was not there: there was only the odour in the kitchen of the fierce curry which was the only thing he knew how to cook. David, robot-like, began to wander round the living-room picking up newspapers from the floor and stuffing them, no more tidily, into the magazine-rack, taking ashtrays through to the kitchen and emptying them into the pedal-bin. Once he found himself standing with an ashtray in his hand unable to think for the life of him where it went. It was a rather awful mother-of-pearl thing in the shape of a shell. How did it get here in the first place? He had a vague idea that Ron had brought him it from the Canaries. He found too that in his other hand he still held a jumper of his that he had picked up from the back of a chair. 'I'm getting old, my mind's going,' he said aloud. He put them both down on the settee and went to the telephone.

On the pad beside it was a message in Nicholas's big scribbled writing.

You're in trouble sunshine. Your Uncle Alan rang about three. He reckoned you'd promised to go to his for dinner today and you didn't turn up, he was in a right state. I told him you were enjoying splendour in the grass with Miss Selfridge. No not really. I tried to make some excuses but anyway you're to ring him back. N.

David stared out of the window at the soaking garden, swearing under his breath at Uncle Alan, as an alternative to swearing at himself. A whole screen of excuses flashed on his mind at once, and with the same immediacy he saw that only the truthful one was viable: I completely forgot. Uncle Alan's face, seen in memory when they had bumped into each other in Sainsbury's last week, seemed already to take on a hurt resentment. The invitation had been kind, and sincere, and a suspicion that it sprang from loneliness hopefully recognising a similar kind of loneliness had not prevented David from accepting. Anything had seemed better than a Sunday alone.

He dialled Uncle Alan's number and got an engaged tone. He made himself a cup of tea, thinking the while of apologetic phrases. His heart was beating rather fast. Must have been that running this afternoon. Stupid thing to do.

He dialled again, and again got an engaged tone, this time half-expecting it. He papered over his unease with excessive annoyance at having to get the car out of the garage again. He drove fast, on roads now awash, the tyres making a reluctant sticky sound.

He rang Uncle Alan's bell and then knocked loudly with the heavy brass knocker. He shuffled his feet on the doorstep and looked round at the geometric garden, the silent faces of the other houses in the cul-de-sac, and round again at the brass LNER plate, salvaged from a steam engine, placed above the porch. It shone like the sun, beautifully kept. He knocked again and then peered into the bay window of the front room. He saw the glints of polished surfaces, Alan's railway memorabilia: steam models ranged on the sideboard, a brass lantern, more engine-plates mounted on plinths.

Alan's pristine Morris-Minor was parked in the drive. Lashed by rain, David hurried round to the back of the house. The kitchen too was empty, but the back door was unlocked. He stepped in and called, 'Uncle Alan? Are you there?'

There was a faded smell of roast and on the stove were three saucepans full of vegetables. In the dining-room David found the table set for two: carefully folded white napkins were placed in glasses. There were even a few stiff bright daffodils – the first he had seen this year – in a cut-glass vase in the centre.

David took the stairs at a run. Stupid thing to do.

CHAPTER 9

'God, what did you do?' said Nicholas.

What did I do?

I must have shouted when I saw him. I must have taken him by the shoulder and shaken him. Shaken him fit to kill him, ironically. Shaken the life out of him. Shaken the life back into him.

Then I must have looked on his bedside cabinet for an empty bottle. That's the way it's supposed to be, the empty pill-bottle beside the bed. Except I couldn't find anything, which must have made me panic even more. I must have yelled at him, 'What have you taken, what have you taken?' I think he could speak, but he just wouldn't say anything, just moaned a bit like somebody in their sleep.

Then I suppose I must have run downstairs and phoned an ambulance. Thinking all the time, are you supposed to make them vomit? Or leave them alone? How do you make someone vomit? Thinking too, absurdly, of Marilyn Monroe. I must have sounded a bit apologetic, too, on the phone, the way you do. I mean you never think you're going to need them. And I couldn't remember the number of the house – had to run out to the front and check – like I can never remember the registration number of my car.

There was a woman down the road when I was little who stuck her head in the oven. But she used to do it regularly. That was in the days when the gas was different. They were a funny lot. Her husband had fits. Mum used to tell us always to smile and say hello to that woman, she was convinced that people ignored her and she got depressed.

I must have stood outside waiting for the ambulance. I didn't want to stay in there with him, I must have been afraid he'd stop breathing before my eyes. He was in a jacket and tie, but he'd taken his shoes off. Mustn't put your shoes up on the bed. Face as white as a sheet, but then it always was. He never looked well. Never was, with his asthma.

I must have gone in the ambulance with him. They don't smell clinical, funnily enough, just like an ordinary van. I must have thought he was going to die, because I kept crying. The ambulance-men didn't take any notice.

'I just did what you'd do in such a situation,' said David. It was Monday morning, raining still. 'It's all a bit of a blur.' He stuffed his shaver into his bag. 'They kept him overnight, he's coming out this morning.'

'Did they pump his stomach?' Nicholas made it sound rather obscene. Which it was, really.

'Yes, I was surprised they still do that, but apparently it's the only way.' He did not much want to talk about it. 'Anyway I'm going to pick him up and I'm going to stop with him a couple of days. He can't go back to that house on his own. Besides . . .' He zipped the bag. 'I've rung up work, I'm taking two service days. I'm trusting you with the house. If anybody calls you know where I am.'

Nicholas stiffened and saluted. 'Count on me, sah,' he said gruffly. Then he added: 'You'll not be going to the drawing class tomorrow then?'

'I hadn't thought of that.' He thought of it now, and of Ruth, and it had an effect of a finishing touch of sadness. 'No, I don't suppose so. Er – ' he felt suddenly embarrassed before Nicholas, who was watching him closely, 'perhaps you'd explain for me.'

'Yup.' As David turned to go, Nicholas tapped him on the shoulder. His face was grim. 'He's a stupid bastard, trying to top himself like that,' he said. 'Tell him so from me.'

That, David supposed, was Nicholas's version of 'Don't go blaming yourself.' Marian had said it more straightforwardly last night as they lingered about the hospital corridor. He hadn't been able to think of anyone else to get in touch with.

'Are you the next of kin?' the nurse had asked, in that accusing way they had; and he supposed they were. Alan was their dad's brother. 'He damn near worshipped dad,' Marian said, as they talked round and round, in widening swirls of irrelevance. David was dying for a cigarette. An admonitory poster on the wall developed this theme sarcastically. 'Why do they have to keep drumming it into you?' he said.

'I've stopped now, on account of Fred here,' said Marian, patting her belly. She had been huge with Tracey, but this time it was hardly noticeable.

'It's just another drug, David,' said Richard, who had sat there reading a magazine – actually reading it. 'And you've just seen what they can do.'

'I know it's a bloody drug,' said David. 'That's why I want one.'

'Don't swear in here,' said Marian, as if it were a church. 'What tablets was he on then?'

'Some sort of tranquillisers,' said David. 'They asked me if I knew why he was taking them, whether he was in a depressed state of mind and so on.'

'I hope you made sure they realised that you don't see him much, that you're not really involved in this,' said Richard. This was another variation on 'Don't blame yourself.'

'Well he was always in a depressed state of mind, wasn't he? Bit of a misery. Oh dear . . .' She was shocked at herself. 'That sounds awful . . .'

'It's true though.'

'Don't keep saying "was", Marian love,' said Richard, 'he's still alive.'

'Well, I told them that I was supposed to go to his for dinner today, but I forgot, and he must have got upset. And that he was a bit of a lonely type. They seemed to quite understand.'

'Of course they would,' said Marian. 'How were you to know he'd do a thing like that? I'd never have . . . He always was a bit of a neurotic I reckon. A right Methodist.' She stopped again, with a guilty look: bits of talk from normal gossip-life kept creeping in to this situation where they seemed inappropriate.

'Had he asked you to dinner before, David?' asked Richard, with an unfortunate air of prosecuting counsel.

'No. It was out of the blue. I suppose he thought he's on his own, I'm on my own . . . it was kind. I meant to go – '

'But you were busy, and it slipped your mind,' said Richard helpfully, this time the counsel for the defence.

'You'll have to get a diary, David,' said Marian, with a pale smile, touching his hand. She seldom made jokes.

'I've never needed one before,' he said, returning the pressure. Marian was what you called 'good' when this sort of thing happened. No, that wasn't fair, she *was* good, he couldn't have done without her. It was just that so many people telling you not to blame yourself was a pretty good way to make you do so.

He had barely had a couple of hours' sleep overnight, and his eyelids were prickly as he arrived at the hospital again to pick his uncle up. Under a curtain of grey rain the morning seemed abased and hopeless, and the car park was jammed full, as if the whole town were sick. But Uncle Alan, though he looked ghastly, was oddly cheerful. To the nurse who brought him down to out-patients he kept offering effusive thanks.

'It just feels wonderful to be alive, David,' he said. 'You just can't imagine how it feels.'

Alan's face, normally pale, with a weak receding forehead and chin and watery blue eyes behind thick-rimmed spectacles, was drained utterly of colour, even his lips. The stomach-pump was a shatteringly horrible experience. But even as he talked of it on the way home David had a sense that this was somehow part of what was almost exhilaration in his uncle. And in his old brown duffle-coat, with his skeletal twitching hands with the gingery hairs on the knuckles, he was really still the same Alan: surely a Brush With Death should leave you changed more?

'When I woke up this morning I felt so glad to be alive. I

had to keep thanking God. I wanted to shout and sing or something. I just can't tell you . . .'

Only slowly did David begin to grasp, as Alan spun out this endless mantra of gratitude, that what his uncle was seeking to convey was precisely that shame and contrition that David had expected and half-feared would be his reaction. And he began to perceive too that this evasive tack was a desperate manoeuvre to skirt round his own part in what had happened. Alan's brightness rose to almost hysterical pitch when they arrived at his house.

'Oh, it's good to see the old place again! I didn't think I would. I really didn't think I would.' He ran a finger along the front door sill. 'This could do with repainting. Another little job to do.' The paintwork was in perfect condition. He turned to David smiling, his eyes behind the spectacles curiously enlarged and still, as if half-blinded. 'Thank you for bringing me home and everything, David.' He affected amiable surprise at the overnight bag David carried. 'Really it won't be necessary,' he said. 'I shall be quite all right. Really.'

'I dare say you will,' said David. 'But I'll stop anyway.'

'Oh, but I was going into work this afternoon. I really ought to put in an appearance – '

'You're not fit to go to work and you damn well know it.' Through the screens of his own pity and guilt David was glad to find a little impatience emerging. 'You'll stay here and I'll stop with you until – until you're better. Now get the door open.'

'I don't want to put you out . . .' Uncle Alan was weeping, suddenly: he did not put a hand to his face or turn aside but stood there staring out across the street, ashen, painfully exposed as if taken by surprise. He was entirely helpless. David took the key from his hand and opened the door, steering him in. He felt almost relieved now.

The roast and vegetables that lay untouched David threw in the bin when Alan was out of the way. They had a salad instead – at least David did, for Alan could manage little. Then David washed up, insisting that his uncle rest in the sitting-room. As he moved about the kitchen he found himself acutely aware of the objects that testified to Alan's existence like so many exhibits in a courtroom: a calendar on the wall featuring paintings of locomotives by David Shepherd; a pile of dry washing, grey socks and white Y-fronts; on top of the fridge a Toby-jug, inscribed 'A Present From Great Yarmouth', filled with pencils, paper-clips and odd clothes-pegs; a brass log-box with a print of Gainsborough's *Blue Boy* on the front; all the furniture and décor like a tape-recorder on to which the minutiae that made up one life was faithfully wound. He caught a vivid, acrid whiff of loneliness. Not loneliness in the way it was commonly represented, in the concerned, social-workerish tone you heard in those songs – 'Eleanor Rigby', 'Streets of London' – which carried the patronising subtext that these people are lonely because they are ugly and old and poor and stupid and boring. Just the sheer horrible banality of being alone, of seeing on everything around you the same, single, so-readily identifiable fingerprint.

Uncle Alan had a tin of Brasso and a rag and was vigorously polishing a model traction-engine.

'I know I've done a very stupid thing, David,' he said.

David sat in the chair opposite: it was of the uncomfortable sort with upholstered seat and wooden arms. 'Do you not want to talk about it?' Somewhere down the street a shut-in dog was barking, a single monotonous yap every few seconds like the dripping of a tap: it was impossible for the ear not to anticipate it.

'There's not much to say. I've been unforgivably selfish and silly.' There was something of relish in his voice, a pleasurable self-laceration. 'I'm not about to start making excuses for myself. That's always the easy way out these days, making excuses, not taking responsibility for what you do. Like these young hooligans who end up in court for mugging an old lady. They say they come from a broken home or something and they pat them on the back and tell them to be good boys.'

'That's rubbish and you know it.'

'It's like that lodger of yours,' said Alan, ignoring him.

'Nicholas? What's he got to do with it? He doesn't go round

mugging old ladies.' David remembered that Nicholas had pointed out that Alan was an anagram of anal.

'I don't mean that. I just mean – the way he carries on. It's the same kind of thing. No responsibility. It wouldn't have been allowed in my day.'

David felt oppressed in the uncomfortable chair, as if pinned down by intolerable pounds of pressure. 'What do you mean? Because he's gay?'

Alan looked up with a hostile glitter of his spectacles. 'I'm surprised at you using that word, David. It's a silly word. It's just condoning – '

'Condoning? It's not a crime.'

'You know what the Bible says.'

'Oh sod the Bible.' With relief David burst upward out of the chair, like a cork coming out of a bottle. 'Now listen, what Nicholas does is up to him, and it's got nothing to do with this. Now I'm sorry for you and I want to help, but if you're going to go all tight-lipped and pious on me then you can forget it.' He paced across the room, which was north-facing and dark: it would always be sunless. 'I know I was supposed to come to dinner yesterday and I had every intention of doing so. But I forgot and I went out to the country with a friend. That's all there is to it.'

Uncle Alan had stopped his polishing and was staring at David. 'A lady-friend?' he said, and David almost laughed at the antiquated gentility of the phrase.

'Yes,' he said. 'If it's any business of yours,' he added as an afterthought of bad temper which he did not really feel.

'No, no, I'm not being nosy.' Alan still looked genuinely surprised – and almost pleased. 'It's just that I thought you hadn't come deliberately. When I asked you, I thought you'd said yes out of politeness – but when it came to it you thought "What am I doing – going to spend Sunday getting bored to death with this fussy old man. I won't bother." I honestly thought that.'

David sighed. 'It wasn't like that.'

'Well, that makes it all the worse,' said Alan, resuming his polishing with even greater vigour. 'What I did, I mean.

Assuming that people have nothing else to do . . . feeling sorry for myself.'

'Everybody's allowed to feel sorry for themselves,' said David. 'I do it all the time.' He felt for a cigarette. 'Will it bother your asthma if I smoke?'

'No, no.' Alan disappeared into the kitchen and came back with a saucer. 'I'm afraid I haven't got an ashtray,' he said – a sentence that always filled David with guilt.

'I'm glad you've found a lady-friend,' said Alan, going back to his model engine, with an air of hoping the subject was closed.

'Oh – well, it's nothing serious really.' Now why had he said that? He didn't even want to believe it. Even as he thought of her he felt the old sensation – he thought he had forgotten it – of a tightening at his chest, a quickening anticipation. I'm in love, he thought with a delight pleasurably leavened with absurdity. Just the idea was exciting. Forcing himself not to think about it, to come back to the point that Alan seemed ready to evade again, he said, 'I didn't realise you were on tranquillisers,' and immediately regretted the word 'on' which had a doleful sound.

'They're for my nerves,' said Alan.

'I take beer for that,' said David, which was insensitive.

'Drink never did anyone any good,' said Alan, but abstractedly, automatically. 'I do realise the image you've got of me,' he went on. 'I'm the person nobody wants to end up like.'

'That's not true,' said David, acknowledging the truth of it.

'But just because you live alone doesn't mean you're lonely. It's wrong for people to think that. There are a lot of advantages to being alone. There's too much fuss made about togetherness and sharing and all the rest of it.' His tone had become starchy and hectoring: he emphasised his words with tight budgerigar-like dips of his head, as he crouched over the now gleaming engine. 'Look at me. I've got my interests. They're quite enough for me. But people think they're silly, that you're just trying to fill in the time. As if chasing round trying to get into somebody else's pants isn't silly.'

David registered a mild surprise at this indecency. 'Well, I hate being alone,' he said. 'I can't stand it.'

He stood at the window seeing through a proscenium of looped net curtains a tableau of a suburban street on a spring afternoon. Rain had coloured the pavements a dark rust and by the post-box on the corner two young women with pushchairs shook out transparent rain-hoods, frowning and laughing. With a vertiginous sensation the image of the street as it had existed for the whole of his life threaded through David's mind as if on time-lapse film: summers bouncing light off the bay windows and forcing flowers in the front gardens, winters choking the roads with ice and slush, people darting with Charlie Chaplin steps up and down and back and forth; yet the street still unchanged, and indifferent.

'You just have to get a hold of yourself,' said Alan. He placed the engine on the sideboard and stood back to survey it. 'Become self-reliant, that's the secret. A question of self-discipline.'

His uncle gave him a proud, unfriendly look and then took a brass clock from the mantelpiece and began polishing it. It might have been David who had taken the overdose. But at least Alan had stopped saying how good it was to be alive.

There was a little colour in Uncle Alan's cheeks the next morning. He began to frown at the cigarette stubs in the saucer on the coffee table and he refolded the *Daily Mail* with excessive care after David had finished reading it.

'I don't think it's too early to start spring-cleaning, do you?' he said. 'Put my day off to some practical use.' He pushed his glasses up the bridge of his nose eagerly.

David was bored, restless, beginning to appreciate anew what an easy person his mother had been to live with, and glad of any activity to pass the time. Alan, like some houseproud Goth, sacked his pantry and cupboards: four, five, six complete teasets came blinking and virginal into the light, demurely nestling in corrugated card; redundant cruets were dusted and polished and then returned to their ceramic limbo. The drone of the Hoover filled the house: Alan probed beneath beds for dust that was not there and rammed the nozzle down the sides of armchairs. He was like Mole in *The Wind in the Willows*. David elected to clean the windows, and made something of a smeary mess of the job: Alan tut-tutted delightedly. Once David told him not to overdo it and tire himself, and his uncle flapped his hand testily, as at an irrelevant remark.

Uncle Alan talked to him about the war, and David encouraged him: this fantastic upheaval which occurred only a few years before he was born and yet seemed so remote always fascinated him. 'Our side of the family were lucky in a way. I mean your dad and me having bad chests. We didn't know your poor dad had TB then, God rest him. He wanted to fight, you know. He tried to join up twice, but they wouldn't have him. I was in the Home Guard later. It was quite enjoyable in a way. Though of course the invasion scare was over by then. They did some good work you know. It wasn't all drilling with broomsticks the way people make out. But they're always ready to make fun nowadays, there's not the respect.'

From white-painted cupboards came neat stacks of railway magazines, in chronological order, to be re-stacked even more carefully and replaced.

'It all seemed a long way away most of the time. But I do remember watching from my bedroom window and seeing a German bomber very clearly over the south side of town. It was trying to bomb the water bridge. The searchlights picked it out so perfectly. The ack-ack guns were blazing away like mad, but they didn't hit it. It was exciting in a way, but rather frightening. The next day we went over to look at the two houses that had been bombed. There were lots of folk there gawping. They'd been sliced right in half – you could see in, like doll's houses. Nobody was killed though, which is remarkable. So many people were lost in the war. It was a regular thing for women to come in the shop and say they'd just heard about their son or their husband. Such a waste.'

'What about that chap in uniform in the photo upstairs? Was he a relation?'

'No, no. He was a friend. What's the name of this lady-friend of yours, then?'

'She's not really my lady-friend.' But David, pleased, told him.

'It would do you good to settle down. I think you're the settling-down type, really. In spite of everything. Better late than never.'

David had never doubted he was the settling-down type. But it was the associations of the phrase that he baulked at – that suggestion of resignation, a deliberate lowering of the temperature of experience. For him it promised the opposite: a liberation, a new beginning – indeed the real beginning of his life, the time that he felt, obscurely, he had always been anticipating. But perhaps that was how everybody felt no matter what happened, that sense that the moment when life would begin is always just in the future, the moment when the trundling gives way to a breathless acceleration and you realise that *this* is what you've been waiting for, *this* is what at last vindicates all the suffering and boredom – especially the boredom. And perhaps – most pessimistic idea of all – you went on feeling like that until you died, and everyone's last, outraged thought before they were extinguished was: Hang on! – It hasn't even started yet!

Eventually Uncle Alan, as David had suspected he would, began to feel a little weak and sick. David sat him down at the kitchen table and made him a cup of tea and told him to take it easy. He continued the excavation of the cupboards and drawers himself, bringing each item to his uncle for inspection, to be told it was to be thrown away or, much more frequently, kept.

'Your mother's side weren't so lucky of course. Your Uncle Frank flew right through the war without so much as a scratch – though it was sending him peculiar towards the end, I reckon, the constant pressure. But there was your Uncle Joe dying in that Japanese prisoner-of-war camp.' The subject of death seemed not to disturb Alan now in the slightest. 'Terrible way to go – no grave for the family to visit or anything. It was months and months before they even knew.

Cruel little people, those Japanese. They'd do it again if they had the chance, you know. Only they channel it all into making money now.

'Thing was, everybody did their bit. Even your Aunt Aldyth, going on the land. Though I reckon she did it for the men. Those land girls soon got a reputation, piling into trucks and going off to dances and not giving a damn about anything. Responsible to no one. She'd be in her element there.'

David, fascinated by the unmistakable glint of malice, did not say anything but waited for more.

'Of course a lot of standards slipped in the war. They had to, really. But we never found them again afterwards, that's the worst thing. Your generation had it so easy. It was as if the war had never been.'

David didn't deny it. 'I do just remember, when I was little, sweets being still rationed,' he said. 'Although mum never let us have many anyway.' He lifted out a bundle of yellowing sheets of paper tied with cotton and unthinkingly turned it over to look at them.

'Give those to me,' said Alan.

'Sorry,' said David, embarrassed, and not quite knowing why.

Alan held the bundle lightly in his long spindly fingers as if judging its weight. 'Someone else the war took away,' he said. And, with a gust of great bitterness, 'Always the best ones, too. It left the rubbish behind, that's why we're in such a mess now.' He put the bundle down on the table with a show of casualness. 'Just letters from Philip. The one in the photo upstairs. Twenty-one when he died. The best friend anyone ever had. This is all that's left of him. It makes me very angry.'

'I understand,' said David.

The defensive glitter had come down over Alan's glasses again, masking his eyes. 'I don't expect you to,' he said shortly.

By the evening the house had been scoured, purged, as if Alan had ritually submitted it to an operation like the one he had undergone in hospital. 'You're looking a lot better,' David told him as they sat watching television. 'You should be all right for work in the morning if you want to go.'

'Well, I would have been all right to go today,' said Alan. 'But you insisted, so I thought I'd better go along with it. As you made such a fuss.' He smiled.

David said nothing, reluctantly admiring the way his uncle had shifted the burden of being a finicky nuisance to him. Only one more night here, thank God. It was nearly nine o'clock. He calculated the hours till he could be free of the restraints of his uncle's house. Funny how much you missed being able to slump and loll in your chair, scratch your bum whether it itched or not, give cavernous trumpeting yawns for no reason.

Nine o'clock. The life class would just be coming to an end. Nicholas would have explained, of course . . . but perhaps Ruth would think it merely the feeblest of excuses: that he was really backing out in some cowardly way.

Backing out of what? She might not give it a second thought. But no, that was an unbearable idea . . . Surely – surely . . .

He looked down at himself, in the blue light of the television, trying to see himself as others saw, and judged. He saw long legs, big feet, a pair of large hands with fair hairs running in a line from wrist to knuckle. He wondered if he was getting a suspicion of a podge – yet no, he was big-boned more than anything, like Marian.

But it was just an identikit of disparate parts. He had seen himself once on a home movie taken by Auntie Jeanette – somebody's wedding – and had been horrified. Was he carrying this appearance round with him all the time, this so bulky, unignorable presence, this terribly unguarded expression?

He found himself picturing Ruth, walking slowly round the life class, her rounded, uplifted profile as she inspected the drawings, the green angora sweater with its hints of soft small breasts. The thought of the presence of the nude model in that same room, normally the complete opposite of arousing, produced a strange combustion in his mind. He was alarmed to find himself excited, and shifted quickly in his chair.

Uncle Alan looked across at him. 'Why don't they show some good news for a change?' he said.

David made a non-committal noise. He cast about in his mind for the nearest pub to his uncle's house: supposing Alan went to bed about ten, he should have time to get there before last orders. Any later was pushing it . . .

'I think I'll have an early night,' said Alan, getting to his feet. 'Be fresh for work in the morning.' He yawned, a stagey, optimistic little sound. 'Don't forget to unplug the television.'

'OK. Sleep well. See you in the morning.'

Alan paused at the door. 'And do make sure your cigarettes are put out properly. I don't want to be burnt in my bed.'

'I will.'

This was a bit of luck: but perversely, David continued to stare at the television while a jolly weatherman made conjuror's passes over brightly coloured charts. He did not much fancy going alone into a strange pub. His mother had never minded him drinking, but had always warned him against drinking alone: it made you introspective and gloomy. A documentary about Beirut came on, and he felt the usual guilt about not giving a toss. He switched it off, and in the abrupt silence the gentle knock at the front door sounded loud and urgent.

As he opened the door the hall lamp laid a square of light on the darkness outside, framing the figure of Ruth peering up at him uncertainly.

'David, hello. I hope you don't mind . . . is your uncle – ?'

'He's gone to bed,' said David. 'Come in, come in.'

She stepped inside, bringing with her a fresh outside smell like clean washing and a darker scent of perfume. David inhaled dizzily. 'I've just stopped by on my way home,' she said. 'Nicholas told me the address . . . well, told me the whole story during break. It must have been awful for you.'

She came into the living-room but did not sit down, and

neither did he. The radiator gave a loud metallic bang as the central heating went off, making her start.

'It was upsetting,' he said. 'But he's better now. We've had a long talk about it.'

'He won't mind me coming in, will he?' She spoke softly. 'I don't want to disturb him.'

'It's all right.'

'I'll bet you blamed yourself, didn't you,' she said.

It was rather a relief to hear it put plainly. 'Yes, I did,' he said. 'If anything had happened . . . well, you know. But as I say, we've talked about it. It's just one of those things.'

'And you came out with me – I can't help feeling a bit awful – '

'Hang on – don't you start blaming yourself now.' He laughed strainedly. 'He's a bit of a nutter anyway, to be honest. But I thought I'd better stay with him. Till he was himself again. I'll go back home tomorrow. Well, I've got to go to work anyway.'

She was wearing a short black coat with a hood and it made her seem large and magnified as she slipped her arms around him. Her skin was cold with a faint dampness and he tasted lipstick on her mouth. They both made a little satisfied Mmf sound and he was aware from the rough noise as she brushed her lips across his face that he had not shaved today.

'That is nice,' he said. 'It's lovely,' she said, her fingers twiddling in the hair at the back of his neck. They stood, squeezing each other, huddled as if it were cold in Alan's overheated house.

How long was it since he had held someone like this? It was too long. It was too long by half. What were you supposed to say? He didn't want to say anything. He was facetious. 'To what do I owe this unexpected pleasure?' he said.

She pulled at his lower lip. 'Oh, impulse. You standing there with the little-boy-lost look. An old male trick, but for once it worked. And I missed you, actually.'

'What, after two whole days?' The old delight. Like riding

a bike, you never forget it. It wasn't old. It was brand-new, shining, sparkling new.

She drew away from him and put her hands on his chest. 'What you're supposed to say is how much you missed me.'

'Oh, sorry.' He looked up, thinking of the incongruous presence of Alan upstairs. 'Where are the stars?' he said. 'There should be some stars, really.'

'And a moon. But there's only your uncle's horrible lampshade.'

'Look, you,' she went on, giving him a dig in the ribs, after they had kissed again, 'I've got to get home. What I really came here for was to say, we've got the Regal on Thursday, so can you come then, and also to invite you to tea on Saturday.'

'To tea,' he said. 'I say, how genteel.' The words mocked her a little and she gritted her teeth and made a threatening face at him.

But it was all right. 'I'll be there,' he said. 'Best bib and tucker.'

It was all right, everything was all right. In Alan's chilly little spare bedroom he flicked the ash from cigarette after cigarette into an empty matchbox and could not sleep for happiness and fear.

CHAPTER 10

Night has fallen over the clay fields of the Lincolnshire farm, but in one corner the darkness and silence are incomplete. There is a soft chugging and a wink from a low-power lamp as a tractor is driven slowly up the lane and into a corrugated-iron shed. A young girl in jersey and breeches climbs down from it and unscrews the radiator cap and drains the radiator and covers the engine with a piece of old sacking. Her fingers are cold and stiff and from her mouth comes steaming breath and a constant swearing: 'Sod it, sod it, sod it, sod it.' At last she turns out the lamp and heaves the shed door shut and turns towards the farmhouse. It is Aldyth Russell's nineteenth birthday.

She removes her caked boots before opening the back door, and even through the thick socks the flagstoned floor of the kitchen strikes horribly chill. An oil-lamp still burns on the scrubbed table and beside it stands a mug of milk. She slips past it towards the staircase but a voice calls from the living-room. 'That you, gel?'

'Yes, Mr Millard.' Mustering a smile she pokes her head round the living-room door.

'Did you remember to unscrew that cap?' The farmer sits in a high-backed chair by the fire. His spectacles are perched on the end of his nose, and in the firelight Aldyth can see the clumps of tawny hair that grow out of his ears, so that it looks as if he were stuffed with straw. Which is unfair, as he is a pleasant enough man.

'Yes I did. I'm off to bed now.'

'I left you a mug of milk there,' he says. 'Drink it up.'

'Oh thank you. I'll take it up with me.'

Reluctantly she carries the enamel mug up the stairs. The invariable night-time drink here is milk fresh from the cow, considered a great treat. It is warm and sickly and, having seen the filthy shed where the cows are kept, Aldyth can seldom bring herself to drink it.

In their little attic room her fellow land-girl, Vi, is just getting into bed. The air here is both cold and fuggy. There is only room for one small chest of drawers and so piles of unwashed clothes – jumpers, dungarees, stockings – cover the floor and the narrow truckle-beds. Unwashed bodies add to the smell. Chasewater Farm does not even have a tin bath: they must make do with cold swills under the pump in the yard and fruitless piecemeal pourings from jugs and ewers.

'What on earth am I going to do with this?' says Aldyth. 'I can't drink it. I'd be sick.'

'Chuck it out of the window,' says Vi, sitting up in the bed and drawing the coverlet round her, 'that's what I did. I say, aren't you late? I finished half an hour ago. The old bag had me mucking the stalls out today. I still stink of it. Listen, though, we'll have some of my whisky to celebrate your birthday. Look in that bottom drawer. There's plenty left.'

Vi is from Nottingham, and quite posh. Her father is a retired major, and lacking a son insisted that his daughter should do her bit as soon as war broke out. 'I think he would have sent me to France to get killed if he could,' she confided when they first arrived, unpacking bottles of French perfume and silk pyjamas, 'but he decided this was the next best thing.' Expensive, unheard-of gifts still come her way: a cake with real chocolate, jars of best marmalade, and most recently the bottle of Scotch from which Aldyth now pours them two half-mugs.

'What a pity we've nothing to put in it,' says Vi.

'It's best this way.' Aldyth sits on the edge of her bed, makes an attempt to pull off her socks, and then gives up and leans back against the wall and takes a long drink. 'I'm too tired to get undressed.'

'I think I've gone deaf with all those aeroplanes screaming over today,' says Vi, sipping her whisky with a shudder. 'I think most of them were ours, but I can never tell. I think I ought to have glasses. A flock of geese went over the other day and there was me peering up trying to see if they were Germans.'

Aldyth laughs. 'Oh, Vi,' she says weakly.

'Well, I did!' says Vi with mock indignation. 'They fly in a *V* just the same.' She is secretly pleased at making Aldyth laugh: they get on so well but she is a little bit afraid of her and sometimes exaggerates her own 'jolly' persona to amuse her. 'They've started on Nottingham, the pigs,' she goes on. 'Daddy will be in his element but I'm a bit worried about mummy, she's very nervy. What time's your sister coming tomorrow?'

'Five o'clock. They're bringing Harold's brother too, for a day out. Apparently he's been in a bit of a state. His best friend was killed last week. Just twenty-one.'

'Oh Lord! In a raid?'

'No. Ethel says he was a sergeant-instructor up at Spilsby, on the rifle-range, and a new recruit who hardly knew what he was doing shot him dead by accident. Bullet right through the head. I remember him at Ethel's wedding, a very nice-looking bloke.'

'Oh Lord!' says Vi again, and then twists round and pulls a letter from under her pillow. 'I got a letter from Charlie today. He's still in Ulster and he says things are quiet at the moment and he's rather bored waiting around. I shall write back and tell him he shouldn't complain about being bored. We'd jump at the chance of being bored here.' She looks at the letter and re-reads something with a little laugh and then gives Aldyth a slightly abashed glance. 'I do think it's rotten you not having a sweetheart to write to.'

Aldyth smiles. 'Do you?' she says, and Vi is discomfited, but she plunges on. 'Well, yes. It makes things so much more bearable. I'll bet you could have the pick of the men with your looks. But how can one meet any stuck out here?'

Aldyth's looks are not at their best. Dirt and the scorching summer that has recently come to an end have coarsened her complexion and she has cut her black hair short. But there is still much to admire for Vi, who is small and pretty, but fancies herself mousy and plain.

'Sometimes the best men are already taken,' says Aldyth, and finishes her whisky.

'Oh, have some more,' says Vi, agreeably shocked, 'it'll keep the cold out.'

'Besides,' says Aldyth, pouring another good measure, 'I've got an admirer here. He was following me around again today.'

'Horrors, not the Child again.'

'The same. He offered me half of his apple. Teethmarks and all.' They fall into giggles that grow louder until they have to beat their hands on the beds and shush each other. The Child is their name for Mr Millard's sixteen-year-old son Ray. He is an ill-tempered youth with his father's straw-coloured hair and a habit of staring for which Mrs Millard still clobbers him. Once Aldyth and Vi found him squatting in the yard with a half-dead fieldmouse that he had cornered. He had a length of watch-chain and he struck the creature with this, conker-style, each time it tried to crawl past him. He went scowling away when they saw him and Aldyth had to put the mouse out of its misery with a shovel.

'So he actually spoke,' says Vi.

'Well, he sort of mumbled. I feel sorry for the old Millards. Fancy having produced that.' Aldyth yawns and begins to undress, slowly at first and then with more and more haste as the cold air hits each piece of exposed flesh. A grumbling noise in the distance grows to a booming drone that seems to pass right overhead and then is gone.

'Ours,' says Aldyth. She drains her whisky and then slithers shivering into bed.

'Please God keep them safe,' says Vi in a small voice. When they first came here she would say a prayer every night but somehow the presence of Aldyth made her stop this.

'There's a good reason for not having a sweetheart now,' says Aldyth as she burrows down into the chill starched sheets searching for warmth, 'at least you haven't got to worry about his safety.'

As a birthday treat for Aldyth, the Millards are laying on a tea at the farm for Ethel, Harold, and the last-minute addition of Alan, with real eggs and the home-made butter that is laboriously cranked in a wooden churn in the 'dairy', as the scrubby little room behind the kitchen is called. But the morning is taken up with work as usual. It is October 1940, and Aldyth has been here since January and has been awarded her six-months' service armlet, and has overcome her fear of the bullocks in the wash field. 'Goo and water them beasts,' Mr Millard would say, and so reluctantly she would descend to the dyke that runs at the bottom of the field and with straining muscles hoist bucketfuls of water into the bullocks' tank and then edge out of the way as they came slummocking forward to drink with their big fleshy mouths. Now it is an automatic task, and one of the less unpleasant ones, like searching about the yard and the outhouses for eggs, left by the chickens that wander where they like, even in and out of the kitchen with their scaly feet scuttering and slipping on the floor. She still dislikes the horses, however, and sometimes when she passes the stalls at night on her way to the toilet they make her jump with their sudden whinnying and stamping.

The toilet is a cesspit with a wooden seat. There is a lid over the hole and in summer to lift the lid is to release a volcano of fizzing, frenetic, shiny bluebottles. This toilet is one thing she knows she will never, ever get used to.

Sometimes she wonders what the Millards did before the land-girls came. Ray the Child works, after a fashion, though he has a tendency to slope off; and Mrs Millard cooks, after a fashion, for meals almost invariably include slices of the reesty fat bacon that hangs in fly-blown flitches in the living-room, and the rest of the time the range seems to be permanently occupied by a vast pot boiling up small potatoes for the pigs. But Mr Millard does little except sit in his high-backed chair, it seems, sometimes under pretence of 'doing the books'. 'The books' is a little exercise book that the farmer holds open on his knee, with a stub of moistened pencil poised above it. Meanwhile Aldyth and Vi have undergone a crash course in everything from hedging to rat-catching to shocking and tying sheaves – this the first occasion Aldyth has known herself break down and weep in sheer frustration as she struggled to enclose the recalcitrant corn in arms that seemed just an inch too short.

The sheer monotony of life in the country is matched by a lugubrious gloom. The Millards allow themselves an occasional chuckle, and are rays of sunshine compared with most of the people Aldyth and Vi come across. There is an imperturbable quality about everyone that is perhaps admirable but sometimes seems like mere idiocy. The planes that screamed above them heading south throughout the summer excited no comment. In the farm living-room, where the couch is always taken up by a sleeping sheepdog – and why a sheepdog? they have no sheep – there is a radio set, but it is only tuned to the news, and even ITMA is switched off. On Saturday nights Mr Millard walks two miles to the village pub, drinks a single pint of beer, and walks back again. On Sundays they sometimes sit in the parlour, where there is a Bible (though no one opens it) along with a table covered with a fringed chenille cloth on which stands an arrangement of deathly, hypnotically hideous lilac flowers under a glass dome. Of course, the war is making dreariness something of an institution. But they scarcely seem aware there is a war on anyway.

Aldyth spends the morning on the tractor, and then at noon Mr Millard sends her down to the village with the accumulator from his radio with twopence to get it recharged. The day has turned mild and pleasant and she takes a route across the field-paths. Heavy black clay with a purple sheen stretches from horizon to horizon, and the sky is for once empty and silent: the country is for the moment less forbidding, a place to have a good think, and so she does. But as it turns out this does not refresh her spirits, and she arrives at the long street of cottages that calls itself a village rather low.

After taking the accumulator to the garage, a shack of rusting corrugated iron with a petrol pump and no petrol, she stops at The Bird in Hand to talk to the two sisters who keep it. They are friendly old bodies in voluminous skirts and petticoats that brush the floor: the place is part-farm, part-pub, with a saloon-room of wooden benches where morose farmhands wait for the old ladies to bring up cold jugs of beer from the cellar below and never say thank you. The sisters got to know about Aldyth's birthday and have saved their sweet ration to bake her a miniature cake. Aldyth is touched when they, a little bashfully, present her with this, and her eyes moisten: perhaps also she is affected by a ghost of Spinsterdom that they raise. And then Aldyth walks back to Chasewater carrying the accumulator and the cake in a tin and has another sniffle unobserved except by the cows.

'You goo and git ready for your company,' Mr Millard tells her that afternoon, and as Vi is on the tractor and Mrs Millard has retired to an outhouse to 'do the bulbs' – the place is full of tulip bulbs but what 'doing' them entails Aldyth has never found out – she takes the opportunity of boiling pans of water on the range and slopping them up to the attic to wash her hair and as much of her body as she can manage, spreading one of her pair of WLA-issue towels on the lino and shiveringly rubbing herself with a dwindling cube of Lifebuoy.

The attic door, like all the doors in the farmhouse, is made of planks, with a latch, and she would probably never have noticed the crack in it, about half-way down; nor, probably, would she ever have noticed Ray's eye pressed to it, which makes her speculate afterwards on how many times she has been spied on before. But it happens that on this occasion, moved by who knows what impulse, he pokes his tongue through the hole, and she catches sight of the pink wriggling thing.

She is quick enough to gather the other towel round her and yank the door open just as he is stumbling up off his knees.

'What the hell do you think you're doing!' she hisses, but for a moment he can say nothing for his hand is stuffed into his mouth. 'Got a splinter in my tongue,' he manages at last, with a whimper.

'Well it damn well serves you right!' Her anger is giving way to contempt: he really is a very ugly boy, with his raw chapped skin and oily hair and stains down the front of his sleeveless pullover. And a sly look comes down over his eyes. 'I were only looking,' he says, and she realises that, insecurely wrapped in a towel as she is, he is still looking.

'Clear off,' she says. 'I've a good mind to tell your mother and father about you!'

The sly look gives way to fear, and he backs to the head of the stairs. 'I won't do it again, honest. I promise. *Honest*,' he whines. He starts noisily down the stairs and then turns his face to her again, this time pinched and hateful. 'I reckon you and Vi touch each other's things in there,' he says.

'Do we? What things? What things do girls have then?' she says, curiously, and he looks alarmed. 'What things do they have? The same as boys' things? Do you know? Do you actually know?' She takes a step towards him. 'Do boys touch their things then? Do you?'

Ray disappears at a run down the stairs, with a little sound that suggests he is going to cry.

'Such lovely bacon,' says Ethel. 'Honestly, the meat we get nowadays is rubbish, just offal most of it. Ooh, I shall be fat as a pudding at this rate.' Her pretty hazel eyes roam over the table with unashamed greed, and she laughs at herself. Harold laughs with her, and their fingers briefly seek each other across the tablecloth. Marriage has suited them, it seems, and even Harold's slightly frail handsomeness has been overlaid with a healthy tan from working on his allotment all summer.

'Finish it up, finish it up,' says Aldyth. 'Mr Millard left us lots.'

'Where *did* they go to?' says Vi, who sat down to tea still in her work clothes, and immediately endeared herself to Harold and Ethel by gusting, 'I say, I'm famished!'

'Visiting some relations on the other side of the village. The Child's still lurking about somewhere, though.'

'It was nice of them, wasn't it?' says Harold. He has egg on his chin, and Ethel absently dabs at it with a handkerchief.

'Oh, we deserve the odd treat, don't we, Vi? Alan, would you like some more?'

'No, thank you.'

'Go on, you need feeding up,' says Vi, for the second time, and realising now that her well-intentioned jolliness does not wash with this thin pale young man who sits straight and solemnly, not looking at anyone, as if he were in church. 'Poker-faced', she thinks, for it is only gloominess, which she cannot comprehend, that ever prompts her to be uncharitable; and she quickly reproves herself, and thinks 'Poor boy, how it must have upset him.'

Harold and Ethel and Alan arrived having driven the fifteen miles from town in Harold's new Ford Popular: he has been saving his petrol coupons for this trip. He is very proud of the car, in a hushed, maternal sort of way, and when they walked up to the farmhouse he turned several times to glance back at it parked in the lane.

'I believe you're afraid that car will run away,' said Ethel.

'Oh! no, it'll be all right,' he said, and then blushed with his amiable smile as Ethel and Aldyth, arm in arm, laughed together at him. 'He pets it,' Ethel said, 'I swear he does, like an animal.'

Gossip is swapped across the tea-table. Joe Russell still hasn't been posted; Frank was home on leave recently, and has taken to using peculiar posh phrases like 'bang on' that he has picked up in the RAF, and about which his father is devastatingly sarcastic; Ethel, prompted by Harold's mother, has joined the WVS. 'I'm sure they do a lot of good work,' she says, 'but sometimes it seems like busybodying, really. Nothing like what you and Vi are doing.'

'Hearing what you girls have to do makes me feel pretty silly with my little allotment,' says Harold.

'But you've got a full-time job as well,' says Aldyth.

'Full-time's the word. Women are starting in the factories now too. There's all sorts of changes at work. They're even taking on people who would never normally have a job at all.

People who are a bit funny – ' he taps his temple – 'old chaps who retired, didicois. We've got one who comes to work on his old horse. Leaves it tethered by the bike sheds. Honest!'

There is laughter and, excepting the figure of Alan, there is an ease amongst them that seems actually to take them by surprise, so that they laugh more and more, sometimes at nothing in particular. How nice-looking the three of them are, thinks Vi, each in a different way. And poor Harold's brother, who is not a bit handsome, with his eyes screwed up behind his spectacles, and his sandy hair that will soon recede. When he does laugh, he seems to look towards Harold for a lead, and Harold looks at him in a worried, encouraging way.

'Harold tried to join up again,' says Ethel. 'He thought with things as they are they'd be getting less choosy.'

'Gosh, why won't they have you?' says Vi through a mouthful of bread.

'Bad chest,' says Harold. 'Makes me feel pretty bloody useless, I can tell you.' It is unusual for him to swear, and he does it without fluency, like a man struggling with a foreign language.

'Of course you're not bloody useless,' says Aldyth, much more readily, and with a certain heat that makes Vi look at her in surprise. 'What do you want to go and volunteer to get yourself killed for? You ought to count yourself lucky.'

Harold and Ethel are both silent; though something that is like a smile lifts the corner of Ethel's mouth.

'Oh, but Aldyth, you mustn't think like that,' says Vi, wriggling in her seat as she does when she is excited, a habit for which her mother used to reprove her. 'We're fighting for our lives. I mean, what if a German parachutist were to come floating down here one day, what would you do?'

'Give him a chair and a drink and send for the police,' raps out Aldyth.

'She would as well,' says Ethel amidst the laughter, 'she would.'

Vi has a habit, as well as wriggling, of blurting: she cannot help it. 'I say, I was so sorry to hear about your friend, what a terrible thing,' is what she blurts this time, to Alan, resigning herself almost simultaneously to having been clumsy. Alan flinches as if at a blow. Harold touches his elbow gently and says, 'Yes, a terrible thing. We all knew Philip, it's a great loss. But I mean – there was no pain, perhaps it was better – '

'It would have been better if he'd been killed in action,' says Alan. Though he is sixteen, his voice still has a fluty wobble that gives it an effect of primness. 'That's what he would have wanted. He always said so.' He looks round at them all with a juvenile, wounded pride that is moving and pathetic.

'Look, the old ladies who keep the pub in the village made me a cake,' says Aldyth. 'Have some, Ethel. You always had a sweet tooth.'

'Well, I don't suppose I ought to, but I shall. As long as I don't break the springs on Harold's precious car.'

'I don't believe in God any more,' announces Alan. He rubs his palms up and down his thighs. 'If there was a God, he wouldn't have let it happen.' There is a contrast in the agitation of his hands and the level, almost priggish sound of his voice.

'I understand how you feel, old son,' says Harold. 'It's quite understandable. But I don't think mother would. Perhaps best not say anything to her about it, eh?'

'Why not?' says Aldyth. 'He's quite right, if there was a God he wouldn't let it happen. Or if there is, he's a right so-and-so if you ask me. That's what I've always thought.'

'How would you know?' says Alan, curt and white.

'Now then, Alan,' says Harold.

'Oh, sorry.' Ray Millard has sloped in to the kitchen, and stands in the doorway nursing his left arm in his right, staring.

'Hello, Ray,' says Aldyth. Introductions are made, and Ray, in the manner of adolescents, does not acknowledge them. He stares round and finally says to Alan, vaguely: 'Want to come and see the horses?'

'Yes, go and have a look round, Alan,' says Ethel. Alan obviously does not much want to see the horses, but he goes.

'They bite,' Ray observes, leading the way. 'Sometimes.'

'Oh, dear, all my fault,' says Vi, giving herself little smacks on the temple as if in self-punishment.

'Nonsense,' says Harold. 'Better to mention it. Mother was saying he's been impossible since it happened.'

'He must have been a fair bit older than Alan,' says Aldyth.

'Took him under his wing a bit, you know. Ever such a nice chap. Alan's never really had many friends. I think it was a bit of hero-worship on his part.'

Dusk is gathering, and it will soon be time to light the oil-lamp in the kitchen. Vi produces her whisky, and they drink a toast to Aldyth, though Ethel drinks it in tea, and only at Aldyth's persuasion does Harold have a drop. Then he takes off his jacket and rolls up his shirt-sleeves and volunteers to do the washing-up, so they boil some water and set the bowl on the table. 'You've been working hard today, Vi, you sit tight,' says Aldyth. 'I *am* a bit tight,' says Vi, to a laugh, for the whisky quickly goes to her head. So she sits and watches as Harold washes and Ethel dries and Aldyth puts the crockery away, and feels light-headed, and the three of them, all on the tall side, all rather good-looking, seem peculiarly matched in more than one way; so that as the sisters move round the table, interchanging, fussing, and laughing as they hand back to Harold pieces of cutlery that are not properly clean, and he tuts and raises his eyes in mock exasperation, it seems as if they might be any related combination, or all siblings, or even a man and two wives. And when they have finished Aldyth dives on the little bottle of scent they bought her for her birthday, and dabs some behind her ears, saying, 'Damn it, I just want to remember what it's like to smell nice again. Even if it's only to charm the pigs,' and then dabs a little on Ethel's cheek, saying, 'Here, you too, Ethel. You never know what might happen.' And they laugh together, and Harold laughs too, though not quite with them, for he stands a little apart, like a passer-by caught in the edge of a snapshot.

He thinks they had better go, for he is uncertain about driving in the dark; so Vi fetches their coats, and Aldyth goes out to find Alan. A couple of chickens run before her feet in their panicked, stupid, straining way: she always feels like kicking them when they do that. There is no-one in the stable: the two old carthorses grunt and shuffle their big hooves in the muck. She finds Alan and Ray at last in the Dutch barn, sitting on bales of hay. Alan is thrusting back some pieces of paper at Ray, and weeping.

Aldyth snatches the papers from Ray, who merely looks up at her in a more gormless way than usual. One is an arty photo of a naked woman peeping out from behind a tree: she recognises it as having been torn from an issue of *Lilliput*. The other pictures are similar, but older, and much cruder.

Alan takes off his spectacles and wipes his eyes with the heel of his hand.

'I was only showing him 'em,' says Ray. 'I thought he'd like to see 'em.' He backs away, with his gait that is oddly cringing, as if he always expects a blow. Which she feels like giving him.

'Well, perhaps Alan's not as childish as you,' she says. She shoves the pictures back into his grubby hands, and he lopes away slowly, staring back over his shoulder.

Aldyth frowns down at Alan, who is polishing his spectacles with a clean handkerchief and trying not to sniff. 'Harold's getting ready to go,' she says. 'Shall we wait a minute?'

'They didn't bother me, you know,' he says, with the short breath of tears. 'I've seen those things before.'

She frowns again. With most people, you would pat their back or put your arm round their shoulder. But not with this strange boy. Or perhaps not so strange.

'Is your mother getting fed up with you, being so upset still?'

He looks up at her now, in a startled way.

'Well, she probably doesn't understand how much he meant to you. She's older.'

Alan keeps his head down, so she cannot see his eyes. 'He was better than me, much stronger and cleverer and everything,' he says. He sounds very adult; then he sounds very childish as he says: 'But nobody was friends with him like *I* was.'

A single aeroplane makes a bee's drone, invisible in the dusk above.

'Well, if you lose someone you love, you're bound to be upset, that's natural,' she says. His shoulders move in an irritable way, and he mumbles and she catches the word 'Sissy.' His ears are crimson.

'That's a stupid word. That's one of those words that doesn't mean anything,' she says. Pity, as is its nature, is infected with exasperation. 'There's nothing wrong with loving somebody, you know. Whoever they are. No doubt that mother of yours wouldn't think so.'

He stands quickly and turns to her, his face completely suffused with red. She is startled by the stare he gives her: it is like hatred.

'Don't you talk about my mother like that. She knows about *you*. She says you're no better than you should be.'

'I dare say she does,' says Aldyth, and there is the merest glint of an edge in her voice. 'But like I say, there's things she probably doesn't understand.'

He puts on his spectacles, and his face is frozen tautly, impenetrable, behind them as he walks past her towards the house.

Soon after Harold's Ford grinds off down the lane, Mr and Mrs Millard return and a cold drumming rain falls. While Aldyth and Vi chase the chickens and cover the hay and close the stalls it grows harder and penetrates their sou'westers, crawling down their necks and plastering their hair to their faces, and their clothes fill the attic room with a steamy fustiness. Shivering, wrapped in prickly blankets, they finish off Vi's whisky by candlelight. Or rather Aldyth has most of it, but then Vi never really liked it that much anyway.

'I should never have come,' thought David several times, and several times a rising panic threatened to lift him from the tea-table and scoot him out of the house.

But instead he filled his mouth with food and acted normally, the way you do, and Ruth was there and that was the whole point.

'There's been a change,' Ruth whispered to him, meeting him at the door. 'My brother's here too and now the Olivers have turned up as well. Relations of mum's, horrible. Keep smiling.'

She removed his coat, running her hands lightly down the outside of his arms. There was the sound of laughter from the dining-room.

'You don't live in the townships, do you, David?' asked Mrs Lacey. 'Well, thank heaven for that. I think those places are dreadful, so soulless. Those rows and rows of identical gardens. With those twirly things to hang your washing on – what are they called? Like umbrellas.'

He did not know what to say.

'I don't think they're called anything,' said Ruth.

'Like umbrellas.' Mrs Lacey delicately lifted a forkful of salad and popped it between her lips. She smiled, a sheen of dressing on the sheen of red lipstick.

David walked to the Laceys' house, cutting across the park that smelt of earth and coolness, and in the evening after the tea Ruth walked partway back with him and said, 'Mum loves company. Although I don't think she actually likes people very much. The Olivers came round this afternoon out of the blue, and then of course they had to stay to tea. She calls them all the names under the sun when they're not there. But that doesn't mean she doesn't want to see them. Company, that's the main thing.'

Ruth was wearing a collarless shirt of a pearly grey colour. Her skin was of the waxen sort of whiteness that often goes with very black hair and dark eyes and it inched out at wrists and neck so that he could not stop himself, throughout tea, from looking at it at these places. She was next to him and whenever she turned to him her face was neutral, friendly, and unrelaxed: once beneath the table she laid her leg against his and kept it there for a while, comfortably, with unbearable intimacy.

The Olivers were in their forties, and both very fat. David kept thinking of Oliver Hardy. Mr Oliver had the same dapper, exaggerated courtesy. 'They're not all so bad, you know, Barbara,' he said to Mrs Lacey. 'The Lady Lodge estate is rather nice, I think. But I know what you mean. They don't seem like part of *our* town to me. Not the real town.' A tiny fragment of bread escaped his lips as he said this, and he retrieved it with a long prehensile tongue.

'That's just it,' said Mrs Lacey. 'The old identity's gone. You don't feel you belong any more. We shall end up like Coventry or somewhere. A great big nothingy sort of place.' Her pencilled eyebrows, with a head start over her invisible real ones, travelled upwards, and she looked at David.

'I suppose the town's got to expand,' he said.

'But *why*?' she said. 'I don't see.'

'Well, look at Corby. A whole place can go under very easily these days.'

'Oh, these days.' Mrs Lacey tossed these days away with a ringed hand.

'Progress,' said Mr Oliver, with a deep chuckle, and sent progress to join these days with a hand that was also ringed, and dimpled like a baby's.

'Well, the town's changed, and you can't change it back,' said David.

'That I realise,' said Mrs Lacey. 'But I don't have to accept it. And I don't accept it.'

'Good old Barbara,' said Mr Oliver. 'Barbara has spoken.'

'Yes I have,' said Mrs Lacey, and there was a little grating of temperaments in the air, hers and David's and Mr Oliver's, so that they all smiled in a cheerless way.

It did not seem to affect Ruth. 'You live in the past, mum,' she said, 'that's your trouble.'

Mrs Lacey sighed and with a gesture of great charm laid a finger on David's arm and said, 'Never have children, David. They turn on you when you're old.'

'You're not old,' he said.

She was in her mid-fifties, and did not look it. Well-preserved was a curiously appropriate term, for there was a kind of accentuated dewiness and bloom about her face, a softish heart-shaped face, that suggested fruit and flowers; even the wrinkles became a feature, taking their place in an act of pleasing contrast with the smooth neck and brisk body that was wide-hipped but by no means heavy.

He was not just trying to be flattering. He quickly fell victim to the charm, which was there in abundance, whilst guessing that it was meant for just that – the taking of victims – and perceiving the vein of iron that ran through it. When he first arrived, and Ruth brought him into the lounge where Mrs Lacey was talking to the Olivers, she rose with a smile that was directed right at him, as if in warm recognition: a shy, almost impish smile that established a secret between them which he did not understand.

'I am on foreign territory,' he thought several times.

There was a photograph of a young Mrs Lacey in the lounge on top of a black, carved *thing* – sideboard, bureau, medieval altar, he could not guess – quite a beauty, remote, old-fashioned, her hair up. He remembered that she had been on the stage for a while.

'She was an actress for a couple of years, very small-time stuff,' said Ruth later as they walked through the park. Greenish and decaying evening light withdrew behind the branches of the conifers, slowly, decorously, making oriental bows. She held his hand in a restless way. Her forefinger and thumb encircled his wrist. 'But it's never left her. If anything it seems to have taken over more and more. Didn't you get that impression?'

He was uncertain, the question seeming cloaked, not asking something about Mrs Lacey but about himself. 'Maybe,' he said.

'Either you did or you didn't,' she said. Her smile was disquieting, coming from somewhere he had not been with her before; his very footsteps as he walked were not confident, the grass untrustworthy.

She talked frankly, dispassionately to him about her

mother, in a way that somehow absolutely precluded malice. She talked to her mother in exactly the same way, without stress. 'Oh, mum,' she said at tea, 'David doesn't want to hear about your boring bridge. Give it a rest.' And Mrs Lacey sighed and rolled her eyes at David, extending something to him again, including him. Almost as if she were saying, 'The young . . .!'

Walking to Park Crescent that afternoon, he had felt nervously that this invitation placed him as an object of scrutiny: it was a formal introduction. But that was overturned by the presence of the Olivers and Gordon and, while part of him was relieved, another part managed to feel slightly resentful at being diluted thus. Only gradually did he realise that the real centre of attention was Gordon.

'Another of these arty-farty types, eh?' said Gordon to him, as they sat in the lounge before tea. 'Budding Rembrandts.' But he said it in a way that turned the mockery chiefly on himself. He had an amiable, defenceless smile, and David rather liked him. Unlike his sister and his mother, he was not good-looking: he had mousy, sparse hair and an old man's face, fiddle-shaped. David remembered that he was an accountant and lived in London, and wondered why he was here.

'How's the world of accountancy, then, Gordon?' said Mrs Oliver at tea. She was eating as voraciously as her husband: they seemed to have a race on. 'Wheeling and dealing, financial wizards, dodging the taxman, all that.' She laughed musically.

'I haven't been exactly in that world, as you put it, for a while,' said Gordon. 'Due to circumstances.'

'Well, last time you were in it, I mean,' said Mr Oliver – as if he had asked the question – and frowned down studiously at his plate.

'There's a point,' said Ruth in the park, 'that separates drinking a lot from being an alcoholic. Gordon recently passed it. We've known for a while, and mum tried to get him to come home. He'd been to a clinic, and he'd stopped work. But he wouldn't come back here to dry out, as they call it.

He wanted to be on his own. Suddenly he changed his mind. I think he got really frightened when he couldn't remember things. There was one weekend when he spent the whole time drinking in his flat. A friend found him on Monday in a terrible state. He couldn't remember a thing. The lost weekend in fact.'

'Have you seen that big new "Welcome" sign they've put up by the railway station?' said Mrs Oliver. 'Awful. Meant to be a townscape, as far as I can gather. Modern art sort of thing.'

Mrs Lacey closed her eyes and hunched her shoulders in a shudder. 'Oh, Ruth's the one to talk to about modern art. That's Ruth's thing.'

'It's not my "thing", mum. And you think anything that's not *The Monarch of the Glen* is modern art.' She looked at David.

'It's funny how the term "modern art" is really very old,' said David: he felt he was being invited, somehow, to join in the ritual debunking of Mrs Lacey. 'Not really modern at all. But people are still afraid of it.'

'Rubbish by any other name,' said Mr Oliver, and ate celery with a noise like a crash.

'No one more Philistine than the displaced middle class,' said Gordon. He smiled unhappily. 'I hear you're at Barlow Watkins, David. Booming place that. Amazing profits last year. Any of it come your way?'

'Not much,' said David.

'David,' said Mrs Lacey, sitting up with a hen-like fluffing that indicated, with some but not complete self-mockery, that she was about to make a pronouncement, 'the name of your boss is Kenneth Musson, isn't it? I know him. Or his wife, mainly. Very nice man, isn't he? Oh, but of course you won't think so. Nobody likes their boss.'

'Yes, he is a nice man.'

'Are they taking on any apprentices this year?' said Gordon. David noticed he seemed to be ignoring everyone else at the table.

'No. They haven't done for several years, even though they're making money hand over fist.'

'I hear Heigham's aren't either,' said Gordon. 'That's the trouble. How this place thinks it's going to thrive just on all those nice new empty office blocks – '

'Well, I do think, really,' put in Mrs Lacey, 'that before we start blaming these firms we ought to remember that the young people used to *jump* at those jobs once upon a time. Isn't that, really, the heart of the matter?'

'Go on, mum,' said Gordon. 'Tell us. They don't want to work.'

'I didn't say that. I'm not entirely stupid, Gordon. But the incentive isn't there so much these days.'

'The state keeps 'em,' said Mr Oliver to his plate. 'Too well.'

'Well my lodger is one of these young people,' said David. 'And he gets less money than I was getting fifteen years ago.'

'Perhaps he doesn't want to work.' Mr Oliver addressed his plate again.

'He does work,' said Ruth. She had sat, not eating, apparently bored, through this. 'He works voluntarily at the Salvation Army thrift shop. Change the subject, mum, you're good at that.'

'Not what you'd call a proper job though,' said Mr Oliver, with a pleased nod, and his plate had no answer to that one.

In the park David lifted Ruth's hand as they walked and kissed it and studied it a moment.

'Mum wants people to argue and get exasperated with her, she encourages it,' she said. 'That way you never really can. Gordon gets wild sometimes. I mean, that scene today. I think all he wants is for mum to acknowledge that there is such a thing as an alcoholic, never mind that her son should be one.'

Once during the tea David went to the toilet, which was hidden away behind a churchy-looking door beneath the stairs; and when he came out into the big hall he could not remember for a moment where the dining-room door was. Just like when he was a child, coming out of the toilet on the caravan site in Skegness and standing, staring, unable to recognise their caravan; and that little itch of panic in his chest.

He saw no photographs of Ruth's father in the house: in fact there was only that one of her mother and one of Ruth herself, at a graduation ceremony, with long hair and a smile the confidence of which annoyed him. Perhaps because its confidence was in a world that did not include him. His own family filled their houses with photographs, like primitive ancestor-worshippers. The eyes of dead relations observed your life, as if in envy. And live relations too. Like mementos mori: it was ghoulish really. Photographs were remains.

'They were separated when I was quite young,' said Ruth. The streetlights beyond the trees hid amongst the branches; a few birds were singing, a depleted chorus. 'It's still quite a painful point.' She did not say for whom.

'And so how's *Carousel* going then?' said Mrs Lacey.

David found himself addressed. 'Oh, well, it all seems fine to me,' he said, 'but I mean, I'm really a backroom boy.'

'He paints very well. I think this will be the first good scenery we've had,' said Ruth.

'It is important, of course,' said Mrs Lacey. 'I remember the set for *Gigi* was especially poor. A shame, it was a lovely show. Bill played Gaston. That was when you and Bill met, wasn't it, Ruth?' She did not look at Ruth. She was talking straight at David. She obviously assumed he knew who Bill was. 'He was marvellous in the part. But there was a bit when they're by the sea – you know the scene – where he and Gigi – that was Vivien, wasn't it – had to ride a tandem across the stage. And he could *not* ride this damn bike. Everybody roared. Bill took it in the right spirit though. He always did.' She leaned forward and smiled, and David smiled back, and realised – with something of real fear, so subtle was the shift – that the act of charming inclusion that she had practised on him was now being used, unmodified, to exclude him utterly. Ruth was watching in what seemed a dispassionate way.

'I understand you were in the theatre yourself, Mrs Lacey,' he said, while little humpbacked suspicions and jealousies did a quick caper in his mind. Flirtations amongst the amateur theatricals always happen, never anything serious. You picked up the leading man once, why are you settling for a scene-painter, declaimed an inward voice, with maximum drama, relishing its opportunity, knowing it would never have access to his mouth.

'I just knew she'd mention Bill,' said Ruth. They walked along beside the tennis-courts and the putting-green and there were smells of crushed grass and creosote from the pavilions. 'I was prepared for it. She was fishing to see if I'd mentioned him to you. I think he's still a going concern in her imagination. Oh, God, I'm making her out to be some sort of monster or something aren't I? When you've just seen for yourself that she isn't. She's perfectly ordinary.'

'You're forgetting,' he said. 'I know what it's like to live with one's mother, how it affects you.'

They began kissing against the side of the pavilion, in the smell of timber and creosote and dusk dampness, he with his shoulder-blades against the ridged boards, she folded into him, pressing him back and pulling him forward. 'I know one thing, I couldn't cope like you have. If my mother died I don't know what I'd do, I'd be lost.'

'That's what I always said. It doesn't work out like that.' He was aware of her in a fiercely detailed way, and an overwhelming closeness, as if it were part of some outside agency, seemed to bind them together. Yet he felt himself up against a mysteriousness, an aggressive presenting of her self, made stranger by the fact that they had not spoken much together in the house and had sat at the tea-table like any fellow-guests.

'You're not eating much, Gordon,' said Mrs Lacey, in the casual manner of close observation.

'I had a big dinner.'

'He's all right, Barbara,' said Mr Oliver. 'He doesn't have to stuff himself.'

'I know you, just making sure there'll be more for yourself, Ray Oliver,' said Mrs Lacey brightly. 'Whatever happened to that diet?'

'This,' said Mr Oliver, caressing his belly upwards, almost lasciviously, 'this is all solid muscle.'

'Go on!'

'He's ever so light on his feet, though, for a big man,' said Mrs Oliver. 'When he gets up for work in the morning he never wakes me.'

'I do like a drop of beer, though, that's my trouble,' said Mr Oliver. 'Can't resist it.'

Mrs Lacey wore a stillborn smile, like someone listening to a joke that turns out not to be funny.

'Sorry, Gordon, that was a silly thing to say,' said Mr Oliver.

Gordon looked relaxed. 'Actually, whisky's my tipple,' he said, and rolled his eyes and gave a mock maniac's laugh. 'By the pint.'

'Gordon, I'm sure we don't want to talk about it,' said Mrs Lacey.

'Well, perhaps it makes it better to talk about it, eh, Gordon?' said Mr Oliver, with an earnest reasonableness.

Gordon shrugged. 'I don't think anything makes it better,' he said.

'Least of all feeling sorry for yourself,' said Mrs Lacey, shortly, for her.

'That's the way men are, feel sorry for themselves,' said Mrs Oliver, who was looking with concentration at the last of the tiny fluffy cakes that lay on a silver tray in the middle of the table. 'You ought to hear the fuss Ray makes if he so much as cuts his finger.'

Ruth had rested her leg against David's again, and a kind of inappropriateness added to the sudden rush of excitement he felt.

'David, are you interested in motor-cars?' said Mrs Lacey, and he could not tell if there was a humorous self-consciousness in the dated phrase. 'Gordon turned up in the most exotic thing. It's got some continental name I can't pronounce. Perhaps he could show you.'

'Mother,' said Gordon slowly, 'please do not treat me like a kid.'

'Eh, mind your manners, lad!' said Mrs Lacey in an accurate Northern accent, and laughed in David's direction. He laughed, and for the first time in looking at Mrs Lacey was reminded of Ruth.

'I'm not old-fashioned, but manners aren't what they were,' said Mrs Oliver. 'The way some of the kids talk to you nowadays. I mean not the teenagers, I suppose you expect that, but little kids.' She leaned over and picked up the last cake and took the tiniest of bites out of it, as if leaving herself the option of putting it back again. 'Little kids of nine or ten.'

'Kids are still kids,' said Gordon. He looked sour. 'They're no different from what they used to be. It's parents that make kids what they are.'

Mrs Lacey was calmly alert. 'I hope you're not suggesting what I think you're suggesting.'

'What, that you made me an alky? No, mum, much as you'd like to take the credit.'

'It is a medical thing, though, isn't it?' said David quickly, catching on, and realising that he was putting on a Helpful Interested face. 'I mean, treatable, like any illness . . .'

'Pathological, I think is the word,' said Gordon, smiling a yellow smile.

'You didn't have to go trying to be all helpful and diplomatic this afternoon, you know,' said Ruth, as he stroked her face, which was smooth and hot, while a pigeon warbled, invisible, in the trees. 'Just let them fight it out, that's the thing to do.'

'Why?' he said. He was pleased, as at a challenge successfully met, with the normal inflection of his voice, with the ordered logicalities of their conversation, for their hands were suddenly everywhere, moving restlessly over buttock and crotch and breast.

The tea was insubstantial – thin gammon and oily salad and slices of wafery bread-and-butter and a pale currant loaf and those airy cakes – in a way that left you decorously unsatisfied. It was in contrast to the house, which was full of unnecessary bulk. Mirrors hung on chains, huge and heavy, seemingly about to pull the plaster away from the wall. Chair-legs poked out into the middle of the rooms, like jokers trying to trip you up. Big clocks in wooden cases made guttural tickings, half an hour slow. David always found the interiors of houses interesting: the sheer fact of other people's private lives. But part of the interest was the shock of recognition. This house was different: he could not connect this house with Ruth, could not imagine her growing up in it.

'Don't start using those long words, Gordon,' said Mr Oliver, with joviality. 'Spare a thought for us peasants.'

The park seemed vastly, primevally empty. Their bodies filled it. Enough to explore for a lifetime. Her tongue, booming, clicking, amplified, outlined his ear. 'How long have you lived in that house?' he said.

'All my life,' she said. 'Why?'

'I was just trying to imagine it,' he said. 'You as a little girl in that big dark place.'

'You and your nostalgia.' Her breath was warm and noisy, enveloping him.

'That's not nostalgia.'

'You and your past then. Always poking into the past.'

'So you think you know me that well, do you?'

'Yes.'

Later they moved to the lounge. It must have been dim even in full daylight with its mullioned windows and heavy curtains: Mrs Lacey got up to switch on the wall-lights. 'Anyone for more tea?' she said. She wore a shortish skirt and her calves had the same kind of rosy, distended youthfulness as her face.

'Barbara, why don't we have a drop of that wine I brought you?' said Mr Oliver. 'Celebrate a bit.'

'I don't think that would be a good idea,' said his wife.

'Oh, come on. Surely that won't hurt you, Gordon? No need to be melodramatic about it, I'm sure you'd agree.'

'You have some if you want, but I really don't want any,' said Gordon. David was rather glad to see there was no mad dipso's glint in Gordon's eye: he just looked weary and cross.

'I'm sure you'd get on better – '

'Just drop it, will you!' Gordon was pale, angry, and David saw for the first time that he looked ill.

'I'll go and make some more tea,' said Ruth.

'Gordon, really,' said Mrs Lacey. 'All this silliness.' She made the word sibilant and withering.

Behind the tennis pavilion an embankment sloped up to a screen of lilac bushes. The ground was dry and hard as she pulled him down. Her face and hands looked luminous in the deepening dusk. All the tension of the afternoon, that had shown in her as a flatness, even a boredom, in himself as a coiled attentiveness, a constant jaw-aching smile, seemed not to break but to twist to a finer and finer tune as they embraced, almost clawing, almost grappling with each other like fighters. 'God, I thought once I was going to grab you right there and then in front of everybody,' she said.

'Silliness,' said Gordon, and his eyes were mutinous, roving around the overfurnished room before settling on Mrs Lacey perched rounded and apparently self-effacing on the edge of her chair. 'That's it, mum, turn it into silliness. Pretend there's nothing *really* wrong.'

'We've got guests, Gordon,' said Mrs Lacey in a voice that carried though it was low.

'Well, so what? Let's put on the family circus for them. I thought that's what you liked. Anyway this pair have seen it all before, haven't you? And David doesn't mind, do you, David? See what he's letting himself in for.'

Ruth had come back into the room, and her expression remained strangely neutral.

'I'm quite sure David doesn't want to hear you shouting about it, at any rate,' said Mrs Lacey, and David was disconcerted to find both her and Gordon looking at him with a kind of appeal and yet also with a kind of accusation, as if it were all his fault.

The air struck suprisingly warm on his exposed flesh. It flashed on his mind that he had not been to this park since he was a child when his mother used to bring him and Marian to look at the aviary on Sundays. His brain seemed to race, hurtling, detached, yet compelled by the same alarming momentum that filled his body, like a clockwork toy that has been wound up till the spring is on the point of snapping. There were bits of grass in his hair, in her hair, on his fingers, on her belly, clothes, impatiently pushed, fetched up in tangles around neck and knees, diminishing zones of rationality. At the last moment his voice said, sounding hollow and absurd, 'I haven't got anything.' 'It's all right,' she said.

The Olivers left, it seemed to David, when there was nothing more to consume. Mr Oliver gave him a plump handshake. Shortly before, Gordon had gone out in a half-hearted sort of huff, first to the kitchen, where Mrs Lacey followed him and there was a muttered row culminating in an audible 'Go to hell' from her, said in a flat way like 'Go and put the kettle on', and then upstairs. He did not re-emerge. But Mrs Lacey's serenity did. And so did the peculiar confidentiality, the special treatment: 'Now then David,' she smiled on returning – as if to say that all these unimportant people had gone at last.

He felt himself made part of an inner circle, perhaps even a circle of just him and Mrs Lacey. She told him stories of Ruth's and Gordon's childhood, of Ruth at college – 'She did nothing but cry for the whole of the first week – not so unusual, maybe; but the thing was she couldn't bring herself to *tell* me she'd done nothing but cry the first week until the very day she qualified' – of Ruth going through a 'hippy phase' – 'Once she had a joss-stick burning in her room and in my ignorance I thought "that's it – drugs – she's finished". But I suppose you went through the same thing.'

'Well, I did try to grow one of those Zapata moustaches at the time. But my mother said I looked like Groucho Marx,' he said, and Mrs Lacey laughed, satisfyingly, and Ruth watched him, amused in some different way.

He was charmed again, and something else that he could only call unconvinced. It was not simply the feeling that this beguiling inclusion was extended to everybody – that was quite plain. It was as if this profusion of anecdote and confidence and instant familiarity, this admission to view the interior scenes of a crowded life, a life that precluded him, was curling round and swaddling him in ease, only to clamp him like a trap, and pose the question: 'So where do you imagine you fit in with all this?'

The pigeon had continued to coo, unseen and for a while unheard, in the twilight. Ruth still had one shoe on and the heel dug into the clenched muscle on his calf.

Small stones were digging into his elbow: he slowly became aware of discomfort as of some impossibly distant and arcane memory. It had not been over as quickly as he had feared when he entered her, excited to a frightening degree.

The human body was noisy, a great Victorian factory of a thing: in the quiet of the park their hearts were huge shuddering hammers, their breath giant bellows, rasping.

Mrs Lacey took off her shoes and put her feet up on the chair, a thing he somehow could not imagine Ruth doing. 'She used to paint a lot,' she said, 'but now she hardly ever does. She says teaching art puts you off, which I can't see at all. That one on the wall behind you is Ruth's.'

He turned to look at a still life of glass bottles and a basket, startlingly good. He felt jealous, and then for a moment proud, a feeling that was dispelled almost guiltily – for in what relation did he stand to Ruth that he was entitled to feel 'proud' of her?

Her face was almost completely in shadow as she shifted to lie on top of him and her lips brushed his face. He had never felt, in his small experience of this, the traditional sadness, and he did not now. 'You must ask me to tea again,' he said. Facetiousness was wrong, and he acknowledged it by holding her tighter.

CHAPTER 11

You'd never believe it's like this. The way it seems to cause as much worry and pain as pleasure. And yet you don't care about that. Complete absorption. Like playing an exceptionally compulsive game. But all worthwhile. Being in love, that is. David Barber, close on thirty-six, undergoing adolescence. All I need is a few spots.

Only now did he begin to feel really free, as he had not done at the death of his mother. Then there had been amputation, he had continued to feel pain in absence, effectively imprisoning him more than any putative dependence could do, and his gestures of freedom were strained, mere flourishes that emphasised all the more his frightened, floating sense of detachment. Now his life had clattered out of its grooves and spun off: he began to enjoy impulse. He found himself spending a lot of money. He would dash into town and buy a shirt or a bottle of wine. He could not pass a junk shop without going in and poking around and emerging with a parcel of books, or a print, or something battered in brass which his mother would not have given house-room. ('Ugh, it's so old-fashioned.') It became a point of honour with him to spend all his wages before the next pay-day. He became impatient, though not in a bad-tempered way: he would cook his dinner early and wolf it, messily, because he was starving. ('Only little children in India are entitled to say they're starving.' His mother.) He began to find he rather liked being on his own – because he was not on his own.

The euphoria belonged to the times when he was on his

own, rather than when he was with Ruth. Being with her was an absorption in itself, a roller-coaster ride with no time for reflection.

Routines went out of the window by virtue of the simple fact that he suddenly became aware of them. Baths he took at odd hours, scrambling himself dry and zooming out of the house with his hair sticking up. He did the week's shopping in a hurtling fifteen minutes before the supermarket closed, sweeping tins with a crash into his trolley and steering it like a dodgem: he ended up paying by cheque because he never had enough cash with him, and people in the queue blew out extravagant sighs and shuffled their feet, as he used to.

The warm weather began midway through April, accompanied as usual by a foul pervasive smell that settled over the city centre: the river that wound its way within a hundred yards of the cathedral was low, exposing sludgy banks, and choked with silt from the fens. But after a few showers the stink was gone, the weather stayed fair, and the town in its lopsided, brash way began to look handsome in the sunlight. The sleek new office blocks of impenetrable black glass and the stone cathedral gateways seemed to look across at each other mildly, as if in a truce. At Barlow Watkins the secretaries shed stockings to expose winter-white legs. Along the pounding carriageways and parkways the baby trees made an attempt at foliage, and the view from the flyovers was bounded by a rim of bright yellow where fields of rape encircled the town. Mr Carelli next door seemed to live in his garden permanently, like an animated plaster gnome.

Most large towns David had ever been to were built at least partly on hills, so that you could see streets climbing off in steps and terraces to the distance. Here the land was so entirely flat that each row of houses you came to might have marked the edge of the town for all you could see: even the cathedral was built on a horizontal principle, not soaring and domineering but seeming to lie low and expansive with the land.

But the sky came into its own. Clouds were huge, stately, and entirely visible. In the evening you drove along the parkway and beyond the efficient fluorescent streaks and blobs of the arching lights the clouds made a progress, piled and crenellated, rising on indigo keels that seemed to be moored to the fields beyond. Marmoreal or sooty or raw Disney pink, they converged ponderous as medieval jousters: slowly they parted to reveal glowing canyons of vapour, like the skies in the Bible picture-books he remembered at infants school – God came sprouting out of one of them with a square beard and his hands akimbo in a karate-chop and that was still how David pictured him – the same skies he saw from the bottom of the garden across the allotments when he was small and the keen, savoury moment came when he finally had to go back into the house and eat his tea and the day seemed to roll with a grand sort of dissolution over the horizon and the world to recede to the known limits of the kitchen where his mother was frying something and the living-room where Marian was shunting Dinky cars across the circle of blue-lit carpet in front of the television.

'The summers *were* hotter and sunnier then,' Ruth said. 'And they lasted about a year as well. It's true.'

'It's true,' he said. 'We've been robbed.'

'We have. All this stuff about the way you remember things as a child being all distorted. Crap. We're being defrauded. It's a conspiracy.'

They were on a bus – they were going out to get drunk so neither was driving – and they made pinching grabs at each other's knees, embarrassing the other passengers, and giggling – sniggering – all the unpleasant words for laughing. It was a conspiracy: it was them against the world, delightfully. They were like two people who have discovered they both went to the same place for a holiday, and excitedly compare notes – 'Did you go to – ?' 'What about that awful place near . . .?' They were discovering that the past, that most intimate and fundamental element of the personality – the past, that can only really exist for the individual, or else be relegated to the never-never world of persuasive sepia photographs and cottage museums giving frozen testimony to the fact that other people existed, and were uncomfortable – could be shared, and need not be divisive.

He felt, in the heightened, hurried manner that characterised his life now, proud and fond of the town. It was large and diverse and yet he felt it as peculiarly belonging to him – to him and Ruth. In the regular ten-minute halt in the thick traffic at the water bridge on the way home from work he would look out at it and his mind would explore further: across the narrow rows of terraced houses, mined by a network of windy underpasses with their frescoes of graffiti, the tiny corner pubs where old men were silent over folded newspapers beneath framed photographs of alsatians; to the office blocks and banks where schoolboys wore their first suit and pawed cheques with red unpractised hands too big for their wrists; to the railway station where French teenagers slightly smaller than their rucksacks arrived alongside big-eared soldiers and commuters; to the old council estates where the wind bowled fish-and-chip papers down the back alleys of moribund shopping parades and stray dogs nosed among the pallets of squashed cardboard boxes and overweight women struggled to descend from the steps of shuddering buses. He was generous and expansive, embracing these visions, and skittishly in love; he liked the town, and even began to like himself, as a harmless, transparent sort of fellow, where before, contemplating some mistake or omission of his own that had landed him in trouble, he would look at that blundering, idiot former self with angry contempt. Bung-full of emotions, he sprayed them everywhere, like a baby that has learnt its first word and applies it to every object. At night he slept as if poleaxed, in the morning he was dredged numbly into waking from impossible depths of sleep.

He could not have expressed, except in words that even to himself would have seemed foolish, what they did most of the time as the days grew longer and warmer and softer: how they sat in cinemas laughing at crude American comedies that formerly he would have disliked, and on the way home laughed again as they did poor impressions of the characters; how they drank cheap bottles of cider in his kitchen while he cooked the easy one-pan meals that to his surprise she liked – she was too impatient for any sort of cooking and would constantly dip a spoon into the pan to taste it; how they wandered around the city centre – she dragged him into shops he would never have thought of entering, and she did not mind as he always had about picking up and inspecting articles that it was obvious they had no intention of buying – and took photographs of each other, posed by the river, in the cathedral cloisters, anywhere.

The sight of her in his house filled him with pleasure. 'What are you staring at?' she would say, as he looked at her sitting in front of the television, with that total, unconcerned relaxation that always gave him a feeling almost of envy: 'You,' he would say, and she would smile; but more exactly he was looking at her against the background of his room, his world, that had never seemed capable of containing anything like her.

Though she still ribbed him about his propensity for nostalgia – 'Old "Those were the days" Barber' – he found a pleasure in marshalling it anecdotally for the right effects, though they often missed the mark. And in the same way that he began to find it possible to like himself, the past began to lose its dramatic significance, to lose that quality it shared with its physical effects – keepsakes and photographs and letters – of the brooding and private and obsessive, of the locked drawer and 'These Foolish Things' and Miss Havisham in her wedding dress. He had not been so much a prisoner of it as a voluntary recluse, retiring for a sterile sort of comfort to its airless chambers. It became public, accessible, its power sapped; entertaining, indeed, like a well-told story.

In the leafy environs of Park Crescent spring had made its appearance in the most pastoral and traditional forms. 'So much money round here they have the seasons specially laid on,' said Ruth, sourly. She was very scornful of this world. Once, when an old lady neighbour talked to them at her front gate for several minutes, and David said afterwards, 'She seems like a nice old girl,' she almost turned on him. 'Oh,

David, she's not, she's an awful old snob, and she was just being nosey, measuring you up.'

On Sundays he would walk over to the house and in the fine weather they would sit out on the large, ill-kept lawn and sometimes he would stay for tea when Mrs Lacey came back from her bridge, though often Ruth would discourage him. 'It seems a bit rude to clear off before she gets back,' he said.

'She's got nothing to do with you, she just happens to be my mother,' she said.

Gordon was still there and often David found him sitting outside on a canvas chair, very still and looking rather perplexed, as if someone had told him to go and sit there without giving any reason, and he was just beginning to expect a practical joke. He always seemed glad to see David, who felt again a puzzling sense of being liked.

'What do you find to do all day?' David asked him, not so much solicitously as out of real curiosity.

'Bugger-all,' he said. 'I ought to go back to London. I'm all right now. As all right as I'll ever be.'

'Why don't you?'

Gordon looked wry, and also helpless. The gold rings on his fingers looked too big for him. 'I don't know. It's so easy to slip back, somehow, once you're here. The Enchanted Ground.' He frowned down at his cup of tea, as if unsure what it was. '*Pilgrim's Progress*. Sunday School.' He took a tentative sip. 'Funny how these things stay with you.'

The last Sunday in May was Ruth's birthday, and he walked over early with her present in his pocket, an expensively slim wrist-watch. The sunshine had suddenly become not only bright but very warm; even in his shirt-sleeves he was sweating. The trees that screened the house were shiny, sticky green as if they had just been painted. He noticed Gordon's car was not in the drive and Ruth pulled open the door before he could knock.

After the glare outside the big hall was cool as a cellar and full of a greenish blinding darkness. He found himself almost shivering and the stabbing, searching kisses with which she covered his mouth and face were exactly like the rays of sun that had been beating down on him: sharp and intensely pleasurable.

'Happy birthday,' he said.

'Gordon's out,' she said, and her voice was dry with a breathless kind of strain. 'We've got the place to ourselves.'

He had never been upstairs in the house before. On the landing a stained-glass window directed lozenges of bilious colour on to the thin, threadbare carpet. There was a musty smell. 'When will they be back?' he said, and she shook her head. 'Not yet.'

The windows were open in her bedroom. Through the bellying curtains a garden-scented breeze brought with it the droning of an electric lawn-mower pitched shriller by distance. All the time the sound seemed to get caught up in his head as if in a kind of web till he too felt suspended, taut in a magnified wakefulness and a desire that was tangy as unease, until they subsided amongst sheets that were tangled like ropes and the droning slackened, faded off into the patchwork of sound that made up reality with his thundering heart and her breaths drawn in long and painful beside him. A shaft of sun, full of imprisoned motes, swirling, parted the curtains and bisected the bed, and he saw for the first time the couple of drawings pinned to the wall, the board with a few postcards and photographs, a squat bottle with flowers in it: all oddly cursory and temporary, a sketch of a room.

After a while he said, 'Your birthday present' and scrambled to get up. His feet were caught in the contorted sheets, and she laughed as he nearly fell swearing on to the floor. Being laughed at was something he had almost, but not quite, got used to. 'I laugh at people I love,' she had told him. 'You mustn't take it the wrong way.'

She laughed too as he covered himself up before bringing the little parcel back to the bed. 'You hardly need to do that,' she said. 'Not after what we've just done.'

'Well – you don't look at your best in daylight,' he said.

'Don't I? Nice compliment.'

'Not you. I mean I don't. *We* don't. *One* doesn't.'

The bed scranched again at his weight: it was an old

wooden one and not very large. She lay back on the pillow looking flushed and comfortable, like an invalid making a rapid recovery. 'You look all right,' she said.

'You look all right. You thirty-three-year-old crock.'

The watch, as he had thought it would, looked good against her white skin. The sun was still pouring warmth into the room and in a hot, almost tipsy way he kissed her wrist below the gold strap. But when she began lazily to caress him again he thought of the watch and the time and she sensed his nervousness. 'It's all right,' she said, 'nobody'll be back for a while.'

'How long's a while?'

She smiled. 'As long as I want it to be.' Outside the lawn-mower had been switched off, exposing the chirruping of birds and a far-off buzz of traffic. 'Don't be so nervy. You're not afraid of mum, are you?'

He was, in a way, and wondered if she sensed it. It was something too about being in this house.

'After all, I've stayed over at yours several times. She's not a complete innocent.'

'That's different.'

'How is it different? Look, how old am I? Thirty-three. We don't have to carry on like frightened teenagers, do we?' Her voice was low and coaxing. 'I've told you, she's nothing to do with us. Relations are just a sort of natural disaster you have to cope with.'

'You haven't met any of my lot yet, have you?'

'No.'

'I don't think I want you to. I want to keep you all to myself.' He stroked her hair, then stiffened. 'What was that?'

'What? I don't know. The old place creaks like anything. It's on the point of falling down. Do you want me to go down and look?' She stirred and then sank back again. 'Oh, I don't want to go down. It's nice here. That sun's nice. I hope we have a really long hot summer, don't you? Something for you to get nostalgic about. Here, relax. You're like a cat on hot bricks because we're up here, aren't you?'

He reached across her for a cigarette, trying to show no

expression. It was strange, as he had noticed once or twice before, that words could sting you like this while you lay in a naked embrace with someone.

'It's this house, I know. You see, it's that hidden prig in you – now, it was you who once said it, I remember – the old solid Protestant thing coming up. Somehow not decent. Well it's my birthday so you have to put up with it. And it's not so bad, is it? Anyway, Gordon won't be back yet for sure. It was me who put him up to going out for the day. Come on, sweetheart, cheer up and give me a drag of that cigarette.' She slid on top of him, smiling, her face filling his view, backlit with a dusty aura from the sunlight that still flowed in a molten column into the room; and he felt again awed, overwhelmed, his life writ large and dramatic in a way that almost intimidated him, as if he had only a small reserve of self with which to meet it.

At last, hot and curiously drained, like a child that has stayed up late on a special occasion, he got ready to go. She did not come down with him but lay still on the bed watching him, and just before he left knelt up on the bed, her small breasts and slender belly pale in the adulterated light, and kissed him and thanked him for the watch. 'You're supposed to get a watch on your twenty-first,' she said.

'So what,' he said. 'That's about how old you look.'

'Oh! dear,' she laughed, 'well, I handed you that one.'

He continued to think of her amused face as he last saw it, watching him with dark eyes from the tumbled bed, as he walked across the park. There were many people there today: defiantly amateur tennis players crowded the courts, children pulverised the grass, old couples sat unspeaking on benches in puddles of viridian shade. He was so abstracted that even when Mrs Lacey stopped in front of him, smiling, he looked at her for a moment as if he did not know who she was.

'You've seen Ruth?' she said. Lack of preamble was common with her: it established you, charmingly again, as a person too sensible for all that nonsense. 'And no doubt you took her a birthday present. I thought so. Just to make me feel guilty. Because I haven't got her anything yet. I couldn't think of a single thing. How are you, David? You look well.'

'So do you.' She was wearing a summer dress, which made her look young, with an old cardigan thrown over it, which made her look younger.

'Well, I shouldn't. This afternoon's put years on me. My bridge partner was seventy-five years old – ' she said these last words with an amusing mock-senile quaver – 'and also, I think, mentally subnormal. Well, young man, for all your flattery, I notice you left before I got home. This is something we elderly folk have to get used to.'

'Really – I've got to get back . . .' The sun was behind her, so he had to squint at her: it was almost as if she had arranged it so as to place him at a disadvantage.

She made a gesture that vestigially expressed putting a hand on his arm. 'Don't be silly, love. Just you make sure you stay to tea another time. What did you get for Ruth, if you don't mind me being nosy?'

'A wrist-watch.'

Mrs Lacey sighed and nodded. 'I thought about that, briefly,' she said. She did not say anything more. The sun struck at him, strewing blobs in front of his eyes.

'Well, I'd better be going. I shall play patience this evening, and only have myself to blame when I lose. See you soon, David. Take care.'

The scenery for the Musical Society's production of *Carousel* was finished. There was really no need for David to attend the rehearsals any more, but the director encouraged him to keep coming, in case of last-minute repairs, and to help with the setting up. He did not seem to notice that David turned up mainly on account of Ruth. Roberta, though, leading them all out to the pub after a rehearsal one evening, said, 'Come on, we're all going: actors, technicians – and camp-followers,' and though there was a laugh at this against the man who played Jigger Craigin, who camped it up and liked to pretend he was homosexual, David suspected the remark was meant for him.

Ruth had an enviably deep and rich singing voice. Singing had always been completely beyond him: whenever he had opened his mouth to attempt hymns in church the note seemed at least an octave out of his range. The fact that he was left in the wings, an onlooker, seemed to be the main object of Roberta's malice. Several times she mentioned Bill to him – how well he sang, how popular he was – and so, by inference, what a pale second-string replacement David was.

He knew Roberta did not like him. It was not that she ignored him or even was openly hostile to him. Rather, when she saw him approaching she would say, 'Here comes David,' in a way that was perfectly friendly and perfectly horrible. That he did not like her, found her irritating, thought her silly and pretentious, was not entirely relevant: to realise that you are heartily disliked by someone, even someone you yourself hold in contempt, is always a nasty shock.

'Ignore her,' said Ruth, who seemed to find this easy. 'Anyway, she fancied Bill too, we had a sort of friendly rivalry about it.' He did not find this at all reassuring.

He was surprised to learn that Roberta was a secretary at a firm of solicitors and was having an affair with her boss, a married man. How much was apocryphal he did not know: it was a well-publicised secret, and he suspected her of being behind some of the publicity. The ups and downs of this affair were recorded in her moods at each rehearsal. They reached their apparent nadir when she arrived one evening pale and stiff and dry-eyed, spoke to no one, and burst into tears half-way through her big song.

Ruth was closeted with her for half-an-hour in the dressing-room. When she finally emerged she drew David aside and put her fingers on his chin. 'I'm sorry, David, I can't come to yours afterwards. I've got to go and dispense Kleenex and listen to the Whole Story.' That she spoke so lightly showed she expected his reaction. 'I'm sorry, love.'

'What's happened, then?' he said. He caught himself trying to sound reasonable. Prig. 'It can't be so bad, can it? She just likes to be melodramatic.'

'So do we all sometimes. Look, I know it's a pain, but I'm

an old friend, for better or worse, and – you just have to do these things. She'd do the same for me.' She touched his arm, a little tensely.

'She'll never have to,' he said, hearing a little quaver in his voice, as with a rush he felt the need to re-establish a warmth that seemed suddenly to have dropped between them.

She smiled briefly and kissed his brow. 'Good lad,' she said. 'Ring me tomorrow'; and his love seemed to bubble within him, stronger than ever but cramped and frenetic, contending with an intenser dislike of Roberta.

He went home and cooked the dinner they should have had and called down Nicholas to share it. Standing at the stove mechanically slopping the chilli round the pan he was struck with an unpleasant realisation that he was in danger of becoming what he had always set himself against with an almost ideological rigour. Loving couples, with their intolerable egotistic selfishness, their rejection of everything beyond their smug, gazing-into-each-other's-eyes circle of two, their righteous worshipping of their own emotions; the couple, who mystify and annoy everyone with their private jokes, who are always the first to leave the party so they can hurry off and gaze at each other some more, who confound with the arrogance of their giant jealousies and insecurities. Oh, no, he wasn't that bad, but still . . . He thought of what Ruth had said about Roberta: 'I know you don't like her, and I can see why it is – but you must understand – I mean you have some friends, say, that you get on with but you wouldn't ever let them mix with certain other friends. You know what I mean.' He was both hampered and fortunate in having few friends. Ron, solid and reliable, old drinking partner: since Ruth he had hardly seen him, hardly given him a thought, but then they had never needed to be demonstrative, could go long periods without seeing each other and nothing would change. People at work . . . they hardly counted. Nicholas . . . well, living in the same house meant he was in a different position.

Family had always been more important; or they bulked larger in his life. Marian had rung him one evening last week when Ruth was there, asking if it was all right to come round.

'We haven't seen you for ages.' He had felt a momentary guilt, then put her off. 'You didn't have to do that,' Ruth had said. He tried to explain, in a nice way, that he didn't want to see Marian; and had to admit to himself that it didn't come out very nice. He felt quaintly ashamed, as Ruth, with that divination that he often enjoyed and occasionally found disturbing, had perceived. 'There are more people in the world than just you and me,' she had said, gently. He was abashed – sufficiently so to prevent him voicing a comparison with her attitude to her mother.

And as it happened, disappointment at her not being there turned into a sort of enjoyment. 'Nothing wrong I hope?' Nicholas said a little warily when he came down. 'I'm not about to hear the gruesome details of the end of the affair?'

'No, no, she can't make it, that's all.' Nicholas got on well with Ruth, but whenever she was there David discerned in his lodger a kind of watchfulness over the two of them: one felt he missed nothing, rather as his mother had missed nothing.

They drank the bottle of wine and Nicholas wolfed the chilli. 'Not hot enough,' he said.

'You going out tonight?' David asked. Nicholas had been out a lot lately, and though he remained rather quiet, David sensed that he was no longer in his Mood.

'Yep.'

David studied the half-smile on the young man's lean face. 'I'm not to know any more, then?'

Nicholas waggled his empty glass at him. 'Let's just say you're not the only one with a hectic love life,' he said.

'I'm glad,' said David, filling his glass. 'No, really. Who's this then? Is it Bez?'

Nicholas folded his arms over an imaginary bosom and pursed his lips. 'Ask no questions and you'll be told no lies,' he said, and belched. 'Better out than in. As the actress et cetera. Anyway I haven't gone as gooey as you.'

'Gooey? Me? What do you mean?'

'Puppy-dog eyes. Singing in the bath – *I've* heard you. The way you stand there with your hands in the washing-up bowl staring into space.' He trilled in falsetto: '"Ah, sweet mystery of life, at last I've found you." A bad case.'

'Sarcy sod.' David hiccoughed painfully. The wine had gone to his head. He stretched out his legs, feeling pleasantly bloated. 'Funnily enough, I think this is the first time I've really relaxed for weeks.'

'Does you good to get away from each other for a little while,' said Nicholas. 'I should know. And now, as you are plainly too pissed to ask me to help you with the washing-up, I shall go up and make myself even more unbelievably handsome and be off. Oh, did I tell you I'm going for another job? Oh, not a paid one, don't expect miracles. Voluntary again, at the Citizens' Advice Bureau.'

'You? I know what your advice would be to people. Go and get drunk and have a good screw and then you'll feel better.' He stopped suddenly, afraid he had offended: it was too easy to treat Nicholas like a comic turn. But Nicholas laughed. 'Well, you're a one to talk, you senile debauchee. But they're always glad of volunteers. And the thing is it's more useful experience for proper jobs, as you're supposed to call them.'

'True. I shall probably be joining you soon. When I turn up at work and find a computer sitting in my chair.'

'That won't really happen, will it?'

'No, I don't think so. They made several redundant two years ago when they reorganised the office. They can't really get rid of any more. In fact I might be up for promotion soon. Musson's retiring.'

'Blimey, everything's coming up roses,' said Nicholas.

David thought he detected a touch of asperity in his tone. 'Well, I don't think I'll get it. Jack Erskine's been there longer than me.' He sat up suddenly, as if galvanised by the question he suddenly and desperately wanted to ask. 'Nicholas, this isn't the wine talking – do you think I should ask Ruth to marry me?'

Nicholas looked uncomfortable, even embarrassed, and ran his fingers through his bright yellow hair.

'Is it a bit soon, do you think?'

'Maybe. Couldn't you ask her to come and live with you?'

'Hmm. I hadn't thought of that.' He had thought of it, but the idea, for some reason, seemed perplexingly hedged round with the thought of Bill and of Mrs Lacey, so that he approached it on mental tiptoe.

'I would have thought you're all right as you are.'

'I'm not getting any younger,' said David, and laughed. 'Well, funnily enough, I feel as if I am.'

'There you are then.' Nicholas grinned. 'Wait till you're twenty-one, and then ask her.'

At work he was alarmed, whilst asking Mr Musson's secretary to do some photocopying for him, to find that he was touching her arm: he realised that he was thinking of Ruth. She didn't seem to notice, but he was disturbed again by the implication of such unthinking preoccupation. He had a vision of himself as that boring Lover, irresponsibly lost in his private cotton-wool abstraction. Self-reproach moved him to make an effort to talk to Jack Erskine, perhaps rather obviously. For weeks they had exchanged only commonplaces; David had felt it not worth the bother, a wasteful use of the vocal cords. The humming on the office grapevine that Erskine and his wife were going to be divorced had even made David avoid him more.

He felt a surge of pity, dangerously close to condescension, at the childish readiness with which Erskine responded, and at the signs which he noticed for the first time – his crumpled suit, his pallor, and most absurdly his ears which seemed pathetically raw and big and red as if perpetually pricked for gossip about himself.

'You all right, Jack?' He knew he might unleash a flood, but he was vain with magnanimity. 'I'm not being nosy, but you don't seem yourself lately.'

'No, I'm all right, mate. Usual bloody trouble, that's all.' He looked up, half-suspiciously, half with appeal. 'I imagine you've heard some tattle about it.'

'Well, you know. You don't know how much to believe.' He felt himself playing a part.

Erskine nodded. His phone rang and he ignored it. 'She's

got me well and truly fucked this time,' he said with great violence. 'Well and truly fucked. I never expected this. She's getting a divorce, isn't she?'

'That's what I'd heard.'

'Thinks I won't be able to do without her. Well she's fucking wrong there.' He tapped his pen against strong yellow teeth, looking at David. 'Don't suppose you fancy going down the club at dinner-time?'

There was no getting out of it now. In David's car Erskine shifted and wriggled in the passenger seat, occasionally throwing him glances of the same vague mistrust. He was a plumpish man, not especially big, but he always seemed to take up a disproportionate amount of space. There was a strong smell of after-shave, and David wondered if he put it on his beard.

'You're a funny bugger, Barber,' he said, irritably twitching his shoulder against the seat-belt. 'One minute you're going round with your nose in the air, the next minute you've suddenly decided to speak to me like I was human.'

'Is that how I've been? I'm sorry, I didn't mean . . . I've had a lot on my mind.'

'You're not the only one,' Erskine grunted. And then, with a renewal of hostility, 'Like what, for instance?'

'Well, I've had a bit of luck, Jack.' To crow about it would be extremely tactless, but he could not entirely restrain his delight. 'I'm – well, I've really fallen for someone. I'm like a teenager again.'

'God help us.' Erskine stared out of the window. 'She's fallen for you several times by the sound of it. Nobody I know, I suppose?'

'Oh, no,' said David, and it came out a shade patronising. 'Just out of the blue really. Anyway, my head's been in the clouds about the whole thing. You know.'

Erskine made a dubious sound. 'Lucky old you.'

In the Barlow Watkins Sports and Social Erskine swallowed a pint and ordered another before David was half-finished. 'Now don't start telling me this is no bloody answer,' he said, indicating his glass. 'I don't care about that, it makes me feel better.'

'I'd be the last one to say that,' said David. 'It's the best answer I know.' I'm being just a bit too Understanding, he thought. He tried to drink his own beer quickly, so as not to appear disapproving.

The bar was nearly empty. A few retired members sucked their dentures as they shunted dominoes, wattled necks trembling. Taped pop music was blaring from speakers on the wall. 'Bloody row,' said Erskine, leaning forward. Close to, David could see his gingery hair was matted and unwashed: only in the pervasive smell of after-shave and the expensive tie did the traces of the rake remain. 'Look at these hands,' he said. 'I never used to shake like this. It's destroying me, this, I tell you. Destroying me.' Oddly enough, this sounded convincing as well as melodramatic. 'I don't deserve this. I'm no bloody saint, all right. But she's stabbing me in the back. I don't *want* a divorce.'

'You were always fighting,' said David.

'Not always. You don't want to believe all the rubbish you hear, mate.' The truculence faded into his voice and then out again. 'Things weren't perfect. But you don't expect them to be, do you?'

David shook his head.

'It's just a cop-out, that's what gets me. Taking the easy way out.' He put his glass down heavily. 'I've never been unfaithful to her. That's what gets me. All this jack-the-lad business – it's just fun. But I've never been unfaithful.' He stared at David as if challenging him to deny it. David said nothing. Whether it was true or not – he suspected, after all, that it perhaps was – it seemed irrelevant if she simply couldn't stand him any more. But it was out of the question to say that. 'She's not prepared to give it another go, then?'

'Fuck she is.'

A voice called his name, and David turned to see Louise waving from behind the bar. He waved back, and when he turned round again Erskine was looking closely at him, his mouth half-open. 'That's the one then, is it?'

'Eh? What, Louise, no, no.'

'Mm? Doesn't seem so long ago since I heard you were taking her out.'

'Oh, that was only once. It wasn't anything.'

'Well, you're certainly getting your share just lately, aren't you?'

'I've told you, it wasn't anything. She's engaged, for Christ's sake.'

'So. Stranger things have happened.' Erskine scowled into his glass. He seemed to be sinking again into a pessimistic sagacity about things in general that got on David's nerves. When without saying anything Erskine reached for David's glass and went to the bar to refill it he felt further irritated, for by buying him another drink Erskine was virtually sealing a bargain: in exchange David would have to keep listening. He allowed his mind, as a quick treat, to think of Ruth and look forward to seeing her tonight.

'I'll tell you one thing, though.' The pints of beer slopped as Erskine banged them down on the table. 'If she thinks I'll be lost without her bloody regal self she's got another think coming. I'll be all right, mate, you see. Start having a few good times at last.'

'Come on, Jack. You don't have to start all that defensive stuff. If that's how you feel, then you wouldn't be upset about the divorce.'

'You're a smug bugger sometimes. Think you're so clever. Who's this bint of yours, Sunday School teacher?'

David inwardly winced at this, and hoped nothing showed in his face. 'All right, I'm sorry. I'll stop being clever. Carry on, I'm listening.'

Erskine's frown deepened. The beer was making him look, if anything, healthier, or at least more like his old self. 'I'm not stupid, you know. Maybe I act it. Thing is, there's more to married life than you can realise, old son.'

'I dare say there is.' Fearing he had been pompous again he added hurriedly: 'Did you and Pauline never want children?'

Erskine sighed. 'We did, but we kept putting it off. I mean, the fucking money you get when you start at Watkins. And then, when things started getting bad . . . it just didn't seem . . .'

David was suddenly afraid that Erskine was going to cry, and almost leapt from his seat, muttering 'I fancy some crisps.' Once he got to the bar he glanced back; but Erskine was merely staring at the table in front of him, his glass held under his chin.

'Haven't seen much of you lately, David.' Louise was smiling at him. He felt grateful for the sight of her. There was a reassuring friendliness between them: something more positive than embarrassment had come from that disastrous evening. 'I didn't really mean to come today,' he said. 'Packet of plain crisps, please.'

She nodded towards Erskine. 'He's found a listener, then. He's been moping here all week.'

'He's got a few problems.'

'He won't make 'em any better here. What have you been up to, then, love?'

'Me? Oh, this and that.'

'Not the other, eh?' They laughed. 'All right, I won't be nosy.'

'Your Terry got any leave lately?' It was, he was pleased to find, a subject entirely without pain.

'He's coming back next month as it happens. Just before the works' centenary dance. Sounds as if it's going to be a good do. Shall you be going?'

'I might do, if there's some free beer.' He glanced over to Erskine. 'Well, I'd better get back to Happy Harry,' he said, and then felt a twinge of disloyalty. Oh, sod it, he didn't even really like the man.

Erskine did not look up when he came back. 'What were you two cooking up then?' he said into his beer.

'God, I was only speaking to the girl.' David picked up his glass and then put it down again. He didn't want to be here listening to maudlin problems being poured out; he wanted to be at home listening to the football on the radio whilst doing the whirlwind tidying-up that passed for his housework nowadays.

'Something about me, was it?'

'It was nothing about you. What makes you think everybody's talking about you? Who says they're even interested, for a start.'

Erskine flashed him an unfriendly look; but then he said, 'Yeah, maybe you're right. Who gives a fuck.' Abruptly he wriggled forward in his seat. 'You know, if I found out she'd been screwing around, I'd kill her. Literally, I mean that. Kill her.' He spoke very low, clenching his stubby fist, with a menace that was grotesque and yet still disturbing.

'Come on, I'm sure it's not that. Jack, why don't you go home now, eh? Maybe if you do that you could try and – '

'You're sure, are you? I'd like to know what you fucking know about it.' His voice was growling, slurred. 'Just because everything's rosy in your bloody garden. Not saying I begrudge you. But you're carrying on like some spotty teenager over it, you said so yourself. So how can you say – '

'All right, I'm not saying I do know anything about it. But you're telling me all this so I'm giving you my advice for what it's worth.'

'Your advice.' Erskine gave a strained barking laugh like a cough. 'You giving advice to somebody who's been married ten years. You make me laugh. You don't know bugger-all. Bloody mother's boy all your life, going home to mummy and putting your wage packet on the table and being given your tea. And now you're on your own you're acting like Lord Muck because you've had your first screw and you liked the feel of it and you think no bugger else has ever done it before.'

'OK. I've had enough.' David did not feel particularly angry, yet, but resigned, even relieved. He got up. 'Go home, Jack. It might do some good even now if you went home half-sober.'

'Here, wait, have another drink, Dave, come on,' Erskine said, almost piteously, as he went.

Half-way home he stopped the car and went across to a newsagent's and bought some peppermints, feeling suddenly apprehensive that he might be over the limit. What good the peppermints would do if he was breathalysed he did not know. But he needed a few minutes to cool himself: he felt woozy with a potent mixture of righteousness and a bitterer dash of a suspicion that he had not come out well. An equilibrium seemed to have been lost somewhere, and he wanted to get it back.

Mr Carelli next door was standing at his front garden gate when David drew up outside the house. There was nothing unusual in that: he always seemed to be there when he was not in his garden, his arms folded and a philosophical look on his face as he attentively watched the sparse traffic that plied this street. But when David got out of the car Mr Carelli beckoned him over.

'Your young friend,' he said gravely. 'We got him in the house.'

'Eh? Nicholas – my lodger?'

Mr Carelli nodded slowly, frowning, as if David had used an unnecessarily crude word. 'Lisa saw him going in. She was in the kitchen. The kitchen looks out on your back door.' David was aware of this. 'Something's happened. Come and see. She said to bring him in. Come and see.'

It was years since he had been inside the Carellis' house. Mr Carelli, like hundreds of other Italians in the town, had come over after the war to work in the brickyards. When David was small his mother had once smacked him for saying Mr Carelli talked funny in Mr Carelli's presence. The place was beautifully kept and curiously old-fashioned, with the sort of glossy tubular furniture that had flourished briefly in the 1950s: the figure of Nicholas sitting on the settee was doubly incongruous in it. He had obviously been beaten up. One eye was closed in a big crooked purple wink, and a corner of his mouth was cut and swollen, so that the general effect was of a horrible mockery of a cheeky grin. There was a smell of antiseptic: Mrs Carelli stood by him with a cotton swab in her hand rather like a proud artist.

'Lisa screamed when she saw him. I heard her, I came running,' said Mr Carelli. 'She's soft-hearted. He says he's been to the football match. I told him, I used to go, years ago. Then it was nice, but not now.' He frowned at Nicholas. 'This happens now. Best not to go.'

Nicholas's good eye watched David and then swivelled to Mrs Carelli. 'Thanks ever so much,' he said. 'You've been very kind.'

David took him back next door. Nicholas held his hand to his ribs as he walked and David held his other arm to steady him. There were spots of dried blood on his white T-shirt.

'You'd better have a drop of Scotch,' said David, fumbling in the sideboard. He felt like some himself.

'Thank God for that,' said Nicholas. 'The Carellis have been pouring tea into me.'

David sat down opposite him: he was shaking like a leaf, whilst Nicholas seemed quite calm. 'God, you're a mess,' he said. 'What on earth happened to you?'

'Like the man said.' He chanted gruffly: 'Un-i-ted.'

'You don't go to the football. Besides, the game'll only just have started.'

'Can't fool you, Maigret.' He swallowed his Scotch in one go and coughed.

'Were you in a pub in town or something? Was that it? A bunch of skinheads or whatever?'

'What are you, Agatha Christie's favourite nephew?' said Nicholas, holding out his empty glass. 'It doesn't matter now, does it?'

'You should have gone to casualty. You should have gone to the police. Your ribs, are they hurt as well?'

'Just a bit.' Nicholas pulled up his T-shirt to show a large dirty-yellow bruise on his side.

'Bloody hell.' David stood up, feeling sick, unable to keep still. He was out of cigarettes: he was always running out these days. 'You got any cigarettes?'

'In my jacket there. Chuck me one. Oh, don't stomp around. It wasn't what you think, it wouldn't have been any good going to the police. It was what you could call a private thing.'

'What? Not Bez?'

'Well, not exactly. Even a willowy welter-weight such as myself could have stood up better to him.'

'What then? I want to know.'

'Oh, you are all masterful today.' Nicholas' calm was deceptive: whenever he was really in a state he camped it up like this. 'All that happened was, I was at Bez's house, in his room, a clinch was in progress, more a smooch really, anyway nothing that hadn't happened before. All of a sudden one of the blokes he shares with barges in without knocking, horrible greasy motor-bike fiend, you know the sort. And Bez starts yelling and swearing. Making out I'd jumped him. Get this bloody queer off me sort of thing. The troglodyte was happy to oblige, and they both laid into me. Not the sort of lay I was expecting for this afternoon.'

'Oh, Christ, Nick, don't joke,' said David, sitting down again, feeling sicker than ever.

'Must admit it has its funny side,' said Nicholas, but he was beginning to sniff. 'This bloke started going on about letting me into the house – could catch AIDS, you know. Worst thing, Bez was standing there agreeing with him. Obviously he's never let on about himself. Have to feel sorry for him. Probably didn't dare, see.'

'Don't waste your pity on him,' said David. He was surprised to find that he was absolutely livid: it was as if this irruption into what had been the euphoria of his recent life were directed at him personally. He felt as if he had been beaten up himself, struck without warning by cowardly thumping blows. 'You're all right now? You're sure you don't want me to drive you down to casualty?'

Nicholas shook his head. 'Broken heart only,' he said, trying to control a wobble in his voice. David knew he hated appearing pathetic.

'Where does he live?' he said after a moment.

'What?'

'This Bez, what's his address?'

'Oh, no. You can forget it. I've had enough machismo for one day. Look, don't you bloody dare – '

David had sprung up. 'I know, you left me it one night in

case I needed to get in touch.' It was on the telephone pad; he snatched it up. As he left the house Nicholas's voice cried, 'Don't you *fucking* dare.'

The house was a shabby villa in a run-down street near the railway station. There was no gate or fence and the front garden was a wild patch of long grass littered with dog turds. He had driven fast, and as he rapped at the door he panted a little as if he had run there.

A girl with long henna-stained hair answered and stared at him neutrally. 'Is this where Bez lives?' he said, and heard himself sounding stiff, framing the word with an older-generation frigidity of distaste.

She nodded, and let him in. He stood in a dark hall where the wallpaper was peeling in little twirls like the peelings of an apple, and there was a smell of patchouli. 'I'll call him for you,' she said, and shouted 'Bez!' up the stairs before disappearing into the front room, where there was the sound of television. Her accent was posh in a strangely dated way. From above came a muted pounding of music. A fat cat was asleep on a cushion on the third stair. David had never been in a house like this before.

Bez was plumper than he remembered him, and his eyes behind the round National Health spectacles were small and timid. He felt a renewal of disappointment and puzzlement at the fact of Nicholas's involvement with somebody like this, which somehow had the effect of diluting his anger.

'Yeh?' Bez came halfway down the stairs and stopped. 'Oh, hello.'

'Don't you bloody hello me.' He wished he had something pat to say. The idea of hitting this insignificant youth, which he acknowledged now must have been at the back of his mind, seemed altogether out of the question. 'You know what I'm here for,' he went on.

'What's Nick been saying?' His voice was very faint.

'He didn't need to say anything,' said David. 'For fuck's sake,' he added, a bit lamely: he felt a compulsion to swear, as if to establish a common level between them.

The stairs creaked behind Bez, who had gone pale. A

young man with long lank hair, dressed in a black T-shirt and jeans with gaping rips in them, stood on the stair above him. 'Who is it, Bez?' he said. He had a moustache and a beard which accentuated his youth: his face showed unused and soft beneath the wispy teenager's-floss, straw-coloured and interrupted by spots.

'It's Nick's landlord,' said Bez, and David saw that he was really frightened.

'So you're the brave pair, are you?' said David, and was reminded for a moment of his headmaster at school.

'You want to watch him, mate, he's a poofter,' said the beard, hesitantly, and David realised that he too was searching for some common ground.

'Just you try saying that word again,' he said. He put his foot on the bottom stair. He detected another smell under the odour of patchouli, a ghost of cheap over-spiced cooking that was rather like his own. 'You're better than him, then, are you? Gives you the right to kick hell out of him, does it?' His hand grasped the banister, and Bez took a step back. '*You.* You're a coward and a fucking hypocrite as well.' Bez looked at him, frankly imploring. It occurred to him that if he said any more – and perhaps that had been enough – he was potentially exposing this Bez to what had happened to Nicholas. Bez's fear was of more than him. He hesitated, debating whether that was what he wanted, and knowing it was not.

'Look,' Bez said. 'We never really meant to – '

'Maybe you didn't,' said David, and moved another step up the stairs. 'Perhaps that's what I could say as well afterwards.'

He realised that it was highly unlikely that he, unfit and pacific, could really lift a finger against these two young men without being beaten to a pulp: but the realisation was cancelled out by another, simultaneous, that such stuff was irrelevant. For from the moment he had come in the door he had represented not My Big Brother come to duff you up, but something far more powerful: he was Old Authority, the cold irresistible wind of adulthood blowing into the fuggy fascinating crannies of youth. Dispiriting and disorientating as the thought was, he saw that to these two worried figures on the stairs he had appeared not bristling with fearsome revenge but simply girded with the instantly admonishing status of the parent, and that was enough.

When David got back, Nicholas was reclining on the settee, eating a takeaway Chinese meal off his chest; and Ruth was there.

'I've been looking after this invalid,' she said. 'Even fetched him a beef chow mein, he said it was his last wish.'

'He can't be that bad, if he's stuffing that down him,' said David.

'Peel me a grape, Beulah,' said Nicholas from the settee; and cocked his good eye at David.

'You've been to see this chap then,' said Ruth. 'Nicholas told me all about it. What did he have to say for himself?'

'Not a lot.' He sat down. He had not offered to kiss her. He felt heavy and bad-tempered. 'Don't know what I expected him to say really. He said he was sorry, if that's any comfort.'

'It isn't,' said Nicholas.

'He just looked worried to death,' said David. 'I don't suppose it's any good saying you're well rid of him, is it?'

'No.' Nicholas sucked a flailing noodle into his mouth. 'True though,' he added after a moment.

'Sounds as if you haven't had a very peaceful half-day,' said Ruth, sitting down on the arm of his chair. Clearly she sensed his mood. That, and the smell of her perfume that was the smell of her, a thorn of undeniable pleasure sticking into him, seemed to compound his irritation, twisting and sharpening it into irritation with himself.

Nicholas put down his plate and jumped up. 'I'm going to wash my hair.'

'What for?' said David.

'Because, Rigsby, my looks are not exactly at their best at the moment, and any little improvement will be welcome.'

'He seems cheerful enough now anyway,' said Ruth.

'It's an act.' He sat back in his chair, avoiding her eyes.

'Hey. Little ray of sunshine. Remember me?' She held his hand. 'I was all disappointed when I arrived and you weren't here.'

'Sorry.' He sighed, aware of some last corrosive bubble of cantankerousness rising in him like indigestion. 'You know, it seems like I've done nothing but think about other people's troubles today.'

'Oh, you poor thing,' she said, and he caught the inflection of sarcasm. How easy now to slip his arm round her and slide with her into a comfortable, conciliatory hug; how easy to open his mouth and let forth a halitosis of ill-humour.

'What are we going to do tonight?' she said.

He shrugged. He disliked himself very much at this moment.

'What we ought to do is take Nicholas out somewhere.'

'We won't be on our own then,' he said, frowning, as if his vision were obscured by the lump of his own stubbornness.

'Well, at this rate we're not going to have much fun on our own, are we?' she said. 'I think I'd prefer an evening with Nicholas,' and there was a light hardness in her voice, as of a shiny tough metal.

He sat up and looked at her, as he should have done before. 'I don't know why I'm like this. I started to feel old today all of a sudden. Well, not old. No, I'm not whining now. I went drinking with Jack Erskine at dinner-time.' He realised he had not eaten, and was hungry. 'I shouldn't drink at dinner-time, it doesn't do me any good.'

She smiled briefly, and patted his knee. 'Daft. You're not old,' she said. 'I'll make you a cup of tea,' and he realised as he watched her go into the kitchen how close he had brought her to utter exasperation. He got up and walked around, as if to shake apathy from his limbs, full of a heightened and relieved awareness. He was like someone who has stepped off the kerb in a daydream and narrowly missed being run over and reels back with the blare of the hooter ringing in his ears.

The evening was a success. It turned into a sort of pub-crawl, ending in a taxi-ride home with the three of them squashed in the back singing: Ruth's good voice, rendered slightly flutey with lager, Nicholas, an unsteady tenor, and David rumbling a bass so off-key it became a counterpoint, making Ruth cough with laughter, so that he laughed too and deliberately made it even worse in a kind of clownish contrition for that earlier self of this afternoon – the Ur-David whose baleful retrospective influence he had thought not so long ago was permanently erased. Nicholas was in the middle, and put an arm round each of them. He spoke loudly for the benefit of the taxi-driver: 'Here's where the action is! Right in between you two! Coming between your desires – if you'll pardon the expression. A fruit sandwich . . .'

They were quiet as they sat in the living-room after Nicholas had gone to bed: a quietness that seemed an acknowledgement of something. With the sound turned low they watched Ronald Coleman sacrificing himself in *A Tale of Two Cities* and sipped coffee and he stroked her hair, which she liked and always said made her sleepy. He had changed this living-room a lot since his mother had died, tentatively at first, but recently more radically: repainting the walls cream instead of beige, putting down new rugs he had bought, replacing vases and figurines with potted plants. But their quietness breathed an intense familiarity because his mother, and as far as he could remember his father, had been quiet, and he and Marian too; even when most fractious and restless as children, screaming and yelling did not come naturally to them. He was often amazed at how loud other people had their radios and televisions.

He fell asleep, though shallowly, and woke with the thread of his thoughts unbroken. Ruth had turned off the television and was standing at the sideboard looking at his mother's old photograph of Auntie Aldyth that he had placed there.

'It's not your mother, is it?' she said.

'No.' He held out his hand and she came back to him. 'It's her sister Aldyth. The one she fell out with, the one I told you about.'

'I would have thought having a picture of your mother would be more appropriate.'

'Well, I can remember my mother. Aldyth's different. I never met her.'

'I don't see the point of having a picture of someone you never even saw,' she said. He wondered for a moment if she was being awkward in some kind of retribution for his mood of earlier; but he saw nothing quarrelsome in her pale composed face as she turned, leaning against him. At the same time he felt a keen pang of love for her, transfixing him, so that he felt warm, helpless and clumsy. 'She's been pretty well disowned by the rest of the family. I just felt a sort of identification with her. I still want to get in touch with her. I must remember to ask Auntie Jeanette if she knows anything.'

'I thought we'd finished with all this family stuff,' said Ruth, and her finger moved on his cheek, somehow quizzically, as if tracing the shape of a question-mark. 'Just you and me.'

'Just you and me,' he said. He felt fully awake now, and both quiescent and pleasantly anxious, wanting things to be not only as good as before but better, a new contract.

She looked around the room again, as if seeing it for the first time, and she indicated a single watercolour landscape, his own, the first that he had been vain enough to hang. 'It is good, that,' she said. 'Didn't you ever want to carry on with art when you left school? Maybe go to college?'

'I don't know. I don't think it even occurred to me as an option. Nobody in our family ever did that sort of thing. And when I left school what I really wanted was a job and money of my own – be grown-up, you know. And jobs seemed to be going begging then. Just one of those things you slip into, not conscious of anything else.'

'And you don't regret it now?'

'I can't honestly say I do. But you know me. I could regret everything I've ever done once I got started thinking about it.'

'Everything?'

'Not everything.' His heart seemed to get big, a dilating balloon in his chest. 'You said about just you and me just now. Would you consider moving in here with me?'

She did not look surprised, but she was silent for a while. 'I haven't thought about it,' she said. 'Well, that's not true, I have thought about it.'

'You don't have to,' he blurted, not knowing why, and shocked at the trembly humility he heard in his voice.

'Oh, I'm not saying no,' she said. 'It's just I can't really imagine it. It's . . . I mean, we're all right as we are, aren't we? More than all right, I should say.'

He nodded. 'That's what Nicholas said.'

'You discuss me with Nicholas, do you?'

'Yes. Do you mind?'

'No . . . no, I quite like the idea, I don't know why. Thing is . . . like you said, about not being conscious of things, it's the same with me at home. I've just carried on living there, you know . . .'

He nodded again. He did not mention Bill.

'Then there's mum. It's not that she's not capable, it's just . . . I can't imagine it. Am I hurting you?'

He was startled, for she was not at all. 'No, God no. When I say it was only a suggestion, I really mean that. I don't mean to put any pressure on you or anything.'

'It's just – having to start thinking about things, and – what's been so lovely is not thinking about things – just living for each day, sort of . . .' He was rather charmed at the way she was floundering; she usually talked with such precision. 'Let's blunder on for now, eh?' she said.

That night they made love slowly and kindly and said how much they loved each other in drugged muffled voices against the stark silence of the grey early hours. At last Ruth went to sleep and before he dropped off he looked at her burrowing down against him, cocooning the sheets around her; for the first time he had known her reminiscent of a child.

CHAPTER 12

10th November 1943

Dear Aldyth,
I hope everything is all right with you and that this letter finds you in good health.

Jeanette Russell pauses and sighs. Beginnings are always so stuffy for some reason. She hates stuffiness. It's not as if you would ever speak to your sister in that way. She puts down her pen, already discouraged, and reaches for the packet of Camels given to her by a fellow-student at the teacher-training college, who got them from a Yank her family had to dinner. She coughs at the harshness of the cigarette and stares out through the kitchen window at the cold gardens of Corporation Road. There are no lawns to be seen: all have given way to vegetable plots and Anderson shelters. None of the family are great letter-writers, and though Jeanette, in spite of being The Daft One, is also The Bright One, it is not a task she relishes either. But poor Aldyth must appreciate a letter stuck out in that hostel; and she feels even more compelled to write by the growing coolness of the others, especially her father, who scarcely ever mentions Aldyth's name.

I hope this winter isn't too unkind to you. It's freezing in this house too if that's any consolation!

Of course Aldyth always tended to be a bit wild . . . but with the independence that the war has brought she just doesn't seem to give a damn what anyone thinks of her. Of course there are plenty of girls who go with Yanks; but her mother definitely disapproves, and really they are often . . . not quite the thing. That crowd at The Bell and Oak in town: the place is jammed with Yanks, with their big sloppy behinds and their money spread out on the tables, and some of them sitting on the floor of the passage with their legs sprawled out playing dice, so that you have to step over them; and there are girls there who are obviously after one thing, girls with ankle-bracelets, which is a sure sign . . . Jeanette feels disapproving at the thought of her sister associated with girls like that, but is also stirred with a little excited curiosity. Instead of writing these dull trite comments, it would be nice to ask Aldyth a few things quite frankly.

Reg hasn't been sent abroad yet, but he expects to be any day. He says he is quite looking forward to it, anything is better than waiting around. Obviously I don't agree! I'm glad now we got engaged, though it seemed a bit hasty at the time. It makes me feel more secure somehow. Frank still comes home occasionally. He still swanks like he used to, but he doesn't talk much about his flying, his 'ops' as he calls them. No word from Joe. Mum's very worried. I don't know whether you hear from Ethel, but she and Harold are well. Grandma thinks it's very odd that there's no children yet, but they say they want to wait till the war's over, it's no world to have children in according to them, and till they've got a house of their own.

Of course her friend Vera's mother goes with Yanks – and Yanks emphatically in the plural, but then she always did have a reputation. She remembers what happened at Vera's house last week, and wonders if that story might liven up the letter. Such a nice girl, Vera, in spite of her upbringing. You'd have thought she wouldn't stand a chance; but her mother's a nice woman, really, and it can't have been easy . . . Vera's dad cleared off years ago . . . But the house is such a filthy place, and Jeanette never likes going there, but she wouldn't hurt Vera for the world. When she went round that afternoon Vera's mother was there with a Yank – much younger than her, and he wore spectacles. Jeanette was embarrassed at first and so, clearly, was Vera; but then this Yank, whose name was Hank – she thought it must be a joke at first but no, that was really his name – produced this paper parcel of pork chops. Real, juicy, inch-thick pork chops such as they hadn't seen for years. She fairly drooled at the sight of them. And he put them in this filthy black frying-pan and fried them and they ate them just like that, on their own, without any vegetables or anything, in the middle of the afternoon. She thought nothing had ever tasted so delicious. Afterwards she and Vera went up to Vera's bedroom which was the cleanest place in the house, to have a good gossip; and Vera's mother's bedroom door was standing open, and she saw the most unbelievably dirty messy bed, left just as it was, and in the middle of the floor the jerry, absolutely full to the very brim so that you couldn't have lifted it without spilling, and such a reek . . .

Jeanette smiles to herself, and feels her face go hot. Her tendency to blush is a family joke, and she is regarded, as she is well aware and admits, as very naïve for twenty-one. Perhaps they would not think her so naïve if they could know of the experiments she and Reg got up to before he was called up, she thinks, and feels her face go even hotter. But they never went beyond a certain point and never intended to. And some things do shock her, or if not exactly shock her, take her up short somehow, as if she is constantly unprepared, living in a dream world. She no longer takes the short cut home through the cathedral precincts, for those dark quiet lanes amongst the trees and the ancient tombstones are, since the arrival of the Yanks, littered with used condoms, and she will never forget that audible squelch beneath her shoe.

Jeanette puts the kettle on the stove and sits down again. She ought to hurry and get on, for soon her mother will be back from town and Maggie home from work and then there will be no hope of finishing. She looks at the letter. This paper is discouraging too, flimsy and grey and woody. It seems you can't get decent writing-paper now either. In a rush she writes with a sudden recklessness:

I suppose you see lots of Yanks down where you are, with all those bases round about. They say James Stewart and Clark Gable are there, have you ever seen them? We see our share of Yanks here too, mostly Air Force, especially at weekends. Great truckloads of them come in to the pubs and the dances. A lot of people don't like them, in town they sprawl about and sit down on the kerb, in fact some were actually sitting on Lacey's windowsills as if they owned the place, which caused quite a stir. The officers seem quite different, they tend to go to dances at the Town Hall. Anyway you can't judge by appearances, and a lot of them seem very nice, for instance Auntie Min was on the bus the other day and a Yank stood up straight away to let her have his seat, and you won't find many of our lot doing that.

Well, it would look much worse, and ridiculous, if she didn't mention them at all. Last time Frank was home he told them a joke: 'Have you heard about the new utility knickers? One Yank and they're off.' It was rude, but it was rather funny. Her father hadn't thought so. He seemed to be growing more crusty these days.

I don't know how you're managing for stockings. Maggie bought a pair from a dodgy sort of character on the market, and it turned out they didn't have any feet. Some girls I know have tried painting their legs with gravy browning, but it goes all streaky and looks awful. Do you get enough to eat at the hostel? We wonder if you were perhaps better off at the farm in that respect, but then I imagine it's less lonely for you now, with lots of other girls for company, more cheerful.

Jeanette notices with relief that she has filled up two pages. Though her writing has been getting bigger towards the end. She gets up to make the tea, and feels guilty for wishing to get the letter over . . . But after all she just hasn't got much to say to her sister, and can find no common language between them. Aldyth had always had a certain remoteness about her, a situation that seemed to Jeanette perfectly reasonable; her sister, beautiful, daring and independent, was everything she herself was not; moreover, though she is studying to be a teacher and Aldyth was always academically lazy at best, Jeanette suspects that Aldyth's are the real brains of the family. And yet she is not entirely of the family, somehow.

Jeanette thinks pleasantly of Reg for a few moments, allowing her mind a respite from handling the thorny thought of Aldyth, and then with another sigh she writes what she has decided will be the last paragraph of her letter.

Do you ever think about what you'll do after the war is over (and that can't be really so very far off – or can it)? Harold says women will find themselves in a different position after the war, they won't go back to what they were before and a good thing too he thinks. I don't suppose you'd fancy going back to the railway offices, even if they'd have you. Oh dear, that last bit sounds rotten. But she can't scribble it out. In desperation she adds: *But of course you deserve better than that place anyway. Well, I shall be glad just to have the war over, and have my Reg back in one piece, that would suit me down to the ground. Take care of yourself now, and write soon.* *Love, Jeanette.*

She hesitates over that *Love*, not because she doesn't want to say it but because there seems a hint of insolence in signing herself thus to Aldyth. The gawky schoolgirl, drably overshadowed by her lovely sister who walks with her head in the enigmatic clouds of adulthood, rises again for a moment in twenty-one-year-old Jeanette as she bends over her letter, chewing the end of her pen. Oh, well, why not *love:* there is really no other way of saying it.

Down to the south and west of the town, the gently rolling, brook-sown fields of Northamptonshire have undergone their own trauma of war. This country of the old, with its water-meadows and spinneys, its ragged red-brick farms lost among apple-trees at the end of lanes leading nowhere, its damp mists and silent market-towns where the solitary hotel is a crumbling limestone mausoleum and there is a pub for every two houses, has had youth forced with startling suddenness upon it. In a Victorian shooting-lodge, staring across the fields hoary and glassy-eyed as one of the stuffed animals in cases that clutter its attics, the dust of years has been blown away by a hundred girls of the Women's Land Army, including Aldyth Russell and her friend Vi. And a somnolent landscape of ploughed earth and fox coverts and low church steeples is ringed with air-bases, its long congealed quiet torn by the thunder of bombers and the violent vitality of thousands of strange young men, and the ancient names of English villages, Deenethorpe and Apethorpe and Luffenham and Polebrook, have a brash new resonance.

Dear Jeanette,

Thanks for your letter. I was glad to hear from you.

Cunning draughts that no amount of matting and drapery will shut out haunt the old pile that is the hostel. They whip around Aldyth's aching shoulders as she sits hunched up on her truckle-bed, with Jeanette's letter beside her and a writing-pad propped on her knees. Its whiteness glares back at her under the naked light-bulb that hangs from an elaborate plaster ceiling-rose. On the next bed a large fat Welsh girl lies still dressed in jersey and jodhpurs and snores with her mouth wide open.

'Pretty as a picture,' Don would say with that gruff seriousness of his, and she would laugh. Yes, she would laugh.

And now what should she write to Jeanette, forty miles away secure in her good-natured innocence and her wholesome thoughts of Reg? What should she say that can begin to answer that absurd commonplace with which one is faced all one's life, 'How have you been?'

Perhaps she should try to say something of the constant agitation of the skies here, the way your neck aches from looking up into them, the way your ears throb with the throbbing of the engines. Or the sight of the great B-17s taking off, and the incredible, searing noise that shatters the morning peace and seems to go on for ever, until you think the huge bulk will never get off the shuddering ground. Or in the dim late afternoon, when with a dull pain in your back you straighten up from the sugar-beet and see across the fields the runway lights winking on and hear a distant rumbling and realise they're coming back. And perhaps too she should say something about the little feathery panic she would feel inside, thinking of Don and his coming back; but perhaps Jeanette would not understand.

There is no sound now from the sky, no sound but the

snores of her companion and the soft talking of other girls in the chilly unfurnished rooms. Vi has gone to a dance: some Yanks brought a truck to the hostel. Aldyth has rarely missed a dance, but did not feel like going tonight.

Perhaps then she should write about the dances at the Victoria Hall in Oundle, and the girls from the little town in rows against the walls, looking half-scared and half-excited, with sometimes a few WAAFs, rather snooty and making no secret of what they think of the land-girls who arrive in vigorous sweaty droves; and the Yanks coming in late from the pubs, looking almost painfully big in that cramped smoky hall; and the strange accents, not one but many variations, loud above the sound of the band. And the girls dancing at first with the stiff ballroom steps they had learned at school and then copying the loose-limbed Yanks with a gradual teetering awakening of confidence like people who have never used their bodies before.

Strange accents. Don's was a soft, blurred voice, uniquely easy on the ear. Sinus made it lower and softer: he suffered badly from sinus, from being at high altitude too long.

His plane: the *Attagirl*. He took her to see it. A painting on its hull, in painstaking childish detail, of a mermaid who looked like Betty Grable, and had breasts of ridiculous size. 'Well,' he said with that deceptive slowness and hesitancy, 'I guess you could say it's a little gaudy. But the boys like it.'

Aldyth sits, her pencil frozen in her fingers.

Perhaps then she should just write about Don: his bristly blond hair that at first sight made her think of a convict's haircut; his ambling walk and warm, chortling laugh; his liking for English beer, a subject of endless ribbing from his buddies. Perhaps, though it would be beyond her to describe it, she should write about the night she had met him, when she and a group of other girls were stacking wheat through dusk and on into evening until they were working by moonlight, and half a dozen Yanks who had heard about this weird custom had come laughingly to lend a hand. Their laughter soon faded and they were worn out in no time, except Don, who worked on beside her quietly until they had finished.

Going with Yanks. She can see with perfect clarity her mother's face and behind her, in diminishing perspective, lines of set mouths and small petrified eyes full of uncomprehending hostility, images of narrowness, like the constricted rows of grey houses in the pinched air of which she had grown up, the identical privacies of square back yards, tarred sheds and pigeon-lofts and cinder-paths, private lives that must be jealously guarded and yet constantly exposed, offered up in challenge to the other jealousies beyond the wooden fences.

So, she had gone with Yanks. Perhaps she should write that down, and write too that it had been kinder, healthier, more good-humoured than the times she had had with men before, snatched with a hurry and furtiveness that ultimately turned everything to so much greed and recrimination in the suffocating atmosphere of the town.

And perhaps she should write – though she doubts it would be believed, since once the borders of respectability have been crossed and left behind then even the good things that lie within it must be for ever inaccessible to you – but in spite of this perhaps she should assert that it is possible for her to fall in love.

The dances at the USAAF bases themselves are the best – not only are the bands better but there is always a vast quantity of food laid on. Rich food, and often peculiar – fried chicken, sauerkraut, salami, waffles, doughnuts. Don looked on admiringly, the first time he took her to one of these dances, as she unashamedly stuffed herself until she could hardly move, let alone dance. 'You go right ahead,' he said when at last, coming out of a gorged daze, she apologised. 'I'm happy just to watch you.'

Perhaps – since now she knows she can write none of these things, and her letter is becoming a ravelling up of memories in her head, a soothing mental knitting – perhaps if that *How have you been?* is not for once to be dovetailed with the usual phrases that it invokes as if by contract, but an attempt is to be made to answer it, then she should mention how she made love with Don: how once they went to a very weighty and crusty country hotel and just booked in for the night, carrying it off with sheer cheek, so that the tiny dusty lady peeping over the mahogany top of the reception desk made never a murmur, and how in that hideous expensive room amongst ponderous furniture muffling itself in genteel mortification with drooping fringes and drapes and antimacassars – there was a painting of a watchful Victorian gent garotted with starched collars and Don gravely turned it to the wall – they undressed each other by the corridor-light that filtered under the door and she inspected the glowing sketch that it made of his pale rangy body. Or if that is too singular a picture and maybe half-way acceptable, in its romantically anecdotal way, then perhaps she should try to convey how defying all odds they managed to find all sorts of places to be together, simply because when you must, you do – though to say that may well be to meet with incomprehension again – anywhere where there is darkness, and solitude of a sort. And though it is even more incomprehensible, and liable to be blasted by gales of scepticism, perhaps she ought to write about the many times when he was curt and exhausted, brooding after a mission of ten hours, hours that turned his face as closed and expressionless as the face of the clock that had measured them; when there would be none of the rabbity enthusiasm that the instant myth demands, but a slow anxious tenderness, as hesitantly he placed his hands on her body, now here and now after a pause there, as if with a pleased perplexity he was discovering something for the very first time. And – this is perhaps most incomprehensible of all, she thinks with a spike of malice rising like heartburn – how that was often enough for them and nothing more scandalous than mutual comfort would follow, and how they would subside into an embrace – a cuddle – to all appearances obviously the Yank and his tarty partner, post-whatever-the-current-word-was that spluttered from the legion of tight lips to spray muddily on whatever it was that pulled them so tight in the first place.

He liked to go and look at old buildings and churches. Rarely did he jibe at England, its shabby smallness, as other Yanks ('Jeez, I don't believe those little trains with that tin whistle – peep peep! How do you stand it?') so often did: he liked England, sometimes with an inclusiveness that surprised her. He enjoyed quietly drinking tea in the sort of tea-rooms, where there was a smell of naked gas and worn grey table-cloths and a tiered cake-stand with one or two mummified cakes; and he in turn was surprised when she said how unutterably dreary such things would have seemed to her before.

'Where's he from?' Vi asked her, for she loves to hear the sound of American place-names.

'St Paul, Minnesota,' she said. The name meant nothing to her. The actual place he came from would have meant even less: 'When I say St Paul, that's just the nearest city,' he said. 'Home's a little one-horse town way out, smaller than your Oundle.' He never talked much about things like that, unlike many of the Yanks who would spin out tales for hours. 'Seems a long way away,' he said. Because of this, somehow, she knew he was telling the truth when he said he was not married, as so many of them were. Nor did he talk about his flights over Germany, except once to say he had got his thirteenth over – he was very superstitious – and now he knew he would survive the twenty-five you needed to complete a tour and go home. It was the frequent cancelled missions that bothered him. 'You get all tensed up and then they tell you it's off and – hell, you feel sick.'

But if all this is to be expressed, then she must also say about the jolt, the shock like a blow in the stomach, that night when they were drinking in a village pub. Ironic, now, to remember how they were with a group from the Combined Operations HQ that was stationed at a stately home outside her own town – Americans, British, Czechs, Poles; an interesting bunch, and all getting on well. She scarcely took any notice of the black GI at the bar. He was only there a few minutes, quickly drinking a glass of beer, obviously feeling out of place. But as soon as he had gone a Yank who had been playing darts with a couple of locals went up to the bar and picked up the empty glass and smashed it against a table.

'Don't worry, I'm paying for it,' he said to the barman, and gave him a careless handful of pennies and shillings.

The noisy conversation, a patchwork of accents, rose again after a momentary lull. She did not join in. The barman without comment had swept up the glass. Eventually Don turned to her. 'What's wrong, honey?' he asked her gently.

'You saw it too, didn't you?'

'That?' He shook his head. 'There's always some crazy fellah.'

'He should have been chucked out.'

'Oh, come on,' he said, his face divided across, the easy-going smile below and a frown above. 'Like I say, there's always some who react like that. I know how he feels.'

'You what?'

'Wait, I'm not saying I'd ever do something crazy like that – '

'But you know how he feels.'

The smile was gone, and the frown was deepening into puzzlement. 'Listen, I hope you're not about to read me a lecture, honey, because if you are I'm afraid I'll tell you where to get off. You may mean well but you don't know what you're talking about.'

His face set, closed up as it very occasionally could so that he was as far away from her as if he were in Minnesota. She did not give in, but he shrugged at her questions. She asked him about various tales she had heard, of white GIs going round in trucks to find and beat up their black comrades, of more gruesome things. He shrugged, and each shrug grew more emphatic, until they amounted to his turning his shoulder to her.

She had looked up Minnesota on a map in one of Vi's books. It was in the north, and she had always had some vague idea, culled from the films, that prejudice against the blacks really only existed in an archaic hothouse South.

She brooded, and there was coolness between them for a while; then she got lonely for him and when he flew on a mission one day she was convinced he was not going to come back; and when he did they were reunited almost violently, making love with fierce urgency in a barn with an old farm cat watching them from yellow eyes.

One weekend he had a heavy cold and was fit for nothing. 'You make sure you go on out to a dance tonight and enjoy yourself,' he told her huskily. 'You earn it. Me, I'm going to get some medicine and just sleep till I'm better.'

The next time she saw him he was not completely better. They had arranged to meet in a pub in Oundle and as she waved to him across the bar she saw his nose was still rather red: she thought it made him look, as he would have put it, cute.

His eyes were fishy as he looked at her. He had risen, as all the Yanks did, when she came up, but he did not offer to get her a drink. 'You go to a dance on Saturday?' he said.

'Yes. You wanted me to.'

He nodded: with restless fingers he stood a threepenny bit on its edge on the table and then flicked it over again. 'Well, I want you to be straight with me, honey. I heard something and I don't believe it's true but, like I say, I want you to be straight with me.'

'Go on.' She felt weak, and was aware of the landlady behind the bar watching them with obvious interest, a fat woman with a home-made permanent wave and lots of lipstick, a large generous mouth painted over a small mean one.

'Buddy of mine says you went to the Negro dance.' He sighed and rubbed his hand over his eyes, as if struggling to say something very difficult and painful. 'And danced with 'em.'

'Yes,' she said. 'What if I did?' But it swam in on her, horrible and absurd, the realisation, she could almost laugh. She had simply enjoyed the dance, such as it was: she had not even thought about it. There were different nights at the hall for white and black servicemen, but she and virtually all the girls she knew had never taken much notice of that: the black GIs were strange, but so were the white ones; they were all Yanks. 'I've danced with black soldiers before,' she said, all defiance. 'It's up to me what I do,' but she knew it was all over bar the token fuming and snapping, all over. It was she who left the pub at last, with the sight of him still sitting there, playing with the coin, hunched. 'Christ, it makes me sick to my stomach to think of it,' he had said. 'That you could . . . Just the thought of it.' He shook his head.

He had once written his name on the ceiling of that pub with a candle-flame: it had become a custom with the Yank regulars. He had beautiful old-fashioned writing: even with a candle-flame it looked good.

Aldyth stretches on the hard bed and closes her eyes, wishing for a drink of water but reluctant to make the journey down cold passages to fetch it. Perhaps, finally, she should mention that she heard Don's plane was lost over Stuttgart on the twelfth of October, during a terrible week when, though they were not supposed to talk about the figures, the bombers had suffered ghastly losses. But perhaps now that is not relevant. She reckoned he must have been well short of his twenty-five, so no ironic significance there either.

She opens her eyes and picks up Jeanette's letter, a finger of Family reaching out across the miles and across the gulf of experiences that can never be shared, and then looks again at the sheet of paper with *Dear Jeanette* at the top. Perhaps then she should turn to old reminiscences, immerse herself in the warm suds of domestic familiarity. Jeanette, do you remember the time . . . ? Do you remember when you were nine, you tried to climb on to the little hall table to see out of the window, and it collapsed underneath you? You were so startled you didn't even cry. Children always assume everything will bear their weight. Perhaps adults go on assuming that too, and go on being startled when they are proved wrong . . . But she is not fond of extracting such morals, does not believe in the deft picking out of kernels of truth without touching the husk. She yawns, and then with a feeling of weariness and of relief she crumples up the sheet of paper and throws down the pen.

There is the hum of a plane in the sky far off, so faint that it is the instinctive straining of the ears that one is first aware of and not the sound itself. Aldyth is suddenly filled with an acute regret that she did not go to the dance with Vi: she should have gone, instead of moping about here. She is damned if she'll miss another single dance.

David looked at the baby curiously, for he had no experience of them: what was going on inside that fluffy apple-sized head? The idea of being a godfather was weirdly archaic.

'Makes me feel like I should wave a magic wand,' he said. 'Or join the Mafia, really.' And when Ruth shushed him, he was a little surprised, for he seemed to be seeing a different side of her, a side that was at home with the conventional pieties, or at least those of his family, which he thought were unique.

And it was unexpected when Ruth said, peering at the swathed dollish figure in Marian's arms, 'Oh, I can see David there. It's in the mouth.' Marian agreed, and she and Ruth laughed. Marian and Ruth laughing together, seemingly at his expense – though he did not mind that – was a strange sight. And it was strange that common features should be discerned between him and this tiny homunculus: he could not imagine babies having any sort of individuality. He had never considered children as being human beings, only, in a vague way, potentially so, as a sketch might perhaps be built up into a painting.

At the same time, he found the baby charming, with its unambiguous demands and its small customised physique, so unlike the adult body which was complicated and temperamental in the manner of an old car. His curiosity, he perceived after a while, was more than academic: he began to speculate on what it would be like to have one of these; and he was going to say so to Ruth. But a fear of being shushed again, and a fear of her reaction to the joke (not entirely a joke) that he was going to follow the remark up with, how he felt the same about buying a video recorder, shut him up.

Marian's second child had been born at the end of June. The day before, David had suddenly remembered she must be due and at once drove guiltily over to find the house dark and empty. He stood there ringing and ringing the bell and feeling guiltier still whilst an unseen dog next door hurled itself against the fence in paroxysms of barking. He resolved to ring her first thing next day, forgot, and was just going to bed that night when the phone rang and the unfamiliar voice of Richard – unfamiliar on the phone, for he never rang David – told him he was an uncle again.

Marian in the bed in the maternity hospital looked rosy and attractive, and pleased to see him. They kissed warmly, as they scarcely ever did, and he was conscious of the bond between them that he often disregarded. It was a family group, the rightness of which impressed him; even Tracey came and sat on his knee and wriggled there for a while.

'I wish I could get up,' said Marian. 'I feel ever so well. I was awful afterwards last time. Must be one of those things that get easier.'

'What are you going to call him?' He peeped at the baby, sleeping with intense concentration. As if he were steeling himself for the overwhelming life to come.

'Mark. We decided a long time ago, didn't we, Richard? Sarah if it was a girl, Mark if it was a boy.'

'That's a nice name. What about a middle name?'

'Oh, we're not sure. Just something ordinary. Kids always get made fun of if they've got those funny middle names. Like mine. Winifred. Whatever were mum and dad thinking of? Oh, David, if only mum was here to see him.'

'She can see him,' he said. 'She knows what's going on, I'll bet, and she's pleased as punch.' Marian strongly believed this sort of thing, and though he had long since ceased to do so, he was determined to say everything that was right for the occasion. This was partly because he still felt guilty about not having seen her for so long, but also because of a reawakened sense of fondness, and of solidarity. She seemed ready to let bygones be bygones, but Richard was stiff and reserved with him.

'Now you've got to come to the christening, David. Because we want you to be godfather. Don't we, Richard?'

'If you want to take the responsibility,' said Richard heavily. 'You can say no.'

'I'd be delighted. Really.'

'And you must bring your lady friend as well.'

'What lady friend?' He did not know why he was still being evasive about this.

'Oh, I've got my spies you know.' She winked and grinned, looking like a little girl as she often did. 'No, Richard's spotted you in town with her several times. I can put two and two together you know.'

'I see.' He felt faintly embarrassed at the introduction of Ruth into this conversation: for some reason he had immediately thought of her lying in his bed, and had blushed as if they could read his mind. 'Well, I'm sure she'd love to come.'

Ruth said so too, when he told her, but the root of what threatened to become a fully-fledged quarrel between them was his reluctance for her to go.

'I've got to go, but that doesn't mean you have to. It's one of these dreadful family get-togethers. Marian's very big on this sort of thing.'

'Well, I've told you, I'd like to go.'

'It'll be awful.'

They had met for lunch in town, and were in the stone-clad Macdonalds that looked out over the cathedral square. The place was hot and packed, and the only seats they could find were the kiddie seats: his legs were wedged painfully under the plastic table.

'What church is it at?'

'Oh, it's one of those modern ones in the new town, look like multi-storey car parks.' He sipped at the bitter boiling hot coffee. 'You don't really want to go,' he said, supplying no question mark.

'What's the matter, ashamed of me?'

'It isn't that . . .'

'Oh, thanks. What then?'

She was in brisk mood, as she often was when she had been teaching, and not to be crossed. He looked at her miserably.

'I'm just trying to spare you.'

'Well, it's my decision, I'll answer for it.'

'It's only a bloody christening. Who makes a fuss about them nowadays?'

'Your sister does, apparently, and I don't know why you're making such a fuss about going.'

Undigested hamburger yo-yoed in his gullet. 'You don't know my family.'

'Seems like I never will the way you're going.'

'Look, it's like we said, surely? They're nothing to do with us. Just you and me, we said.'

'Oh, David – ' she did not often use his name: when she did it was usually in special tenderness, but now it was curt and sharp – 'that's all very well and all very romantic . . .'

'I rather thought you meant it at the time.'

'Of course I did.' A brief softening, and impatient. 'But in day-to-day life it's different.'

He sighed, a forced sound and not a nice one, and leant back as far as he could in the squeaking chair. He looked at the garish cartoon frieze above them. 'Fancy making cartoon characters out of hamburgers,' he said. 'When you're going to eat them.'

'I think what's behind all this is you're really a snob.'

'Me?'

'Yes, you. You don't want me near this extended family of yours, all the embarrassing old aunties and whatnot. I don't know what makes you think you're so different, as if you've got to deny all that. As if you've just popped into the world on your own. I know you didn't.'

'That's a rotten thing to say.'

'Well I'm sorry but that's what I think. Sometimes I wonder if all your nostalgia bit's just a blind. You don't really want me to have anything to do with your past.'

'All right. Maybe that's because I thought you were the break from it.'

She would not be turned aside. 'I sometimes feel like I'm some sort of fantasy figure for you. Just something you indulge in. Well perhaps that's nice, but I'm not, I'm real. I'm not going to be a – a ration of escapism in your life.'

His ears were tingling; he knew his face must be bright red.

'What's brought this on?' he said.

'Oh, for Christ's sake.' Violently she screwed up the greaseproof paper in front of her and threw it down and folded her arms and then unfolded them again. They did not look at each other.

'I wish you'd tell me these things instead of brooding on them.'

'I just have.'

They both had to be back at work soon, and the row, if that was what this was, would have to be crammed in, hasty and nasty as the junk food meal.

'This is a bit hypocritical, isn't it? You do everything you can to keep me away from your mother.'

'That's because I have to live with her, and she can be an interfering old so-and-so. You're just going to have to be more realistic. Remember your age. Remember my age. We're not bloody Adrian Mole and Pandora.'

He was silent: he already felt drained, as if they had argued the toss for hours.

'Can I take it then that I'm coming to this christening?'

'If you must.'

She blew out a hissing breath. 'If you ever say "If you must" like that again I'll murder you.'

Standing in the church, which had a fresh pleasant varnish smell like a do-it-yourself warehouse, David felt a thrill of horror as he recalled this scene. The row, in the way of rows, had not ended: it had tailed off into longer and longer silences and an unbelievable exhaustion.

The baby cried a bit when the water touched its browless forehead, but soon went quiet again. Richard's mother, who had come down from Manchester, also cried a bit, which seemed affected: weddings yes, but not christenings.

And the curious thing was David was glad Ruth had come. He felt proud: not just proud of being with her – that pleasure had never palled – but proud of her, as a person of obvious and eminent worth. When he had picked her up at Park

Crescent he was struck by how marvellous she looked. She was wearing a tailored charcoal-grey suit with black buttons and piping: it seemed to go perfectly with her short glossy black hair and pale skin. That this woman should be climbing into the car with him afflicted him with an intense happiness and an entirely new sense of wonder, making him tongue-tied. It was as if, given the ugliness of their argument over this occasion, he had expected an ugliness in her. And his admiration was so manifest that it immediately established a warmth between them that carried them to the church smiling almost shyly and nervously deferential as new lovers. He had often told her how beautiful he thought she was, and she liked that, but for herself she was insecure about her looks: she did not like looking in mirrors, and she always closed his wardrobe door to hide the one that hung on the back, whereas lately he rather liked looking at himself.

Marian and Richard's house was designed for nuclear families: its functional square rooms did not take to being filled with Richard's mother and father, his brother Peter, Great-Uncle Bob in his wheelchair, Auntie Jeanette and Uncle Reg, Uncle Alan, David's cousins Duncan and Tricia, and David and Ruth. Jammed into unlikely corners, they juggled paper plates of sandwiches and sausage rolls and glasses of wine: there was a constant whooshing noise from upstairs as the toilet flushed and flushed again.

Ruth was the only person here who was not a member of the family, and the significance of Marian's insisting that she should come did not escape David. He was a little annoyed; interested, too, at the thought that his sister was in some way taking on the office of their mother.

'She's very nice, David,' Uncle Alan told him emphatically. Ruth was circulating in an unforced way that he knew he could never achieve in such a situation. Alan spoke with a special intimacy that David realised was inevitable after what had happened in April.

'I'm glad you like her,' he said.

Alan nodded vigorously. 'I've been thinking about you a lot lately.'

'Oh, dear, don't do that,' said David, with a stilted laugh. He had been hearing stilted laughs all day, and despising them.

'Just thinking about what's best for you,' said Alan. 'I mean we feel a certain responsibility for you.' We being the family, presumably.

'Well, that's nice of you.' He gave the words a sincere intonation, whilst in his mind sarcasm raged.

Alan nodded again, a ludicrous sort of confidentiality. 'I think you'll be all right.' They were wedged in the hall with only Tracey – glaring resentfully about at having a houseful of people who were not all exclusively interested in her – next to them; but still Alan formed the words almost soundlessly, lip-reading style. David smiled and looked down at the sausage on a cocktail stick that lay on his plate. He could not imagine how it had got there. What he had feared, then, was happening: Ruth was being sucked into the Family, that new, strange, delightful life was receding into the distance; your significant self that in the dreams strode about performing significant actions vaporising as you become aware of your unsatisfactory limbs lying sweaty and too-familiar beneath the patched sheets.

'Now then, David.' His cousin Duncan had squeezed in next to them. He had had a drink in the pub beforehand 'to wet the baby's head', and his breath smelt of whisky. 'What have you been up to lately?'

It was one of those questions to which there is no real answer, that seem designed to make you stand there looking sheepish. 'Nothing much. Earning a crust, you know.'

'Managing all right on your own? Well, you certainly seem to be. Still in your mum's old house?'

'My house, yes.'

'Ah, should have sold up like I told you, you could have been quids in. How about you, Alan? Everything OK?'

'Yes, fine, thank you.' Alan looked more than usually disapproving, perhaps at the smell of drink, perhaps also at the interruption of his tête-à-tête.

'That's the way. Christ, where do you suppose Richard

gets this plonk? Enough to take the enamel off your teeth. Well, I must say, David, you seem to be doing pretty well for yourself.' He inclined his head sideways towards the kitchen, where Ruth could be seen talking to Richard. The sight of her there unexpectedly made him catch his breath, leaving him balanced on the pin-point apex of a pyramid of desire, not simply for her but for everything in the future that included her. Again, he did not know what to say.

'I was just telling David she seems very nice,' said Alan. An edge of hostility: for whatever reason, he seemed to be allying himself with David.

'I'll say.' Duncan gave a rugged smile, then looked serious. 'That Lacey as in Lacey's?' he said in a lowered voice.

'The store, yes.'

Duncan raised his eyebrows, pulling in his chin. 'Good for you. Barbers going up in the world, eh? No offence, mate. Best of luck to you.'

David managed a sort of smile. 'Mm. Will you excuse me?' He wanted to go to the toilet, and he wanted to get away from the pair of them.

In the bathroom a concentrated blast of summer sunlight poured through the frosted glass. David splashed water on his face. He had shed his jacket but still his shirt stuck clammily to his armpits. Ruth, he had observed, did not look hot.

For a splintered moment he felt not merely envious but hated her for being so unruffled. So damned amenable and helpful. Always coming up trumps. How come you're not hot? I'm just not. Well, you ought to be. He leant his forehead against the cool surface of the mirror above the sink and prickled with remembered moments of irritation, little border-incidents of argument that blew up over trivialities, when it seemed she was setting herself up as a disinterested guardian of a helpless lamb of objective truth which he, cruel brute, was trying out of some inexplicable spite to kill.

He rubbed a towel over his face. He was crotchety with love. He opened the small window and breathed in a waft of fresh air, not wanting to go downstairs again. The melody of *Romeo and Juliet* from a record of Tchaikovsky that Ruth had lent him was stuck in his head. It seemed his life had become suddenly cramped, run into a chicane, and he felt an obscure longing for something with the largeness of tragedy, an injection of that lush, spurious savagery and lyricism.

Richard was waiting on the landing.

'How's the proud father?' David said. Sort of thing Duncan would say.

'Proud,' said Richard without humour.

'So you should be. You're a lucky man.' This was forced too.

Richard nodded his large curly head judicially. He always gave considered attention to the most throwaway remark. 'We were a bit anxious,' he said. 'Marian had a bad time with Tracey, as you know. And now of course, she's that much older.'

'Yes, of course.'

From downstairs came a yelping laugh that he recognised as Duncan's followed by a girlish one that he recognised as Marian's. Dear God, how well he knew them all: in comparison he didn't know that elegant stranger down there at all.

'Anyway it's nice to see you around again, David,' said Richard. He stopped, and did not move.

David made an effort. 'I realise I've been rude. Not being in touch more.'

Richard looked relieved. 'Just that we got in the habit of worrying about you after your mother died. You know. Pair of interfering beggars we are,' he added gustily, digging his hands deep in his pockets as if to puncture them. 'Marian got a bit upset, that's all. We should have realised.'

'Well, I have been busy, but that's no excuse.'

Richard extracted his hands again, bringing bits of fluff with them. A cry came from downstairs: not the baby's thin wail, but Tracey in a temper. Richard smiled and sighed together. 'Getting over-excited,' he said. 'Have to watch out for jealousy, she's been used to all the attention. Sibling rivalry and all that. How did you feel when Marian was born?'

David thought back. 'I don't know. I think I saw her as a sort of animated teddy-bear at the time.'

'Did you?' Richard looked perplexed. 'Ah, well.' He indicated the bathroom, as if it had just become empty. 'Have to go.'

How well he knew them: each one was fastened to him by a tenacious root of memory. Auntie Jeanette, a single glass of wine going to her head as usual, gave him a vigorous powdered kiss on the cheek. 'You are looking well, David,' she said. 'Do you still have that nice young man in your spare room, what was his name? I did like him. I always thought that was rather brave of you to have someone so young as your lodger. I like young people, but I mean they could take over, couldn't they? How do you manage when he wants to bring girls home and things like that?'

'Oh, well, you have to compromise, you know.' He saw Ruth out of the corner of his eye suppress a smile, and was glad he had not hesitated.

'And Ruth tells me you've been helping out with the Musical Society.' Strange to hear the name on her lips. 'I thought at first she meant, you know, actually singing, and I couldn't quite believe . . .'

He laughed. 'Good Lord, no. Rodgers and Hammerstein would twirl in their graves.'

'That's our side of the family in you, you see. Decidedly unmusical. Your father used to play the piano, of course. I did hear him once, he played beautifully. Taught himself.'

'Yes. I can just remember. He used to play on Saturday evenings. He let me sit on his knee sometimes, though I must have got in the way.' He remembered too as a boy going to visit Auntie Jeanette on Sundays with his mother – his father was dead by then – and fidgeting in an over-stuffed chair and waiting, in the acquisitive way of childhood, for the time when Jeanette would reach into a drawer for the halfpennies and pennies she had saved for him. He recalled the satisfying feel of the big cold coins dropping in his hand.

He shuffled his way past Duncan to speak to Great-Uncle Bob, and Ruth reached out a hand to touch his arm as he went. 'Everything OK?' she said, smiling. He was grateful for the gesture, a flicker of genuine intimacy amongst the pressed bodies.

'All right, Bob?' he said. 'So they've fitted you with wheels now, have they?'

Bob, with a glass of beer and a captive audience, was in his element. His trilby was tilted back on his bald head. 'Aye, you get it free, so I thought I'd have it. There's not much you get free. Good thing is, I can get as drunk as I like without worrying about falling over. Got a light, have you?'

'Here, have one of mine.'

'Oh, you smoke these, do you? Bloody woman's cigarette. Can't get a puff out of them.' Bob took the proffered cigarette. 'What do you think of this babby then? Funny, he reminds me of your Uncle Joe.' He sucked in smoke and coughed, a rich, productive, old-man's cough. 'Course, you wouldn't remember him.'

David did not; but he thought of the pennies again and remembered Christmas Eves when he was young and Bob would come sholling round from the pub with a Christmas card for his mother and would peel out a ten-shilling note from his wallet for David. 'No wonder Bob's never had any money,' his mother would say, shaking her head. She would change the note into silver and make David save half of it and the rest she would take him to town to spend the day after Boxing Day.

Everyone went out into the garden for the taking of photographs, and it was scarcely less crowded on the small square of immaculate lawn than it had been in the house. The camera was passed from hand to hand as they rang the changes of group: parents and baby, parents and baby and Tracey, godparents and baby – and, as she would not be left out, Tracey again – relations, various, and baby – Uncle Alan held the child stiffly like an assistant showing a lot at an auction; and then whole family group and baby, when Ruth had to take the picture.

Perhaps because this made her seem left out, Marian then insisted on taking one of Ruth with David holding the baby.

As they stood there squinting into the sun, Ruth's arm through his and the warm surprising weight of Mark in his hands, Great-Uncle Bob called from his wheelchair: 'Ay up, David, I think they're trying to tell you something!' There was a laugh, and he felt peculiarly self-conscious and embarrassed, exactly indeed like a little boy again stranded amidst the indulgent adulthood of aunts and uncles.

While they drifted back into the house, Auntie Jeanette spoke to him. She was looking slightly misty-eyed and she laid her bony hand on his. 'What a lovely day it's been,' she said. She reminded him at that moment of Marian; the same utterly unguarded expression, the large attractive teeth. 'You know, David, I'm ever so glad things are working out for you. We were worried, you know. I mean it can't have been easy.'

Again he did not know what to say. Perhaps he should work out a formula reply for this.

'I think it's smashing when all the family gets together like this. Your mother would have liked to be here . . . but there we are. Can't have everything.'

She must have known what this would prompt him to say: whether she had forgotten or the sherry had made her incautious he did not know. 'Yes, it's a pity. Seems a pity too that Auntie Aldyth's not here, really.'

He fancied that she looked at him with a sort of appeal from under the brim of the flowered hat that was plonked on her head, but he went on. 'I mean I know there was this thing between her and mum. And I respect that. But it does seem a shame. I've been meaning to ask you about her.'

'Oh! goodness, I lost touch years and years ago. No good asking me I'm afraid.' Her eyes roamed this way and that, alarmed.

'You've no idea where she is now then?'

Jeanette shook her head. She waved away a bee that was buzzing near her with a fluttery hand.

'Not here, in the town, then?' he persisted.

'No, no.' She sighed. 'Well, I think I've got an address

somewhere – at least I did have – mind you, that's years and years old too . . .'

An eagerness beat in his head under the stinging sun. 'Well, that's a start, could you – '

'Of course, I might have lost it. I must have a look.' She smiled briefly and plunged up the step to the back door. 'I'll ring you, shall I?'

The inside of his car was like a kiln when he drove home. Beside him Ruth, he saw, was sweating too, her forehead shining and a damp patina on her throat and upper lip. They had scarcely had the chance to speak to each other all afternoon, yet he felt close to her in a new, almost disconcerting way.

'That's a sweet nephew you've got,' she said.

He thought so too, though he did not say so. 'Niece isn't so sweet.'

'No, I know what you mean. But that's her age. I've never been to a christening before. I think it's nice, much nicer than weddings. Shall we have our kids christened?'

This was so unexpected, and so unlike her, that she laughed at his startled face. He was oddly vulnerable today, constantly unprepared. He mumbled something about burial in consecrated ground.

'Trust you to think of that.' Her hand rested lightly on his shoulder. 'I like you in a suit. Your old uncle, great-uncle, he's a character, isn't he? They were all very nice to me.'

They were avoiding any direct mention of the quarrel, and he was glad. 'Nobody could ever be anything else, if they're any good,' he said, confusedly, from deep feeling.

Her hand massaged his shoulder. 'It was funny seeing you with them all. I was having a good look at you. You were so different. The way you behaved in a different way with each one.'

'Well, you have to be.' He stared ahead at the road, where shimmering mirages of tar disappeared and reappeared in the distance.

'I know. That's what was nice. I felt really proud of you, you came out so well.'

He was not aware of having come out well, and felt almost too puzzled to be pleased.

She came back to his house for tea. He was astonished when he started crying: she seemed less so. He thought later it might have been coming back to his mother's house after being with all his relations: whatever, he spluttered and groaned into paper hankies, crouching helpless on the settee and deeply embarrassed. They had agreed, in the course of pleasantly earnest discussions, that the trouble with men was their overweening misplaced sense of dignity, and that they ought not to be ashamed of such things as having a good cry. He found it different in practice.

Ruth was less troubled about the whole thing, and kindly amused. 'Church, babies, family, memories: bound to happen,' she said. 'Eternal verities sort of thing. You should know that, you with your country-and-western music.'

He chafed at his nose with balls of sodden tissue. 'Sorry . . . I'm sorry.'

'Go on, have a good blow. I know you have mucus in there too, we all do.' She sat beside him, stroking his back. 'It's funny, all the songs about crying, they never mention that. It is the main ingredient after all. "Snot for Souvenirs". "Snot of a Clown". No, I suppose it wouldn't sound quite the same.'

During a week of searing July heat the Musical Society gave their three performances of *Carousel* to a full house at the Regal.

The hot weather became a constant subject of conversation as nothing else short of the outbreak of war could. On television and in the newspapers the usual statistics were quoted; on the streets of the town there were strange sights. Old gentlemen broke out in baggy shorts that revealed baggy knees and long tartan socks, looking as if they had strayed from a walking-party in a 1930s travelogue. Builders, always ubiquitous in the town where office blocks that were weird amalgams of black plate glass and 'traditional' Dutch gables were constantly springing up, turned sore pink and lobster-red and finally deep copper; at lunchtime they piled into the pubs in the city centre, swarthy as Moors, noses peeling. At Barlow Watkins Mr Musson, dry and taciturn, licked brightly-coloured ice-creams shaped like feet or space-rockets. Each day David waved across the back garden fence to an increasingly nude Mr Carelli, who finally called a halt to his quotidian striptease when he had got down to the briefest of swimming trunks and a pair of gardening gloves.

The night before the opening of *Carousel* David had his friend Ron to dinner along with Ruth. They pushed a table out into the garden to eat, vainly hoping for coolness in the breathless evening; even the salad made them sweat. Ron, who had looked like a policeman when he was at school and still did after five years out of the force, would not even loosen his tie. Stalwart and running to fat, he sat upright in a creaking garden chair, light blue eyes ringed and hollow with circles of perspiration. The manager of the town football team had just been sacked in disgrace and Ron, who was a passionate and pedantic fan, was in a state of only half-facetious mourning. He talked about this in staccato, self-deprecating bursts, breaking off and looking from David to Ruth and to David again with an innocent sort of deference. David was full of vanity.

When he was gone they stayed in the garden, lifting their faces in concentration as cats do to catch a whiff of breeze. They sat side by side in canvas chairs, each with an arm dangling so that their fingers touched. It was still too stiflingly warm for any greater contact. Cirrus cloud sloped in a ribbed canopy behind the rooftops, harshly luminous.

'Poor Ron,' she said. 'He takes it very seriously, doesn't he?'

He nodded. 'I used to, too. Till I found I just couldn't care that much about it. Seemed a waste of energy.'

'Men are strange.'

'Am I strange?'

'Stranger than most.'

He squeezed her fingers.

'The awful thing about being a football fan like him is you have no control over your own pleasure,' she said. 'I mean, if your thing is stripping down old cars or whatever, then you control it, it's never going to turn against you. Whereas if your team keeps losing and losing, your chief source of pleasure and relaxation is actually becoming a source of pain.'

'That's very philosophical.'

'I do have my philosophical moments, you know.'

'I know you do.' He had sounded condescending.

She sighed, pushing her feet out of her shoes and stretching her bare feet on the grass. 'Not many though,' she said. 'I don't believe in too much thinking. Leads to all kinds of trouble. Makes trouble that wasn't there before.'

'In what way?' He was not feeling argumentative, but enjoying listening to her.

'There you are you see. Analysing, probing. You must learn, Mr David, to . . . to . . .' Her voice was soft and slow, almost tipsy. 'To sail along the surface of life, and not . . .'

'Plumb its depths?'

'No. Oh, I don't know. One philosophical statement's enough for one evening.'

The hushed clunking sound of a goods train slipped in and out of the still evening beyond the houses. One or two birds piped a few last messages of shrill morse among the apple trees.

'Well, you're my pleasure, and I don't have any control over you,' he said.

'Your only pleasure?' she said.

'Yes. You're all I want.' The words had a satisfying solidity in the shimmering quiet.

'I'll hold you to that,' she said after a moment.

The first night of *Carousel* he spent backstage, in case of problems with the scenery. There were none. The second night he joined the audience and watched from the auditorium, though at the last minute Ruth tried to dissuade him. 'I bet I look a prize idiot,' she said, confidence suddenly vanished. 'But I've seen you in rehearsal and you don't,' he said. 'Looks different from out there,' she said gloomily.

It did: he was surprised how good it looked. The two leads could both really sing, which helped. Roberta, as the second lead, was not much of a singer, but he grudgingly admitted to himself that she could act. It was a good choice of show, with its emphasis on the lyrical: the few choruses and dances worked less well. The thudding of feet on boards sometimes threatened to drown the orchestra, and massed voices – recognisably Midland even in chorus – gave the 'Bus – ' in 'June Is Bustin' Out All Over' a most un-American flatness. Ruth did not look a prize idiot; in fact he had difficulty picking her out amidst the identical costumes and wigs. It was a peculiar sensation to stare straight at her knowing she could not see him. The middle-aged man sitting next to him hummed along with all the numbers through his nose and clapped himself silly: David was amazed as the lights came up at the end of the first act to see the man had tears standing in his eyes.

During the intermission he bumped into Mrs Lacey whilst queuing in the bar. 'I didn't realise you were here, David,' she said.

He was going to say the same to her. She had a way of pre-empting your conversation: it had the effect, deliberate or not, of leaving you naked, unable to take refuge in prepared remarks.

'Can I get you a drink?'

'Small vodka please, no ice. I thought you might be backstage.'

'Not much for me to do there now,' he said.

'You're well out of it. I know what it'll be like, they'll all be running round like rabbits blaming each other.'

He bought the drinks. The bar was called the Hollywood Bar. It was painted aubergine and turquoise, with low plastic tables on a migraine carpet, and framed photographs of debatably 'stellar' stars like Vic Damone and June Allyson on the walls.

'I won't say shall we sit down, because there isn't anywhere,' Mrs Lacey said. 'It's going rather well, don't you think?'

'Marvellous.' It was not a word he would ever use.

'I always come to the second night. The first night's often

wobbly and the third night they're so pleased with themselves they overdo it.'

This light astringency pleased him. She smiled, and he saw again what a good-looking woman she was. Her hair, dark as Ruth's with only a touch of grey, was thick and waved: she wore little make-up.

'I imagine this must bring back memories for you,' he said.

'Oh, goodness, it does,' she said warmly, and he felt the glow of having said the right thing, like a child who makes a grown-up laugh at his joke. 'This place was a second home to me for a while. Of course when I think about it I realise what horribly stilted stuff we used to do. Enough to make one cringe. But then we did work hard. It was a new play every week or so, you know. And the Court Players were very popular then. Not so much as the pictures, of course, but still the theatre had a place in the town. And it was a small town then, in the fullest sense. Now, of course, there's that awful place by the river, all smoked-glass and girders . . .'

'The Warehouse,' he supplied.

She smiled. 'That's it. Pop groups and Japanese mimes and all those things that antagonise an old reactionary like me. I'd better hurry and finish this, they'll be starting again soon.' She grimaced. 'Whatever it is, it certainly isn't Smirnoff. Some sort of Spanish import perhaps. Or even Australian. Am I right, there are such things as Australian wines now? The spirit shudders.'

He found himself about to apologise, as if the cheapness of the vodka were his fault. His pint of bitter felt large and unwieldy in his hand.

'I knew your mother, David, did I tell you?'

'I – think Ruth mentioned it.'

'Long long time ago.' He was going to say, 'How did you meet?' but she anticipated him. 'When I say knew, it was through mutual acquaintances really. Like I say, it was a small town then. Now it's a . . . Hydra-headed monster. Who was it said that, I wonder?'

He was lost, and knew he must look it.

'You see a lot of Ruth,' she said.

'Yes. Do you mind?' At that moment there seemed no option but to be bold.

'The only thing I would mind would be Ruth's seeing a lot of someone who made her unhappy. And here the case is quite the opposite.'

Pleased as he was at this, something was pierced and deflated within him. The great triumph of alchemy that had conjured gold from the clinker of his life was a case amongst other cases.

'I think she's been good for you, too, David,' she said. Then she frowned and looked down, wryly, into her glass. 'I also think that was a patronising thing to say.'

'Not at all. I've learnt how to – well, all sorts of things. Take things as they come – play it by ear.' He was disgusted at his own inarticulacy.

Mrs Lacey nodded, understandingly. It was remarkable how, supremely resentful of her, you could also be grateful: full of mistrust, you yet felt she probably understood you as nobody else could. 'That's it,' she said. 'Play it by ear.'

That was all the drink he had that night, which made it all the more frustratingly inexplicable to find when he got up next morning, he had left his car headlights on all night. To get to work on time he had to borrow Nicholas's bicycle, and when he came out at five o'clock he found that the back tyre was as flat as his car battery had been.

He stood looking at it in a stupefied sort of way – it was years since he had had anything to do with bicycles – and he was still standing there as Jack Erskine's Cavalier drew up by the bike sheds.

'Oh dear, oh dear,' Erskine said leaning out of the window and grinning. 'You won't be able to give her a crossbar now.' He was in one of those desperately comic moods that alternated with black temper nowadays.

'Funny,' said David. He did not want to be late this evening: he would be backstage again, this time to attend the party after the performance.

'Don't suppose you've got a puncture repair kit. Too down-to-earth for you sensitive romantic types.' Music blared from his car stereo.

'It's not my bike,' David said with a deliberate flatness, for his head was thumping.

'Well, I'd offer you a lift, but I suppose you don't want to be seen with an oik like me.'

'That's right. Piss off.' It came out suddenly and surprisingly, a gout of bile, as bitter and irrevocable as actual vomit. Erskine revved his engine, saying something David could not catch, and drove off.

Afterwards it occurred to him that that bitching of Erskine's was par for the course for him, and that he was quite prepared to give him a lift. But it was done now. He walked to town and then queued for a bus at the station for half an hour. The bus was packed to the doors: he had to stand, and the heat was unbelievable, turning that uniquely stale bus-smell into a fetor. It was half-past six when he opened his front door. Nicholas was not there. He scribbled him a note about the bicycle and Blu-takked it to his room door. This was standing open and he looked in. The place was like a pigsty: there was even an old apple core on the carpet. He must remember to say something to him. He didn't want his mother's old room treated like a tip.

The performance had already started when he arrived, by taxi, at the Regal. When Ruth came off after the first scene he sought her out amongst the milling, sweating players and hurriedly tried to explain why he was late.

'Well, it doesn't matter.' Her make-up looked garish close to. 'God, that didn't go very well. Philip forgot a line and he couldn't hear the prompt. We all stood there like spare parts, you could have heard a pin drop. This damn wig's getting all caught up in the buttons at the back. Can you undo it for me?'

'What a terrible day,' he said, fiddling with the blonde stuff that felt like horsehair. 'I had to get a taxi here.' He felt impatient of the wig, knowing the real person underneath it and unable to reach her.

'Did you? There's some little kid crying all the time in the front rows. They shouldn't bring them that young. The music's too loud, it scares them.'

'There, it's out. I couldn't believe it when that tyre was flat as well.' His hands were not clean, he noticed: he had changed but had not had time for a shower or a wash. He felt grubby, and also superfluous. A man bumped into him in passing, and he gave him a look.

'The party's going to move on to Roberta's place,' she said. 'We're not really supposed to start boozing in here.' She had found a splinter of mirror and was rubbing at the smudges on her face with a tissue. He was full of desire for her, keen, inappropriate.

'Oh, Christ,' he said. 'It would have to be her place.'

'All right, you won't have to speak to her unless it's absolutely necessary.'

'I love you, you know,' he said, and offered to kiss her, but she said, 'Mm-mm, make-up,' and instead kissed him quickly on the cheek.

He didn't know quite what attention he wanted for his tale of misadventure, what hero's approbation he expected for the fact of having to come in a taxi; but it seemed she hadn't been listening to a word, and it fixed him in a bad mood, and for the rest of the performance he hung about backstage, at first getting in the way by accident and then, perversely, on purpose. How stupid it all was, a bunch of bank clerks and typists and fitters scurrying about in daft costumes and carrying on like it was the National Theatre or something.

It was Roberta who said to him, 'You all right, David?' when she found him sitting on a stray chair in the dressing-room passage. She put a hand on his shoulder, and for once he could not detect any irony.

'Just feeling like a spare part,' he said, unable to keep self-pity out of his voice.

'Well, you've done your share of work,' she said. 'You did it well, that's why you've got nothing to do now. There always used to be problems with our sets in the past, right at the last minute. Had to act in front of a plain flat once.'

Whatever prompted this, he was grateful: he was ready to accept any ally.

'You are coming on to my place after, aren't you?' she said.

'We'll cheer you up.' She smiled at him: it was the sort of smile that she had given him before, and only the abrasiveness between them stopped it short of flirtation. He closed that gap by giving her the same smile, with an exciting chill of treachery at his heart.

For the whole of the party, which started with a few bottles of cheap champagne and plonk in the dressing-rooms and moved on to beer and spirits and considerable drunkenness at Roberta's, it was rarely possible for him to be alone with Ruth. He should perhaps not have expected otherwise: the show had been a success, and by nature it had been a joint effort; she wanted to share in the general celebration. Roberta lived alone in a flat in the centre of town, above a physiotherapist's surgery, so there were no restrictions about noise. And it was very noisy. Crushed into the three smallish rooms, members of the cast shouted and shrieked and bellowed snatches of the songs with vulgar embellishments: 'You're a Queer One Julie Jordan' lent itself especially well to this. There was some sort of punch in plastic cups that had an aloe's bitterness and was probably very powerful; he began to drink a lot of it.

It was the poshest members of the company – the people from accountants' offices, the small executives who came from the Park Crescent world, or from the newer gentry that was taking root in the luxury development estates – who seemed the most rowdy and bawdy. Still in bits of costume, they cradled arms around each other in groups, faces red with laughter. An arm went convivially round David, drawing him into one of these caucuses, and he disengaged it, seeking the kitchen. Here he poured himself more of the punch: he did not feel the slightest bit drunk yet. While he stood there a youngish man with a boater perched on his head lurched in and grabbed at the edge of the sink with both hands, swaying. After a moment he looked up. 'Thought I was going to puke,' he said, with an expression of bewilderment and even disappointment.

'I know how you feel,' David said. Ruth came in shortly afterwards. There was a long paper streamer round her neck which he rather wanted to pluck off. 'This punch is strong,' she said. There was a floating sort of serenity about her that he knew meant she was very slightly tiddly. 'What are you doing in here?'

'Getting a drink,' he said, though it was obvious he wasn't. There was a renewed explosion of laughter from the living-room and a rising squeal of 'Don't you *dare*!'

'Haw haw old boy,' he said.

'Eh?'

He inclined his head towards the door. 'The bourgeois at play.'

'They're allowed to as well, aren't they?' she said lightly. She turned to go back.

He could not believe he was nearly thirty-six years old, so exactly like a child did he feel; importunate, irrational, unable to negotiate the world. 'Hey,' he said. 'We're not seeing much of each other, are we?'

'It's a party, sweetheart,' she said, putting a hand up to his face. 'Now don't be a pooper. Don't be a kitchen-hanger-abouter.'

'I wanted to talk to you,' he said – what about he didn't know, was only sensible of the longing, 'and I wanted to be with you because I love you and I don't love all these other people.'

'What a speech,' she said, and her eyes were amused.

'I'm glad you find it so funny.'

'Don't be so touchy. We'll have plenty of time to talk.' Roberta's voice called, 'Ruth! Come here.'

'You're being paged,' he said.

'How much have you had?'

He disliked this question and drained the metallic stuff in his cup. 'No more than those Hooray Henrys, why?'

She said nothing and went back into the living-room.

He waited in the passage for the toilet. The director, with his little beard and loopy eyes, was waiting too. 'David,' he said, and beckoned, leaning towards him and almost sliding right down the wall in the process. Pissed as a newt. 'Next year. You're going to do our set again.' His tone was hushed, ridiculously earnest.

'Am I?'

The director nodded vigorously. 'Beautiful,' he said. 'Magnificent. Not many things are,' he added with abrupt melancholy, looking at the floor. Silly old fart. The toilet door opened and Roberta came out. The director zoomed in, saying with a wave of his hand, 'Bladder!' Like a benediction: *Salut!*

'Aren't you enjoying yourself, David?' said Roberta. It was exactly the sort of thing she could say in a way that set his teeth on edge. But it seemed somehow different. 'Not particularly,' he said.

It was pretty rude, as she was the hostess, but she nodded and said: 'No, I'm not either. These things are always a bit forced.'

The director was emptying his salutation very noisily: there was a watery thundering behind the toilet door. It suddenly occurred to David that he did not know how old Roberta was. 'Your flat will be a mess in the morning,' he said.

'I know,' she said with a sigh. 'And what annoys me is it's always got to be at my place, never anybody else's.' The director emerged bashfully smiling, as if expecting a round of applause for his urinary Niagara.

Well, presumably it was her who suggested it. But perhaps the others took advantage, and she didn't like to say no. Magnanimity towards Roberta rose vaporously in him: he began to realise he was drunk as he found himself leaning his forehead on the old metal cistern while he peed. He performed the usual, utterly ineffective ritual of splashing cold water on his face to sober himself up: the stooping over the sink only made him more conscious of his intoxication. He was startled when he came out to find Roberta still there, waiting for him. 'What do you think of the flat?' she said.

'It's great,' he said. She looked very attractive, in the way that people do – rounded, dark-eyed, well-dressed, vulnerable – to eyes foxed with drink and frustration: the sort of eyes that create temporary cataracts to obscure imperfections, bad skin, crumbly toenails, the past and most especially the future.

'I used to share. Ruth says I still ought to, she says she'd find it too depressing on her own. But then she's still stuck there with her mother, how can she know?'

He nodded vigorously.

'Sometimes she's a bit too ready to give advice. Let's get another drink.'

Oh, it was flirting all right, and though when he saw her slopping drink into the cups he realised with a last spark of wakefulness that she was deeply, dangerously drunk, he went along with it. Even though hidden under the fog also was the suspicion that she was playing him off against Ruth, acting as a kind of maleficent go-between. Roberta fancied him, whatever the ambiguities behind it, and that was enough. (See. Other people do, you know, it is possible. I don't have to wait around until you deign to speak to me.)

'I don't really like half of these people here,' she said. A few minutes ago she had been shrieking along with them. 'I don't suppose you believe I get lonely, do you?'

'Why shouldn't I?'

'Because I'm not the sort of person people imagine as lonely.' She was already pouring more drink. 'I suppose you've heard all the – all about me and my boss.'

'I've heard some of the usual gossip.' How easy it was to be a hypocrite! It was like discovering you had a natural aptitude for something, a card game, skating.

'Well?' Her eyes were fixed on his in an earnest, smashed way.

'I think people should mind their own business when they don't know what they're talking about.' In the living-room someone had put on a record of *Carousel*, as if they weren't sick to death of it.

'So they should.' She was belligerent for a moment, then downcast. 'Not that it matters what rubbish they talk. If there was anything in it there certainly isn't now. Not any more.' She looked into her cup and then drained it.

'I'm sorry.' So absorbed was he in this game that he actually did feel sorry.

'Dear me, drowning of sorrows?' Ruth's voice was bright and caustic against their opaque mutterings. Roberta tilted the bottle once again and then held it towards her. Ruth shook her head. 'I was just boring David with my troubles. He's a good listener, you know, Ruth.'

'You weren't being boring,' he said.

'I'll go and rejoin the jollity,' Roberta said, looking at them both from under lowered lids. She took the bottle with her.

'You shouldn't encourage her,' said Ruth. Someone had plonked a straw boater on her head: she looked beautiful in spite of this, and somehow sharply-defined, like a line drawing against a wash. His chest heaved. 'What's that supposed to mean?' he said.

'She'll get completely plastered once she starts feeling sorry for herself. It's happened before. What else would it mean?'

'You tell me.' He knew at that moment that the row was here. You could ignore the signs for as long as you liked, but in the end it was no good trying to fool yourself: it was like feeling sick, and trying to ignore it, and then thinking perhaps you are going to be sick, but no, it was a false alarm, and then in that fraction of a second before you open your mouth and the vomit spews out you *know*, with serene, perfect certainty.

'God knows what's got into you, David, but I tell you I'm not going to let it spoil my night.'

'Obviously not. I'm surprised you even remembered I'm here. But oh yes, you soon came barging in when I talked to someone else instead of waiting for you in a corner while you hammed it up with the Rotary Club or whoever the fuck they are.'

Her expression was more of distaste than anything. 'I was well aware of what you were up to.'

Fear seized him in the midst of rage. 'Look, you don't think there was anything – Roberta – '

'If I thought that was anything but a childish little plea for attention, anything serious, do you think I'd even be *speaking* to you now?' A low voice, but the effect was as stunning as if she had yelled. She bypassed red heat and went straight to white.

'I've had too much to drink,' he said, but not with contrition. The director came swaying amiably into the kitchen, looked at them, and swayed out again, holding on to things as he went like a man on a tossing ship.

'Well drink some water or eat something and sober up a bit,' she said.

'No,' he said, 'let's go. I've had enough of this do anyway.'

'Well I haven't,' she said. He could not look at her, but she was looking at him steadily. If he was ready to retract, she certainly wasn't. 'This is a big night and I've been looking forward to it. I'm not going home yet.'

'Well I am.'

She raised an eyebrow slightly and shrugged. 'That's up to you.'

There were a few taxis left in the cathedral square. With a half-full bottle of wine that he had taken from the party he slumped in the back of one and as he rode home he inspected the wreckage of the day, his mind fearfully turning the pieces over in dread of finding something much more valuable shattered amongst them. Once the Pakistani driver turned and said, 'Are you all right?'

'No,' he said, swigging from the bottle.

The darkness of his house oppressed him: he went round switching on lights, and then he stormed up the stairs because he wanted to shout at someone, and Nicholas would do. That filthy room. If he was asleep he would wake him up.

Nicholas's light was on anyway. David banged open the door. He found Nicholas lying on the floor with another young man who had his shirt off.

'What the bloody hell's this?' said David. His voice sounded surprisingly normal.

'What does it look like?' said Nicholas. He looked embarrassed, but within bounds: the other young man just looked terrified.

He threw them out, more or less. The young man – not Bez, but a good-looking youth with spiky black hair – scooted out with no need of encouragement, scrabbling his shirt on; Nicholas protested, swore, joked, attempted to reason, and was finally half-bundled out of the front door, and only then seemed to realise that David was serious and cried, 'Where on earth am I going to go?' before the door closed. David, meanwhile, had heard himself swearing, and shouting, and sobbing: 'Not in my house you don't . . . how can you . . . go on, get out . . . how dare you . . . my mother's room . . . my mother's room . . .': delirious, dream-like with fury and miserable frustration, shocked to find that the sight had shocked and also obscurely excited him, and stinking drunk. He was crooning snatches of 'June Is Bustin' Out All Over' when he fell asleep on his bed.

CHAPTER 13

If the man in the bath-chair at the end of the Arcade has a name, nobody seems to know it. He never says much beyond 'Ta', when you give him money for the shoelaces and pipe-cleaners and odds and ends that he sells, and it follows that nobody knows how he lost both his legs. There is also a certain mystery about where he goes at night. The popular supposition is that he simply sleeps in his chair in the Arcade. This in 1945 is spruce and busy (forty years on it will be known as the Old Arcade, to differentiate it from several new arcades of mirror-glass and steel, named after local celebrities, and will be a shabby place down which a mournful wind blows hamburger wrappers) and contains select little barber-shops and jewellers, and as such the archaic and unattractive figure in the chair might seem to be out of place. But he is so familiar that only visitors to the town give him a stare, and he takes no notice of that.

Neither does he seem to take any notice of the flags that suddenly break out like a rash one May day all along the Arcade and across the cathedral square beyond the entrance: though a few little Union Jacks appear on his tray of goods, to be eagerly bought: perhaps, in its circumscribed way, a nose for business is the chief sense that remains to this silent, immobile figure. He never goes further than The Greyhound across the square, where he parks his chair outside rather than struggle to steer it into the bar, and where the barman always brings him out his pint of mild; but if he did go further, he would see those flags all over the town, hanging from windows, strung across the narrow streets, pinned to front doors. And if he were an individual involved in the current of historical time, rather than moored arbitrarily in it, he might perceive that these flags mark the end of something else. They themselves are already part of the past, a time when every household has a flag to display. Some indeed have several flags: against the dull grey brick of sooty terraces Union Jacks dangle alongside the Stars and Stripes, the hammer and sickle and the tricolour, bright primary colours for bright primary emotion. On the front of one house an enthusiastic old lady has hung the flags of the allies saved from the First World War, and so the Rising Sun of Japan flutters there, whilst Mrs Russell, joining in the street party at Corporation Road, maintains a ceaseless inward prayer that her son Joe be all right, whilst his body has lain for six months in the graveyard of a Japanese prisoner-of-war camp in Burma.

And this is the tenor of many of the hopes that find noisy and tearful expression across the town amongst the flags and the parties: that the Family can now reassert the primacy temporarily overshadowed by the Nation, the West, Democracy, Freedom and a progression of more nebulous ideals. But for the man in the Arcade this, like so much else, would seem to be irrelevant. Dispossessed, he might be called, him and others like him: but perhaps it is an innaccurate word for those who slip through the fibres of life separate from warp or woof. And perhaps the fact people do not notice him is not down to familiarity, or to a pained shunning of disability, but is like an aversion of the eyes from a naked body: a state so single, so unconnected, is as shocking as nudity.

Now the war is over Harold Barber mourns the death of his father, who collapsed in his shop a week before VE Day, his activities as ARP warden – as well as everything else he could volunteer for – finally taking their toll on the bad Barber health, a strain that will only end with Harold's two children; whilst Ethel begins to inspect furnishings for the new house, not with much success, for the word Utility will soon become common; whilst Frank Russell returns from his base to

Corporation Road, an unscathed hero, and is restless, and in the local pubs regales sceptical railwaymen with stories of his flights over Germany and drinks himself blind, wistful for the concentrated excitement which, if it had gone on any longer, would have shattered his nerves for good, and finally marries on impulse a girl he hardly knows, whom he will make unhappy for the next thirty years; whilst Mr Russell rejoices at the election of the Labour government, and privately grieves for Joe, whom he has long believed will not come back; whilst Jeanette welcomes back her fiancé Reg, full of tales of the Western Desert, and marries him immediately; and Aldyth leaves the Land Army and returns briefly and unhappily to Corporation Road before taking the unprecedented step of going to share a flat with two other girls who are clearly incorrigibly bohemian from the simple fact that they live in one.

Changes, great changes, as shattering in their impact on these families as the bombs that have made a cratered mess of Europe; but there remain those like the man in the bath-chair who are impervious, as he will be impervious to the new bout of changes to the town in which he exists. It will grow again, not on some easy organic principle, but shooting up in leaps and starts like a gawky child. Ancient hamlets in its hinterland, uselessly protesting like small nations before a benevolent civic Reich, will be swallowed up by its estates: the hooters of the old factories will sound meekly in the shade of faceless office blocks: the name of the town will appear in advertisements, alongside other products, and there will be a kind of inverse colonialism, as the railways come to be run almost entirely by Asians, and the Central Library will contain shelves of Fiction in Hindi and Urdu: the dirty stone of the cathedral will be scourged and an acquisitive antiquarianism will canonise little old disregarded buildings and slap plaques on them, to the surprise of the dwindling number of town-natives, who had never spared them a second glance.

He will not be there to see, or not see, all of them, but he is there, in his usual place, in December 1951, when Vi passes him. She is on her first visit to the town, and has come from Nottingham for the day to see her friend Aldyth.

She is a smartly-dressed young woman, Vi, with real fur trimming on her coat collar and sleeves: she was never short herself, and the man she wrote to throughout the war and married after it is now a partner in the firm. But the overlay of a certain severity on her pretty features is merely another inheritance from her parents, and she is still as disingenuous as when she perched on a tractor in the Lincolnshire emptiness, and basically timid: she had to pluck up courage to ask a passer-by the way to Lacey's department store.

It was her husband who indirectly suggested this visit. 'Whatever became of that other land-girl you were friends with?' he asked the other night when they were reminiscing over the war. Vi thought of their letters, ever shorter and ever more infrequent, and felt guilty. A brief telephone-call – Aldyth as coolly friendly as if they had last met just yesterday – and they arranged to meet for lunch on her half-day.

A chill wind is whipping round the corners of the shopping streets: there are Christmas trees and lights in the windows. The spires of the cathedral reach up to a bitter iron-grey sky. Vi stops a moment to admire them, and thinks how wonderful it must be to go to the Christmas service there. But then she supposes that is not the sort of thing to interest Aldyth.

She is relieved to see that Lacey's is so large and impressive and decorous. She is not, she earnestly hopes, a snob like her mother, but some instinctive residue within her had caused a little perplexed recoil when she first learnt that Aldyth was working in a store. 'A shopgirl' – a catchall of disapproval for her mother. But of course, she tells herself, lots of women have found their wartime usefulness abruptly disregarded, ending up slotted back into second-string occupations, with marriage the only alternative. And Aldyth – she must be nearly thirty now – is still single.

Vi ascends in a clanking lift to the third floor of Lacey's unbuttoning her coat. It is warm in the store, with a pleasantly stolid smell of varnish and thick carpeting. Even if she isn't married, perhaps Aldyth has settled down a bit. She thinks of that American airman who was killed . . . such a pity, she thought he was terribly nice, though there was always something about the Americans – no 'bottom' her father might say – which she had been dubious about. Anyway, after him it had really started; Aldyth got a reputation, even amongst the land-girls who were often pretty easy-going. Vi would always defend her – not that Aldyth gave a damn. That was what was so striking: plenty of girls would brazen it out as if they didn't care – but Aldyth really meant it.

A floorwalker points her towards china and glass: and the sight of Aldyth produces, though Vi despises herself for it, a certain relief for she looks very respectable. (Well, whatever were you expecting, little prig, Madonna of the Seven Moons? she tells herself crossly.)

Intensely respectable, in fact: a dark grey suit of anonymous sobriety, black hair up, no jewellery. She is patiently helping an old gentlewoman choose between two cut-glass fruit-bowls, neither of which, it is obvious, she is going to buy. Vi pretends to look at some china figurines, whilst struggling inwardly to overcome her shock: not at the respectability – in a store like this, after all, it is mandatory – but at Aldyth's enhanced beauty, which had struck her almost with furtive embarrassment, as if she had arrived at a party in a comfy frock to find it is formal dress. Any trace of skittishness, of prettiness indeed, in Aldyth's looks has gone: the beauty is mature, a painting in which one more brush-stroke would spoil everything, and the word pretty would almost be an insult.

'Vi! Sorry I kept you waiting. You're looking well!'

Vi is thrown into such deprecating confusion at having her own looks mentioned that she stammers and can only say 'Aldyth.'

'Have a good journey? What's the time – five to, well, I'm off in five minutes, we can pretend you're buying something till then. I'm not supposed to talk to people, except to say Yes madam, no madam, three bags full madam. Did you see that old crow? She's often in, never buys anything, just wastes your time. I don't think she's got two pennies to rub together really.'

Vi, conscious of the fact that she was always the talkative one, strives for something to say. 'It's been such a long time. Five years, isn't it?'

Aldyth nods, smiling. 'And you a married woman.' And though she says this with no irony, Vi feels almost ashamed, as if she had compromised herself. She begins to look distractedly along the glass cabinets. 'I think I ought to buy a little something while I'm here,' she says. 'There are some lovely things . . .'

'Oh, Lord, you don't want to buy this junk. There's a little shop in Priestgate that's much better, cheaper too.' Aldyth laughs, a low discreet version of the laugh that Vi remembers. Vi feels a little more at ease.

A man steps out of the lift as they get into it, and after a fractional hesitation says 'Morning' to Aldyth. He is tall and elegantly dressed, youngish but going slightly grey. 'We'll go to Peel's,' says Aldyth. 'Big portions there. I'm always starving at this time – still can't eat breakfasts.'

'Who was that distinguished-looking man, do you know?' says Vi.

Aldyth smiles, seemingly into space, before turning and resting the tail-end of the smile on Vi. 'I ought to, he pays my wages.'

'Oh, your boss?'

'Well, ultimately. That's Mr Lacey – Mr Lacey junior, really, though he's the one in charge. His father's pretty well retired.'

'I say, what a good-looking chap.'

Aldyth smiles again. 'Don't get excited, Vi. He's taken, I'm afraid.'

In Peel's tea-rooms they talk about their life in the Land Army, and they laugh together as they used to, so that Vi, who is vulnerable to nostalgia, feels herself transported back to that time of dreary darkness that now seems rather romantic and monotonous labour that now seems rather heroic and tense gaiety that now seems rather hilarious. 'The funny thing is,' she says, 'that I'm the most hopeless gardener. Our garden is just nettles, as far as the eye can see. Charlie's started to say he doesn't believe I ever was on the land, he says I'm just making it up.'

'Are you happy with Charlie?' Aldyth comes out with this, not rudely but directly: it is an Aldyth Vi recognises, but in peacetime, without the hothouse forcing that war gave to such confidence, it seems an overly confrontational question. For Vi there is almost a whiff of impiety about it – how can she be unhappy with Charlie, she asks herself unhappily: it is an inquiry that delves in ground that, though she did not consecrate it, she respects as consecrated. 'Oh, yes,' she says. 'Everything turned out for the best. And what about you – ' only her discomfort could make her brave enough to dare this ' – no thoughts about marriage?'

'Only unrepeatable ones,' says Aldyth quickly, drinking her coffee: then she seems to relent and adds, 'No, that's not fair. Let's just say I haven't got tired of being single. Perhaps I will eventually.'

'And how's your sister? The one I met, Ethel?'

'Oh, didn't I tell you? She's made me an auntie. Last winter, a boy.'

'How lovely!'

Aldyth raises her eyebrows. 'You could say that. I don't like the idea of auntiehood myself. Not that I have to do anything about it. I'm pretty well out of bounds as far as my family are concerned.'

'That's a shame,' says Vi.

'Depends how you look at it. I'm going to have another cake.' There is something in Aldyth so assured – not brittle or cold, but formidable – that makes Vi feel disadvantaged, as if she were attempting to bargain with someone in possession of something obviously priceless. 'You seem – quite content at Lacey's,' she ventures.

'It's not too bad. Have to take what you can get.'

'And – the money, I mean . . . ?' Vi experiences a genteel diffidence about the subject. She is just beginning to realise with distaste how far she has slipped back into a mousy prissiness since peacetime.

'It's rotten of course. More than I was getting at the railway offices, but not much. I suppose I was vaguely expecting to go back to an office job, but for most of them you need shorthand and typing. I thought of taking a course at the college.'

'But . . . ?'

'But I didn't.' Aldyth smiles suddenly, broadly, as if catching sight of Vi sitting there for the first time. 'That coat's lovely. You got it from London, I should think.'

'Oh, yes.' In a confusion of admiration and dim guilt, Vi almost feels like handing it to Aldyth, it would look so much better on her.

'You can't get really good clothes here,' says Aldyth without rancour. 'Let's go for a drink.'

She leeds Vi into the bar of the Bull Hotel across the street. Vi was going to demur, but thought better of it. It is just so long since she had been into a pub – not since the war in fact. So many things she has got out of the habit of, without noticing.

'Oh – not in here – the lounge,' Aldyth says. 'Some of the men from Lacey's come in here sometimes. Won't do to be thought a pub-crawler on top of everything else.'

'Why, they're surely not that stuffy about things, are they?'

'Poor Vi,' says Aldyth, not unkindly, with a shake of her head. 'You haven't worked in a place like Lacey's.'

'Well – ' Vi bursts out in a little flurry of shame and vexation – no-one likes to suspect they are being laughed at – 'really, why do you put up with it?'

They sit at a table by the fire, amongst potted palms and heavy chenille curtains with tassels and pier-glasses that yield a spotty reflection: on the walls are prints of galleons at sea rendered abstract by the dirt of years, and a flock wallpaper gone shiny like the seat of an old suit.

'Sorry, that was a silly thing to say,' says Vi. But Aldyth smiles again, the smile of overwhelming attractiveness, so that Vi smiles shyly back. 'Don't be daft,' Aldyth says. And they talk some more about the old days. Aldyth rapidly polishing off several whiskies: 'D'you remember your Scotch, at the farm, how it was the only thing that kept us warm at night?' she says, and Vi nods and laughs, still choking on the burning sourness of her first – Charlie does not approve of women drinking, and she has lost the taste: but she gets it down, and is warmed, and talks about her smart house in Nottingham, a red villa with a conservatory and a splendid parquet-floored hall and all mod cons, but impossible to heat upstairs, and Aldyth is good-naturedly envious; until Vi falls quiet, drowsy with the whisky and the heat of the fire, and muses on whether she can tell Aldyth also how the house sometimes makes her feel like a prisoner, and she wanders in it from room to room, like someone who has lost something they don't really expect to find, and how all the fun seems to have gone out of Charlie, who has become pompous, and endures caresses restively, like a cat intent on something else; and various other things, which she wonders if Aldyth will understand . . . She thinks perhaps she will, too well. Aldyth is looking at her with a patient speculation, as if to say she is quite prepared to listen, but will not smooth the path for her. Vi talks about plans for Christmas.

Vi stands on the platform at the North station, waiting for the four o'clock train. She will be glad to get back, in a way. It went off well, really, better than she had thought: she was afraid they might have nothing to say to each other. And when they said goodbye, after a brief hesitation they kissed and hugged warmly, and for a moment they were back in the dream-like loneliness of the war, when emotions were written large and luminous, and people seemed simply important, impinging on one's life with a directness that is gone. Vi flinches at the wind that roams, vicious and lost, across the cold spaces of the station. But Aldyth is now a person of remoteness, engaging and solid as a character in a play on the stage, but just as inaccessible. Vi realises, with a rare certitude, that they will not meet again. She pulls up the fur collar of her coat, willing the train to come. It is quite a nice town really, not so very different from Nottingham, but it does not feel welcoming. She has a feeling – something like seeing that poor man with no legs in the Arcade – of not belonging. And she needs to belong – even in the loveless household to which she is returning – as it seems Aldyth, supremely, does not.

In the window of Fairlie's, the big toyshop, a curlicued sign says, 'Come and meet Father Christmas'. Aldyth thinks of the Father Christmas at Lacey's, who is incomprehensibly Czechoslovakian and as thin as a rake under the padding, and smiles. She walks down the alley at the back of Fairlie's to the Odeon car park, where a gleaming Wolseley is waiting. The engine revs as the driver sees her.

Whoever is the more nervous – and there is a strangely exaggerated relaxation in Aldyth's body as she sinks into the musty leather seat – it is John Lacey whose breathing is so noisy and who scrabbles in a silver case for a cigarette before starting off. There is silence but for the stertorous throbbing of the big car's engine until they have left the city centre behind: it is as if they are afraid to speak with the town landmarks pressing round, church cupolas and the pillars of the town hall and the corn exchange and cathedral gates and cinemas and Lacey's department store, listening like the trees of an enchanted wood in a fairy-tale.

At last Mr Lacey pulls up in a quiet road that runs beside the cemetery on the east side of the town. With hands still shaking he lights a fresh cigarette from the stub of the old one.

'You might offer me one of those,' Aldyth says.

He looks at her in a startled way, as if he had forgotten she was there. He has eyes of a pellucid shadowless blue, that look out perennially young and veracious from a lean face. 'I'm sorry,' he says. He gives her a cigarette and she cups her hand round his as he holds out a match. He stops shaking then and with a quick movement raises her hand to his lips and kisses the inside of her fingers. For a moment they both look away. 'Did you meet your friend?' he says in a flattened voice.

'Yes.'

'Nice time?'

'Very nice. She hasn't changed a bit.'

He has taken her hand again, and is holding it with a desperate tightness, so that the fingertips go red, but he does not look at her. 'That's good. Often don't work at all, those reunions.' He gives an apologetic little laugh. 'As I sat there just now, I suddenly started thinking, "Perhaps she won't come this time".'

'Did you?' She frames the syllables with an odd hesitation, like someone short of breath. 'And were you relieved when I did? Or would you have been relieved if I didn't?'

He frowns and shakes his head and squeezes her hand again, as at an absurd question. 'There would be an element of relief if you hadn't come, of course,' he says. 'All over. Problem solved. But then there would be another problem.'

'What?'

'How to live without you.' He says it in a vehement, choking voice, looks at her and looks away again, hurling his cigarette out of the window.

Cold moisture is glistening on the car bonnet. The winter evening is coming down swiftly, the fogged darkness stretching like gauze over the cemetery. The mossy tombstones for a few minutes stand out pure and pearly, memories of whiteness.

'You don't have to live without me,' Aldyth says. 'That's the point of this, isn't it?'

'I suppose so.' His eyes rove helplessly over the dashboard, as if he cannot imagine what these dials and switches are for. 'Is there anywhere we can go?'

She shakes her head. 'One of the girls is bound to be at the flat by now.'

The windscreen is steaming up. He wipes it with his glove. 'I suppose this is the point where one of us ought to say "We can't go on like this".' He laughs softly. His is a quiet tenor voice, unaccustomed to irony, unaccustomed to being raised.

'We've said that enough times. But we've got to go on, haven't we.' This is not inflected as a question.

'Yes, we've got to.' He runs his hand through his hair, the

stiff and bushy kind that often goes with early greying. 'I wonder, if things had been different – '

'Things would have been different.' She disengages her hand and allows it to cover his, restlessly, her fingers mapping and touching it, like the heightened thoroughness of the blind. 'It might have been me who's married, we might both have been, we might have been pushed together with all the blessings of the world on us. And it still would have been the same. If we can't see that, then we're nowhere.'

He stares at her and then, as if the sight is too much for him to bear, looks away. 'And the fact remains that I've got a wife and a child and another on the way and I'm not free,' and there is a straining sing-song in his voice, as of someone chanting a code that they fear is slipping out of memory.

'Neither am I. I could get run over by a bus tomorrow. There's nothing I can do to stop it. I have to work, I need money, because I have to eat, it goes on and on. Nobody's any more free than anybody else. Where there's no choice, like whether or not to breathe, it's simple. Where there are choices, you make one, it's simple too.'

He turns to her, about to say something, and sees for the first time the shining agitation in her flushed face, the coiled tautness of her still body, the words that seem so insouciant spinning out of her in desperate release. His mouth is dry. 'The choice has been made, hasn't it?' he says. He leans over to kiss her. She puts her hands to his face, and they hold each other, chilled, trembling, wordless; and lost.

A few last shoppers are hurrying down the Arcade as the winter afternoon dims and the cold is pitched higher and sharper like a string tuned to snapping-point. Wrapped in muffler and cap, the man in the bath-chair stays put, counting his change. His breath steams but the cold seems not to affect him. It is a fruitless question, whether he knows love, whether that imperviousness of his extends to what the couple in the car by the cemetery feel: but certainly, so apart and unconnected as he is, he might understand what they are just beginning to: the utter isolation of desire.

*

Once when David was about seven or eight the son of the old lady who lived three doors away was killed in a road accident. The morning after they heard the news he saw from the window the old lady walking her dog as she always did, looking stooped but otherwise just the same, and he had craned excitedly to look at her saying, 'There she is!', so interested was he to see the person caught up in such a drama. His mother had given him a very angry telling-off and it was just about the only occasion he could remember her really smacking him. But it was not this that made the incident memorable, but the fact that for the first time he was troubled with genuine guilt. He was familiar with feeling bad like any child after being naughty and being punished, but this time he realised what he had done: the actual thought of it pricked him and made him cringe, rather than the thought of the punishment. It was the beginning of the age of embarrassment.

And that was an age you never grew out of. Groggy, dreadfully hung over, tasting sourness on his own breath, his face whey-coloured and unshaven, he felt exactly the same as that little child, chastened, admitting everything. As he washed he avoided catching his own eye in the bathroom mirror.

He was surprised, then unsurprised, to see Nicholas calmly eating toast in the kitchen.

'You look terrible,' he said.

'Any tea in that pot?' His voice was husky, as if he had been to a party and smoked too much and had to shout because it was so noisy. Which he had.

'Should be a drop.' Nicholas was probably enjoying this, but then he was probably entitled to.

'I feel terrible.' The tea was stewed but he gulped it thirstily. 'Not just physically. You know.' He felt too weary to say any more. Nicholas gave him a wry glance and applied himself to his toast.

The sun was streaming in: it would be another hot day. The kitchen looked shabby and grimy as rooms kept with a minimum of housework look in the brightness of morning.

'How did you get in?' David said, staring without seeing at the paper.

'Well, I do have a door key, you know. That's how I usually get in and out. Weird, I know. And you were too – how shall I put it – pissed out of your brain to put any bolts on, if you really meant that I should never darken your doorstep et cetera.'

'Christ, I didn't know what I was doing.' He closed his eyes against the light. He wished he could shut out memory too. 'What time did you come back?'

'Oh, it wasn't long, but you'd obviously crashed out by then. I just walked Mark home, and – '

'Mark?'

'That's his name. Don't tell me you've forgotten him as well.'

'Oh, your friend.' For a ridiculous moment he had thought of his new nephew and imagined the little figure toddling down the street. He was in that reptilian stupid state where even the fact that two people in the world can have the same name bounces dully off the consciousness.

'Uh-huh. And still no more than a friend yet, thanks to you.' There was no belligerence in Nicholas's tone, but there was a kind of defiant invitation, as if he were testing David for reaction.

'Look . . . I was in a bit of a state last night, so – '

'I could see that. It's all right,' said Nicholas cheerfully. Whether something had been permanently undermined between them could not be discerned, yet: Nicholas was clearly making allowance for the fact that he was still wretchedly fuddled.

'I'm going to have to make some more apologies before the day's out.'

Nicholas got up, looking healthy and raring to go, and perhaps playing a little on that also. 'I guessed that too.'

It was Saturday, but he had to work that morning, for he had been stretching his flexitime to snapping point, and Musson had been on to him about it: besides, he was in the mood for hair-shirts. Someone came round the office selling tickets for the works' centenary dance next week, and gloomily he bought two, as he had intended: whether this was tempting fate or the other way round he could not work out. At dinner-time he rang Ruth's, but there was no answer.

Mr Carelli recharged his car battery for him. The Carelli garage, he noticed, was cleaner than his own kitchen: there were strips of well-hoovered carpet round the edges, and a picture of the Pope on the wall. He found a restful comfort in talking to Mr Carelli, who had no opinions about him, or if he did kept them to himself. Afterwards he went to pick up Nicholas's bicycle and to do the shopping in town. In Tesco's he embraced frugality as another penance, and fought with the old ladies for the knocked-down meat pies. In the cathedral square he queued for a call-box, while the drunks and nutters on the benches waved their bottles of cider at him and loudly accused him of being the murderer of their sisters: there was no answer again.

At a loss, he wandered into the city museum, where there was an exhibition of watercolours by the Norwich school. He walked round for twenty minutes, liking their monotonous dexterity: it was as soothingly pleasant as a drive through Norfolk countryside. When he came to the last room he saw from the corner of his eye Mrs Lacey seated on the banquette across the other side. He studied the painting in front of him, debating whether it was possible to escape, but she was looking straight at him.

'David,' she called, as he turned: if she could see he was acting, she was playing along. She patted the seat beside her.

'Nice, aren't they?' The word was slightly mocking and also appropriate. 'A bit parochial perhaps.'

'I suppose they're not meant to be anything else.' Oh, come on, he thought, get it over with.

'I gather the party after the show was rather riotous,' she said. She left a pause that indicated he didn't have to say anything if he didn't want to, and went on: 'Ruth was looking somewhat the worse for wear this morning. She's always been sensible about drink, and I didn't say anything – of course the position is rather difficult, what with Gordon's problem, as you know.'

He hadn't thought of Ruth herself being queasy and regretful: this gave him such an injection of hope that he only obliquely noticed Mrs Lacey's acknowledging Gordon's 'problem' for the first time. 'I didn't feel too clever myself this morning,' he said cautiously. 'I – tried to ring Ruth earlier, but there was no answer.'

'She's gone out. Where I don't know. Often she goes off sketching somewhere. Comes back and more often than not throws what she's done in the bin. I used to think this was done for – well, shall I say dramatic effect?' Her eyes crinkled attractively. She had a good tan from the summer already: she had the sort of skin that responds to the sun. 'But now I don't know. She's got this very low opinion of herself, you see: or, well, her self-image is very vulnerable, if that doesn't sound too modern and social-workerish. That self-possession of hers has been very carefully acquired.'

He was unprepared for such confidences, and groping for their import said, 'Oh, really?' which was not a very helpful response.

'Well, whatever the trouble was last night, I'm sure it wasn't that serious. I would have been able to tell from Ruth if it was.' She smiled at him.

'She didn't say anything, then?'

Mrs Lacey touched his arm with a finger. 'When you've lived with someone for thirty years, you get to read them like a book.' She had the knack, always disarming, of saying banal things with a flicker of irony, so that you believed they were not banal.

'I'm afraid I didn't behave very well last night. Made a bit of a fool of myself.'

She shrugged. 'That's between the two of you. She'll soon tell you if you did. She even ticks *me* off.' With a little wave of her hand, as if admitting the weakness of the moment of humour and dismissing it, she went on: 'The thing is, when that confidence of hers does get destroyed it gets destroyed utterly. In many ways Ruth's had it very easy, and in another way very hard. With her father leaving like that – '

'I thought he was dead?' said David, in one of those outbursts as unpreventable as a sneeze, little seizures of stupidity.

'He is. But we were separated when Ruth was very small.'

'Oh – I'm sorry.'

'I don't imagine it's something she talks much about. Anyway, suffice to say she didn't grow up in the – happy environment a child should.'

Ruth as a child – it was no good, he still could not picture it.

'So what I mean is she's really incredibly vulnerable. She's never considered things as her right – even things that are.'

'Well, I'd hate to think I've made her unhappy,' he said, a little impatient of what she was driving at, and delicately fired anew by the thought of Ruth.

'Oh, tiffs. Everybody has them. I'm not worried about that, and don't you be. Remember, I know she can be difficult too.' She gave a serene smile here, as of having given a gratuity gracefully, then she got out a handkerchief from her bag and to David's surprise dabbed at his chin. 'A little crumb, I think,' she said. With the sudden reviving of hunger following a hangover, he had been scoffing a packet of crisps before he came in. Her action was the sort of thing Ruth did, the sort of lovers' nonsense, like both drying your hands in the same towel or playing footsie under the table, that he frankly delighted in. At the same moment he descried the outlines of a warning, draped by the reasonable friendliness of her words, but bulking unmistakably. Resenting this, he said: 'How is Gordon, by the way?'

She sighed, and for the first time he had made her avoid his eyes, instead of the other way round. 'I can't pretend it's something I understand,' she said. 'But one must give him all the support one can. He's still my son whatever happens.' She spoke with emphasis. A closing of ranks, while he had drifted in here, solitary, with crumbs on his chin.

He nodded, and remembered, mundanely, that he had

frozen food in the shopping-bag that he had left at the desk. He mentioned this and said he had to be going. Only afterwards did he reflect that it sounded like a terribly lame trumped-up excuse; but she had accepted it, as if truth and falsehood, in that regard, were all one to her.

He phoned again when he got home, with no luck. Feeling the need for some such emotional wallpaper, he played his favourite, most sentimental country-and-western records; but he soon got tired of them – all that stuff about loving and losing, which could melt him when he was really quite content, seemed now simply a cop-out – and turned them off. Only as he stood at the window staring out at his jungle of a garden, where in spite of his negligence a few vagrant flowers had appeared like kind thoughts in a bad mood, was he afflicted by a bona fide sadness, tinted with prescience: the lovely summer, so seamlessly lovely as to be untrustworthy, would end. An idyll, perhaps – and so perhaps everything about it would fade. 'And it was all a dream'. Alice waking up to find the vivid creatures only chess-pieces. Perhaps it was as finite and treacherous as the school holidays he and Ruth had talked about, when he and his friends played rounders in the rec every day, all day, oblivious; and then you were taken to town to get a new blazer, and the evenings got cooler, and you started to wonder what your new teacher would be like. Reality, always sticking its nose in: nothing so dramatically immediate as a slap in the face or cold water or the usual images, but breaking out small and irritating like a rash on your body, until you have to stop pretending it's heat or acne, and admit there's something wrong.

The telephone rang, a shrill sceptical sound.

It was Ruth; and it was all right. He talked to her – on the phone and half an hour later when she came round – in clogged, halting phrases, all the time feeling – like someone who comes down in the morning and finds they have left the gas on all night – both grateful and propitiatory, resolving in honour of the god who has spared them never to let it happen again.

'I was going to have a go at you,' she said. She was wearing jeans and a T-shirt: unlike her mother, she was still pale-skinned despite the sun, and it suited her.

'What changed your mind?' he said. He did not want to push his luck but, still full of penitence, he did not want to slimily evade anything that he had coming to him.

'Oh, I don't know.' She lolled in an armchair, with her legs over the side. 'Perhaps I still might. No, you were in a foul mood anyway, looking for a fight, it wasn't just me. If it had been I wouldn't be sitting here now.' It was a light, clear reproof, and they understood each other.

'That'll never happen,' he said. As if in deference to the laid ghost of discord, they were still sitting some distance apart, with a careful casualness.

'Besides,' she yawned and stretched, 'I'm on holiday now till September. You forget what good holidays us teachers have, as the *Daily Mail* never tires of pointing out. So I just want to be lazy and happy.'

'That's not much to ask.'

She looked at him round the corner of her uplifted arm, and smiled. They both smiled. 'And I'm too lazy to come over there. So you come here and be told off.'

A person who applied a strong control over her own life, Ruth was also, he began to realise, often willing to let it slip into a sort of overdrive: highly diligent and responsible within limits she had set herself, beyond those limits she submitted to a law of the arbitrary. It was extremely likeable, but also disturbing. She had sometimes taken him to task for his lack of ambition, about which he made no bones – such ambitions as he had were of a cloudy romantic sort, with no more relevance to the everyday than the possibility of an afterlife; but whereas it was she, if anyone, who thought about her job in terms of the word 'career', she frankly admitted to a kind of fatalism about futures. On the hottest days they had taken a blanket and a bottle of lemonade down by the river, and she had lain there, curling up and uncurling, and said she could stay there for ever, delivering herself up to the temporary as he never could. Understanding this – if that was what it was – seemed to him to stiffen his love for her, toning up its pliant, sentimental limbs, imbuing it with a stamina that would never fail.

He thought of what her mother had said to him earlier that day, and as it happened Ruth had the sketches she had done today in her car. He insisted she fetch them so he could look. He tried for once to still the feeling of plain envy that glimpses of her work gave him – it was so gormless and childish to say, 'I wish I could draw like that' – and make some constructive comment instead. But she was impatient. 'Yes, they're all right I suppose,' she said. 'But it's only actually doing them that's enjoyable. Once it's done you don't want to have anything more to do with it. There's enough pictures in the world already.'

When later they lay, limbs cooling, on his bed, he told her in a sudden wordy rush – she had once said that post-coital sadness was replaced in his case by verbal diarrhoea – about what had happened with Nicholas last night.

'Not as broad-minded as you thought, then, eh?' she said.

'No. I suppose that's it,' he said. He had wished almost immediately that he hadn't brought it up: the memory of that seemed more contorted with pain than the memory of their row last night. He blurted into the darkness: 'I think it was more jealousy than anything.'

'Who of?'

He thought for a moment she was being facetious, but she was looking at him in an interested way. 'Both of them, I suppose. I mean it was – it was after we'd – well, parted on bad terms – ' he was glad of the extra squeeze she gave his hand here – 'and there were these two . . . I don't know. As if they knew something I didn't. It wasn't that I felt disgusted or anything, I just felt – resentful.'

'I think I see.'

'Well, I'm glad you do. I'm not sure I do. But God knows how I could explain it to Nicholas.'

She dug her chin thoughtfully in his shoulder. 'Women see these things differently,' she said. 'You must have had the proverbial Phase at school?'

'Yes. Yes, I did, though I didn't really understand it at the time.'

'It's in everybody, somewhere, even if they don't admit it. I'm sure Nicholas will understand.' She tapped her finger on his chest. 'That's men again, you see. Always trying to analyse themselves. Because they think they're so interesting, I suppose. But they don't like to find anything they're not expecting. Want to have it all weighed up. Shift your foot, lovey, I'm getting cramp.'

He accepted what she said, as he often did, because he had also often found that it was true, especially when he had baulked at it; but he did not like the idea that there was anything that subsisted in his life, in their lives, subterranean, lurking, inaccessible to scrutiny.

For a long time they had been saying they would have a bath together – it was promoted as the ultimate in romantic sensuality in a certain class of 1970s' films which as hopeful young adults they had both seen – so, as there was no sign of Nicholas, they did it, as a kind of flourish on the signature of their renewed contract. It was uncomfortable in the extreme: he had not reckoned with sitting on the plughole with the taps digging in his back, and neither of them had reckoned with unarousing crinkliness, or standing on the bath-mat puffy and lobster-coloured, dripping like fleshy stalactites. But laughter did the work of libido, with overtime, as if in an assertion of faith in the company.

CHAPTER 14

'You'd think they'd have got a decent band, wouldn't you?' said Louise in his ear.

'Well, they're loud enough.'

'Eh?'

'I said they're loud enough!' he shouted, and she grinned.

The band on the stage played pop tunes to unsuitable Latin American rhythms: the electric organ covered everything with a tawdry shimmer, like a thin scraping of margarine across bread. From time to time a strobe light was played across the dancers on the floor, turning their skin an unwholesome puce and freezing them in gawky attitudes.

David returned to Ruth and sat down.

'Oh, I like this one,' she said. 'If it's what I think it is. It's hard to tell. Anyway, come on snakehips.' Ruth pulled him up out of his seat. Neither of them was much of a dancer: they were content to shuffle in the couple of square feet of space that was all they could find. 'Remember that disco?' he said, and they laughed and grimaced. Rejecting the time-warped dreariness of 'Over-25s' nights – flared suits and little frightened women sipping Babycham – they had ventured recently into a new nightclub where the clientele was young and trendy. How young and how trendy they had not realised. They had slunk away, mortified, after half an hour. 'I couldn't have felt more antique if I'd marched in there with my fan and my little dance-book with a pencil on a chain,' Ruth said.

It had been insufferably hot in the crowded club dance hall until the double doors at both ends had been opened: now moths were zooming in and hurling themselves to a colourful death against the strobe lights. There were so many people he knew from work here that David felt worn out with making the appropriate nods and smiles to the faces that loomed by him and exchanging the same shouted pleasantries time after time.

'Not getting fed up are you?' he asked Ruth eventually, but he could see she was not: she was quietly amused by it all, and she had the knack of extracting what pleasure there was from any occasion.

Louise was not serving behind the bar tonight, and had brought her fiancé to the do. She was steering him round, presenting him like a debutante. When it came to David's turn she gave him a nervous private smile. 'You remember Terry, don't you?'

'Of course. How you doing?' Meeting the man whose absent presence, as it were, had once caused so much embarrassment was peculiar, like saying hello to a ghost. And that time did seem impossibly distant, part of a previous life.

Terry had the uneaseful look of the soldier in civvies. It must, David thought, be something to do with the haircut, which even now when short hair was the fashion stuck out like a sore thumb. 'How long are you home for?'

'For good, actually. I've just left the army. Knocked around a bit. Knew when I'd had enough.' 'Sah!' David almost expected him to add, which was a bit unfair.

'We'd both had enough,' said Louise, hooking her arm in Terry's. 'Now I've got him where I can keep an eye on him.' Terry smiled in a restive, self-conscious way, like a schoolboy when a teacher jokes with him.

'Can I get you a drink?' David asked him: he had a feeling of well-being, and of wanting to share it.

Terry looked relieved to come and stand at the bar and be gruffly monosyllabic as men are together. 'Not really my sort of thing, this,' he said, drinking his beer to attention.

The band shut up for a while and made way for a brace of bosses to make speeches and present a few retirement watches to old men who all seemed to be called Fred. Above the stage was a banner saying 'Barlow Watkins 1885–1985', the letters rather boastfully encircling a globe.

'Which one's Barlow and which one's Watkins?' Ruth asked him.

'Oh, there aren't any. Never were. It was a German firm originally. When the First World War broke out they changed the name to the most beefy British one they could think of. That's the story anyway.'

'By the way, your friend came up and introduced himself while you were away.'

'What friend?'

'Said his name was Jack.'

'Oh Christ.'

'It was that Jack, was it? I thought so. He seemed plastered already.'

'What did he say to you?'

'I think it was "So you're Dave's little secret, then, are you?"' She did a passable imitation of Jack Erskine's belligerent jocularity. 'So that's how you refer to me.'

'God, I hope I can keep out of his way.'

'Last I saw of him he was making a fool of himself trying to chat up some girl half his age. Dear me, how long are they going to drone on?'

David pushed the unwelcome thought of Jack Erskine away. It had no place in his serene mood, which had in fact been set earlier by a phone call.

Auntie Jeanette had found that address for him: an obscure little town, on the Norfolk coast, that he had never heard of. He was surprised, but full of thanks, which Jeanette had been strangely reluctant to accept. 'That's from years and years ago, David, you know. I doubt it'll be any good to you, really.' Her voice was fluttery and uncertain down a crackling line. But he was delighted, and confident. He had vague visions of Auntie Aldyth being slotted into place in the beautifully complete edifice of his life: of reconciliation, of righting of wrongs and laying of ghosts. He had come through. Armed with love and rationality, he would cut through the Gordian knot wound by years of mystification:

lives need not be spoiled, the past and the future need not be peered fearfully into like darkened rooms. He thought of his mother, with tenderness and without pain, and felt she would be proud of him.

He finally met up with Jack Erskine in the corridor on the way back from the toilet. Erskine was dangerously drunk: he had gone past the stage of slurring and blustering into a fierce articulacy. 'Dave,' he said, taking his arm in both hands and propelling him along like a Hoover. 'You ought to come and see this girl I'm after, she works in personnel, she's got these brilliant tits, and they're just about popping out of the front of her dress. I keep buying her drinks, God knows if I'm getting anywhere, she don't give anything away. What do you think of the do then?' Before he could answer Erskine went on, rather to his surprise, 'Fucking excellent I reckon. Best do in years. I'm well tanked up.'

The girl wore a backless dress and a witless expression. Jack said 'This is my mate Dave,' and she said 'Hullo' to a space about three feet to his left. David had the unmistakable impression that she and her friends had been laughing about Erskine, and felt uncomfortable. 'Oh, good, there's the food,' he said, hoping to get away, but Erskine came with him, still gripping his arm. 'Silly cow, I'll wait till she's pissed,' he said. 'I could do with something to eat. I never have anything during the day, now. Can't be arseholed. Drink instead, it feeds you just the same,' and David was aware of Erskine's tense vitality stretching and cracking, wedged into a vice of desperate unhappiness.

He found Ruth already at the buffet tables with Louise, who with her usual friendliness had struck up a conversation with her: Terry was hovering behind them holding plates, like a footman.

'Oh, here he is!' Louise said. 'I was just saying to Ruth, you'd think it would be a sit-down, wouldn't you, the price of the tickets. Still, it's a good spread.'

'Ignore me Louise, why don't you,' Erskine said. David managed a 'Couldn't get rid of him' glance at Ruth and got a 'Never mind' glance in return.

'Sorry, Jack, I didn't see you,' said Louise. 'How you keeping, all right?' Prudently she did not await an answer but went on: 'I don't think you know Terry, do you, my fiancé?'

'Oh, you're the squaddy one, are you?' Erskine was gobbling sausage rolls and pickles straight from the table, using his plate to catch the crumbs.

'Well, not any more,' said Terry equably. 'You want any of this cheese, David, I've took too much.'

'Oh, it's "David", is it?' Erskine said, still chomping. 'I don't reckon you'd be talking to this one like that if you knew what he'd been up to.'

David felt nothing but a great weariness, as if a weight had been hoisted on to his shoulders.

'Why, what's that then?' said Terry, in the voice of someone expecting a joke, and amiably prepared to laugh.

'Oh, you mean she didn't tell you? Well, I'd better say no more.'

'Jack, you're drunk again, and you'll go too far one of these days,' said Louise. 'He means when I went out with David for a meal while you were away, love. Same as I used to go out for a drink with Tony from behind the bar.'

'Oh, that,' said Terry, looking uninterested and faintly disappointed, as if he had still hoped to hear a joke.

'Which I did tell him, Jack Erskine. Your trouble is you're dead old-fashioned, for all your talk.'

Erskine was stock still now, the veins showing painfully in his temples, a man who had found insinuation to no avail and hopelessly resorts to volume. 'I should hope I bloody am old-fashioned.' A spray of crumbs made an arc from his red shouting mouth. 'If it meant letting you go screwing around like the village bike while I was away . . .'

'Shut it, mate,' Terry said. David felt a guilty relief that he was no longer centre stage.

'You're a mug, sunshine.' Erskine was improvising, anything to keep the oblivious words flowing. 'A right mug. Everybody in this place knows what a slag she is, and – '

The blow was a smart practised one, so that hardly anyone

around them was even aware of it: Erskine simply folded in the middle like a book being snapped shut.

'It's a wonder he didn't throw up, what with all that drink and food,' Ruth said later as they drove home.

'Well, I caught sight of him later, he was still putting it away.' David, who was driving, had been drinking shandies and tonic waters all night. 'Must admit, I felt a bit righteous and goody-two-shoes, standing there, keeping out of it.'

'Why? Always keep out of it, that's my motto.' She leaned her head against his shoulder: there was a lovely sort of drowsy suspense about her. 'I enjoyed it.'

'What, the bit of violence? You savage. I bet you're one of those women who sits at the front of wrestling matches going "Kill him!"'

'No, the whole thing. Well, I enjoyed that too in a way. I mean you said it was a real Wheeltappers' and Shunters' Club, and I even got the drunken brawl thrown in.'

'True. Trouble is, I've still got to work with him.' He braked for the traffic lights. 'Anyway, where to, m'lady, home?'

'Yes Parker.' She moved her head about on his shoulder, looking for the comfortable places that she knew. 'Of course, where else would we be going?'

'Oh, my place, you mean?' He had been about to take the turning for Park Crescent.

'Yes, home. That's where I like being.' Her voice was sleepily muffled against his shirt. 'I think I ought to start calling it home. I wonder if your offer still stands.'

He was silent for a moment. 'You know it does.'

'I've got no end of stuff. Boxes full. Depends if you've got room.'

'All the room in the world.' Deep feeling, as so often, came out trite in words, as the breath of one's body comes out in steam that evaporates and is gone. He shifted his shoulder, cushioning her, aware of her face, a patch of upturned luminosity close to him. He felt he understood the phrase 'pride and joy': he was glad he was sober, to savour the delight with no loss of keenness.

There seemed something entirely new about the way she loafed on his settee that night, about the way she pointed the remote control panel at the television with a Pow! Pow! face like someone pointing a toy gun, about the way she beckoned him to hold her hand with a mock imperiousness. She was leaning over, her back to him, to light a cigarette, when he told her about getting hold of Auntie Aldyth's address, and he was standing by the sideboard looking at the old monochrome photograph: it was a perfect tableau, as he realised later.

'Shut up.'

She had never said that to him, except in fun; and he could tell, though she had not altered her position, that every muscle in her body was tensed.

It was only two hours later by the clock – 'the clock', as people say, as if there were only one Clock in the world, like the Holy Roman Emperor, instead of millions all exhibiting the same smug face – that David was walking alone around empty streets, stunned as if his mother had risen out of her grave and spat at him. The sound of his footsteps dropped into the silence of the summer night as into a deep well.

He had thought she must be ill at first: he bent and touched her shoulder, still holding the photograph of Aldyth, and she whipped round and knocked it out of his hand. The glass cracked and fell out of the frame as it hit the floor.

There had been a temporary reprieve, a last clutch at fugitive normality. 'Sorry, I'm sorry,' she said. 'I got sick of it . . . hearing about that bloody woman, you keep going on . . .'

'I only mentioned it.' He could not believe she was about to cry over this: his mind hurried back and forth looking for some reason – Louise, perhaps, Erskine, something –

'Forget about it. Talk about something else, will you.'

Moved by some helpless fear, he blundered on. 'All right. I'll talk about something else. I don't see what's wrong, though. I was just pleased about it, you know I've really been wanting to get in touch with her, it's something – '

'I'm going home.' She was at the front door before he

realised she was serious. He pulled her back, recoiled at the anguish distorting her face.

. . . He was on the footbridge over the parkway, though he did not know how he had got there. The woods of the boating park massed on either side, green lost in darkness. The cars were moving trails of light beneath him, a hoarse smell of exhaust rising in mild air.

She had leaned against the front door, like someone at the last gasp of fatigue. The tears were simply leaking out, like sweat: there was no sob in her voice, which was flat, seared, automatic, the mind leaving the words to come while it retreated to an inner distance where it could not be followed.

When she said, 'Promise me you'll shut up about it now and forget all about it or I'm going', it was not stubbornness that made him say, 'No, I want to know what this is all about', but utter bewilderment.

'Your Auntie Aldyth. Right. Aldyth Russell. Remember it was you who dug this up. You wouldn't bloody leave it alone. You had to keep going on.'

He had never seen her cry at all, let alone like this. He put his hand on hers, and she brushed it off like a fly.

'Your dad died of TB, didn't you say? That's terrible. It's awful. Like my dad. He died of your bloody Auntie Aldyth. Well, I didn't have a dad really. Other children say Where's your daddy, haven't you got a daddy? You know what children are like. But I couldn't really say he lives with another lady, could I? I couldn't say he cleared off with her when I was a little baby. OH, did he? He must have took one look at you and up and went. Oh, well, that's all old history now, isn't it? No doubt mum soon got over it. And he's dead now anyway. Of course, your lovely auntie had got fed up with him then, so he was left with nothing. No damage done. It's all a long time ago, yes. But that's what you like, isn't it, David, things put away all nicely in the past so you can look back at them. No damage done.'

It was instinctive to attempt to put his arms round her. But his arms hung out stiffly, nerveless and useless: she might have been cased round with glass.

'Families. You must admit they're important, for better or worse. She didn't think so, obviously. Ask my mum about that.'

Her mouth was square and red. Tears scored her face, sketching a vizard of ugliness over it. He thought of how he could never imagine her as a child. He suddenly could. He was not surprised to hear her gasp 'I want my mum, I want my mum.'

She was already out of the door and running down the path when he burst out, 'But it's got nothing to do with us!' and the words bounced dully across the street, idiot words, plaintive, idiot words, conjuring a faint echo that was like a snigger, at the foolish banality of lovers, setting up their ramshackle shrine of Us, and as full of ignorant reverence as savages before a little grinning idol on a stick. She was quickly gone, the noise of her heels diminishing. Somewhere a dog gave a single yap.

He roamed around the house, looking about him; like a man suspecting a trick, someone about to jump out of the cupboard and cry 'Fooled you!' Then his legs took charge, leading him round the streets on a mysterious itinerary. They took him on and on, they seemed supernaturally tireless: he was like the character in the fairy-tale who puts on the magic shoes.

He was in a windy underpass. Graffiti crowded the walls: there was a pile of crushed beer-cans and dog-ends in the corner, like picked bones in a primeval cave. Down here the noise of the traffic was only an aural suggestion, a slight tinnitis. He realised he was alone: the sense came unmistakably to him, like the smell of an unloved but familiar home.

Harold Barber, tired of contemplating death, begins to contemplate his life instead.

And he is surprised at how much of it there is. A circumscribed life, spent in the town where he was born, and not a long one: he is just turned forty, and will not see forty-one. Yet reviewing it is more than enough to fill the long hours, lying flat and still in the wooden whitewashed hut, with its open door admitting sweet scents from the autumn world outside. No hospital smell. He likes that.

He has always been a great believer in luck, and does not see this as incompatible with his religion. Which is sincere, and deeply felt, and personal without any of the humbug that word suggests. It never had to be drummed into him. He was infected by it, insensibly, as he supposes he was infected by the tubercule. Unlike poor Alan, who had it drummed into him by his mother, and subsequently embraced it with an over-compensating fervour. Always does more harm than good that way, Harold thinks. Poor Alan . . . And this is one of the things that troubles him – more, perhaps, than the pain, the terrible coughs that go on and on, which he has become accustomed to, as you would to someone violent and unpredictable if you were handcuffed to them – the sense of things likely to go wrong in the future, as things will, and his impotence to do anything about them.

Still, he believes in luck, and concludes that his life has been, on the whole, lucky. His death, no; but he is thinking about his life. And indeed when the tiredness comes over him – not real tiredness, for he doesn't get tired, but sleep seems to keep stubbornly coming out of habit, like some muddle-headed old night-watchman, turning up to do his rounds although the factory has closed down – and the scenes pass more rapidly and hazily across his mind, then it seems the chain of chance runs so blatantly through his life, through everybody's lives, that he can make no sense of it, and is troubled again.

Poor Alan . . . Harold doesn't know what he could do for his brother, but he wishes he could do something . . . something perhaps that will sever that 'poor' from his name, for it is beginning to be attached automatically by many people, and Harold guesses it will eventually be said with impatience and even contempt. Alan can hardly find a word to say when he visits: he just sits there by the bed, pale, thin-lipped, looking old – oh, too old – and forlornly resentful. And he carries his resentment out with him again, and Harold fears that he is constantly adding to his store of it, and that it will be a burden to him.

They all put on different faces when they come here. His mother grim and worn, as if all that bird-like vitality had not ebbed but disappeared in one go, and nothing in reserve. Ethel's sister Jeanette – good of her to come, and like her – full of a big-boned schoolmistressy good health, and looking guilty about it. Ethel herself – well, they have never put on special faces for each other, and are not about to start now. And the children, both very sturdy he is glad to see: Marian only two, toddles around the hut and plays as she would wherever you put her. Gets a bit panicky when she finds a spider or something on the floor and it frightens her. And David, nearly six, and probably beginning to understand what is happening, though he doesn't let on. A good-natured child, but with a sort of unawareness about him: when he falls down or hurts himself, he does not cry so much as look startled, as if each time it is a complete surprise to him. But healthy children, and Ethel will bring them up right, of that he is certain.

Harold dozes in the autumn dawn, the hut rinsed with cold blue light. He dreams of his father, advising him with that sallow gravity of his. 'Always do what you believe to be right.' Then he is aware of being awake, though he was not aware of being asleep, and is thinking of Ethel, and how when he had told her about this she had said, 'Right for who?' There is a vein of scepticism in Ethel; likeable, and hard and clear as agate. He loves her so dearly. And the worm of trouble moves in him again, tickly and ominous like the beginning of a cough. A feeling that perhaps he had not told her so . . . but no, that is not it, for he had told her often. He tries to follow the thread the end of which dangles in his mind, but it becomes tangled and lost among so many other threads, and he dozes again.

Often he sees a thrush through the open door of the hut, darting across the grass, stopping every few seconds and cocking its head before hurrying on again. Sometimes it comes right up to the threshold, with a snail in its beak, to break the shell on the edge of the concrete path. Harold has tried giving a little chirrup of encouragement; but the bird just looks at him beadily, with a look as if it could tell him something if it chose, but on second thoughts it won't. And darts away again, with a pattering sound on the fallen leaves.

. . . There is a nurse here who he slowly realised was fond of him. He hardly sees her now: not since it became clear that he was not going to get better. He must cut a poor figure, of course: not that he has ever quite understood about his good looks. When visitors come a nurse combs his hair and shows him his face in a mirror. Haggard and colourless certainly. But the same old face, and he has never really thought about it in any other way. The idea of anyone falling for him has always struck him with quizzical amusement: not Ethel, of course, but that is different. And there is a dangling thread here too; but if he could follow it he does not do so.

Instead he savours the faint smell of sugar-beet that comes on the wind from the town. Some people don't like it, but for him it is delightfully evocative: he thinks of burning leaves in the garden, putting things away in the potting-shed where there is an equally pleasant smell of wood and creosote, of preparing for the winter in the knowledge that summer will come. He is, unashamedly, pleased by these cycles and repetitions, the assurance of domestic life. He is a homebody, has firmly believed always in the solidity of home and family.

Outside in the hospital grounds the trees are bending and shivering restlessly in the wind, as if they wished to pull up their roots and run for shelter. Harold has had a bad night, and has been in pain, and he passes out of pain into a waking dream, or memory, in which he is sitting in a cinema alone, and is fidgeting in his seat unable to attend properly to the film. The film is *Lost Horizon*, of that he is sure, so it must be getting on for twenty years ago, but he is leaving before the end. He is standing in the noisome little toilet, with the one dim light bulb that is never enough feebly glowing in the corner, and he is trying to come to a decision; but he knows the decision has already been made. And now the dream is confirmed as memory, and is unrolling relentlessly like the film he had been half-watching while he fidgeted and struggled with something he did not know then to be passion, for he had not known it before and has scarcely known it since; and he sees himself walk out of the cinema into a chilly March night, and remembers how he half-hoped the figure in the grey coat would not be there waiting in the walk behind the Bishop's Palace, and how his heart dived and mounted again when she was. And then pain, like a bluff, bullying sort of friend, comes to his rescue and seizes him again and pushes memory away.

. . .The doctor is a jaunty, ginger-headed Scotsman with a jaunty ginger-headed way with patients that often seems to brace them into health. When he comes in he always gives Harold a humorous frown as if to say, 'What, you still here?' and Harold feels a little ashamed, as so many people are getting better and leaving. He would like to please the doctor by getting better, instead of getting worse.

Memory returns, and as if it too is ashamed guides him to gentle scenes. There is Ethel, as he saw her soon after David was born, sitting up in the hospital bed with the boy in her arms, lovely as ever; and in her face a kind of triumph and a new peace. For she presented the baby, and he took it, with a special solemnity; it was the ratification of a treaty . . . and memory betrays him again, like the baser part of man rallying always when the better part seems ascendant . . .

He is in the front room at Corporation Road, the place that was tacitly given up to him and Ethel when they were courting, and is remembering details about it he thought he had long forgotten – the old prie-dieu in the corner, strangely strayed into such an Anglican house, the wireless, with a sunburst front and a pile of gramophone records on top, that doesn't work, the silver-topped vase – Mrs Russell pronounces the word *vaize* – that is supposed to be valuable, and is certainly hideous enough to be so. This time they are not on the sofa kissing. They are standing a long way apart, and he is glancing at himself in the butterfly-shaped mirror above the mantelpiece, and at the reflection of Ethel, her face set, her eyes fierce. It is a cruel memory, and his ruined chest labours beneath the sheets and he closes his eyes and opens them and closes them again as if he would erase it. That young man standing distraught and hopeless before Ethel's anger is suffering the pain of knowing he has thrown away his happiness with a single act, and has only himself to blame.

There are no raised voices in that long terrible evening, but the rest of the household has tiptoed around and let them be – even Mr Russell – sensing something wrong. At last he is leaving: he remembers meeting Joe Russell coming in as he goes out, and Joe in his friendly way patting his shoulder as they pass. And then he remembers sitting down on a front garden wall, after having gone only a little way down the street. Feeling exhausted, drained, and profoundly disorientated. For he is still engaged to Ethel. He sits on the wall and takes off his hat and rubs his brow, drinking in the cool air like a man saved from drowning. He has betrayed her, and deserved and expected no mercy. In a way, perhaps, he has received none . . . But they are still to be married.

'I'm still going to have you. So that *she* can't.'

Ethel in a quiet, complete fury; something he had never seen. But rational, also. A bargain. Out of love for her – which has never faltered, and that is the bitterest truth: the passions that whipped him seemed so utterly foreign to it – he will keep it, and not expect to regain what he has forfeited. Harold remembers swearing that to himself, as he sat on the garden wall and breathed in the evening air.

Pain has come and gone again with a promise to return, and he is very weak. But he is thinking calmly again of luck, and how lucky he has been. How what he had forfeited was given back to him by degrees, until the final redemption, and Ethel smiling at him from the hospital bed with their child in her arms. And his mind lingers pleasurably over the simple thought of Ethel, like a warming of the hands before a fire; and even his weakness seems hazily agreeable, so that he feels he might waft off the bed and slip between the floorboards.

. . .And as memory now is having its own way, as it is sure to do, he thinks too of Aldyth, and the last time he and Ethel saw her, the last time she moved into their lives. Four or five years ago, it must be, when all the dire predictions about her seemed to have come true. An unsavoury business, and he would have kept well out of it . . . The breaking up of a home and family, of all things the most painful to him. But it was Ethel whom she called upon to act as a kind of go-between for her, and Ethel agreed, negotiating the unpleasantness, able as ever. There were two children, he remembers, boy and girl like their own, poor mites. The wife was a proud sort of woman. He admired her; apparently she was taking it hard . . . And so Aldyth was gone. He supposed she had got what she wanted. But he could not understand Aldyth's turning to Ethel for help . . . but then he has never really understood the pair of them and what they really think of each other: unless this floating, supernatural sort of insight into which he is slipping be understanding – that in spite of everything there is an unbreakable bond between the sisters, and he is it.

. . .Ethel is by his bed again, and he is contemplating her with pleasure as he does the thought of her. She is telling him there is someone here to see him, and then goes out of the hut again, and in a moment the face of Aldyth is looking down at him.

He is so surprised he would not know what to say; but his extreme weakness excuses him, and indeed prevents him. Aldyth looks down at him for a long time, until her face seems to freeze into the familiar background of the hut, and take root there as if never to move again. Then she leans over and kisses him on his dry lips, and is gone.

The clumps of trees around the sanatorium are almost bare. The wind has raked the leaves in crisp, curling drifts against the walls of the huts and the grass has an old ragged greenness. Ethel and Aldyth walk down the path from the hut where Harold lies.

'Did he say anything?' Ethel asks. Her breath steams.

'No.'

'He's very bad.'

Aldyth nods. 'That's why I came.' She pulls her fur coat around her: she dislikes the cold. They stop at the edge of the drive. Away beyond the trees a large car waits, a man at the wheel.

'It was nice of him to bring you all this way,' Ethel says. 'Are you still happy with him?'

'Yes.' Aldyth looks at Ethel and then looks away. 'How long has Harold got?'

Ethel shrugs.

'You hate me very much, don't you, Ethel,' Aldyth says.

'It doesn't matter.' Ethel does not look away. A rook wheels above the trees with a scraping cry. 'He was always yours, really, wasn't he?' she says, in a conversational tone.

Aldyth shivers, and draws a deep breath. 'I'd better be going.'

'I don't think we shall see each other again, Aldyth.' Ethel stands very erect and still: the cold seems not to affect her. Aldyth turns and murmurs 'Goodbye' and walks away towards the car. Ethel watches her figure, slightly hunched in the stiff wind, diminishing until it is lost among the trees.

CHAPTER 15

The spade slid into the earth with an easy motion. It was perplexing, and half-annoying, that after such long neglect the soil should be so easy to turn. He wanted stubbornness, wanted back-breaking toil.

Nicholas had come into the garden and stood at his elbow. 'I know this perhaps isn't the time . . .'

'What time's that then?' Nicholas's sensitivity to mood was for once not welcome.

'Well – if you're busy.'

'Yes, I'm looking for buried treasure.' He dug on for a few moments, then stopped and leant on the spade. He felt too tired even to be sullen. Sunlight stung the nape of his neck.

'It's just that I think I'm going to be moving out.'

'You think?' Half of a chopped worm was wriggling feebly on the blade. He stared at it.

'Well, I am. I'm not sure exactly when, but – '

'You'll have to give me an exact date.' He bent and plucked the worm off. 'So I can advertise the room.'

He looked up, and saw that Nicholas was hurt. Skinny and white in the sun, he looked very young and unprotected.

David looked away. 'Where are you going? Back to your parents?'

'God no. It's Bez's house. Oh, he's moving out, you see, him and that hippie bloke, you remember.'

'I see.' Across the fence Mr Carelli's brown round back was visible, astonishingly hairy. He wiped his forehead and made an effort. 'Why are you going?'

'Eh?'

'If it's because of what I said the other week – '

'Don't be daft. It's Mark. We're going to move in together. So . . .'

'Ah.' He was restive under Nicholas's gaze. 'Is he the Biggie, then, Mark?' The Biggie had been Nicholas's name for Mr Right.

'Oh, well,' Nicholas laughed, an engaging careless sound David wished he could appreciate, 'I'm only nineteen, remember. Bit early to start hoping for that. But – well, you never know.'

'Never too early,' David said. 'Well, tell me when you've got a definite date. Although I might not take anybody else anyway. I'm thinking of putting the house up for sale.'

'That's a pity.'

David shrugged. He knew he was wearing what his mother used to call his mardy-face. 'Can't stay in one place for ever.'

'No.'

'Still. If it doesn't work out, with thingmy, you know, there's always – '

'Yeah. Thanks.'

'As long as you realise.' Feeling stirred in him, cramped and constricted, and quickly smothered like an incommoding ache one has made up one's mind to ignore.

'It's half-five,' Nicholas said, 'I'm going to make something for me tea. Can I do you something?'

'No. No, I'll stay out here a while yet.' He slammed the spade in again and dug. He ought to have some proper shoes for this: his trainers were rapidly getting ruined.

'Okay.' Nicholas touched him lightly on the shoulder and went in.

He stayed in the garden till after eight. He might have been vying with Mr Carelli in some horticultural marathon. The pile of uprooted weeds and rubbish stood higher than the fence. He thought about making a bonfire: his weariness, rather than the fact that the neighbours would complain, decided him against it.

He went in and made a sandwich, ate half of it and put it

down, went to the telephone and sat in front of it. Nearly twenty-four hours now since it had happened. A sort of plimsoll-line, BC, AD. Earlier, at work, he had dialled as far as the fourth digit of Ruth's number and then stopped. (Ruth, that was her name, wasn't it? She had become slippery, diaphanous, a black hole in his mind.) Now he just sat and looked at the phone, as if expecting something Delphic from it. It did not ring. That was Delphic enough, he supposed.

The photograph of Auntie Aldyth, with its broken glass, still lay where he had set it on the sideboard. He did not want to touch it. He averted his eyes, as from a deformity.

The next day, Saturday, was the beginning of the three-day country-and-western festival. He had intended to go with Ruth in that other, BC life. He thought he still ought to go: it would take him out of himself. He had never felt so firmly in himself, as stiflingly as if he were in a coffin underground, nose to nose with his own corpse. He drove into town and watched the opening parade and then wandered around the stalls and marquees pitched on the river embankment. Steel guitars pined from scores of amplifiers. In an open marquee a hypnotist was doing his act with people from the audience. He had told them they were members of an orchestra. Eyes closed, they sawed at imaginary violins, tootled invisible flutes. Complete absence of control over themselves. It was horrible. He left.

The equilibrium of the summer had wobbled. It was still warm, but fragmented clouds had stolen in overnight and as he drove up Park Crescent they tussled with the strong sun, so that the light dimmed and brightened every few moments, shadow rolling across the road and then rolling back again like a carpet. Ruth's car was not in the drive. He stared at the doors of the double garage

The front door was open. Mrs Lacey was standing on a stool in the lounge, unhooking one of the curtains at the big bay window.

'Now, don't expect me to get down, David, it was bad enough hauling my old bones up here,' she said. She took off the last hook and heaved the curtain down on to the settee behind her with an exaggerated groan. 'This is my equivalent of spring-cleaning. Three months late, I know. But there's something about this house that discourages you. Like a mausoleum. No, I don't mean that, I love it dearly.'

He stood looking up at her, feeling physically sick. That she should stand there fluttering on in this way seemed outrage, blasphemy. It confirmed her real opinion of him; and, he supposed, of his family.

'Is Ruth here?' Yes, that was her name.

She looked over her shoulder at him and began to tug at the second curtain. In the raw, dancing light she looked less young, her skin more worn and sallow. 'No she isn't,' she said. 'And I hope you'll believe me. I hope you don't think so badly of me as to imagine I'd fib about that.'

That word 'fib' was typical of her, he thought. 'She told you, then?'

'My dear, as I've said before, she doesn't need to tell me things. And you must realise, there were certain things I of all people didn't need to be told in the first place. Oh, come off, you wretched thing! They've been up so long the hooks go all stiff, and then the curtains won't pull properly. You have to yank at them.'

Suddenly he thought she might well have been waiting all this time for him to turn up, with the stool in position, so that she could do this when he tried to talk to her. If it was true, he had to admire it.

'Can you tell me where she is?'

She stopped, and looked down at him with a frown, a disappointed sort of frown. 'Really, David,' she said. 'You can't expect me to. Ruth's not here because she wanted to get away for a bit, and I can't go against that.'

'Why not?' If she was determined to place him in the position of a child, he would be one: piqued and obstinate.

She tugged at the last hook, and broke her fingernail in doing so. 'Damn. Takes me ages to grow them.' She sucked her finger. 'You said to me you didn't want to make her unhappy. I believed you. And I'm still willing to believe you.

No doubt you think I should have said something. Well . . . it doesn't matter now. Things have sorted themselves out. I don't think there's any need for any more unhappiness,' and her voice rose a little, flutey and optimistic. She bundled the curtain up in her arms and then held it down to him. 'Would you take it please?'

He took the curtain. Brushed nylon, thin light stuff, it was voluminous and ungainly as he tried to gather it up in his arms. It was like trying to come to terms with Mrs Lacey – soft, gauzy, impossible of negotiation. Like trying to wolf candy-floss – it would choke you. He thought of Aldyth, and Ruth's father, this woman's husband, and the past seemed to well up in the same way, frothy and insubstantial, a drowning pool.

She took a cloth from her pocket and began to wipe the curtain-track. 'By the way, I was talking to your boss the other day, Ken Musson. He's retiring shortly – well, of course, you know. Not a minute too soon, I think, his health's never been good. Anyway he spoke quite highly of you, and though I don't suppose I've got any influence, I made sure to put in a good word for you, and I think when the time comes – '

'Oh, Lord.' A little chuckle had escaped him. It really seemed sad, somehow: it was an attempt, in its way, at buying him off. He laid the curtain down and went out.

As he started up the car there was a tap on the passenger window. He wound it down and Gordon poked his head in. 'Thought I heard you,' he said. 'Looking for Ruth, are you?'

'Yes, d'you know where she is?'

Gordon nodded. 'Oh, come on, let me in and we'll get away from the house of Usher. Mum put you off, I suppose? Uh-huh. We'll go for a drink. Wheatsheaf, it's only up the road.'

Gordon was panting as he settled in the seat. 'Thought I'd missed you,' he said. He was looking better than when David had last seen him. He was sunburnt, and his nose was peeling: he fingered it tenderly. 'Doesn't half hurt. It's because I sit in the garden all day like some bloody gnome. Back to London next week, thank God.'

There was a noisy lunch-time crowd in The Wheatsheaf. David shouldered his way to the bar and then looked round at Gordon in sudden perplexity.

'Oh, orange juice, any damn thing,' he said. 'It's all right. Part of the treatment is to get you to go into pubs and feel at ease, you know, without ending up under the table.'

They took their drinks outside to the beer garden. David, noticing again the dissimilarity between Gordon and his mother and sister – there was something leaner, something closer to the surface about him – speculated for a moment on Mr Lacey's looks.

'She's at Roberta's,' Gordon said, swallowing his orange juice. 'Often goes and holes up there for a while, when there's trouble. Now don't go whizzing round there yet. I want to know what she said.'

'Well, depends how much you know – '

'Oh, dad and your scarlet woman, yes, that all got dug up, I guessed that.'

'How was she, when she came home that night?' He felt faintly hurt and resentful at Gordon's breeziness.

'Oh, in a right state.' A toddler, falling over in the grass a little way away, began to cry. 'Bloody kids, I can't stand them. Of course, you know it's all mum, this – ' he flapped his bony hand – 'don't you?'

David lifted his beer and then put it down again. 'Perhaps you don't realise how – how upset she was, how everything seemed to just – '

'Oh, I do. I do indeed. David, don't look at me like that. It's no good going all tragic over this. That's the whole idea as far as mum's concerned. Just what she wants. As if any of it bloody matters now.'

'And it doesn't to you?' he said, coldly.

Gordon sighed. 'I'll tell you what it was like when we were little. And dad cleared off with what's-her-face. It was horrible, of course. But the thing is, mum wanted it to be horrible, as horrible as possible. She didn't try and make the best of it and cover up like people do with kids.'

'Perhaps that's best.'

'What?' Gordon frowned and shook his head impatiently. 'Mum has quite simply never got over it, that's the point. Or she made up her mind not to. She took it out on us. "Daddy doesn't love you. He went away with that other lady because he doesn't love mummy and he doesn't love Gordon and Ruth." All this crap, I mean you swallow it when you're a kid – '

'And you're saying Ruth's stupid enough to still keep swallowing it?' That remark about going all tragic had been rather close to the mark: he was pricked into perversity.

Gordon ignored him. 'Another thing, in that situation you expect to still see your dad. Oh, no. For a little while he used to come and take us out once a fortnight or so, but that soon stopped. It didn't fit in with mum's little melodrama. Dad gave up after a while – you know what she's like. Anyway it was a pretty grisly environment. The point is, I got out. Flew the nest. Simple as that. And so it's had that much less effect on me. Ruth stayed.'

David thought of Ruth's saying she would come and live with him, just before the explosion.

'She's frightened, Ruth, that's all. And there's not much that does frighten her. Which maybe makes it worse.' He laughed a little and lit a cigarette, drew on it eagerly, then absent-mindedly shunted the packet across to David. 'Your auntie was like the devil incarnate in our house. Like dad had been tempted to hell or something.'

'When did your father die?'

'Oh, must be ten years ago now. Had a stroke. Never had a day's illness before, as far as I know.'

'Where was he then?'

'Eh? With Aldyth, in Norfolk.'

'Ruth said something – '

'Oh, God, the mum version. She sucked him dry and left him to die. Look, as far as I know, there was never any suggestion . . . How happy they were's a different matter.

As it always is. The original Different Matter.' He shot an aggrieved glance at the toddler, who was now screaming with delight as his father pretended to chase him round the lawn. 'I've told Ruth lots of times she ought to get out, but she stayed . . . The thing is, you've got to remember this is nothing to do with the two of you.'

'That's just what I said.' A bitter thrill travelled through him, coppery-tasting fear.

'And it isn't. God, it all should be dead and buried. You're neither of you spring chickens – ' He looked at David and laughed, apologetically. David suddenly laughed too.

'What do I say to her then?' he asked. I'm asking.

Gordon slumped back, as if his spate of talk had suddenly exhausted him. 'That's where I can't help you.' He flicked at his empty glass with his finger, making it ring. 'If she comes home this weekend, which I don't suppose she will, I'll ring you. But . . . I'd say tell her to snap out of it, but that's a piece of advice that's been offered to me before now.'

He sat with the telephone directory in his hands, trying to remember Roberta's surname. To be thwarted by such a thing seemed absurd, surreal. He was actually toying with the idea of going through every name in the book until something clicked, when he remembered it.

The phone at the other end trilled, chirpy and business-like. He let it ring twenty times before giving up. He rang again at half-hour intervals. At last, in the evening, he drove to Roberta's flat, a sizzling summer rain percussive on the car roof, the streetlights dangling ribbons of yellow reflection in the wet road like luminous raffia.

He could see no lights up in the flat. He rapped at the door, twenty times, for symmetry, and went home again. He had slept the previous two nights, but did not this time. He lay awake, and tried to keep in mind Gordon's bracing practicality, but it kept slipping away.

Ruth had redeemed Sundays, conjuring life out of that terrible deadness: they had always been together, as they could on no other day. This Sunday threatened him with the old pattern, and worse. He rang twice in the morning, with no reply. The third time Roberta answered, and told him Ruth did not wish to speak to him. And that was that. An eminently civilised instrument, the telephone. Unpleasant conversations could be terminated, sealed off, like the ladies in Victorian novels, summoning a servant to show you out: 'Sir, not another word, or I shall be constrained to ring.' He went to the flat again, and knocked again, and got no answer. This was like some television comedy sketch of the 1970s: 'Hasn't this happened before!?' Cue canned laughter.

When he got home again he looked through the local papers and noted down the best estate agents.

The letter came with the first post, as he was getting ready for work.

Dear David,
I heard from Jeanette the other day. Apparently you were going to get in touch with me. Well I've beaten you to it. Come and see me straight away. Never mind work, say you're ill. Or say your auntie's ill. I'm not, but I'll swear I am if that would help. Just come.

Aldyth

All across the flat farmland as he drove east, the sun and wind pushed tides of rippling shade, ruckling the tawny wheatfields so that he might have been driving on a causeway above a saffron-coloured sea. Lorries pounded past him on the narrow road throwing the car into brief shudders and flinging up whorls of bright dust. Once he saw a cattle transporter coming the other way with a crowd of sheep on the open top, looking complacently around them like an outing of pensioners on a seaside tram.

He was still in the suit that he had put on ready for work, and it was hot in the car, with a baking musty smell of rubber. He pulled his tie off and opened his shirt. There was a peculiar, abstract sort of excitement in the fact of driving out to the coast like this on a Monday morning: a sense of escape. He found himself eagerly anticipating the first glimpse of the sea just like when he was a child with a bucket and spade.

The address at the top of Aldyth's letter was not the one Jeanette had given him: it was in the same tiny seaside town, a few miles west of Cromer, but this time it was obviously a pub, The Crab Pot. As he struck the road into the little town he was aware of dryness in his mouth and his stomach muscles hard and tight; but he felt nothing. Feeling was dissolved in anticipation: a simple awaiting. The road dipped, and over the roofs of big genteel villas and the green of a wooded golf course he caught a glimpse of a wedge of shining sea.

He left the car in the narrow strip of high street and walked down to the front. There were holidaymakers on the beach, hobbling on tiptoe across the slaty shingle, breasting into a boisterous, full sea. There were crabs and cockles and mussels on sale along the promenade, adding a dash of extra saltiness to the air: it was impossible not to draw in deep breaths. He followed the front until it began to peter out and a rim of distant cliffs edged out across the lip of the sea, and came upon a white pebble-dashed building with the sign 'The Crab Pot' above a pot-bellied bay window.

After the bright sun outside, the place seemed full of a choking greenish gloom: there were fishing-nets and baskets hung everywhere and this added to the first bizarre impression of stepping under the sea. When his eyes adjusted he saw a mixed crowd of old townsmen and holidaymakers in an old-fashioned saloon and a plump elderly woman behind the bar.

'What can I get you, love?'

No, couldn't be.

'I'm looking for my Aunt Aldyth.'

She smiled. 'Oh yes. Come on round the back.'

She lifted the bar-hatch for him and he followed her down a passage and down two steps to a small parlour, where there was the sound of voices.

He recognised the woman in the leather chair as Aldyth at once. She looked up as he came in, interrupted in something she was saying. The other person, who did not look at him, was Ruth.

'Come in, David,' Aldyth said.

Strangely, after all, his first impulse was to walk out. But he couldn't have acted on it: he was paralysed and powerless, only waiting to be told what to do, inert, his life an amorphous putty to be poured into any mould. Aldyth told him to sit down, and he did it. Ruth was on the other side of the room, with Aldyth between: she looked away.

'Well, I got you both here anyway. That's a bit of luck. I'll take back what I said about the post office.'

There was a knock on the door and a young man poked his head in.

'Oh, sorry, I didn't know – Shall you be wanting me any more today?'

'No, that's all right, Graham. Tell Dot to give you your money out of the till. Cheerio.'

'Bye.' The young man closed the door.

Aldyth took out a cigarette: there was a brimming ashtray by her side. She did not offer one to David or Ruth.

'Graham does the cellar work. He's not much good really, but I always take one on for the holiday trade. It's hard enough for them to find any kind of job nowadays. Signing on as well, of course, but I turn a blind eye, though there's often some busybody ready to go tattling on them. And I rather like the idea of people suspecting they're my toy boys.' She laughed.

David stared at her. She did not seem to mind, seemed to expect it, and returned his look.

He found himself thinking of Mrs Lacey, though there was no actual similarity in looks: only the undeniable handsomeness, turning age to its own account. But Aldyth's hair was white, kept short and straight, and there was no disarming dewiness about her face. Nor did she look like his mother. She was a person, and this ridiculously obvious fact sent preconception and association and emotion itself spinning away leaving him stranded and dumb.

She seemed prepared to endure his stare as long as it took. At last he stuttered out: 'How did you know?'

'Jeanette told me. Yes, she sort of keeps in touch, the only one. She's the one I rely on for news of home – ' it seemed strange to hear her say the word – 'when I want it, that is. Though I think she'd rather I faded away completely. And so, I've got the pair of you here. What do you drink, David?'

'Bitter.' He felt he couldn't swallow a drop, but he was compelled to answer.

'Ruth?'

His eyes flicked across to Ruth, sunk deep in an armchair, looking hunched and small.

'Lager,' she said.

'You both ought to have something to eat. It's nearly two o'clock. Have to be bar food, I'm afraid. I'll go and ask Dot.'

He wished her, acutely and with a sort of panic, to stay, but she was gone.

Ruth still did not look at him. She inspected her finger-ends, picking and pulling at each one, left hand, right hand, and back to the beginning again.

'You got a letter as well then?' he said.

She nodded.

'Saying to come here?'

She cleared her throat. 'Yes.'

He seemed to have lost the power of speech: he strained, as in a dream one strains to run from something terrible, leaden legs refusing to budge.

He looked round at the room. It was untidy and covered with dust. The furniture was all old, a random accumulation of pieces clearly kept simply as individual favourites, with no thought of harmony. Books and magazines and records formed toppling piles on any spare surface.

'I tried to ring you.'

'I know.'

He jumped as a grey tabby cat leapt down from its seat on the windowsill. It came stalking over and rubbed against his legs and he put a hand down to scratch its cheek. The feel of the soft inquiring whiskers seemed to wake him a little, a fleeting token of a tactile, sensitive world outside his paralysis. The cat arched itself against his hand and purred and then walked over to Ruth and rubbed against her legs. After a moment she reached down and stroked its fur gently with the tips of her fingers.

Aldyth brought in a tray with two plates of pie and chips and glasses of beer and lager. David noticed how tall and erect she stood: he imagined she would never allow herself to stoop if she could possibly help it.

'Here. We'll make room on this table.' She pushed aside a heap of newspapers. 'You'll have to budge that chair up, David.'

'Really, I'm not hungry, I couldn't eat anything,' Ruth said. Aldyth looked at her, and after a moment she got up and came to the table. David too had never felt less like eating. But the look Aldyth had given Ruth had made him afraid of her. With no word of persuasion or coercion, Aldyth somehow made them sit at the table together and eat.

She had a large gin and tonic for herself, and watched them.

'Sorry I was so long. I had to give Dot a hand behind the bar. She's getting on a bit. Most people are, round here. Did you know that this place has the highest average longevity in the country? It's no wonder really, they'll never wear out, they just sit and vegetate in their damn deckchairs. Part of the reason John bought this place, just before he died. It was a challenge. It was practically falling down when we came here.'

Not the least bizarre aspect of this meeting was finding himself eating chips at the same table as Ruth, neither of them looking at or speaking to the other. At the mention of John Lacey he glanced warily at Ruth, but she made no sign.

'The place is dead as a doornail in winter,' Aldyth said. 'But the old fishermen still turn up, and we keep solvent.' She lit another cigarette: no doubt as a result of these, her voice had an agreeable roughness.

'Do you live here alone?' David asked. After all his anticipation, he could only come out with polite inquiries.

Aldyth nodded. 'Me and this old scrag.' She lifted the cat on to her lap. 'I'm sorry I never got to your mother's funeral, David.'

He began to say something, and choked on a piece of pastry.

'But I wasn't missed, eh? Well, I would have come. But the train service is terrible here, and I don't drive. One of the things I wish I'd learnt.'

'It's never too late,' said David. Somehow he had cleared his plate. He looked round at his aunt, and found she was studying him intently.

'You take after Ethel,' she said finally after she had scrutinised him for what seemed several minutes. She drained her gin. 'Jeanette tells me you've been after getting in touch with me for a long time, David.'

'Yes.'

'H'm. I prefer it this way. I don't like surprises being sprung on me. I get settled in my habits here. I'm allowed to spring the surprises. Prerogative of age. Well – ' and there was a sudden warning crackle in her voice and he saw her ringed hand tap convulsively on the arm of her chair – 'I think I must have got it wrong, I understood that you two were something more than friends, and you're sitting there like total strangers and you haven't said a word to each other. And you'd better bloody well start talking because I've got plenty of things to do.'

Ruth got up. 'I'd better go – '

'Sit down, Ruth.' Again the crisp voice, not raised, but vital. A woman not to be crossed.

'A lot of people have tried to interfere in my life in the past,' she said, and coughed on her cigarette. 'And now I'm doing a bit of interfering on my own account. Not necessarily for your sake. I just want to set my own record straight, as it seems I'm a bone of contention again. Isn't that so?'

There was silence, and David became aware of the weighty ticking of an old clock on the mantelpiece.

'Why did you come today, Ruth?' Aldyth said.

Ruth looked, for a moment, as sulky as a schoolgirl. 'Because you asked me to.'

'I know. But you didn't have to. You never came to see me and your father, did you?'

'No.'

'No doubt because you hated me.'

'No doubt.'

David looked at the two women, and a new nameless anxiety overtook him. He felt almost like a child whose future is being discussed over his head.

'I've often thought about you. You and Gordon. Your dad used to talk about you all the time.'

'Did he, that was nice of him.' Ruth was picking at her fingers again: they would bleed soon if she were not careful.

Aldyth frowned. 'I don't need that rubbish, Ruth.' She went on as if carefully controlling her voice. 'As I say, he talked about you a lot, and worried about you. He cared. That's a much misused word these days. But he cared. No doubt that's not in your mother's Holy Writ. Nor, I suppose, that I loved him, but I don't particularly care about that.' She drew a sharp breath. Everything about her conduced in David a feeling of unease: there was something brilliantly jagged as broken glass about her. 'I must admit I was interested to hear about you two. I was asking Ruth about it just before you came, but I didn't get much out of her. I used to think a lot about you, too, David.'

He noticed that a tear was running down Ruth's cheek. Aldyth seemed to have noticed too, but her expression did not change. He caught for the first time the sound of the sea, a susurration straying across the borders of hearing. Aldyth's long fingers burrowed in the cat's fur. It lifted its head, eyes slitted in enjoyment.

'I'm not bothered about banging heads together. If people can't manage to make their own happiness when they've got the chance then they don't deserve it as far as I'm concerned. That was my principle years ago. And I've stuck by it. I've not regretted it. Are you listening, Ruth? But what does bother me is this. I'm sixty-four, I've got my own life such as it is, and I just want to be left alone.'

'You are bloody alone,' said Ruth, heaving back a sniff. 'I've never come near you.'

'I didn't say you have. But it's obvious that my name's getting dragged in, somewhere it doesn't belong. And I've had a bellyful of that. I'm sick of it. It doesn't seem to occur to people that I don't want anything to do with them. That goes for you too, David. Very nice of you to worry about me I'm sure. But I'll manage, thanks. Like I say, I really don't want anything to do with either of you. But I'm damned if I'm going to be used as anybody's excuse for anything. For people being too frightened to make something of their own lives.'

Ruth wiped her eyes and looked down at the half-empty plate in front of her and then swept it to the floor with her arm. The cat started and then jumped down and began to lick at the fragments of pie on the carpet.

'Well that's human at any rate,' said Aldyth. She seemed undisturbed, and did not even look at the mess.

'That's what you reckon, then, is it? That's what you've got to say. You loved him,' Ruth said. It flashed on David's mind that it was absurd to strive to picture people as they were as children: they carried the child about with them, as they carried every day, every hour, every second of their lives. They were like Russian dolls, the layers infinite and always multiplying.

'Oh, God, Ruth.' Aldyth shaded her eyes. 'If I've got to repeat that then there's no use you being here at all.'

All at once Ruth was crying again, in noisy gasps, and David was on his feet and putting his arms round her. He felt it to be as exclusively and instinctively and naturally his job as a mother's is to suckle her child. As he stood holding her he looked at the room and at Aldyth, as if the shift from sitting to standing made an entirely new perspective. He saw that the room with its aggregation of shabby, disparate objects was designed to be comfortable to one person only: it was a den, built out of that one person's past, that you had no more right to be in than inside someone else's mind. He noticed for the first time a small faded photo of a man on the mantelpiece. And Aldyth looked old: a fit, good-looking, well-dressed woman, but old, and as she sat and shaded her eyes he sensed the privacy of age, unassailable, and essential.

'I won't see you out,' she said. 'I'm not a fairy godmother. I've said my piece.' The cat jumped on her lap again and her restless hands enclosed it. 'I just hope now I can be left alone.'

Ruth disengaged herself from his arms and wiped her face with a tissue.

They go out, at the same time, though not really together. Once outside the pub the steely glancing of sun on sea and the long sucking crash of waves on shingle and the tangy air swamps him, a sudden blast on his senses, like waking suddenly.

He does feel as if he were waking: the paralysis that had turned him into a frozen spectator leaves him. He steps out into the fresh air and into a new, daunting but irresistible kind of freedom, as the first creatures must have crawled out of the sea and shivered on the sand.

Ruth stands still, looking down the promenade. Her eyes are red and puffy. He guesses she is as helpless, as impotent as he was when he arrived at the pub.

A seagull comes wheeling out of nowhere and settles on the pebbled sea wall. It regards them with a liverish eye and begins to preen itself.

'God, I hate seagulls,' Ruth says. 'They're such ugly great things.'

'How did you get here?'

'Train.'

'My car's in the High Street.'

She turns away from him. Her head droops and he thinks she is going to cry again. Then he sees she is fumbling in her bag.

'I've got a return ticket,' she says.

He comes close to her and they look down at the red-and-white ticket in her hand. They stare at it as if, after all, this small piece of cardboard is the very last obstacle between them, and it is insurmountable.

'Pity to waste it,' he says.

Her fingers relax slowly, and the ticket drops to the ground and the wind plucks at it, listlessly at first, then nudging it and bowling it and then whipping it away, down the promenade and out of sight amongst the litter and the fish-and-chip papers.

Slowly, too, her body inclines towards him, an almost imperceptible tropism, until she is leaning against his shoulder. Only then does she sigh, and say: 'I feel so tired.'

'So do I.' The beginning of this day seems to stretch back, beyond memory, a great gaping rent in time. He is glad to relinquish the effort of recalling it, and just stand there with his body against hers, the salt wind stinging his face.

She clears her throat, and pushes her hair back from her cheek: a show of briskness, with a weak self-mockery, that touches him with a new and almost intolerable profundity.

'It's nice by the sea. I haven't been to the sea for ages,' she says: pressed against her, he feels as well as hears her voice, a throb running like a current from her body to his. 'Let's not go home just yet. Let's go to Cromer or somewhere, shall we?'

He nods, and smiles.

'Make a day of it,' she says, and squints up at the sun. 'Weather's lovely. We needn't go straight home. We've got plenty of time.'